SUMMITT

SUMMITT

A Novel by

William P. McGivern

ARBOR HOUSE
New York

*For Lurton Blassingame—the Count—for
interest, affection and guidance over so many
good years*

SUMMITT

CHAPTER ONE

A girl ran toward him across a rocky beach, crying out in pain, which was wrong, of course, because the day had been lovely except for the flames leaping for her through the slanting rain.

The stewardess moved the pillow behind his shoulder. "Would you fasten your seat belt, please, Mr. Selby? We'll be landing in Memphis in just a few minutes." She smiled at him. "I'm afraid you had the wrong girl or the wrong dream, Mr. Selby. I'm a Monica, not a Sarah."

He had spoken her name aloud, Harry Selby realized. Shouted it, perhaps. That hadn't happened so often lately, but he couldn't be sure since he had slept alone since then.

There must have been something of the dream and Sarah in his eyes when he walked through Memphis's main terminal to the Avis station, because a man he brushed by said, "Dammit, watch it," but stopped and stood looking after Selby, hands tightening on the shoulders of his small son.

The night was cool for that time of year, but the soft, penetrating humidity gave an edge to it. Harry Selby pulled on a topcoat and glanced around the dark parking lot. Slinging his gear into a rented sedan, he drove through a section of the town with neon-streaked windows and found the motel his brother had suggested, the Delta Arms, which faced a shopping mall and guitar bars and used car lots with strings of colored lights.

He didn't bother unpacking; he would be checking out the next morning to drive over to Jarrell's place in Summitt City.

His room was reassuringly similar to the dozens he had known on road trips; beige carpets and couches covered with a hard, nubby material, closet coat hangers almost impossible to free from their slotted metal holders, a blue seascape, sanitized strips of paper crisscrossing the toilet seat, and signs with warnings to keep the door locked, signs indicating the location of complimentary coffee and ice cubes.

After making himself a drink he dialed his home in Pennsylvania. Waiting, Selby looked at the worn leather duffel bag on the floor, stenciled with the smudged names and emblems of pro teams, bulging now with his clothing and his father's diaries and notebooks.

His son answered the phone. "Hey, have you met him yet, dad? What's he like?"

"Hold it, Davey. I just got off the plane."

"Well, he could have met you. I bet Shana he would."

A click sounded from an extension phone. Harry Selby's daughter said in her quick, light voice, "Who is it, Davey? Who're you talking to?" Her tone was amiable, but imperious, a wise and confident fourteen speaking to a nine-year-old brother.

"It's me, Shana," Harry Selby said.

"Oh, hi, daddy. Goodness, it seems like you just left. How was your flight?"

"Fine, fine. I'm at the motel, the phone number's on my desk there, Mrs. Cranston has it."

"Yes, and we've got Uncle Jarrell's number in Summitt. Have you talked to him yet?"

"No, I'm driving over tomorrow."

"I just can't wait to find out what he's like."

"Well, I'll call you tomorrow and let you know. I just wanted to see how everything was going."

The dream of Sarah had left him tense and worried about them. His daughter must have sensed his concern because she said, "Everything here is fine, daddy. You forget about us now and have a good time. I fed Blazer last night's steak with a lot of stale bread and milk. He's up in the meadow now, I can hear him barking. Mrs. Cranston is fixing dinner—"

10

"There's a deer up there, daddy," Davey said. "I'm sure of it. Somewhere in that thick patch of thornbushes."

Shana said, "Oh, every time you see a shadow you think it's some great, atavistic animal."

"Well, Mr. Gideen told me there was a fawn at the pond last spring."

"Daddy, Normie Bride called and he's coming over after dinner. We'll do homework and watch television maybe. Okay?"

"Sure, and take a walk down by the pond."

"Davey, you are incredibly tiresome. So moody and accusatory. Don't sulk, but you are. Daddy, give Uncle Jarrell a hug for us, okay? And tell him I'm a ski freak, or want to be anyway."

When she hung up, Davey said, "I walked part of the fence line before it got dark and found some rails down. Near the logging road at the top of the meadow. I wired 'em up so they'll hold till you get back."

"We'll camp out up there next week. Just you and me. Maybe we can spot that deer you saw . . ."

"You really think there's one up there?"

"I'm sure of it."

When he hung up, he looked out at cars angled into parking slots facing his room and beyond to the glitter of the shopping center and bars.

Talking to his son and daughter, he had visualized the farm he and Sarah had bought after they were married: the driveway flanked with poplars and locusts, the moonlit pond and fir trees, and the garden she had made of honeysuckle and dwarf lilac around the broken stone heap of the old silo.

His phone rang. It was Jarrell calling from Summitt City. Selby had talked to him only once before, when the diaries had arrived from the lawyer, but he recognized his brother's voice immediately. Half brother, he amended, as he said, "Hello, Jarrell. I was just about to call you."

"Well, fine, Harry. The motel's okay and everything?"

"Yes, everything's fine."

"How was your flight?"

"Just fine. I left Philadelphia around four, and we had good weather all the way. Shana and Dave drove out to the airport with me."

"I didn't realize she was that old, Harry."

11

"She's not, she's only fourteen. Our housekeeper came with us and drove them back home."

"And your boy, David, how old is he?"

A piano sounded over his brother's voice, and Selby heard a girl laughing.

"David's nine," he said. "They're both anxious to meet you, Jarrell, and they want me to bring back some snapshots. Shana wants me to tell you she can't wait to play snow queen on our mountains."

"Well, the land my father left—sorry, *our* father—is just a couple of residential lots and it's miles from any decent slopes."

Selby said, "Shana wasn't serious, Jarrell. Mr. Breck explained all that, about the lots, I mean. He suggested we sell them."

"If that's what you want, it's fine with me."

"Jarrell, the land doesn't mean anything one way or the other. But I'd like to find out something about the old man."

"What sort of things, Harry?"

"I don't have a questionnaire, Jarrell. He walked out before I was born. At least, that's one version of it. I'd like to know if there's another. In his letter, Mr. Breck says it could have been trick-or-treaters, or maybe burglars or prowlers. He doesn't seem to know. I'd like to talk to you about that, and what kind of a man he was, about his time in Korea—"

"Harry, I'd better turn this music down. I'll call you back in a few minutes, okay?"

"Sure, I'll be right here."

Selby began to realize that talking to Jarrell was like playing tennis against a wall—everything came back automatically, without excitement or variety or even a touch of spin.

What sort of things, Harry? Jesus! Selby wanted to know *everything*. What Jonas Selby liked for breakfast, how he voted, what made him laugh, what things he was afraid of, did he have a temper, what things riled him, did he drink, was he a cocksman, what—in short—was the substance of the man Selby had speculated about so helplessly all these years . . .

The diaries and the notebooks hadn't told him much. In spiral folders and stiff-backed journals, the entries ranged from the Korean war in the fifties to Jonas Selby's death a year ago. Most of it was written in a cramped but legible hand, except for the years at the army hospital in Boulder, Colorado, where his father's nurse and second wife, Rita Bender (now deceased) had typed entries for him.

Selby practically knew these diaries by heart now, all the scribbled pages tucked away in his leather duffel bag.

The foot-square carton had been delivered to the farm a month ago by Railway Express, accompanied by a registered letter from an attorney in Truckee, California.

"Your father's estate (Breck wrote) consists of two residential lots, not too desirably situated, I'm afraid, and a crateload of personal effects, notebooks, diaries and the like."

Breck then explained his delay in writing.

"I regret to tell you that your father's body was found by neighbors approximately a year ago in the kitchen of his house. He had been shot twice at close range by a .38 revolver. The police have listed his death as homicide at the hands of a person or persons unknown.

"They theorized that Jonas Selby may have returned from work and surprised prowlers. Since no money or valuables were taken from his person or home, they don't rule out the possibility that these prowlers could have been teenagers who panicked when they were caught.

"At the time of his death, neither I nor your half brother, Jarrell, had knowledge of your existence.

"The diaries and other papers were not discovered until six weeks ago. A new tenant found them packed in a crate in the garage. They were partially concealed by rows of firewood and were found when a quantity of wood was moved inside for the winter. Also in that crate was a deed of reconveyance for the lots I have mentioned, consigning the property to you and Jarrell Selby. Attached to this deed was a note in your father's handwriting, requesting me to contact you through the offices of the National Football League in New York City.

"It was his wish that you should take possession of his diaries and other papers, and that the real estate be shared equally by you and your brother."

Harry Selby had no need for alcohol, because he was fairly well adjusted to reality, and had never been forced to try to alter its shape and nature. But he hadn't been able to get through his father's diaries without the occasional stiff shot of whiskey, because in those years of rambling comment on the weather and the terrain and the enemy, in all those angry gripes about the army, and the stockade and the people who had used him so badly, in this welter of detail and nostalgia and how the fucking fish were biting, there was not one reference to Harry Selby, not even a *mention* of the son he had fathered and abandoned, the son he had known about for years but who obviously hadn't been important enough to rate even a perfunctory acknowledgment in his scribbled records.

He needed a little whiskey to help him face the fact that his father had known about him for years and hadn't bothered to do a thing about it. Not one goddamned word over all those years, when he'd needed it and wanted it, at schools where he'd stayed on campus during holidays; there'd never been a Christmas card or birthday greeting, not even a note when the team had made the magazine covers that year; nothing but a stretching emptiness in which Selby wondered endlessly about his father and tried to imagine what he had been like, and how long ago (and in what manner) he had died since that was the only reason he could think of to explain his silence.

Snapshots of his father had been tucked among the diaries and notebooks. In uniform or a GI bathrobe, he was tall with big shoulders, staring at the camera with worried, belligerent eyes. Others were taken around Tahoe, on a dock holding a fishing rod, and standing self-consciously with several men in front of a real estate office, taller than the others, but still regarding the world with those hostile, accusing eyes.

His phone rang again. "Harry, I'm sorry to keep you waiting. How's your schedule now?"

"I thought I'd check out of here early tomorrow. Judging from the map, I'll be at your place around ten. That suit you?"

"Ten, that's fine. Ten o'clock. You've got a car, of course. You want to drive to 64 and head east. Turn off at Summitt City. A bus will bring you right in. No cars allowed in the city limits, you know. But, Harry, there's a hitch. That's why I called earlier."

"What is it?"

"Well, something just came up. I figured you could stay here tomorrow night, you know."

"So what's the problem?"

14

"Well, I've got a girl, Harry, and—" his brother laughed awkwardly, "she's decided to stay for a while."

"That sounds interesting." Selby wondered if he were only imagining something evasive in his brother's voice. "But why is that a problem? I'd say it sounds pretty good."

"The thing is, Harry, I can't put you up. It's a small place, and there just isn't room."

"Then I'd better stay here."

"Yes, you'd better, Harry. I think you'd better."

"Fine, I'll see you tomorrow morning."

Selby felt deflated when he hung up. His reaction made him wonder at the depths of his need for some conduit to the past. What had he expected? Walks along a river, drinks before a fire, leisurely reminiscences which might bring their separate selves into some kind of symmetry? No, but he had hoped at least to be able to add some of his brother's memories to the vacuum in his life, and in that way to catch a glimpse of truth about the tall, narrow-eyed bastard who stared so sullenly at him from those snapshots taken around Tahoe and army hospitals.

Well, he thought, looking at his stained duffel bag, he might as well unpack. And let Shana know he wouldn't be staying at Jarrell's, but right here with the blue seascape and the free coffee and ice cubes.

CHAPTER TWO

Harry Selby left Memphis early the next morning on a highway that ran through pale meadows and stands of dark trees. There was little snow here, but the land was good for soybeans, tobacco and cotton, enriched with shale and limestone from the Cumberland plateau, details Selby remembered from reading about where his brother lived, a model town and plant owned by the giant eastern conglomerate called Harlequin Chemicals.

An attendant gave him a receipt for his car. Selby boarded a white minibus with open sides. When a half dozen other passengers joined him, the driver, a young woman in a casual uniform, started the vehicle's electric motor and they drove off.

The town of Summitt City included parks and lakes, a golf course and green fields where children played volleyball and soccer and baseball, with grown-ups in small clusters applauding and cheering them on. The minibus drove on soundless tires past rows of pleasant homes and apartment buildings with solar paneling and colorful patio furniture. Racks and tubs of vigorous plants stood everywhere. Uniformed maintenance teams in open trucks cruised the streets and recreation areas.

Selby had looked up Summitt City in *Readers' Guide* and had found in the East Chester library a half dozen or more magazine articles relating to various aspects of the city, its ecological harmony, its foliage-aeration program, its noise and pollution control (no automobiles, chemically consumed garbage), its crime rate (nonexistent, in fact), and its auxiliary energy system of windmills, forest farming for indoor fireplace fuel, temperature controlled by sunlight, and so forth.

And yet it was the absence of things rather than their presence that caught his attention and interest—sidewalks and gutters free of litter, driveways without oil drippings, and golfers walking the fairways rather than riding in noisily powered carts.

When the bus dropped him off, Selby realized he had seen no police anywhere, no traffic cops, no patrol cars, not even guards at crossings.

His brother's apartment faced an immaculate lawn crisscrossed with gravel walks. Beyond the low brown and beige buildings Selby saw the green shine of a lake. The wind made a rustling in the trees, but that was the only sound in the empty street.

It was a significant moment for him, a prelude to knowledge and insights he had sought and puzzled over much of his life. Selby didn't know what lay beyond that burnished door to his brother's home, like the king in the old play, he thought, returning from some war or other, unaware of what the audience knew was waiting for him . . .

Sarah would know what he was thinking about; she had studied those classics, savoring the sound of Greek names sounding on the still waters of the Kennebec. Her parents had wanted a place like Dowell for Sarah, humanities, fine arts, anything that was gentle and secure, different from what they had known in Germany.

A girl in a tennis dress opened the door. "Hi, I'm Jennifer," she said. "Come in, please. You're Harry, of course, you couldn't be anybody else, now could you?"

She opened the door wide and looked up at the sky. "My, what a lovely day!" Her tone was approving, congratulatory, in fact, as if the sun and air and clouds had been presented for inspection and she was pleased to give them good marks. "Jarrell's still showering, so how about some coffee?"

"That would be fine."

Jarrell's living room was bright and airy, with an exposed stone chimney and rounded glass walls that gave on the lake. His brother's girl friend went into the kitchen and began looking through cupboards, making a clatter of pots and pans.

Skylights under solar panels filled the house with sun. A partitioned extension from a bay window served as a decorative greenhouse. It contained shelving and trellises and a lush profusion of potted herbs and asparagus ferns. From overhead sprinklers, an irrigating spray created a fine mist around the bright foliage of emerald-ripple peperomia (which he'd read about) and a pair of tall, broad-leafed ficus lyrata, which fanned out behind a crop of varied crotons, green and white leaves striped in red or trimmed in sharp purple.

The colors and textures of the plants were in a nice balance, Selby thought; even the misting waters added a harmony of their own, sharpening the air pleasantly with the fragrance of some kind of citrus fruit.

A bedroom door opened and Jarrell's head appeared through drifting layers of steam. A running shower sounded behind him.

"Make yourself at home, Harry. Be with you in a minute." The door closed, puffs of white steam outlining the edges.

Selby's tension eased somewhat, because that much was over; he had seen him at last, in the flesh, a misted figure, a branch cut from his own genetic roots.

Opening cupboards, Jennifer said, "Jarrell told me this is the first time you've ever met, that you didn't even know about each other. I think that's exciting, starting without any preconceptions. You're from the east, Pennsylvania?"

"Yes, about forty miles from Philadelphia."

"What do you do there? Do you mind my asking?"

"No, of course not. We have about forty acres, but it's not a working farm. We board a few horses, and rent a meadow out for heifers."

"I grew up in New York, on the Island. There was no room for horses, we rode at a stable in Smithtown, but we had a boat. I still miss that."

She looked like she would have a boat, he thought, and a big lawn from where they would watch the Sound on warm afternoons. Jennifer had blond hair and without make-up her features were small and handsome, and symmetrical except for her

18

lower lip which was rather full and added an attractive sensuousness to her expression.

"Jarrell told me about your wife. Do you mind my mentioning it?"

"No, that's all right. It was a rainy day and the car lost traction. It was Spain," he said, as if that explained the rest of it.

"I'm sorry."

"Yes."

She pushed a strand of hair away from her forehead and looked in frustration at the open drawers and cupboards.

"Can I help?" he asked her.

"No, no, I'll find it."

Watching her opening and closing drawers, the sun on her slim, brown legs, Selby let out his breath slowly. To speak only of the rain and the tires and the slippery road put the horror at a remove. It was the way he and Davey talked about it when they had to. (Shana never talked about it at all.) If you just thought of the guard rail breaking, and the little car going through it on the curving sea road between Cadiz and Málaga, if you imagined only the blue Fiat crashing and exploding and burning on the rocks below, it was possible to push away the thought that Sarah had been trapped inside it.

The door to the bedroom opened and Jarrell joined him. Tall and rather slenderly built, he wore jeans and a yellow sports shirt. He was smiling.

"So. My directions okay?"

"Fine," Selby said, and they shook hands.

"Good. It's easy to get turned around coming out of Memphis. It's a pretty big place, half million or more people, I guess. You met Jennifer, of course?"

His brother's smile, Selby noticed, didn't quite touch his eyes, or smooth away the worried frown between them; he seemed distracted as he glanced quickly at Jennifer and then at his wristwatch.

In the kitchen Jennifer asked him something, and Jarrell nodded to a shelf of matched yellow canisters.

"I'll meet you at the commissary for lunch," Jarrell said to Selby. "You and Jennifer can take a walk, if you like, the shopping mall's just a few minutes from here."

19

Jennifer held a canister and was measuring coffee into the mesh cup of a percolator.

"A walk sounds fine," Harry Selby said. "We can talk at lunch then."

His brother didn't answer, and Selby noticed again the persistent frown that formed a crease between his eyes.

Jarrell's hair was light brown, almost blond, and fitted like a smooth cap above his narrow, angular face. His eyes were a pale blue.

There was very little family resemblance. Selby was taller than Jarrell, and thicker through the arms and shoulders. His hair was a reddish brown, and his eyes were darker, a deep gray.

But the most obvious difference between them was in the cast of their expressions. Harry Selby's features were blunt and hard, and something about them usually suggested either coldness or indifference. The look was deceptive, stemming in part from an injury, a triangular scar or groove on his right cheekbone. At certain times, and in certain lights, the slight indentation added a not always intentional belligerence to his appearance.

After Jarrell said goodbye and left for work, Jennifer brought Selby a cup of coffee and went into the bathroom to change.

Summit City had received its corporate charter from the Tennessee State Legislature in 1972. Prior to this—Selby learned from a brochure his brother had given him—Harlequin Chemicals had operated the facility at Summit in accordance with the municipal codes of neighboring townships, paying taxes on a per capita basis for police and fire protection, and school services. Summit City was now fully autonomous, a city of slightly more than five thousand, functioning on a self-contained environmental system, and as an independent municipal entity. A third of Summitt's population worked in the Harlequin Chemical plant, another third was made up of dependent wives and children, while the remainder consisted of maintenance crews, teachers, police and fire personnel and the staffs of local shops and markets.

Selby and Jennifer Easton walked through a wide shopping

mall that stretched like a spoke from the hub of Summitt City, a complex of buildings housing the company's headquarters. Other spokes extended from this central area to the chemical plants, to playing fields, experimental laboratories, schools and churches.

They strolled past boutiques and pharmacies, markets and grocery stores, shops full of sporting goods and electrical appliances. At an outdoor counter with a gaily striped awning, a man in a checked apron and straw hat sold ice cream and praline wafers.

The tone of the brochure was congratulatory. A picture of George Thomson, chief executive officer of Harlequin Chemicals, was featured on the inside of the front cover, with a quotation from him in boldface type: "In ten years we at Harlequin —workers and management together—have given a fresh and exciting meaning to the phrase 'life-style.' With respect for our work and respect for ourselves, we have created at Summitt City a pilot town and plant that is a shining example of the continuing miracle of American industry."

Thomson was in his early or middle fifties, a vigorous man with dark hair and eyes, staring at the world (in this photograph) with a look of aggressive authority.

The pamphlet listed Harlequin's accomplishments: homes, kitchens and greenhouses built into wall spaces, warmed by solar flues running up through the roofs and mist-fed by tiny spray pipes crisscrossed through the plantings; hot water in the bathrooms supplied by solar panels; composting toilets with aerobic decomposition units that channeled household and bodily wastes into fertilizers for commercial truck gardens; a linked system of company structures applying the concept of ecological harmony to human existence; huge city-maintained tanks of tropical fish, a rapidly growing and propagating species which provided valuable edible protein for the community while subsisting healthfully itself on algae fed to them from the town's kitchen wastes—self-contained and self-sufficient, Summitt City was an "interphased and interacting bioshelter," recycling its own natural by-products through biological composting, eliminating polluting sewage treatment facilities while despoiling neither the soil nor the water table with toxic deposits.

The information about "aquaculture" and "homeostasis," the "body-as-machine" and the significance of "mini-arks" in achieving environmental equipoise, this was all fascinating, Selby supposed, but none of it caught his attention as strongly as the worried frown of his brother; thin, anxious lines that were like the iceberg tips of whatever was bothering him.

Selby glanced around, impressed by the silence, the curious weight of it. He was almost lonesome for sounds he was accustomed to, the noise of traffic, automobile horns, people calling to one another, cops' whistles. The shopping mall was full of pedestrians, women and children churning past them, but the flow was orderly and tranquil, no one riding skateboards or roller skates or moped bikes, or carrying transistor radios.

Jennifer had changed into a beige suit and boots the color of cognac. At a vendor's cart, she bought two ice cream cones and a foil-wrapped packet of praline wafers.

She smiled at Selby as she paid the man. "There's a place near the lake with picnic tables," she said, "or would you rather go on reading about Summitt City's plumbing system?"

"I was going to skip to the end and see how it turned out."

"I can tell you about it," she said, and hooked an arm companionably through his.

They walked from the mall and crossed a series of green belts to the lake, which glistened against the woods beyond it. The day had become pleasantly warm. A man in a rowboat cast a lure toward clumps of cattails growing along the banks. A stoutly built man in a warm-up suit was batting grounders to youngsters on a Little League diamond.

Jennifer and Selby sat at a redwood table and watched the fisherman and the boys and girls playing ball. She gave him an ice cream cone and opened the packet of wafers and spread them on the table. In profile to him, she turned her face to the sun, legs stretched and slim, boots crossed at the ankles. A faint, throbbing noise sounded rhythmically and Selby saw a gray helicopter on the horizon beyond the woods, twin rotaries flashing in the sunlight.

"How long have you known Jarrell?" he asked her.

"Four or five months, I think. We met at a jazz concert, somebody shoved some tables together and we began talking, I don't remember about what, probably how crowded and noisy it was."

"That was in Memphis?"

"Yes. I'd been down to visit friends." She nibbled on a praline wafer and licked a crumb from her lips. Smiling at him, she said, "It got to be a habit. Seeing Jarrell, I mean. I flew down yesterday without telling him. It's not a very structured relationship. But that's how I got your bed, Harry. I picked up a car out at the airport, and I also rather dumbly picked up a speeding ticket on the way out here."

She made a comical face, but he could see she hadn't liked the experience; her full lower lip tightened in an exasperated line. "My Yankee sweet-talk jive didn't cut it with the good old boys in the cruiser."

"You work in New York?"

"I'm in fashion photography, free-lance. Eat your ice cream before it melts, Harry."

A second helicopter flew over the lake and trees, the dark tubular shape with blades like insect feelers sharp against the white sky. Selby saw the flash of U.S. Air Force insignia then, and realized the chopper must be settling onto a military installation he had passed on the way out from Memphis, Camp Saliaris, a chemical corps unit, according to the sign he had seen above tall iron gates at a sentry's station.

"Jennifer, is Jarrell worried about something? Did this visit of mine come at a bad time?"

Instead of answering, she straightened up and pointed to the fisherman in the boat. "Look, Harry, I think he's caught something."

The man was standing to reel in his line, balancing himself awkwardly in the rocking boat. The tip of his rod bent almost to the water before snapping up suddenly, causing the lure to surface and fly into the air, a red plug with a white feather tied to it, the tiny triangle of hooks shining and empty in the sun.

"Oh, damn, I wish he'd caught something," Jennifer said. "My father used to fish a lot off the Island. They flew flags when they came home and we could tell what they'd caught by the colors while they were still miles out." She looked sideways at him. "Which doesn't answer your question, does it, Harry?"

"Maybe I was out of line," he said.

She shrugged. "I don't mind. But perhaps Jarrell's worried about meeting you, did you think of that? One minute he was an unattached bachelor, no family of any sort. Next thing he's got a brand-new brother, plus a full-sized niece and nephew. That could take a bit of getting used to."

"That's possible, of course."

"But you don't believe it?"

"I have no reason not to," Selby said. "He may think I'm broke and need money. Or that I'm going to expect him to play a role he's not interested in, the uncle showing up at Christmas in a flurry of snow, armloads of presents and so forth."

She broke one of the pralines in two and offered him a piece. "Try it," she suggested. "It won't spoil your lunch. You'll like it. How did you get that scar on your cheek?" She licked her ice cream. "I'd never ask, you know, if it wasn't attractive."

"A man ran into me," Selby said. "That's the truth."

"No story to it?"

"Not really."

A pair of black youngsters were watching the ball game, Selby noticed, standing together behind the batter's box. They were ten or twelve, wearing jeans and T-shirts. They cheered the players and shouted, "Atta boy, atta baby, way to go!" at every smoothly turned play, and groaned with amiable commiseration whenever a ball shot between a player's legs or beyond the clutching dive of his hands.

"Listen to me, please." Jennifer put a hand on his arm impulsively. "You asked how long I'd known Jarrell. I told you four or five months. But that doesn't mean much, I'm not good at knowing people. I don't try to. I accept them instead. If Jarrell's worried about something, that's his business. I'm no good at belonging, Harry. I just work at, well, being. I try to understand *me*. What Jarrell believes, what he needs, that's private, and I don't trespass. How was that praline?"

She smiled and then waved at a tall, lanky man who was walking toward them across the green belt around the baseball diamond.

"It's Clem Stoltzer," she told him. "Plant superintendent. He said something last night about a guided tour, a VIP excursion. Are you up to it?"

24

With Stoltzer was a heavyset man in a gray drill uniform. His name was Crowley, Lee Crowley, Stoltzer told them. Crowley smiled at them, and touched a hand to his visored cap in a friendly salute. Crowley then joined the black boys who were prancing with excitement and shouting slangy encouragement and good-humored ridicule at the players. "Now that you *got* it, let's see you *catch* it!" they yelled at a youngster calling for a fly ball. "Get y'self an ironing board," they shouted at a batter and shrieked with laughter. "Can't hit a bull in the butt with a bass fiddle."

Stoltzer was in his forties, with a fringe of blond-gray hair neatly hedging his weathered bald spot. His eyes were watchful, but his manner was pleasant as he escorted them along serpentine paths towards Summitt City's plants and facilities.

Glancing back, Selby saw the security guard, Crowley, leading the black youngsters away from the baseball field, walking between them with his arms casually about their narrow shoulders.

With Stoltzer providing what sounded rather like a practiced commentary, Selby and Jennifer visited a small, immaculate hospital and accident ward, a theater building with an editing room and a film library, and toured a complex of antiseptic buildings that housed generators and offices of the EPS—the environmental protection supervisor—"Not even a VP from the Harlequin headquarters in Pennsylvania, not even George Thomson himself, could overrule Mr. Nash's orders," Stoltzer told them.

They inspected a gymnasium equipped with bowling alleys and racquetball courts, mirrored weight rooms and exercise machines fitted with respiratory and blood pressure indicators.

They saw hot tubs, saunas and swimming pools. Most of the facilities were in use, men and women in yoga classes, others playing court games or attending golf and tennis clinics. The pools were full of schoolchildren darting through the water like well-schooled seals under the eye of instructors.

Harlequin's main plant was a brilliantly lighted building where hundreds of employees, male and female, in white smocks, sat at counters and control panels monitoring instruments which (Stoltzer became animated as he explained this) profiled the quality of raw materials before their conversion into plastic end products, such as textile laminates, appliances of all types, insulating foam and so forth.

"Our function here," Stoltzer told them, "is to polymerize particular monomers and convert them to pellets for final molding . . . "

An orderly, hivelike activity flowed from the various checkpoints and stations in this huge factory, which created (Stoltzer told them with pride) epoxy, polyesters and polyurethane from plastic derived from fractions of gas or petroleum recovered during refining processes.

Selby noticed cameras at various vantage points, slim beige cylinders mounted in ceilings and on the top of buildings. "They help us to record traffic efficiency patterns," Stoltzer explained.

Lunch was a comparatively noisy interlude. Selby was grateful for the reassuring clatter of plates and cutlery, and the snatches of talk from adjoining tables.

The commissary was cheerfully decorated, with two walls painted in a buttery shade of yellow and the others sparkling with huge, clear glass panels which enclosed a well-planned jungle of green, leafy plants and tiers of potted flowers, herbs and small vegetables.

Music sounded from ceiling speakers. Air-conditioning created currents which were pungent with earth smells from the wall gardens, and the pleasant sharpness of lime.

Luncheon was excellent, a grilled white fish and mixed fresh vegetables. Selby sat with Jennifer, Clem Stoltzer and Jarrell. The conversation was casual, but sufficiently distracting to prevent Selby from talking with his brother.

The security guard, Lee Crowley, stopped by to tell Stoltzer that the fish stock had arrived for Summitt City's lakes. Crowley appeared younger than he had with his visored cap on. His hair was dark and thick, and there was a high, healthy color in his rugged face.

"If you're a fisherman, Mr. Selby," the guard said, "we've got all the action you could hope for here. I'm putting in a new batch of fingerlings this afternoon, channel catfish, trout and bluegills. The old crop needs some thinning out. I can fix you up with a rod if you'd like to try your hand."

After lunch Jennifer announced that she had a hair appointment. Jarrell mentioned to Selby that some people were stopping by that night, friends who wanted to meet him; not a party, just drinks and a pick-up dinner, and there would be time then to discuss what they wanted to do with the lots in California.

Selby spent the rest of the afternoon strolling about and trying to isolate the source of his frustration. As the day became grayer and colder, he crossed the baseball diamond and sat at a redwood table by the lake. The water now looked like a huge, flat mirror in its frame of dark trees.

It was too bad, he thought, that this brother of his, half brother, that is, seemed so indifferent to their shared link with Jonas Selby. That was his privilege, of course, not to give a goddamn about the past, his father's, his own, or anybody's, for that matter, but it wasn't so easy for Selby; he couldn't dismiss it that way, because his thoughts had a habit of turning backward to where his pain and troubles were rooted, where somebody else had made the rules.

A football landed with a thump on the grass and rolled end over end and toward him, stopping at his feet and rocking slowly from side to side.

Everything was quiet. The baseball diamond was empty and so were the green belts around the groves of trees. Winds made a lonely sound and created a trembling on the water.

Picking up the football, Selby's hand instinctively found the seams and laces. He touched his cheekbone, absently tracing the blade-shaped scar below his eye.

It had happened in a game with an expansion team. The field had been slick with mud. They had blitzed on third and long, it looked like play-action, but it was a weak-side draw and they were caught coming in by the pulling guards. Selby remembered little after the first impact, when the offensive lineman's helmet drove into his face mask, snapping a metal bar and scooping a neat hollow out of his cheekbone. "Like he used a teaspoon," the team doctor told him.

An anxious voice called, "Hey, mister, throw us our ball, okay?"

They were standing near the woods, the two black youngsters he had seen earlier. They still wore jeans and T-shirts, but looked colder now—huddled together as if for warmth and protection. Their buoyant bravado was gone, they were watching

him with nervous smiles. The taller of the pair put out a hand
to him, but they both looked so tense that Selby realized they
were about ready to bolt and run for it.

"This is your ball?"

"Yeah, mister, but we didn't take it. It was on the ground
loose."

Selby said, "You boys live hereabouts?"

They nudged one another at that, and pressed their lips
together to keep from laughing.

"No, sir, I mean we don't know, mister," the larger boy
said. "Stop making like such a fool," he said to his giggling
companion, and shook his arm roughly. "Cut it out, Dookey.
He's my brother, mister. His name's Dookey. Me, I'm Spencer
Barrow and can we please have our ball, mister? It was loose and
by itself."

"Well, sure," Selby said. "Either of you want to go out for
a pass?"

Their nervousness disappeared; they nodded eagerly.

Selby told them to head for the diamond and run a pattern
toward the pitcher's mound. They raced off together, arms
pumping and legs flying, and when they reached the field, Selby
cocked his arm and pumped twice as if to fake out charging
linemen, shadowy phantoms from a thousand distant games,
and then let the ball fly in a high arc into the blue dusk. The cold
leather against his hand and the sight of the spiraling football
brought a rush of memories, priests at St. Ambrose, cassocks
dusty with chalk, but then the past dissolved suddenly and satis-
factorily into the present as the boy named Spencer went up
high, then higher and higher and caught the ball surely in both
hands, tucking it away as he landed and broke toward an imagi-
nary goal line, his brother, Dookey, after him, cheering and
shaking both clenched fists in triumph above his head.

A security guard walked from a trail in the woods and
looked after them with a smile. "Six points, for sure," he said.
"They'll have a story tonight about winning the big game, I can
tell you. I'm Sergeant Ledge, Hank Ledge. You're Jarrell Selby's
brother, I suppose."

"That's right." They shook hands and Selby felt the testing
strength in the sergeant's grip, the fingers cool and hard.

"Picked a good view here, Mr. Selby. Colors and weather

changes every month or so." He released Selby's hand and put a stubby black pipe in his mouth. "The wife and I always come down here after supper in the summer. Light lasts till about ten. There's a nice shine on the water even then."

Selby looked after the Barrow brothers and had a glimpse of them running behind a screen of oleanders.

"Was it my imagination, Sergeant, or is something bothering those boys?"

Sergeant Ledge stared at Selby. "What gave you that notion?"

"I thought they seemed a little frightened."

"Mr. Selby, were you shocked to find black kids here at Summitt?"

"It's not my reaction I was talking about," Selby said.

"Could be they're a little scared at that." The sergeant took the pipe from his mouth and smiled. "They found that pigskin out in front of the gym, and 'stead of turning it in like they're supposed to, they went off larking with it. They're good boys, though. Their aunt's in Purchasing. Their own folks are dead."

"I asked them if they lived here, but they said they didn't know."

Sergeant Ledge shrugged. "What they meant, I expect, is they're not sure where their *aunt* lives. She's moving into a bigger place now they're with her." He put the pipe back in his mouth. "It'll take a while for them to get used to Summitt. They've only been here a week or so."

In a gesture that surprised Selby, Sergeant Ledge drew his automatic from its holster and hefted it in a calloused hand. With an appraising smile, he said, "You know this weapon?"

"It's a Colt .45."

"Then you know it kicks like an uphill mule." The sergeant pulled back the receiver and removed the magazine from the butt-stock. "Which is beside the point I was gonna make, Mr. Selby." He nodded at the gun's magazine and chamber. "They're both empty, you see. That's the story of Summitt, Mr. Selby. This Colt .45 isn't loaded because there's no need for a guard here to carry a loaded gun. That's what them boys aren't used to."

Sergeant Ledge dropped the Colt into his holster. "Maybe you find this hard to believe. You thought them black kids was scared of you. Everybody grows up with fears like that. But here it's different. The people walk the streets night or day in complete safety. Young girls, old folks, they picnic on the grass, sleep out by the lake if they want to. No muggings or burglaries, here. Most of us don't even lock our doors at night.

"I carry a single round of ammo in my belt, and a whistle in case of emergency. To be frank with you, I had to make some adjustments when I first came to Summitt. I didn't put much store in the talk about equal rights for everybody, regardless of their beliefs or color."

Sergeant Ledge picked up a flat stone and flipped it out over the lake, a whipping sidearm motion that sent it skimming across the water and raising miniature swells. "If my grandfather was alive, Mr. Selby, he'd reach for his cane if I told him I was living in the same block with colored and Puertos. I remember him clear, in a big chair with a spittoon beside him, telling me and my sisters, 'A nigger buck can only go so far down to evil, God help his poor lost soul, but beware the nigger bitch—when they go bad there's no bottom deep enough for them to touch.'

"That's all behind me now, Mr. Selby. A man or woman at Summitt is good as they want to be, can make any kind of life for themselves they're willing to work for. We've had our labor organizers come around here and lawyers for civil liberties outfits; even some big shots from the NAACP rolling up in their Caddies, claiming they could do something better for us, or looking for what they called 'invisible or *closet* discrimination,' for Christ's sake, or *tokenism* or *exploitation* or what some of those assholes called 'prejudice by quota,' whatever in hell they thought that meant.

"But Mr. Thomson told them to get lost, to go on about their business, if they had any. So don't worry about them Barrow boys, Mr. Selby. They'll find Summitt a decent place to grow up in, and learn the right values."

The sergeant's eyes narrowed in his deeply tanned face. His cheekbones were high and sharp and prominent. There was a stillness about him, a stoic strength in his powerful frame.

With a sigh he picked up another stone and pitched it onto the water. It skipped a few times before settling within its own

30

spreading ripples. "Well, I've enjoyed our talk. I expect I'll see you around."

Selby said, "Sergeant, do you know how long my brother's been at Summitt?"

"Well, about ten or eleven months, I think. Why?"

"Are you friendly with him?"

"I like to think so. We've spent some times together, playing cards, that sort of thing. We live just across the street from him, my wife and me. He came over to tell us when you called him that first time a few weeks ago. He was real excited, looking forward to seeing you."

Selby said, "Did Jarrell ever talk to you about our father?"

"I seem to recollect a casual comment now and then. But just in passing, like the fellow says."

"What did he tell you about him?"

"Nothing much in particular. Just that he and his father lived out west, northern California, I think. Jarrell told me his father liked fishing, owned a little property—things like that."

"Did he talk to you about the night our father was shot and killed?"

"That was a topic he steered clear of. I knew about it, of course, it wasn't no secret, but he didn't want to talk about it." The sergeant looked thoughtfully at him. "Has he opened up to you about what happened that night?"

"No, and I don't want to press him."

"That's considerate. It was a sad business, prowlers or drunken fool kids. Maybe he wants to put it behind him."

The sergeant's profile was rigidly outlined against the dusk, the jutting nose and high, bronzed cheekbones shadowed in dying light, again the stillness in his expression.

"I spoke to you about my grandfather, Mr. Selby," he said, his voice soft in the rising winds. "I don't think of him much, I try not to, you want the truth, the way he sat making the spittoon ring with tobacco juice, and hate spilling out of him like red ants pouring from a cracked log. I'm better for not thinking of him, Mr. Selby. Better putting it behind me. That's what Jarrell's done, I think, and maybe that would be best for all of us, to put the past behind us and forget about it. I'll see you, Mr. Selby."

Surrounded by the visual hush of twilight, Selby watched the sergeant striding off along the gravel path, his figure merging with the shadows.

Glowing lights began to wink on in the homes of Summitt City, yellow rectangles appearing in orderly unison against the settling darkness.

CHAPTER THREE

At Summitt's headquarters building, Sergeant Ledge inserted an identi-disc in the console slot of a limited access elevator.

Like certain other areas in Summitt—the film lab, the master greenhouses and specific hospital wards—the central Harlequin headquarters were restricted to classified security grades.

When the elevator reached the third floor, Ledge placed his card in an unlocking slot and kept his fingertips on the metallic edge to provide the computer with an identity-reading of his skin chemicals. A tracking hum sounded as he turned his profile to the scanning machines. With the ID check completed, the elevator doors opened and Ledge was allowed to enter a communications center lined with banks of electronic machines and walls of TV monitors.

Snapping on a row of sets, Ledge tracked Harry Selby along a graveled walk through the dusk toward his brother's house. On other monitors, he picked up Jarrell Selby as he answered the door and the blond girl entering the living room with a tray of drinks.

Ledge listened to their casual conversation, Jennifer's laughter, the clink of ice in raised glasses. He heard Harry Selby say, "Jarrell, is there something about the old man's death you haven't told me about, or don't want to?"

"Didn't Breck give you all the details?"

33

"Hey, *quel dismal!* This is supposed to be a party." It was the blond girl. "Harry, how's your drink?"

"It's fine, Jennifer," he said, but went on. "I was out walking and met your neighbor, Hank Ledge. He shut up when I mentioned it. Breck's letter didn't really tell me a damn thing. Wasn't there a police investigation? Didn't they check to see if the old man had been involved in a local feud or hassle?"

"There wasn't anything like that," Jarrell told him.

"What about somebody with a grudge? A business deal that went sour, did he have any enemies around there?"

"He never mentioned anything like that to me."

"You're sure?"

"Of course, Harry . . ." Sergeant Ledge watched Jarrell shrug uncertainly. "I'd have known if he was in trouble . . . I can't think of anything."

"Well, it strikes me as odd his death seems to have an off-limits sign on it."

"If I could think of any reason for the whole thing I'd be the first to tell you, Harry . . ."

Jennifer turned up the music. A high jazz saxophone muted the rest of what Selby was saying. She linked her arm through his. "Let's have our drinks on the terrace," she said. "Come on, Jarrell. The lake is lovely now."

The door opened and Clem Stoltzer entered the communications room. Ledge snapped off the TV monitors. "We got ourselves a problem, Clem. That sonofabitch Harry Selby is just like his old man. I soldiered with Jonas in Korea, remember. A rockhead. Same goddamn bulldog streak, hit him with a club and he comes back for more."

Stoltzer said, "This Harry Selby's no rockhead, Sergeant. I watched him when we toured the plant and grounds. He doesn't just look, he *sees.*"

Ledge rubbed his jaw with the calloused web formed between this thumb and forefinger. "What'd Jarrell tell you about the girl?"

"That she's just a casual friend."

"Where'd they meet? How come she arrived without notice?"

"Some party, I guess. I'm not sure." Stoltzer shrugged. "I don't think Jarrell is, either. She drove over from Memphis yesterday morning. He wants her here, he's entitled to a normal sex life, what could I say?"

"I don't like any of it," Ledge said. "It's Thursday and the green light's on. They can't scrub it now."

"Can't or won't. It's the same thing," Stoltzer said.

Ledge stared at the dark monitors, frowning. "We can't make any decisions on this. Not yet. I'll try to get in touch with the major. Mr. Thomson should know. And, Clem, you call General Taggart direct, put him in the picture."

Returning to his office on the first floor, Sergeant Ledge placed a call to George Thomson's private number at his home in Wahasset, Pennsylvania, an estate that lay just across the state line from Harlequin's offices in Wilmington, Delaware.

The call was answered by Thomson's son, Earl, whom Ledge knew from the summers the young man had worked in the film lab at Summitt. An athlete, Ledge recalled, handsome but reserved, kept pretty much to himself . . .

Earl Thomson explained that his father was still in Europe, Belgium, he believed, but would be back in the States that weekend for a business golf tournament in New Jersey.

"We got a problem down here at Summitt, Earl," Ledge told him, "and I need your father's advice. Will he be checking in by tomorrow? This is urgent."

"That's a flip of the coin, sir." Earl's voice was smooth and assured. "Father sets his own schedules, of course. Sometimes he calls to let me know his plans, sometimes he contacts Mr. Lorso. Is there any way I can help, Sergeant?"

"If you can give him my message by tomorrow, yes," Ledge said. "Tell your father Harry Selby came down here from Muhlenburg. He's asking the wrong questions. He'll understand that. Advise him we need Selby out of here before the operation. He'll understand that too. Anything to get him off our backs before Saturday. You got that now?"

"Yes. A Mr. Harry Selby. Are you suggesting a *ruse de guerre,* a feint to divert the enemy away from the attack?"

Ledge remembered then that Earl had attended a military college in the east, never regular army, and had a habit of using this rookie bullshit, even with the major.

35

"Look, Earl," he said, "just give your dad my message, okay? He'll know what to do?"

"Aren't you suggesting, Sergeant, that you'd like some pressure to get this Mr. Selby out of Summitt City?"

"That's up to your father."

"Then if I can't reach him, this conversation is irrelevant, I'd say. Wouldn't you prefer me to make it operational?"

"Just see that he gets my message, Earl. I don't have the authority to suggest anything else."

Replacing the phone on his father's desk, Earl Thomson stared through the terrace windows at the lawn shining smoothly in the last cool sunlight. He sat in his father's leather chair and stretched his long legs under the desk, putting his head back and listening to the sounds in the busy house. By concentrating, he could track and imagine the activities, maids chatting in the distant kitchen, Santos's footsteps padding above him in his mother's suite. Time for her shoulder rub, her tea tray and the evening news. In the kennel run the Dobermans were barking.

Earl felt at the center of this web of activity, seated as he was at the position of power in the long, shadowed study, in his father's chair, facing the imposing desk with its row of clocks and phones. But it was, he thought, a sensation of spurious privilege; he was, in truth, isolated from the lines of important function anywhere beyond this house. He was bitterly aware of that. Unconnected in any way to the powers of Harlequin or Summitt City.

The feeling he had talking to Sergeant Ledge, the furious, belittling anger, was intensified now by the faint laughter from his mother's room. He was never *really* at the center of things . . .

He remembered Ledge, silent, weathered-burned features, eyes that hadn't respected him. Urgent, the man had said, serious matters, but not for Earl Thomson, those serious matters always swirled tantalizingly beyond him.

The name was in the local phone book, a quick check disclosed—Harry J. Selby, with an address on Mill Lane, R.D., Muhlenburg.

Intelligence was the "eye of the command," they had taught

him at Rockland, and reconnaissance was its "brains and nerves."

Tearing up the notes he had made of Ledge's call, Earl dropped them into the fireplace where they burst into flames on the glowing logs.

A small farmtown on Route One between Philadelphia and Baltimore, Muhlenburg was only twenty-odd miles from the Thomson estate in Wahasset. Within half an hour after Ledge's call from Summitt City, Earl Thomson's red Porsche turned at Pyle's Corners in Muhlenburg and headed up Fairlee Road toward Harry Selby's farm.

A housing park appeared, a lighted sprawl of trailers and motor homes. Several miles beyond it Earl came to Mill Lane, a narrow, curving blacktop. A young girl was riding a bicycle up the road toward a gate marked by split-rail fencing. Thomson saw a sign that read SELBY glowing in his headlights.

Passing the girl in the dusk, Earl had only an impression of blond hair held back with a ribbon, thin white legs pumping hard, and tight denim shorts. In his rear-view mirror he saw the girl turn into the driveway marked SELBY and pedal through a row of trees toward a house where a dog was barking. . . .

At a bar on the main highway, Earl had a bag of potato chips and two bottles of beer. He smoked several cigarettes and played a pinball machine. It was dark when he drove back to Mill Lane. The Selby house was set back from the road. He could see the lights through the trees. Now he didn't hear the dog.

He drove past the gate and down a short hill to Fairlee Road. Making a U-turn, he went back up the blacktop, slowly this time with his window rolled down.

The silence put him on edge, and so did the slow, heavy rush of wind in the trees. At the top of the hill, Earl noticed an overgrown entrance to an old logging road, a narrow trail that seemed to run across the top of the Selby meadow. The gully in front of it was floored with weather-warped logs and the entrance itself was choked with honeysuckle and thin saplings.

Earl turned into the opening, fed gas to his powerful car

and slowly forced a way through the undergrowth. Soon he was clear of it, topping a rise that gave him a view of a shining pond, a grove of squat fruit trees and the Selby house beyond them, bright with lights on two floors, like a small ocean liner in the darkness.

A woman moved about on the first floor. He could see her through the window, a wide-hipped, indistinct figure. She seemed to be clearing a table.

Taking binoculars from the glove compartment, Earl studied the house. Smoke rose from a chimney, a spark flared occasionally. Lamps mounted on tall posts illuminated the driveway and garage. Beyond he made out a small log cabin, a kennel run and neatly stacked rows of firewood.

Movement at the second floor window caught his eyes. It was the girl he'd seen on the bicycle. She was taking the ribbon from her hair. Adjusting the scopes, he brought her face into sharp focus. She was shaking her head, loosening her hair and letting it tumble back and forth around her shoulders.

He could see her red mouth, and the shine of her lips when she moistened them. She looked so close in the scopes that he could imagine putting out his hand and touching her.

Harry Selby's daughter.

The "eyes of command" told him she was the key to their problem. Her father must love her very much. If she had trouble of some sort, an accident, say, Harry Selby would return quickly. No question about it . . .

The excitement he'd felt earlier was intensified by something free and defiant in the way she shook out her hair and pulled off her blouse. They always knew what they were up to, even when they assumed they were alone and no one would see, keeping in practice . . .

She unbuttoned the waistband of her shorts. They were so tight she had to wriggle her hips to get them off. A falling coldness settled into his stomach and loins. He was oblivious to everything else around him. The riot in his blood nearly betrayed him. He didn't hear the furious barking until it was almost too late.

The dog raced toward him across the meadow, huge and black in the moonlight, a German shepherd with a small boy running behind him.

"Blazer, Blazer, what is it?" he had shouted, and it was this sound that alerted Earl and broke his rigid trance.

He hadn't cut the engine, the Porsche was idling softly. Earl backed rapidly from the logging road, smashing recklessly through the thick coils of underbrush.

As he accelerated and drove away, the blast of the engine drowned out the fading challenge of the big guard dog.

CHAPTER FOUR

Later that evening Harry Selby drove back to the motel in Memphis. The party at Jarrell's had been frustrating and—what the hell was the word for it—*opaque*, that was it. He had faced what seemed to be unreflecting surfaces wherever he turned. A dozen or so people had been there, enjoying baked chicken and a huge salad of fresh vegetables.

Clem Stoltzer, Lee Crowley and the Ledges were on hand, and a neatly groomed man with horn-rimmed glasses, the environmental director, Froelich Nash.

Crowley and Froelich Nash chatted with him. "As Mr. Nash can tell you," Crowley said, "Summitt's an old-fashioned kind of place. But it's like a mirror of the future. That's why it works."

Jazz tapes sounded loudly. Subdued lights from fluorescent tubing played across the plants and ferns.

Froelich Nash said, "Crowley's point is simplistic. Summitt works because we control the value of our money." He removed his glasses and polished them carefully. "We control the price of foodstuffs and shelter. We have our own beef and poultry farms. Rents are controlled by the council. We've stopped inflation here."

Sergeant Ledge took him away to meet his wife, a woman with large, calm eyes. Later Stoltzer explained with serious intensity some things he had neglected to mention about productions operations and estimates.

Jennifer brought him a plate of food and told him an amusing story about falling asleep in the sauna that afternoon and waking to find that—he had missed the rest of it because someone turned up the music.

The flow of guests from room to room and the endless, cheerful talk created a porous barrier between him and Jarrell, and prevented them from talking. It wasn't until he was leaving that they had a moment alone.

Selby said, "I've enjoyed meeting your friends, but I think we should get our business settled. I'll come back tomorrow, okay?"

His brother had rubbed the back of his hand against his forehead as if to press away an insistent pain. "It's not those goddamn lots, is it though, Harry? It's the old man, and I understand that. But I'm not sure I knew him myself. Sometimes I'd think I was getting close to him, and then he'd slam a door in my face. Sometimes I almost can't even remember what he looked like. There were times he wouldn't let you know what he was thinking and that drove my mother crazy. A lot of things he didn't leave us, a lot of things weren't included in the old man's estate. Our mutual father couldn't have been so smart after all"—he was speaking rapidly, his voice rising—"spent half his life in the army and ended up with nothing."

They were standing at the curb, darkness around them and sounds from the party spilling out from Jarrell's house.

"Where were you the night he was killed? How did you find out about it?"

Jarrell put both hands on his brother's shoulders and studied him intently. His eyes seemed puzzled, vulnerable.

Selby said, "Easy now. Want to drop this until later?"

"No, I want to talk to you, Harry. But I'm not sure I've got things straight myself. I wasn't there that night, when he was shot and killed. He asked me to stay with him but"—Jarrell rubbed his forehead again—"I had to get back to school, exams or something. But he was expecting someone, I realize that now. He was worried about it, whoever they were. Maybe it would help if we went over everything, made that call to Breck or the cops in Truckee like you suggested."

"All right then," Selby said. "Tomorrow." For the first

time he felt a personal connection with his troubled half brother, a recognition of their relationship that could dissolve the strained civility between them.

"Sure, sure, tomorrow," Jarrell said, smiling. But it was not an easy smile.

Lights had fallen across them from the apartment. The front door was open and Jennifer was standing there with Sergeant Ledge and Stoltzer behind her.

"So this is where you've been hiding," Jennifer called out, and walked out to join them. Her mood was festive, gay. They stood chatting casually until the canopied bus turned into the street and stopped to pick up Harry Selby.

Selby opened up his duffel bag and took out his father's diaries. Skipping through the Korean and court-martial entries, he read what Jonas Selby had written the night he had been shot and killed by "prowlers or drunken fool kids," in Sergeant Ledge's words.

On that night his father had written: "It's worth it, goddammit, no matter what Jarrell claims. He can't be here, he *won't* be here is what he means. Never mind that I said please. Too long ago, he says, but they'll be here, I'm sure of that. It hurts, what Jarrell says. That I can't be sure, that I forget . . ."

The cramped, almost illegible words somehow brought him closer to his father and to his brother. He didn't understand Jonas Selby's pleas to Jarrell, but he could respond to their concern and dependence, and their helpless involvement with one another. Sitting in the bright, dismal room, the yellowed diaries heaped on a coffee table, Selby found himself envying them. At least they were linked together by something, never mind whether it was love, or some kind of fear. Something.

His own links were only a few faded snapshots. He had pictures of his mother too, taken in the backyard of his grandfather's home in Davenport, Iowa, under cherry trees, a pretty young woman smiling self-consciously. He had lived there after her death, and he knew the cherry trees well. He had climbed all over them as a boy.

Selby often wondered why he thought so much more about

42

his father than he did his mother. She hadn't wronged him in any way, that must be it. She had just died. He remembered the funeral and the cut-glass vases of flowers and the smooth ivory feel of her forehead when he'd kissed her before they closed the coffin. The priest had sprinkled holy water over the mourners and Harry Selby's hands had got wet while he looked carefully through the cards on the funeral flowers for his father's name. (As a little boy, his mother had lulled him with the story that his father was "off in the army" and would come back to him one day. But after her death his grandfather made it clear his daughter had never been married to Jonas Selby, although she had given his name to their son, Harry.)

After college, Selby tried to find out the details of his father's military service. A Corporal Thomas Nye at the Department of the Army's Records Center in Washington, D.C., had provided him with information.

Jonas Selby had served in an intelligence unit in Korea with the rank of sergeant. At the time of his induction (in Peoria, Illinois), he had been unmarried and without dependents. After three years in Korea, Jonas Selby had been reduced to the rank of private and confined to a military stockade near Seoul. From there he had been transferred to an army hospital in Boulder, Colorado, for the treatment of service-related disabilities.

Jonas Selby had then returned to the anonymity of civilian life, and his shadowy profile had faded completely from the files of the United States Army.

The charges against his father had not been specified in Corporal Nye's reply. A transcript of the court-martial proceedings were still not available. The trial's referral symbols were K. (Korea), Gen. Crt. (General Court-Martial), Selby, J.—36663864 (Selby's serial number), but the material was classified operative-confidential and, as such, could not be disseminated to unauthorized persons.

Not even to his son, Selby had thought bitterly, a son he had never admitted having, or acknowledged in any other way, not until it was too late. . . .

Unable to sleep, Selby put on his topcoat and went out for a walk. The neighborhood was familiar to him from many road trips, stretches of freeway and neon signs near airport hotels and liquor stores, sex shops and topless bars. In older cities there was always the bus station with Norman Rockwell soldiers, more neon, bag ladies, winos and young girls, and in the luncheonette off the waiting room, the steam counters with breaded meatloaf, watery coleslaw and flat, starchy pies.

At an all-night diner he stopped for coffee. Something about the waitress caught his attention. There was nothing unusual about her; she was plump and clean with her hair tied back behind her neck, but she puzzled him for some reason or other.

It was the way she took his order, he realized; no, not quite that, but the way she reached for the Silex when he asked for coffee. She didn't turn around, just swept an arm back and picked up the glass pot without looking at it. But he couldn't figure out why that simple gesture should have interested him.

When he returned to his room at the Delta Arms the red light was flashing at the base of his phone. It was his daughter, Shana, on the line.

"Where've you been, daddy? I called twice already."

"I went for a walk. Is something wrong?"

"There's nothing to be worried about, nothing at *all* . But Mrs. Cranston, she got all excited and just insisted we call the police, she acts like—"

"Are you all right, Shana?"

"Of course, I just—"

"Is Davey all right?"

"I'm on the other phone, dad," Davey said. "I'm fine, I saw the car first and I told—"

"Davey, please be quiet. I was talking to daddy."

"Goddammit, Shana, don't ever start a conversation telling me Mrs. Cranston had to call the police. Start at the beginning now."

"I'm sorry, really I am. I didn't mean to scare you. That was really dumb. But a car was parked up on the logging road tonight, and Davey went up to find out what it was doing there. Tell him, Davey."

"That's right, dad. It was about nine o'clock and I heard Blazer barking. So I went up to the top of the meadow, and it was a sports car, sitting there with the lights out. I—"

Shana interrupted him. "It's where people used to park for beer parties, daddy."

"They used it for more than that, you know they did, Shana, until daddy and I planted that honeysuckle hedge along the blacktop."

"Dave, did you get a look at the car?"

"No, it was too dark, dad. But it was low and kind of bulky, I could tell that much, a Corvette or maybe a Porsche. The driver was holding something shiny, binoculars, I think. He must have heard me coming 'cause he started the car and drove off. It was either dark blue or dark red, something like that."

Shana said, "Daddy, here's Mrs. Cranston."

Mrs. Cranston's voice was stern. "Could've been some of them drunks from Little Tenn, Mr. Selby. But they're gone now. They never drink where God and decent folk can watch 'em, not that piney trash. They like sucking on their bottles in the dark. But don't you worry none now."

She had called the sheriff's substation on Route One near Muhlenburg; Sergeant Ritter had sent a car out. Ed Jimson and Milt Karec had checked up and down Mill Lane and had found the break where someone had driven through the honeysuckle hedge onto the logging road. She'd have Casper Gideen fix it in the morning.

"We're all snug now," she told him. "The dog's in and Ed and Milt'll be checkin' around again later tonight. Now Shana wants to talk to you, Mr. Selby."

"Daddy, I forgot to ask you! How's Uncle Jarrell? What's he like? Is he coming for a visit or anything?"

"We didn't touch all those bases yet, honey. It's late now, you and Davey had better get to bed."

"Okay, daddy. But don't hang up, please. I forgot. I told Normie Bride I'd call him after I talked to you. Is that all right?"

"Well, keep it short, doll. You'll see him at school in the morning."

"Thanks, daddy. Good night—I love you. And Uncle Jarrell too."

Selby called his brother in Summitt, but Jennifer answered, sounding sleepy and surprised to hear from him.

"I'll try to rouse him, Harry. Hang on."

After a moment she came back saying, "I'd need help from Gabriel, or a bass drum anyway. We had a nightcap after everyone left—" A smile lit her voice. "Then we went off to see the wizard. I told him you wanted to talk to him but he only mumbled something about seeing you tomorrow."

"Did he say when?"

"No, but he and Mr. Stoltzer are driving to Lindville in the morning. I don't think they'll be back until sometime in the afternoon."

"Would you please ask him to call me before he leaves? I may have to change my plans."

"I sure will, Harry. It was a nice party, wasn't it?"

"Yes, it was."

"Have a good sleep, Harry. I'll see you tomorrow, I hope."

But Jarrell didn't call the next morning. At ten Selby rang his apartment but got no answer. He had obviously gone off to Lindville with Stoltzer without bothering to return his call, or Jennifer had forgotten to give him the message.

Selby lunched at the counter of a crowded restaurant where the snatches of talk were of weather and football games. A radio report mentioned that certain local highways and interstates would be closed that weekend. There was a mention of Camp Saliaris, and he remembered that was close to Summitt City. A man beside him was saying that the Vols needed a running game, while the radio announcer was explaining that traffic would be diverted onto secondary roads. Airborne and field maneuvers from the installation would begin at—Selby didn't catch the time because the football fan chose that moment to outline to his companion—moving catsup bottles and mustard jars into positions—the obvious disadvantage of the Veer information against stunting linebackers.

At the Delta Arms, Selby tried his brother's number again. After a dozen rings he broke the connection and put a call through to Clem Stoltzer's office. A secretary told him that Mr. Stoltzer was in a meeting but had left a message for him. He was to call Sergeant Hank Ledge at Security. If Mr. Selby would hold, she would put him through.

He thanked her and waited. In a moment Sergeant Ledge came on.

"Afternoon, Mr. Selby. Tried you a while back but the clerk said you stepped out. Reason I called, your brother called me a while ago from Lindville. Mr. Stoltzer had something come up and couldn't go with him. Jarrell drove over alone this morn-

46

ing. He'd like to have dinner with you tonight in Memphis. He'll come by the motel about seven. Asked me to tell you that, Mr. Selby."

"Thanks, Sergeant. I'll be waiting for him. By the way, do you know where Jennifer is? There's no one at Jarrell's."

"I think she left, Mr. Selby. Earlier today. But I'll check. Hold on a second." The connection was broken. After a humming interval, the sergeant said, "That's right, Mr. Selby. I talked to the guard at the north gate. She picked up her car around eight o'clock. She was on her way to the airport."

Harry Selby watched the fading sunlight darken and soften the pyracantha and squat firs surrounding the motel's swimming pool. Their evasions had nothing to do with him, he was thinking. He was the outsider here, a role he was accustomed to. But he felt oddly dispirited. A bit of doggerel from his father's diaries came into his mind for no reason. "A cannonball took off his legs, so he laid down his arms." That was followed by lists of trains and a poem about the Bonnie Earl of Murray. He would have liked to ask Jarrell about that. But he wouldn't now. The past was a hostile place, Sarah had told him. The addiction of nostalgia was always terminal. "The past is the only place they allow hearsay evidence," she'd insisted.

If his brother wanted to avoid him, he could simply have said so. No need to bring Jennifer and the granite-faced sergeant into it. No reason for all these clumsy lies and charades. Maybe Jarrell had wanted to be honest last night. For a moment or so it had seemed that way. But it didn't matter.

He knew now why the waitress in the diner had caught his attention last night. She'd known where the coffee pot was, had reached for it without looking, it was as simple as that. But Jennifer hadn't known where the coffee was. That's what had been puzzling him all along.

She'd pulled out drawers and opened cupboards until Jarrell went in to help her. A young woman who slept over regularly would certainly know where the coffee things were kept. Which meant she hadn't known Jarrell either very long or very well.

The office door of the motel opened and the clerk called,

47

"Phone, Mr. Selby. It's long distance for you. You can take it in here if you want."

The connection was bad, streaked with what he thought at first was static. He recognized Mrs. Cranston's voice, but it was so oddly cracked and muffled that he didn't understand her. Then he realized she was crying.

"I hate to—because you're so far off, but somebody took her, Mr. Selby. The police are looking . . ."

"I can't hear you. What—?"

"Somebody in a car took her, took Shana. Davey's not back yet. Trooper Karec—"

The motel office was warm, an electric heater glowing in a corner, but Selby's stomach had become so cold and cramped that the sudden pain flattened his lips. Trooper Milt Karec was speaking to him then in a quiet and careful voice.

"— five-fifteen, five-thirty, it happened about then. She was riding her bike on Fairlee Road . . ."

It didn't get through to Selby. The words were unrelated to reality; they were only noises. He knew Trooper Karec, a stocky young man with glasses and a pleasant smile, black hair already graying. He was the solid officer you talked to about fishing permits, dog licenses, when the roads would be clear after snowstorms.

"—a car hit her."

"Goddammit, is Shana hurt?"

"No reason to think that, Mr. Selby. That is, we don't know yet."

Fairlee Road was a stretch of blacktop that ran along the eastern line of Selby's place. From there it curved past a trailer camp known as Little Tennessee (Little Tenn) to the main highway linking Philadelphia and Baltimore. Karec told him that Shana had been riding her bicycle on Fairlee, her smashed bike had been found there. Skid marks indicated that a car had swerved and sideswiped her.

"He deliberately ran into her?" Selby was trying not to shout.

"Mr. Selby, we can't say *deliberate,* and we can't say *him* yet. We don't know if it was a man. We're figuring maybe she was just shook up and he—the driver—took her to a hospital. We've checked East Chester General and St. Luke's, but nobody's treated anyone answering your daughter's description."

"Hold it." Selby said to the clerk, "Call the airport and get me on the next flight to Philadelphia. Tell them it's an emergency."

"You'll have to use the pay phone, Mr. Selby. I can't tie up this switchboard."

Selby reached across the counter and took a grip on the clerk's shoulder.

"Make that call," he said. "Make it now, you hear me?"

"All right, all *right.*" The clerk dialed rapidly, his finger-flicks petulant.

Selby said, "Trooper, tell Mrs. Cranston I'll be on the next flight to Philadelphia. Is my son there now?"

"No, sir, he's still down on Fairlee with Trooper Jimson. We got four squads covering the back roads, Sergeant Ritter is checking the GPs in Long Grove and London Mill. We got everybody out, don't worry." Trooper Karec cleared his throat. "Your daughter could be here waiting for you by the time you get home."

But Trooper Karec was wrong; when Selby got home four hours later, Shana wasn't there. Selby knew that with chilling certainty when he walked in and saw his son and Mrs. Cranston sitting stiffly beside the phone. A growl sounded as their German shepherd came hurtling down the stairs, the ferocious challenge fading into whimpers at the sight of Selby.

"Blazer's been up in Shana's room," Davey said. "He wouldn't come down after the troopers left."

"Can I fix you something to eat, Mr. Selby?" Mrs. Cranston was standing but she kept her large, worn hand on the phone. "There's pot roast, it's cold now, but I could make you some sandwiches."

"No, that's all right, thanks."

Davey sagged against his father and began to cry. His emotional collapse was shattering; he had obviously kept his feelings under control until that instant, but the effort was too much for his years and strength.

"She's lost, isn't she, dad?" The firelight glinted on his tears. "She took a wrong turn or something. Nobody'd hurt her, she's

49

lost, I know it. She's waiting for it to stop raining and come home . . ."

Selby changed into slacks and a sweater, his senses painfully intent on the silent phone.

He and Davey sat in the study with sandwiches and coffee in front of the fireplace. The light glowed on the leather furniture and hardwood floors. Rain came lightly down the windows. A few of the panes were from the original Quaker farmhouse, the glass flawed and burled and smoky, and the rain found these wavy fissures and followed them in swift, darting patterns, a flashy contrast to the newer glass where the water fell in slow, level rhythms.

On the plane ride from Memphis, Selby had forced himself to face the obvious possibilities as unemotionally as possible. Shana would be found safe and sound. At a doctor's office, at somebody's house, somewhere. Or she'd be found injured, or dead. Or she would remain missing . . .

"I brought her bike back up here." Davey had washed his face and dried his eyes. He was Sarah's gift to them, Selby always thought; he had her dark hair, her quick smiles, and warm, brown eyes. "I put it behind the kennel run," he want on, "where it will be out of the way. It's got some red paint on it, the bike, I mean. It's pretty banged up—" His breath caught, and he looked steadily into the fire. "There's some red streaks on the frame and sprocket. I'm thinking about that car on the logging road, dad. Remember we called you about it?"

"Yes," Selby said, but that call from Shana seemed like a time in another world, the plastic motel room, his brother and the girl who loved boats, the grim sergeant, all of them receding now into shadows.

"You said it was a sports car," Selby said, "with a low silhouette like a Corvette, wasn't it?"

"I couldn't tell what color it was because it was night," Davey said, "but it wasn't white or yellow or anything like that. It had to be a dark color, maybe brown or red."

The phone rang. They heard Mrs. Cranston answer it. Selby was up and moving when she said, "Oh, bless you, baby. Your daddy's right here, 'course he is."

Selby ran from the study to the foyer.

"Baby, here he is."

"Shana, are you all right?"

"Yes, daddy, but—"

"Where are you?"

"Daddy, he hurt me."

"Where *are* you?"

"I'm at Barby Kane's in Little Tenn." Her voice became ragged and thin; she was crying. "Come and get me, please. Don't bring Davey or anybody. Promise, daddy."

"I'm leaving now, honey."

"Hurry, daddy. But don't look at me, please, don't look at me. Just take me home."

CHAPTER FIVE

Early Saturday morning an edge of light spread over the trees in Selby's meadow. He was alone in the study, an untasted glass of whiskey beside him. To distract himself he had been glancing through his father's diaries, the words occasionally blurring in front of his eyes.

Merwin Kerr, their family doctor, had been upstairs with Shana since about four that morning, almost two hours. Troopers Milt Karec and Ed Jimson were on their way to East Chester General with the rolls of film and other medical evidence which Paramedic-Sergeant Edith Redden had compiled from an examination of Shana's injuries. This evidence would be developed and classified at the hospital's laboratory, since neither the sheriff's substation nor the East Chester Police Department had the facilities for sophisticated forensic work; such analyses and evidential procedures were routinely processed by local hospitals on a rotating basis.

The paramedic-sergeant had explained to Selby that this was not an ideal arrangement, that the police department should have its own labs and staff for such work, but there were money problems, there always were, and the voters had chosen to cut off their noses by voting down a measure for the funding of such a facility and the personnel to operate it.

Selby suspected there was a deliberate therapy in the

nurse's determined explanation of her department's staffing problem. In those strange and dreadful morning hours, he was numbly grateful for it.

Little Tenn had been a hellish nightmare. The trailer park was originally named Pleasant Acres. Some years before, a sign at the entrance had announced this, a big square sign hanging between tall posts. The lettering was quaintly stylized, a blend of Amish and Old English characters surrounded by yellow daisies, painted to resemble rows of smiling, welcoming eyes.

When the dogwood and wild apple trees flowered, the park was fringed by a profusion of pink and white blossoms. In that season the pathways among the trailers were swept clear and clean by fresh winds. There were parties in the central campground of Little Tenn, kegs of beer and cider, corn-on-the-cob and pork ribs roasting over open grills. Square dancing and Bible readings broke out with the first flush of spring, and the Jessup boy with his second sight and visions shouted prayers and prophecies with such wild-eyed fervor that it made the hand-clapping spectators homesick with longing for revival tents, and pines and swamps and mossy trees.

But the Pleasant Acres sign had blown down and nobody seemed responsible for putting it back up. Rain and snow turned the paths into ribbons of mud. Only Casper Gideen had done anything about it; he and his sons flagstoned a lane from their trailer out to Fairlee Road, giving them year-round access.

As more people from the south moved in, the camp became known as Little Tenn. The migrants worked the woods and tended the mushroom houses that dotted the rolling countryside, low and vaulted, like windowless barns. But the people living at Little Tenn didn't mind the mushroom houses that ringed them in, because the work paid their bills and kept their heads a desperate fraction above the line that separated them from the welfare blacks and Puerto Ricans.

That's what made it bearable for the pineys, Gideen had told Selby, to be able to stand in line at the Muhlenburg stores and markets and pay cash for their vittles while strapping black men (or more likely, their women) handed over, in shame, the strips of food stamps.

Barby Kane lived with her mother, Coralee Kane, in a two-room caravan model, with worn carpets, flowered draperies and a nineteen-inch television set. With her small face and white-blond hair, Coralee Kane looked more like Barby's older sister than her mother. Selby knew Barby as one of Shana's school friends who came to play in the meadow with her, listen to records or drink cocoa upstairs and skate on the pond when it was safe.

He'd found Shana lying in the small, airless bedroom of the trailer, a pale blue blanket pulled up around her throat. Her face was turned to the wall; he couldn't make out her expression, but he saw the damp stains on the blanket, dark, uneven blotches below her narrow hips.

"Didn't you bring a blanket, daddy?" she said, without turning her head. "I've ruined this one. I've made a mess of Mrs. Kane's blanket. Didn't you bring one of ours?"

"Never mind the blanket, honey," Coralee Kane said, fingering her curlers. "You can take hit."

"It's all dirty, it's filthy."

"I said you could take hit. Needs to be cleaned anyway."

"Did you hear, daddy? We can go now."

"Your daddy can bring hit back. Get hit cleaned like new and bring hit back."

"Momma, will you stop talking about that goddamn old blanket," Barby Kane shouted. "Will you just shut up about it, momma?"

"Child, I been on these two feet of mine for ten hours, and I don't want no blasphemy from you, hear? Blanket's ruined anymore, but I told him to take hit."

"I wish you'd stop about that blanket, it's already been worse places tonight."

"You want a whipping, you keep hit up, Barby. Go on, Mr. Selby, take your child home."

Selby lifted Shana and carried her to his station wagon through the rain. Barby walked with them, holding a plastic pillow over Shana's head. Residents of Little Tenn stood in their lighted doors watching them. Selby saw Casper Gideen, tall in a black raincoat, walk up to the staring men and women and speak to them. His words were carried off by the wind, but their effect was obvious; the gawkers pulled their heads in and slammed their doors.

On the way home Selby looked at his watch. It was nearly two-thirty. The interior of the car was warm and close, sour with the mud and the damp and the acid sharpness of his daughter's sweat.

Selby had adamantly refused to allow troopers Karec and Jimson to either question or examine his daughter.

"But we got to get a line on this thing." Milt Karec had been angry and confused, standing at the fire in the foyer, rain dripping in a steady stream from his hat brim to his thick, black boots. "We got to get a description of the guy and a make on the car. The perpetrator could be gone the hell clean out of the country if we keep stalling around. This is a felony, Mr. Selby, and you just can't—"

"Now hold it, goddammit. I'm her father and she won't even talk to *me*. She's been raped and badly beaten. She doesn't need cops standing over her asking for details."

"But we can't—"

"I want her examined by a policewoman. Nobody else is going to talk to her until Dr. Kerr gets here."

Milt Karec had called Sergeant Ritter at the substation near Muhlenburg. The sergeant agreed to contact Paramedic Redden, but warned Karec that this would waste valuable time.

Paramedic-Sergeant Edith Redden had arrived an hour or so later. After assisting Dr. Kerr tend to Shana—the doctor had reached Selby's house only minutes before the nurse—Redden had questioned Shana briefly, eliciting a tentative description of the man who had kidnapped and raped her.

This information had been reported to the East Chester Detective Division, which had the investigative responsibility for such felonies. The description of the rapist and his car was processed for preliminary evaluation and priority by the shift supervisor, Sergeant Burt Wilger.

When Dr. Kerr came downstairs, Selby started to get up, but the doctor said, "Sit still, Harry. Shana's sleeping now. I've given her something that will let her sleep for another eight or ten hours. When she wakes she'll be hungry. I've told Mrs. Cranston what to give her. Then see that she takes the pills I've left, every six hours. She's all right, in one sense. It's her period, I mean. But I want her to stay absolutely quiet for a few days. No visitors and not too much time on the phone. If you don't put your foot down, her friends will swarm around like it's a damn skiing accident, and they'll want all the details and it's too early for that. She needs rest and sedation. If she's fretful or angry, or won't talk to you, don't be upset, that's normal." He winced at the word "normal" in such a circumstance.

Dr. Kerr gripped Selby's shoulder; Selby felt a tremor in the old man's hand. "Goddammit, Harry, a thing like this makes my whole life seem like a waste. You work so hard to bring them into the world, to take care of them, teaching them what you think is right. Maybe the bad old days with a hanging tree and a whipping block weren't so bad after all." He looked at his watch. "If she wants to talk about what happened, I won't put any restrictions on that. But don't press her. It's too late to say good night, so I'll say good morning, Harry. I looked in on Davey, by the way. He's restless but he'll be dropping off soon. I'll see myself out."

Then Selby was alone, the untouched whiskey beside him, a thin white light rising above the meadow. He couldn't quite see the pond, only the beech trees that screened it from the house. The rain had turned their trunks black. They were saplings when Sarah planted them. She could circle them with her hand.

Blazer came down from Shana's room and padded into the kitchen. Selby heard him drinking from his stoneware bowl. The big shepherd then prowled quietly around the first floor, finally settling beside Selby in the study.

Shana hadn't got a good look at the man; her description was emotional, splintered, charged with panic and hysteria. A wild kind of look in his eyes, twenty-five, thirty, she couldn't be sure, dark (the night? the man?), anger . . .

Blazer growled and raised his head. Davey called from the top of the stairs, "Dad, please come up, hurry. Shana's talking . . ."

Selby took the stairs two at a time. Davey stood at the open door of her room, eyes bright under his tousled hair.

"She said something about 'hornets,' dad. It was real clear. I came out here and listened, and she said some other things I couldn't understand. Then she said, 'hornets' again, and she was crying."

Blazer tried to push Selby aside with his head and crowd into Shana's room.

"Hold it, stay, Blazer. Goddammit, *stay.*"

Selby went in and put a hand on her forehead. It was cool and dry. He touched her shoulder, she didn't move. Her breathing was soft and shallow. The room smelled of talcum powder.

Shana's desk was covered with books. A tennis racket stood on end in the window embrasure. An assemblage, covered with glass and framed in dark wood, hung above her bed. The wood was painted in alternating stripes of yellow and green and red, and the bottom strip displayed a narrow brass plate with the etched legend: MUNICH, 1972.

A dozen names were printed on a parchment in a round, childish hand, and traced with pressed leaves and flowers. It had been a project of Shana's for a history class—years ago, she had been only a child, in second or third grade, he couldn't remember which.

But he remembered her looking up the colors of the Israeli flag in the atlas and then finding a plant and flower book at the library, an old curio of a book which listed the traditional virtues and vices associated with flora of all kinds down through the years. Shana had bordered her tribute with leaves and flowers from their own woods and meadow, the leaves and petals pressed and waxed and intertwined . . . oak leaves for valor, white dogwood for strength and laurel for glory, aspen leaf for lamentation, white chrysanthemum petals for truth and orange, feathery strands of wild marigold, fading now, as the flower of grief. A woven design of nature's message to honor the names of the Israeli athletes who had been murdered in Munich, Germany, at the Olympic Games. Selby looked at those names in the lightening dawn, a hand still touching his daughter's slim,

57

young shoulder. Yaacob Springer, Kehat Schorr, Mark Slavin and Eliazar Halfin . . .

He started when he heard Shana's voice. She had murmured the word "hell" and another word he couldn't make out.

Davey came into the room. "Did you hear that, did you, dad?"

"Not all of it. 'Hell' and then something else."

The morning light covered her bed. Her arms were outside the covers, the bandages small and white about her wrists and one of her hands. Her sandy eyelashes accentuated the blue-black bruises on her cheeks.

She stirred suddenly and Selby put a hand tightly on her arm. An expression of panic twisted her features. But her eyes remained closed.

"Mommy, I'll kill it. I'll kill it." Shana's lips barely moved, but the words were clear and spaced deliberately.

"The waves," she said then, and tears started under her eyelids and glinted on her swollen face. Her voice became deep and rasping, as she cried out, "I am worse than men, in my heart is hatred—"

A phone began ringing. "Stay here," Selby said to Davey. "Try to remember everything she says."

He went into his bedroom and picked up the phone from Sarah's worktable, still cluttered with jars of pencils and books and files, recipes and random news clippings.

"Hello?"

"Mr. Selby, this is Mr. Stoltzer, Clem Stoltzer in Summit City. It's early, I know, I hope I'm not disturbing you."

"No, what is it?"

"Mr. Selby, your brother, Jarrell, left Summit unexpectedly this morning. I was wondering if he'd mentioned anything about a change of plans to you?"

"When was this?"

"Around five or six o'clock, according to the guard at the north gate."

"Well, is that unusual? For someone to leave that early?"

"Of course not, people come and go as they like here, anytime they want. But the cleaning crew assigned to your brother's unit reported that his clothes and gear are gone. If he intended to resign, he would have mentioned it, I think, and collected his money from the credit union, seen about his pension and insurance, things like that. He's got a fine future with Harlequin, and it's not like him to leave this way . . ."

Selby wasn't too interested, his mind and heart were with his daughter, but he said, "We were supposed to meet for dinner last night. Sergeant Ledge told me Jarrell was planning to stop by my motel. I don't know where he is or why he left, Mr. Stoltzer. Maybe his girl friend knows."

"That's a thought, Mr. Selby. Do you happen to have her phone number or address?"

Selby told him no, that he didn't even know her last name. Stoltzer said, "If Jarrell gets in touch with you, I'd appreciate it if you'd ask him to call me. Would you do that, please?"

As Selby hung up, his son hurried into the bedroom. "She's talking too fast for me to remember, so I got my tape recorder. She's saying she'll kill something, she said something about a tunnel and something that sounds like poetry. She's talking about birds too."

The phone rang again. Selby said, "You go back and stay with her, Davey."

It was Casper Gideen. In his typically brusque fashion, he said he'd stop by in ten minutes if that suited Selby. If it didn't, he'd stop by when it did.

Selby put on a hunting jacket and went to the parking lot. The sun was up and the meadow was slick and white with frost. Beyond it was the smooth shine of the pond, and the white beeches.

The log cabin near the garage was named for Casper Gideen, who had built it for Shana and Davey. Davey had burned the letters into a piece of notched and varnished pine. When Gideen saw the sign swaying on its chain, he had said slowly, "My name looks funny printed out. But I'm proud to see it. It was Gideon once, my daddy told us."

Gideen did occasional work on the Selby place, keeping the meadow in trim with a tractor and cutter bar, and chopping down old fruit trees when they were ready for the fireplace.

Tall and thin, about Selby's age, with a rough, weathered face, Gideen's cool, blue eyes could become dark and wary at even a hint of disrespect or ridicule. He wanted to be "let be," in his words. Gideen could hunt pheasant and take his limit without a dog to point or flush them. He knew spring holes in local ponds where panfish were layered by the hundreds; and he took Shana and Davey there in the summer and cooked them breakfasts of perch and bluegills before the sun was up. He knew when game was tiring, and had taught Selby to watch for the sign of tracks going downhill. At night, hunting raccoons, they had often sat on frozen hills and listened to Casper's redbones bugling over the valleys, the sound seeming to carry forever on the winds.

One winter night Gideen had got savagely drunk and smashed his truck into a tree. His wife, Lori, had called Selby, who had found Casper half frozen in his truck and had driven him home. It was after this that Gideen built the log cabin for Davey and Shana. But he had never once mentioned the "accident" or Selby's aid.

When the blue van stopped in the parking lot Gideen climbed out with a cardboard box under his arm.

"I came by to ask for the girl." He handed the box to Selby. "It's from the woman, a new pie and a jar of raisins in pepper sauce. She said it would be good for her." From the front of the van, he took out a jug and worked the stopper loose with his thumb. "We could have a drink, you and me, Harry."

Selby nodded and took a swig of the powerful, colorless liquor. He handed the jug back without wiping off the rim of the neck.

Gideen said, "How is she?"

"Sleeping now. Dr. Kerr's been here."

Gideen drank and stoppered the jug and put it back in the truck. "There was some talk at Little Tenn this morning." Gideen's cold, blue eyes were darker now. "Then it stopped. That means something's started, something's coming. I heard enough to know it's touching your daughter and Goldie Boy Jessup. Don't ask me how. They're afraid. And that could mean the law's in on it. It's against my raisin' to go against my people but I'm with you, Harry. I'll find out what it is. And I'll tell you one more thing now. In my granddaddy's day, they catch the son who did it, that'd be the end of him right there. You tell me we do better, I say prove it. Goodbye to you, Harry."

Davey was waiting for Selby in the foyer. "Dad, Shana's bike is gone. I put it behind the kennel run yesterday, where it'd be out of the way. But it's gone now."

"What about the garage? Somebody might have put it inside, the troopers or Mrs. Cranston. Let's look."

But Shana's bike wasn't in the garage, or anywhere else they looked; it was gone.

Selby called Sergeant Ritter at the sheriff's station, but Ritter was no help; he told Selby that neither Milt Karec nor Ed Jimson would have had any reason to bring the bike in, and if they had they would surely have told him about it.

"But maybe the county detectives got it," Ritter said. "It's their case now, Mr. Selby."

Selby thanked him and called the detective division in East Chester. After being switched to Captain Slocum's office, he was put on hold briefly, and then transferred to a Lieutenant Gus Eberle.

The lieutenant said yes, he had picked up the bicycle earlier that morning, and that the police lab had already run a series of checks on it.

"It was our first lead, Mr. Selby, and we put a top priority on it." Eberle's voice was low and rasping, a heavy smoker or drinker, Selby thought, but his tone was amiable. "A sample of paint from the perpetrator's car would have given us solid ID for an all-points. But the bike didn't help us. It checked out negative."

"What does that mean?"

"What I said, Selby, negative, which means nothing. Your daughter's bike is white with green trim. That's all we found in the way of paint. Some mud and tar, bits of stone and asphalt on the mudguards, but no foreign paint."

"That's very strange." Selby saw that Davey was watching him. "There was red paint on her bike yesterday."

"Who told you that?"

"My son did, Lieutenant. There was red paint on the frame and sprocket after the accident."

"Did you see any red paint, Selby?"

"No, I didn't. But it's not likely my son's mistaken about it."

"What you got to take into account," Eberle said, "is that it was about dark when it happened. Your boy might've seen a streak of tar or mud and figured it for paint."

"I doubt it, Lieutenant."

"Well, maybe he just saw what he wanted to see, Selby." Eberle's voice dropped to an exasperated growl. "Now listen, Selby. I'm just a goddamn cop, but give me credit for knowing how to read a damn lab report. I'm looking at it right now. There's scratches on your daughter's bike, the spokes are broken and the frame is twisted. There's mud and tar on it, and pieces of stone stuck in the metal. But there's no goddamn paint on it except the original white paint and green striping that was sprayed on at the factory, which, by the way, was a Schwinn outlet in Buffalo, New York, in case you want to know."

"What time did you come by to pick it up, Lieutenant?"

"I don't know why the hell that matters. Around four or five o'clock this morning. Doc Kerr's car was in your drive. I didn't want to disturb anybody so I collected the bike and took it to the lab. It was ticketed like any other piece of physical evidence, a weapon, stolen goods, whatever. The thing was not to waste time. Get the bastard before he gets clean out of the country. There's something screwy, by the way Selby, about where your daughter was that night. About the time, I mean. But we're checking that out. You'll get a receipt for her bike, don't worry, and we'll ship it back to you when the lab's through with it. Or you can come by and pick it up. Suit yourself. I been on the case all night, Selby. You got any other questions, talk to Burt Wilger, Sergeant Wilger, he'll be the case officer from here on in. We'll be in touch if there's a break."

When Selby put the phone down, Davey said, "Why is he lying about it, dad? I know there was red paint on Shana's bike."

Selby squeezed his son's shoulder. "Let's keep this talk with the lieutenant between you and me for a while, Davey. Don't say anything about it to Mrs. Cranston or to anyone at school. And not a word to Shana."

62

"Okay, dad. But he was lying, wasn't he?"

"It sure looks like it."

Later Selby listened to the tapes that Davey had made. He ran them back several times, trying to make a copy of what his daughter had said under sedation. It wasn't easy because at times her voice rose hysterically, and at others sank into whispers that were barely audible. It was terrifying to listen to her. Blazer lumbered into the room and whined when he heard Shana's voice rising from the spinning reels.

"Take it easy," Selby said, and pulled the big dog close to him, smoothing his ruff.

Finally Selby had a list of what his daughter had said under sedation. With his comments, it read:

1. Hornet—or hornets.
   (Repeated this word several times—frightened.)

2. Waves—waves.
   (Said this frequently, but why? We're a hundred miles from the seashore.)

3. Tunnel—or tunnels.

4. Birds—birds crying.
   (Said this several times, and *she was crying.*)

5. Time to serve and sin.
   (Sounds like the Bible. This is an angry voice.)

6. Mommy—I'll kill it.
   (The voice was blurred and thick.)

7. Waves and birds.
   (All run together here again.)

8. Mommy, my hand hurts—I hate it.
   (Said this twice.)

9. I think she said, "Tishie."
   (Why mention her grandmother?)

10. Hell is alone—always.
    (Have no idea what this means.)

Shana had apparently retreated into metaphor, drugged and hysterical in her dreams. He had to find out where she'd been taken that night, what she was hiding from them.

Selby spread out a map of East Chester County on the coffee table and drew a penciled circle around Muhlenburg and Fairlee Road, an area including woods, open country and many small farms and residential neighborhoods. He knew these woods and meadows. He and Casper had hunted there many times.

Davey came in and looked at the map, tracing the network of roads running out of Muhlenburg. "I could go with you, dad," he said. "I could help, couldn't I?"

Selby put an arm around his son's shoulder. "We'll start tomorrow," he said. "We'll find where he took her, Davey, then we'll find him. That's a promise."

CHAPTER SIX

The Dupree Engineering Company (a division of Harlequin Chemicals) held its October sales convention at a country club in Osmond, New Jersey, forty miles from the Walt Whitman Bridge and Philadelphia. On Friday afternoon, George Thomson, president of Harlequin, had played with a foursome of local executives, shooting an eighty-two; he might have done better if it hadn't been for the call from Clem Stoltzer in Summitt City.

He was also troubled and disappointed because his son had changed his plans suddenly and decided not to join him for the tournament. Thomson enjoyed being seen with him; there was a sense of accomplishment and pride in introducing Earl to people and savoring their reactions to his dark good looks and casually superior manners.

Thomson had flown to New York that morning on a Correll Group jet from Brussels. His chauffeur had met him at Osmond, but Richard had no message from Earl or any explanation of his absence.

Clem Stoltzer's news, however, had been both good and bad; Harry Selby had returned suddenly to his home in Muhlenburg, but Jarrell's attitude and behavior had become a concern. Plus the fact that he'd had another guest in addition to his brother, a girl who had spent the night with him and left that morning.

Thomson had tried to reach Simon Correll. From his offices in New York and Philadelphia he had tracked him to Mount Olivet but Correll wasn't taking any calls; even Thomson's priority produced only regrets. That was obliquely reassuring because only the most serious emergencies could penetrate the refuge on the Hudson.

Thomson went into the locker room for a sauna and massage and tried to dismiss his anxieties, but they continued to nag at him.

They had been caught completely off-guard by the revelation that Jonas Selby had another son. They had postponed a meeting between the half brothers until the older one had got aggressive about it . . . like his goddamn father, Thomson thought.

Meanwhile they had run checks on Harry Selby . . . a widower, two young children, small farm, ample bank account, a National Football League pension, strong ties to his home and family. Nothing to involve him with Jarrell or keep him at Summitt after they'd settled their real estate business. Thomson had okayed their meeting, though the timing was precarious. After all, it seemed wiser than running the risk of deepening Harry Selby's anxieties . . . risking his suspicions . . .

His decision had been sound, Thomson thought. Selby had left Summitt, and now they could handle Jarrell as necessary, without any complications . . .

The massage relaxed him and put him in an alert and sexually expectant mood—Earl would show up, don't worry. . . .

The cocktail party at the fairway home reserved for him was crowded and noisy, with tanned executives and their smartly turned out wives standing about waiting to talk to him. His spirits rose later when an unescorted young woman joined his large table at the dinner dance. Her name was Natalie Winters. Her cousin was an auditor at Dupree, but she hadn't seen him around. Natalie was a graduate student at Maryhill, a local college. She occasionally joined friends here at the club for bridge, she told Thomson.

A Dupree senior executive, Frank Mallon, suggested with a smile that Natalie must have got her dates mixed up because her cousin was in Houston on a research trip. Possibly, she replied casually, she wasn't all that good at dates and things.

George Thomson had been pleased when she agreed to join him later and alone for a brandy. Her hair was black in the smoky light and her body was full, but with a muscular agility that Thomson found marvelously exciting.

A ringing phone woke him early the next morning. As he lifted the receiver he was comfortably aware of the warm darkness and the silky feel of the girl snuggled up behind him.

It was Clem Stoltzer on the line from Summitt, with Sergeant Hank Ledge on an extension. Thomson swung his legs off the bed and listened, his frown deepening.

Natalie Winters went into the bathroom and closed the door. He waited until he heard the water running. The sergeant told him he had talked to Earl on Thursday and that Jarrell Selby was now missing . . .

Natalie came out of the bathroom, her hair smooth and fragrant. She lay on the bed with one slim leg outside the coverlet.

"How long's he been gone?" Thomson said.

"Since yesterday morning, Major," Ledge told him. "Left his apartment at first light, near as we can figure. Gate guards didn't check him out, and his car's still here. So he may not have left Summitt. We're checking. But the girl's gone, that's for sure."

"Call me at Wahasett in about two hours." Thomson's voice had sharpened; it was good to be reminded of his old rank, and the time with Ledge in Korea. "I'll need all the details then for Mr. Correll."

"We'll stay on top of it, Major."

Thomson called the desk for his car.

He then dialed a number in Philadelphia. The phone was lifted on the first ring; he realized with relief that Lorso had been waiting for his call.

"I'm leaving here in a few minutes, Dom. I just talked to Stoltzer. They got problems. But what about Harry Selby's daughter? The papers have anything on it?"

"Just a couple of lines in the *Bulletin*. I already talked to Captain Slocum. Everything's all right."

Thomson drew a deep breath; his stomach felt cold. "Why'd you call Slocum?"

"That can wait, I think, Giorgio. I'll see you at your place. I'll have it all then."

"Is Earl home?"

"Now look, you take it easy. Earl's home, everything's fine. Have some breakfast. Don't drive with just coffee. A salami omelette, that's good, and some white toast with butter."

"Let me have it now, Dom. All of it."

"But there's nothing, Giorgio. Nothing definite."

"Why'd you call Slocum, then?"

"Because I'm paid to worry, goddammit. It was last night, the accident. It came in as a missing persons, a minor child. The dispatcher had a name, Shana Selby, that's how it made the paper for one edition. Muhlenburg sent it over to East Chester, just routine—that's how Eberle got a line on it. There was some talk about a red car, he said. I don't know where the hell that came from. Eberle told Slocum. Giorgio, like I said, Earl's home, don't worry about it. His car's not in the garage but I haven't talked to him yet. I'll have the whole story when you get here."

Thomson said, "Take care of it, Dom. Take care of it."

"Don't worry, Giorgio."

Thomson put the phone down and listened to the heavy stroke of his heart. He poured himself a drink, a splash of Black Label from a bottle on the dresser. It tasted sour. He shouldn't be worrying, Lorso was closer to him than anyone at Harlequin, anybody anywhere for that matter. There was no name or title on Lorso's door, but few people or problems could get to Thomson's desk without clearance from the little Sicilian.

"Is anything wrong, Mr. Thomson?"

Natalie Winters punched up a pillow behind her back, and watched him pulling on the yellow jockey shorts he had thrown off so impatiently a few hours ago.

"No, just a change of plans," he told her.

He was hardly aware of her, she knew, though she could see the soft bulge of a morning hard-on filling the ribbing of his shorts. He was of medium height and build, but looked larger because his shoulders and arms were thickly muscled. His complexion was dark, not only from the sun but because he was Italian, he had told her last night. His hair was black, his face was hard, the features cut sharply, and his eyes told her it wouldn't be wise to antagonize him, not because he was cruel especially but because he had very little patience with people. Impatience and cruelty were closely related, she had reason to know.

He was close to fifty, or maybe older, but in surprisingly good shape. He ate and drank sensibly, made a point of that, he had told her. Took plenty of vitamins. But there was something else he wasn't getting enough of, Natalie could have told him.

He had been quick last night, rushing it as if he were afraid it might not be there, but after an assist from her that he was hardly conscious of, a touch and pressure that brought a glaze of confident anticipation to his eyes, after that he had settled into a secure and relishing rhythm so intense that when it coiled and finally broke free he cried out as if he were in pain, a sound that always touched Natalie and made her feel tender.

His name was Tomaso, he told her before falling asleep, his hands loose and relaxed between her thighs . . . Giorgio Tomaso.

She raised herself on an elbow now, the sheet dropping away from her smooth white legs. "I thought you were playing golf today, Mr. Thomson. Aren't you one of the leaders in the tournament?"

"I guess I am at that, but it can't be helped."

"You said we'd drive over to Atlantic City this afternoon. You told me you liked the casinos. A psychiatrist would know why, I guess, but gambling turns me on. It's scary. I do things, things that are crazy, and I can hardly remember them."

"Well, like I told you, something came up."

She glanced down at him and laughed. "I can see that, Mr. Thomson."

"Look, you got a card? No, you wouldn't have. Put your phone number on a coaster or a matchbook. I'll be in touch, Natalie. I mean it."

"Okay, my man. But you can't blame a girl for being disappointed." She sat up and fluffed her hair out around her shoulders. "Mr. Mallon said you were staying through Sunday."

"I was hoping to."

"So was I."

Thomson turned from the mirror and looked at her, a hand motionless on the knot of his maroon tie. "What'd Mallon say to you?" he said.

69

"Nothing." Natalie smiled carefully. "It was something I heard at dinner, I guess."

Thomson's concentration had been splintered by what Dom Lorso had told him.

If Earl had joined him yesterday, played golf and gone to dinner . . . they might have had a brandy, listened to the dance music and talked about things that interested Earl . . . his cars, the time in London with the Correll Group, the summers he'd worked at Summitt. Now he was at headquarters in Wilmington, the student prince routine, rotating from one department to another with his supervisors reporting directly to George Thomson. This allowed him to live at home, which a doctor suggested was good both for Earl and his mother, the closeness . . .

It was difficult to talk to Earl, but maybe if he'd had the time and opportunity the night before he wouldn't be standing here now tight with worry and Natalie So-and-So's expensive perfume on everything around him.

She had written a phone number on a paper napkin. She smiled and held it out to him. "I hope you'll call," she said. "Would you kiss a girl goodbye?"

He put his bag down and walked to her side of the bed. "So it was a deal, right?"

"I enjoyed it, Mr. Thomson. That wasn't part of the deal. I mean that."

"I asked you, was it a deal?"

She smiled nervously. "Yes, it was a deal, Mr. Thomson. Mr. Mallon said you'd be alone, that your wife wouldn't be with you."

"Where do you usually work, Natalie?"

"In Philadelphia. I only take a few jobs a month. Mr. Mallon said you didn't like things arranged, that you liked them just to happen."

"He's right, I'm romantic. My wife's a cripple, her name's Adele. Did Mallon mention that?"

"He didn't tell me anything personal."

"She was hurt fifteen years ago, it was an accident, but I was responsible," Thomson said. "Did Mallon tell you all about that?" He was close to shouting. "Did he tell you she's still a goddamn beautiful woman?"

70

She moved quickly back from him, a smile straining her face. "Mr. Thomson. It was business, nothing else."

Thomson struck her twice with a full swing of his arm, and when she rolled on her side, covering her face, making no sound at all, he picked up his bag and left the room.

In the lobby of the clubhouse he bought a morning paper and told the manager that someone in his condo had slipped in the shower and needed a doctor. Franklin Mallon should be informed immediately, and he would take care of it. If Mr. Mallon had any questions whatsoever, he was to contact Dom Lorso at Harlequin headquarters.

Thomson joined his chauffeur, who stood beside a Mercedes Benz 600. On the way home he flipped through the bulky paper until he found the story, a single paragraph in the suburban section.

Under a Muhlenburg, Pennsylvania, dateline, it read:

A fourteen-year-old Chester Township girl was kidnapped at dusk yesterday while riding a bicycle near her home. She was later beaten and raped, according to Detective Captain Walter Slocum of the East Chester Police Department. Slocum said the girl was struck by a car on Fairlee Road, five miles north of Route One, and then driven to an isolated farm where she was sexually assulted. The driver of the vehicle was described by police as a male Caucasian in his twenties or thirties. The girl's name is being withheld by police because of her age.

Two hours after reading this, Thomson was at his home in Wahasset, Pennsylvania. At least the surface of his life was serene, he thought, as a maid brought him orange juice and coffee and a tray of hot rolls. Somewhere beyond the windows of his study a power mower sounded faintly, a last autumn trim of the hedges.

Returning here was always an emotionally ambivalent experience. The grounds were manicured and elegant, a small estate given over to lawns and greenhouses and carefully kept woods with brick-bottomed streams running through them. But after the first glimpse of the driveway and gray manor house, after that first stir of pride would come the dispiriting thought of Adele waiting there for him, alone in her upstairs suite.

Thomson tried to organize his thoughts. The maid told him that Mr. Earl was with his mother and that Mr. Lorso had just joined them.

His phone rang. It was Summitt City, Clem Stoltzer. Thomson made a note of the time and pressed the RECORD button on his desk console.

Stoltzer told him they had no news of Jarrell Selby as yet. He had not returned to his house at Summitt City. Everything else was proceeding on schedule.

Thomson said, "Do you know anything about the girl who was with him?"

"No, sir, just that he said she was a friend of his."

"Did Harry Selby know her?"

"I don't think so."

"But you're not sure?"

"That's right, sir. But I called Harry Selby this morning. He told me he didn't even know her last name and didn't have any idea where to get in touch with her."

"He could have been lying. But you think their meeting at Summitt was a coincidence?"

"That's the impression I got."

Thomson was distracted by voices from the hall. "Keep in touch, Stoltzer." He broke the connection.

Earl and Dom Lorso were coming down the stairs from Adele's suite. Earl laughed and called something to Santos, his mother's therapist.

George Thomson hated the tension gripping him. It reflected worries that Adele couldn't understand or tolerate. Criticism of Earl, to her, was the equivalent of a treacherous disloyalty. He was more than her only son, more than flesh and blood, he was an instrument of God, her savior after the accident. Earl had given his life to her then—his legs were hers, his laughter sounded when hers choked away into sobs; he had made a world worth living for. His fierce love had kept her from finding a solution in the bottle of capsules hidden beneath her pillow.

Adele had in time achieved a steely resignation to her fate and a will to live rooted in the mystical conviction that her life had been spared, at whatever cost in personal anguish, for some preternatural purpose which was beyond her grasp to understand but not her capacity to accept and submit to.

Dom Lorso entered the study with Earl, who wore a blue robe and pajamas.

"Coffee smells good," Thomson's son said.

"Help yourself. You, too, Dom. There's orange juice and fresh rolls."

Earl poured himself coffee and settled into a deep chair, propping his slippered feet against an ottoman. "Coffee's fine," he said. "I'm having breakfast with mother. Santos is making what he calls 'a Cuban credit card.' You take it on faith, I guess."

Dom Lorso sat in a leather chair and stared at his shoes. Small and tidily dressed—white shirt, blue tie, dark jacket— Lorso was several years younger than Thomson, but his face was old, gray and deeply lined. His eyes were tired, heavily lidded, always about to close, it seemed. But at times they could become suddenly and disconcertingly sharp. His thick hair, a cluster of white curls, struck an incongruously cherubic note above the weary face and eyes.

The big room was silent, except for the crackle of the fireplace and the occasional clink as Earl put his cup down.

This silence was deliberate, as Thomson knew. It was a testing game Earl played. He knew his father had questions to ask, but he wouldn't cooperate in even a token fashion with anything resembling an interrogation.

Earl disliked being questioned; in fact he refused to tolerate it. Even as a child, a casual query about what he was doing might tip him into dangerous rages. A doctor had explained to Thomson that this stemmed from the trauma of role reversal. Earl the son was playing the mother to the crippled "child," reading stories to Adele, helping her in and out of the wheelchair, operating the controls of her whirlpool bath, coaxing her to eat and giving her smiles and hugs for rewards. "In the boy's mind, at this stage, his ministrations are perfect, even Godlike, perhaps, and therefore they can't even be questioned or criticized," the doctor had told Thomson.

Thomson said casually, "I didn't see your car when I came in, Earl. So this is a pleasant surprise. I assumed you weren't home."

"Well, I'm glad you're pleasantly surprised." Earl sipped

his coffee and smiled, as though oblivious to the tension in the room.

Thomson found himself reluctantly admiring his son's composure. Rockland Military had put a stamp on him, no doubt of that. The benchmark was evident in the tall, aloof way he held himself and the dismissing politeness he could affect when it suited him.

Those were Rockland's endowments, the molding influence of the hard-assed, stiff-necked army brass (retired) who ran the school. They had worked with Earl's contempt for authority and instincts for violence—"harness those horses" had been a colonel's phrase for it, "guide and shape those qualities rather than stifle them."

They had succeeded, you had to give them that. Earl was totally indifferent to what people thought of him. The swastika he often wore around his neck was a case in point. If people were offended by it, they didn't have to look at it. There had been a local but minor furor in the press because—typically—he had asked a firm of Jewish jewelers in Philadelphia to make the emblem for him. They had objected to the inscription Earl wanted, on the back: "Munich—11/9/38," Munich being one of the places where Crystal Night had been successfully "celebrated" (that was Earl's word to the Philadelphia jewelers) in Germany's Third Reich.

The firm had refused to make the swastika and someone, a clerk or a customer present at the time, had tipped off a local columnist. But Earl had found another jeweler who was willing to do the job and, despite the flurry of unpleasant publicity, insisted that the incident proved his philosophical point, which was that people had options and that somebody would always do anything you wanted providing you paid him enough.

"So," Thomson asked at last, "where's the Porsche? In for a tune-up?"

"No, it was stolen yesterday, father. I was just telling Uncle Dom about it. A pity because it was in mint condition for the rally. Let's hope whoever ripped it off is enjoying it. That's the Christian attitude, right, Uncle Dom?" Earl laughed. "But according to Nietzsche, Christianity and alcohol are society's two greatest narcotics."

Lorso shrugged and blew a smoke ring.

74

Thomson said, "Well, when did this happen?"

"I told you." Earl was still smiling, but a line had hardened around his eyes. "Yesterday."

"I was wondering about the time. The insurance people always want to know, for some reason."

"Well, you can tell them it was yesterday afternoon. Five or six o'clock."

"Where'd it happen?"

"On Route One outside a pub called The Green Lantern. I had a beer or two and when I came out the old red hornet was gone."

"The Lantern's near Muhlenburg," Dom Lorso said. "It's run by a colored guy. It's a bar for coloreds." He inhaled smoke and blew it out in a thick stream. "Which is not to say there's something wrong with it."

Earl stood with a fluid grace which transformed the simple action into a performance. "Yes, Uncle Dom. The Green Lantern is an establishment for ladies and gentlemen of color. *Nigras,* that is. But as Colonel Ward was fond of telling us, the function of the elite in an elite society is to emphasize class distinctions rather than to pretend they don't exist. Camouflage in warfare is an art. In social manners, it's just gutless. I wasn't at The Green Lantern to prove the colonel's thesis, though. I was hoping to buy a shotgun, but my man didn't show."

Thomson said, "Did you report to the police that the Porsche was stolen?"

Earl stared at him. "Look, father. There's no big deal here. I didn't call the cops because there are tons of classic wheels in town for the Longwood Show. Probably one of my pals borrowed the Porsche for a quote joke unquote. So be cool. One of those clowns will swing by with the old red hornet. Anything else?"

Thomson's own temper sharpened. "Yes, dammit. Sergeant Ledge told me he called here Thursday afternoon and left a message with you. Why didn't you tell me about it?"

Earl's face became tight. His powerful hands clenched. "*Why* are you always hassling me?" His voice had risen. "You weren't here, you never *are*. Ledge called about a problem he was having at Summitt with a character named Harry Selby. I didn't know what he was talking about. I told him you were in

Europe. He said he's trying to reach you. I'm not one of your clerks in this house, so kindly get off my ass."

He walked stiffly from the room.

Thomson and Dom Lorso sat in silence for a few moments. They had known each other many years. Their relationship was based on a knowledge of what they had done in the past, and what they were capable of doing, now and in the future, out or pride and ambition and, perhaps most compelling, out of sheer habit. They had long been tacitly aware that their union had become like an old and casually attended marriage, with no unanswered questions between them, no sense of adventure or surprise; they had been left finally with nothing linking them and keeping them together but an unwavering trust.

They had never made the mistake of assuming they knew one another truly well. Lorso was a bachelor and lived in a duplex apartment with a doorman and a fine view of a park. Thomson had been there only once, when Lorso was down with a nagging, persistent flu. A man had been in the kitchen fussing about with a tray of cheese and crackers and drinks. He was balding and plump with wens on his face and wore a plaid belt that matched his tie. A woman in a leather jacket and slim brass chains had been watching TV. Lorso had introduced them to Thomson, but Thomson had never seen them again and had no idea how they fitted into the Sicilian's life.

Their own relationship was based on business and secured by Dom Lorso's loyalty to Thomson, but there was one other significant thing between them, which was their shared knowledge of what men were capable of doing to one another.

Lorso lit a cigarette from the stub burning between his fingers. "Earl called Santos from Muhlenburg late yesterday afternoon after his car was stolen. That's how he got home. Santos drove over and got him. They were back here around seven. Earl had dinner with Adele and they watched TV. So forget what you're worrying about. Earl was here all night. All the time. I already checked that out with Adele and with Santos. Earl wasn't involved with what happened to Harry Selby's kid. Get that out of your mind. He's proud of you, Giorgio, although I admit he don't always show it. But where it counts, he's your son. That trouble with the cunt at Rockland, even that was a way of showing you he didn't take shit from anybody, that he's got your kind of balls."

"But you were worried last night."

"I told you, that's what I'm paid for." Dom Lorso waved at the smoke from his cigarette, which drifted between them like gray webbing. "When I talked to Captain Slocum he'd heard something from Eberle about a red sports car being involved."

Lorso waved again at the smoke. "When my grandmother lived with us, Giorgio, you know how old people are, she warned us to watch out if we ever smelled garlic in the wrong places, like the vestibule of a church or anywhere in the house outside the kitchen, like around the baby's room or when you were saying your prayers at night. She always told us to watch out then because it meant the devil was around somewhere. All right, all right," he said hastily as Thomson smiled and sipped his coffee. "Maybe it's old-country bullshit, Giorgio, but I got a whiff of garlic when Slocum told me about a red sports car in that accident on Fairlee Road."

Dom Lorso coughed hard for an instant but when the burn of color faded from his face, he lit another cigarette. "So I drove out here early this morning and checked out the garage. The Porsche was gone. I went to a pay phone and called Earl's private number here. When he answered I hung up and went home. I was scared then, but not now. I can't smell garlic anywhere, Giorgio. He was home when it happened."

"That's all I wanted to know, Dom."

Thomson was relieved because his fears had apparently been unfounded and because Lorso's nervous and superstitious talk of garlic and devils had been a therapeutic reminder of how far they had come from the old times when Harlequin Chemicals had consisted of only a rented, run-down warehouse and a few mortgaged trucks.

"Just one thing," he said. "Where did that talk of a red sports car come from?"

"There were some scratches on the girl's bike that looked like red paint. At least, that's what the Selby kid thought. I mean the girl's brother, I don't know his name. Slocum had the bike picked up and they checked it out at the police lab." Lorso coughed again and put his cigarette out. "But there was no red paint, nothing but mud and gravel."

77

"What about the police report on Earl's car?"

"I'll take care of it, Giorgio. The kid forgot, I'll tell them. Or better, I'll tell them what Earl told us. I'll call Slocum, give him the details. No, I better do it personally. I'll call you after I talk to Slocum."

When Dom Lorso left, Thomson sat watching the birds on the lawn and listening to the faint bursts of laughter from his wife's suite.

Sometimes, when he was out of touch with the world of Simon Correll, as he was now, it was tempting to think of kinder worlds, where the devils that threatened you were as casual and familiar as a trace of garlic on the night air.

CHAPTER SEVEN

After Mass and breakfast that Saturday morning, when the fogs lifted and the sun was sparkling on the river, three men walked the cloisters at Mount Olivet.

The Most Reverend Terence Waring wore a soutane that glistened with silken lights. On his curly white head slanted a purple biretta, the color signifying his episcopal rank. A cleric in a black cassock, Brother Fabius, strolled respectfully behind him.

The third man was Simon Correll, whose mother lived at the Convent of Mount Olivet. A daily communicant, she was assisted to the altar rail by a nun who carefully blotted the spittle from the old woman's lips before the priest, on occasion His Excellency himself, graced her tongue with the consecrated host.

As the years passed, Mrs. Correll's interests had diminished and her only concern and vanity now were the small clay objects she sometimes modeled in the convent therapy shop and the trim of tiny seed pearls she enjoyed sewing along the edges of her numerous black shawls.

When Ellyvan Ybarra Correll first came to Mount Olivet, she had been a young woman in her thirties. At that time the nuns administered only a ten-bed hospital on a few acres of rocky soil. Their garden supplied their table; corn, a few bushels of root vegetables and, in the humid summers, crops of squash and small, pitted tomatoes on rambling vines.

The convent now embraced a dozen or more buildings on several hundred acres, with gerontological and research laboratories, nurses' training facilities and a new chapel with stunning panels of stained glass.

The overall architectural style was light and graceful, arched windows and entrances decorated with pilasters and braced with fluted columns. As a child in Portugal, Ellyvan Ybarra had once received a postcard from an aunt on holiday in the Loire Valley; the card showed one of the famous river chateaux, slim and purple in the sun and winds. Simon Correll knew his mother loved that picture. It had been propped in a place of honor on the altar in her bedroom in New York all through his childhood.

Years later Mount Olivet would reflect the tone of that faded postcard, low, gray buildings with balanced cupolas morticed in white, and parks and flower beds spreading through groves of trees down to the Hudson.

On a river site near the chapel stood a walled dwelling with a garden, a pool and powerful, protected generators. The house, with its own extensive communications facilities and stocked for year-round use, was reserved exclusively for Correll and his staff.

When he was in residence the security was of a high technological sophistication; the river launch, cars and vans in various parking areas, bulky men strolling through the grounds—these were Correll's things and Correll's people.

A man named Marvin Quade was in charge of this security. He had other responsibilities and functions, but the protection of the person of Simon Correll was Quade's overriding concern, since it followed that a failure there would make any other problem academic.

Quade was of average height with a clear, smooth complexion and restless eyes. He wore dark suits and never an overcoat or gloves. His hands were wide and thick, and his hair in certain lights was almost white, the color of cornsilk or wheat.

It was Quade who monitored within the last hour the calls George Thomson had placed through Philadelphia and New York to Simon Correll.

In 1972, *Fortune* magazine listed Simon Correll as one of the ten wealthiest men in America. An illustration accompanying the article pictured the Correll Group's resources in the form of a pyramid—at the base stood Correll's international operations in petroleum and machinery parts. In the middle were the holdings in airlines, trucks and sea transport, and the geological and electronic systems that supported them. At the top were real estate and corporate assets—office buildings in various major cities, apartments and condominiums for convenience and entertainment, executive jets, a courier service, a hunting and fishing complex on the Maryland shore and even the parklike acres of the Mount Olivet convent and hospital on the banks of the Hudson River.

When the *Fortune* article appeared Simon Correll was in Europe overseeing the building of a four-thousand-mile highway complex which would eventually carry supplies from England and northern Europe to the product-starved but cash-gorged nations in the Middle East. The concept had been Correll's from the outset. Nature did not abhor vacuums; in Correll's view it was just the opposite, the vacuums abhorred nature (strength) and thus were always the force to be reckoned with—in the human heart or in the world, synergistic power was rooted in weakness, Correll believed.

Competitors might ask what difference did it make, chicken or egg, what did it matter if *things* rushed into a vacuum in response to their characteristics as *things,* or if they were *sucked* into the vacuum in obedience to laws governing the nature of the vacuum? It all came to the same, didn't it?

Correll was driven and compulsive that season in Europe, supervising the building of docks and canals, the drilling of mountain tunnels and construction of interlocking national highways which could connect west to east and become (in terms of gross tonnage) the greatest overland freight route in the world.

Forty-ton, five-axled trucks bearing the red-and-white initials of the Correll Group ran northwest to roughly southeast, clutching and breaking their way through six time zones and across more than a dozen national borders. From Italy, from

Sweden and Germany, and from England and France, the roads converged like streams into great rivers flowing across Austria and Yugoslavia and Romania to Istanbul and the Bosphorus area into Asia. East to Iran and Afghanistan, south to Kuwait, and through Syria to the Arab Emirates . . . Copenhagen to Tehran, Bremerhaven to Baghdad, the big rigs traveled month after month, sucked toward the vacuum in the desert and beyond.

What difference did it make? Chicken or egg? The difference, Correll knew, was whether you wanted to be in front of an avalanche or behind it. In the path of an invading army or in its wake. Safety was in one place, profit in another.

But about that time Correll had begun to suspect that there was something profoundly irrational and dangerous in what he was trying to accomplish. His goals were not unique or peculiar. Everybody was after the same thing, developers, drillers, dredgers, shapers, levelers. A *zeitgeist* howled around them all. What did it profit a man to gain the whole world? It profited him enormously, as everyone knew. But beyond this fiduciary absolute, something else nagged Correll.

Even if he succeeded in controlling everything he wanted —power, people, money—the winds tramping the world might still sweep him and his empire away. He recalled the Yugoslavian partisan who had said those identical words. But Mihailovich hadn't been granted time to reflect in that philosophical vein to his grandchildren. He had made that statement in the prime of his life to the captain of Tito's—then Josip Broz—firing squad.

Correll was especially reminded of his doubts one afternoon in London's Piccadilly Circus while he observed a crew with jackhammers and an iron wrecking ball demolishing an old stone building near the Criterion Theatre. Fine, chalky silt had settled over everything in the vicinity, from the statue of Eros to the tall, red mailboxes. In the reduced visibility, a two-decker bus had rammed solidly into a taxi.

A man had been struck by the caroming cab. A woman screamed and the wreckers' ball slammed again into a standing wall, bringing down tons of stone and mortar.

A black Labrador seeing-eye dog had been thrown into a panic. After one pathetic effort to protect his mistress by placing his body between her and the waves of noise, his training and discipline had broken. He dropped on his belly and tried to claw a hole in the street, bloodying his paws on the tarred and rocky pavement.

His terrified lunges had jerked the lead from the blind girl's hands. She frantically called out his name, "Kipper, it's all right, good Kipper, good Kipper . . ."

But Kipper had snapped viciously at her hands, drawing blood from her fingers and terrified screams from spectators.

A policeman warned the crowd back. "The dog is dangerous," he shouted. Kipper's mouth foamed white. The wrecking ball smashed its way through still another mass of stone, sending geysers of dust and shale shooting high about the fountain of Eros.

Minutes later the Metro Animal Squad shot and killed Kipper, and blind—in more ways than one—chance alone was responsible for the ricocheting bullet that had blown away one of the blind girl's kneecaps.

The random incident somehow polarized Correll's earlier thoughts . . . chaos, pain, human confusion . . . and no *preplanned, predictable reason for any of it.*

That incident gave him a glimpse of something he was convinced the world—and everyone in it—desperately *needed* and *wanted.* Discipline, order, creating in turn serenity, peace of mind. No chance, erratic and uncontrolled, to destroy senselessly what had been carefully built and presumably was safe. That was what was needed, and that became his philosophic energizer and overriding purpose.

Certain changes occurred then in the direction of the Correll Group. An emphasis was placed on chemical acquisitions and pharmaceutical combines.

Simon Correll took an unusually close and proprietary interest in one of the smaller units of his diverse enterprise—the model plant and town in Summitt City, Tennessee. Delegating much of his European and African operations to Lord Conestain in London and the Van Pelt family in Belgium, Correll moved his personal headquarters to the United States and even set up small offices in the pollution- and crime-free town of Summitt.

*   *   *

In the convent cloister, Suffragan Bishop Waring, whose special title exempted him from the duties of the local Diocesan See, spoke with warmth of Simon Correll's mother.

"Her appetite is good, praise God. Mother Superior tells me she is especially fond of poached chicken and peas with fresh mint."

A gray overcoat slung around his shoulders, Correll nodded thoughtfully. From his father he had inherited height, blue-gray eyes and a realistic view of life. Alex Correll had once told his son, "Remember this. You are the one person you can never get rid of, can never refuse to see . . ."

Correll had received something more exotic from his mother, Ellyvan Ybarra—a Mediterranean sultriness, his dark, olive-toned coloring and thick, black hair. More significantly, he had inherited from her the linchpin of his character, a pervasive but powerfully motivating sense of despair about man's ability ever to be rational. It would follow from that, then, that only an external force, carefully controlled by the wisdom of a man such as himself, could save man from his own hopeless folly . . .

The bishop went on in his deliberate fashion, "I'm certain your mother knows you're here, Mr. Correll. There are, after all, areas of spiritual communication that even your most advanced scientists can't explain. I see a special expression on her dear face when I tell her we are expecting a visit from you. Isn't that true, Fabius?"

"Yes, Your Excellency." A small man with gentle eyes, Brother Fabius had been nodding in approval to the bishop's comments.

"A mother's happiness," the bishop said with a sigh, "is a devoted son's supreme reward. Never mind whether you feel worthy of it, Mr. Correll. The church has never distinguished between those who obey out of love and those who obey from fear."

Earlier Correll had visited his mother in the park above the river where the sturdier residents of the convent rested after Mass. A few could get about on their own, tottering with canes along the level gravel walks. Others sat on benches near a quiet

84

pond, swaying gently with the breeze, almost as if in unison with the lily pads.

Correll studied the list of names Quade had given him. Van Pelt. Kraager. Lord Conestain. Adam Taggart. Senator Mark Rowan. George Thomson.

He told Quade whom he wished to speak to and in what order, then stood alone watching his mother.

She wasn't aware of him, hadn't been for decades. By the time Correll was sixteen his mother had gone wholly mad. She prayed the night long in a high keening voice that had terrified not only her son but the servants and everyone else in the household, including the cats and dogs and caged birds.

Kneeling on shards of stone, Ellyvan Ybarra Correll had begged God to bring her husband home once—once might have soothed her shredded pride—without the scent of other women on his body. A psychiatrist was consulted when Ellyvan tore her rosary apart and stuffed the large beads into her bodily orifices, not neglecting her nose and ears and vagina.

Simon had been nineteen, at college in England, when his mother was first sent to Mount Olivet to recuperate from a series of electroshock treatments. Her stay at Olivet had been regularly extended over the years by her doctors and family; on the death of her husband, Mrs. Ybarra Correll became a permanent resident.

Her hair was now smooth and white and abundant, her dark skin unblemished by care or thought or emotions of any kind.

The park oppressed Correll. The scene conveyed only futility—the patient nuns wasting their gentleness on burnt-out women, meaningless repositories of forgotten loyalties, residues of spiritual exhaustion.

Yet many still played at living, waving at the boats on the water, smiling at birds and falling leaves, distracted like children by sudden movements and sounds. Some chattered to the nuns near them, remembering the names of long-dead pets, kittens, dogs and birds. Others held dolls and rocked them.

Senility was considered a harmless state, a time of comic antics and lapses, but Correll knew it was a living sentence to be served in the mine fields of distant childhoods, where any misstep could trigger explosions of buried guilts and terrors.

Yet a kind of radar, an early warning system, guided these old people through the worst of it. Their shields, it seemed, were the deceit of memory, the blur of time. . . .

"But your mother *will* fast when she's receiving Communion," Bishop Waring was saying. "Holier than the Church, you know. But Sister Clare is patient, and your mother is most happy with us."

"I'm very grateful, Your Excellency."

Bishop Waring led the talk into other areas. He was interested in politics and world affairs, and it gratified him to evaluate Simon Correll's responses to his notions. He insisted on these exchanges; the bishop had too strong an ego and too wide an intellectual curiosity to be content in the role of a spiritual baby-sitter.

Bishop Waring spoke of the significance of human life. ". . . If we posit a God, we posit—do we not?—by the very nature of our longing, a perfect Creature . . ."

Correll's attention was the price he paid for his mother's security and well-being—an offering in kind, because one didn't pay for spiritual comforts in the same coin one used for cellars of sacramental wines, new buildings and the like.

Marvin Quade appeared at an entrance to the cloisters, the wind stirring his light, sandy hair. Correll checked him with a slight headshake.

The bishop noticed Correll's signal and was flattered to be given precedence over whatever Quade wanted to bring to Correll's attention.

With a smile he said, "The important question, my son, is not whether God exists and will give us a sign to let us know He's thinking of us. No, the important question is, has there been any discernible progress or true evolution over the ages? Is the lap dog an improvement over the extinct Siberian wolf? You liberals, or conservatives, or whatever you call yourselves, generally take the short view. You don't see what's already been accomplished. You consider social aggression to be an aberration. You believe in either bigger jails or bigger welfare budgets, or some other kind of behavioral engineering. But social violence serves a purpose."

Brother Fabius couldn't hear everything the bishop was saying, though he could follow the gist of it. His excellency was veering toward Herr Hegel. Oppression was therapeutic, it nourished revolt. Terrorists strengthened healthy middle-class values. The pendulum swung back and forth. Slaves created democracies, action and reaction, grains of sand in bivalves fashioning pearls.

But Correll was presently in no mood to play the bishop's game. Something else was on his mind, and Fabius wasn't surprised—although the bishop, he noted with satisfaction, was both surprised *and* disappointed—when Correll excused himself and returned with Quade to his quarters.

Correll took the call from Senator Rowan in his study, where there was a view of the trees and river. He was asked by an operator at St. Joseph's to hold for a moment: a nurse was attending the senator.

Senator Mark Rowan was chairman of a joint subcommittee which screened military appropriations for the House and Senate. The function of his committee was thought to be largely clerical, an operation designed to control the endlessly proliferating flow of paper to the Congress.

But Rowan's initials on a request for action in certain categories were the equivalent of an affirmative rubber stamp. His approval also guaranteed fiscal anonymity, since the senator's special projects were so deeply buried in the appropriations of the full House committee that only a hostile in-depth audit would ever be likely to blast them to light. Even then, their destination and disposition—the sensitive questions of who got the money and what it was for—would be forever blanketed under security classifications.

The senator's voice sounded weak with pain. "Mr. Correll, the doctors don't want me to tire myself. It's about a month, give or take a few days. That's the word the path lab sent back."

Correll had known this. Marvin Quade had been advised of the pathology report before it had gone to Rowan's doctors.

"Senator, if there is anything you want for yourself or your family, please tell me."

"Thanks to our long relationship with the Correll Group, I want for nothing, Mr. Correll. Except perhaps that those bloody doctors have misread my X-rays. So shall we get down to business? I took the king's coin, I'm still the king's man. By and large I've delivered what I was paid for. But my usefulness will be over in a week or so. Senator Lester will chair the committee then. He's senior, there's no way to prevent it. His people have already been zeroing in on Harlequin and the general's operation at Saliaris. Most of their expenditures we've camouflaged, no seams showing, but somehow Lester managed to get a line on them. He has his own people, you know. We can't touch them. Which is to say we can't buy them."

Quade came in and put a paper in front of Correll. It read, "Holding now: Van Pelt. Lord Conestain. Taggart. Thomson."

Correll said, "Senator, you've earned a rest from our problems. Remember, if there's anything you need, be sure to let us know."

Afterward, Correll analyzed the conversation. A vacuum would exist with Rowan's death, and Senator Lester was rushing in to fill it. But it was probable that someone was prodding him in that direction, possibly an important aide in the Oval Office. Or someone who moved with authority in other official areas. Bittermank perhaps, Ferdinand Bittermank, who also happened to be a social friend of Bishop Waring . . .

Jennifer came in then from the garden, carrying in each hand a shiny glass globe. She wore a white bathing suit, black sunglasses. Her blond hair was tied back with a ribbon.

Smiling at Correll, she placed the twin globes on his desk with a ceremonial gesture. "Gifts from your mother, Simon," she said.

Each globe enclosed a statue of the Virgin Mary dressed in blue plaster robes and crowned with pink-and-white plastic chips set in wreaths of flowers.

"Fabius brought them by. The nuns helped, but your mother did the painting—the robes, those little red dots on the cheeks."

The globes rested on heavy bases of polished black plastic, trimmed with silver and finished off with beveled edges. Tipping one gently, Correll watched a miniature storm of white flakes fly about the colorful statue.

"The Snow Virgin . . ." Jennifer shifted in her chair and the sunlight ran in a golden flash along her slimly molded legs.

"Now what can you tell me, my dear?"

"Jarrell Selby found me agreeable, I think. Certainly credible. I convinced him we'd met somewhere at a concert and that

I was in Memphis on business." She shrugged. "He was gentle and pleasant. To say he was grateful would be immodest, I guess. I suggested we'd have more time together if he asked his brother to stay at the motel in Memphis instead of with him at Summitt City."

She took off her glasses and with the sun on her tanned face, her eyes were strikingly blue and clear. "Do you want to hear all the details, Simon? I don't mind, but I never know for sure what you want. This is the first time you've asked me to—" She shrugged. "Well, it's up to you. You wanted me to keep him distracted and involved . . ."

Correll smiled. "Listen to me, Jennifer. If you're asking if I'm jealous, of course I am. If that pleases you, so much the better. I would have preferred to do this some other way. As you point out, it was the first time and it will be the last. But since it's done, we might as well get to the point. What happened between you and Jarrell Selby isn't the point, although I can well believe he found you attractive. You must have been an entertaining and fascinating surprise, the stuff of lonely soldiers' dreams, the fantasy sex adventure in the middle of an air raid. I'm sure he attended you with care, poured wine for you, sang your praises and then went about fucking you with enthusiasm."

She clearly didn't like this; her full lower lip flattened slightly and gave an aggressive cast to her expression.

She said, "Well, if it's not important, there's no point in writing a scenario about it, is there? But it wasn't like you described it. He did offer me some wine, as a matter of fact. And he told me I was beautiful, that's true. But sleeping with him was—" She shrugged again, pausing for words. "It was comfortable, and that's about all, but I liked him for being . . . gentle and, well, sort of unsure."

Correll said, "Let's leave that. Jarrell's reaction to his half brother is what concerns me. I want every detail you can remember."

"Okay. Jarrell seemed confused or frightened at first. Maybe a little of both."

And then she told Correll about the first meeting between the brothers, the lunch at the Summit commissary that same day, and the party in the evening at Jarrell's with Sergeant

89

Ledge and his wife ("healthy cow-eyes"), the Stoltzers, Fro-elich Nash and the others. She emphasized that Harry Selby and his brother were alone for only a few minutes that night. Which was the desired result of her efforts. That's what she reported, and Correll liked what she had to say. She knew he would . . .

"Stoltzer and Ledge pumped me casually about where I'd met Jarrell, how long I planned to stay at Summitt and so on. But I did what you said. I explained I had to leave on Friday night at the latest, and that cooled it . . . I'm not particularly maternal, I don't collect wet kittens or broken-winged crea-tures, but after the party was over and everyone had gone Jarrell was so miserable that it bothered me some. He wouldn't tell me why. He just seemed very frustrated, and nervous. When his brother called from the motel, Jarrell told me to tell him that he was asleep.

"I don't know when I got him to bed, but I could *feel* it in his body, like a fever. He lay there for what seemed like hours, staring at the ceiling. He wouldn't make love to me. Suddenly he jumped up and put on his clothes. He was so upset that I could hardly understand him. He said he was in danger, that he had to leave, that it wasn't safe for me to be with him."

"What time was this?"

"Four-thirty, maybe five. It was still dark. I tried to keep him from going but he said he had to get to his brother, to talk to him. He left by the patio door. The last I saw of him he was walking toward the lake area. Running. I figured he knew a shortcut to the parking lots. Sergeant Ledge called, about a half hour later. Then Stoltzer called to find out if Jarrell had told me where he was going."

Correll was studying the Snow Virgins.

"How did Harry Selby strike you? Tell me about him."

She hesitated a moment, then picked up a cigarette. "I'm not sure. He's a man, very *manly* looking. We weren't alone very long but I talked too much, I'm afraid. I'm not sure why. Maybe I was nervous. He didn't talk much. So I guess he knows more about me than I know about him."

"That tells me considerable about him."

"Well, I'm not trying to hold back anything. I'm trying to tell you what I felt about him, what kind of man he is." She lit her cigarette and snapped the lighter shut. "Isn't that what you want?"

"Yes, please go on."

"Well then, if I had to use one word about Harry Selby, I would say he's *ready*. That's what impressed me when I first met him, that he would be ready for just about whatever might happen. Not that he was expecting anything in particular, but he made me feel that I'd better be careful. As a woman I'll tell you what that means. If I wanted him, he'd be ready. Not necessarily excited, maybe not even interested, but he would be ready."

A red light blinked on Correll's phone console. "Thank you, Jennifer. We'll lunch together, if you like."

When she left the study he watched the sunlight shift in streaks across her brown shoulders, then put the tips of his fingers to his temples and exerted a steady pressure. His muscles felt coiled like tight springs. The smoky black glasses Jennifer wore created an unwelcome image of his mother, reminding him of her black shawls and unrevealing eyes. He picked up a Snow Virgin and tipped it back and forth, grateful for these distractions—the snowflakes, the beads of tiny seed pearls on his mother's shawls—because he now faced a decision of significant and dangerous consequences, and once he'd made that commitment there could be no turning back from it.

Virtue, however you defined it, was irrelevant in evil times, he thought with gloomy satisfaction, which was probably why tyrants generally took care to make sure their times were as evil as they could make them. They knew the frustration of moderation, and would risk anything to escape the burden of tolerance.

"Yes, Mr. Correll?" George Thomson's voice was alert and expectant.

"Thomson, I've advised you now and then not to underestimate me. I've also told you not to *overestimate* me. I depend on you people for information. But for the past eighteen hours you haven't put us in the picture about Harry Selby's daughter. The information I have comes from a fragmentary police report our people picked up in Philadelphia." This was a deliberate untruth; Correll's source had been a deputy inspector in Philadelphia. "But I want a report now, Thomson. What exactly happened?"

After Thomson answered, Correll said, "All this seems highly coincidental. To be as plain as possible, was there a causal relationship? Did someone working for you have anything to do with what happened to the Selby girl?"

"No, sir. I've checked that personally. The police have kept me up to date. We're not implicated in any way."

Correll glanced at the stretch of river beyond his study, the waters shadowed and dappled by swaying trees.

Picking up a Snow Virgin, he watched the flakes floating around the blue statue, then said, "Thomson, this won't change our plans. Call General Taggart now and tell him that."

CHAPTER EIGHT

It took Selby almost a week to find something that related to the word "waves." He had spent most of that time driving around the countryside looking for clues or leads to what Shana could have meant by "waves" or "screaming birds" or "tunnels" or "hornets."

In the afternoon he picked up Davey at school and they searched until dusk, Davey watching the fields and roads with a map on his knees.

Selby had called Summitt City twice, but Clem Stoltzer had no news of Jarrell. But he had promised to keep in touch and let Selby know when and if he heard from his brother.

Selby had been to East Chester to talk to the detective handling his daughter's case, Sergeant Burt Wilger. He had met the county district attorney, Jonathan Lamb, and a deputy DA, a young woman who had been introduced to him as Dorcas Brett, but who was referred to by the DA as Kelly. Wilger had questioned Selby about his daughter's friends and acquaintances, her hobbies and interests, what homes she slept over at, where she spent her time after school, whether or not she hitchhiked, used drugs or marijuana or alcohol.

The sergeant briefed Selby on their progress to date. "We've checked the sexual deviates we got sheets on. And flushed out some neighborhood PTs—Peeping Toms—and characters who get it off exposing themselves—weirdos we haven't been able to bust so far. Blanks in that area. And nothing on the perpetrator's car. But there's something screwy about the time, Mr. Selby. Lieutenant Eberle told me he'd mentioned this to you."

Wilger, a thin young man with sparse hair and worried eyes, cleared his throat. "Your daughter got out of a car—or was pushed out—at Pyle's Corner in Muhlenburg. That's what she told Nurse Redden. She wasn't sure what time that was. Which is understandable. But we got a fix on the time from a witness, a Mrs. Elvira Swabel. She's an old lady and she lives there at Pyle's Corners, right across the street from a storefront church. Your daughter got out of the car in front of that church, it's called the Tabernacle of the Golden Flame. The preacher is a local piney, Ollie Jessup. But the church was empty that night, there were no services. But Mrs. Swabel was sitting at her window, her apartment is over a hardware store. She saw your daughter walk to the Mobil station at the other corner and buy a candy bar from an outdoor vending machine. There was enough light at the station for her to see everything pretty clear."

"Did she get a look at the car?" Selby had asked him. "Did she notice what color it was?"

"No, the street in front of the tabernacle was too dark. But she saw your daughter start up Fairlee Road around ten o'clock, give or take a few minutes. The point is, Mr. Selby, your daughter didn't get to Little Tenn for another three hours and that trailer camp is only a mile or so from Pyle's Corners. So we'd like to know where she was those hours between ten and one. It could be important. Dr. Kerr doesn't want us to question her yet, but I thought maybe you could help us."

"I'll talk to her, Sergeant."

On that same day Selby found the link to the "waves"—on a back-country road about a dozen miles from Muhlenburg. The sound came to him as he crested a dirt road between the small towns of Embryville and Buck Run.

He stopped the car in open country. Meadow stretched on either side, broken by patches of sunlight and shadow. The

94

woods burned with fall colors, but the fields were still green and hard in patches from summer.

The silence was almost complete, heavy and drowsing, but when the wind changed he heard faint echoing sounds that shook the ground gently.

Selby drove to the top of the hill and stopped again. Below him spur tracks branched out from a small switching yard. It was a marshaling area for local ranchers; beef herds were shipped here from Texas to be fattened for eastern markets. A pair of diesel locomotives were shunting cattle cars around the yard. The noise echoed from the low hills, traveling in muffled waves over the meadows.

Selby marked his map with a penciled line from Fairlee Road to Buck Run and Embryville.

At home, Mrs. Cranston told him that Miss Culpepper from the library had called, she had the material he wanted. Someone from Las Vegas also called, a Jerry Goldbirn. And their insurance man, Jay Mooney.

Shana's bedroom door was closed, but he could hear her talking on the phone. She had been no help in his search. She had listened to the tape but insisted she couldn't remember saying anything about tunnels or birds. She had no idea what any of it meant.

She became impatient when Selby pressed her about the outbursts in the growling and obviously assumed voice—"Hell is alone—" and "I am worse than men . . . more barbarous in revenge . . . hatred in my heart . . ."

She refused to discuss this with him, either retreating into apathetic silences or erupting in anger and running off to her room.

Dr. Kerr had told him to expect this kind of behavior, but Selby wasn't prepared for her reaction when he asked her about her despairing "Mommy, my hand hurts, it's evil, I hate it . . ."

She shouted, "You wouldn't understand, you never did, you were always outside of us."

This was true enough, but it had been a hurtful attack—he

95

had, in fact, been an outsider, although his wife Sarah and mother-in-law Tishie pretended he wasn't. Or simply hadn't made a point of it.

In a way being "outside" had been a source of strength to Selby. Better outside than trapped inside the rigidity of St. Ambrose, the unyielding, arid atmosphere of his grandparents' home in Davenport. Sure, being part of them he'd tried, and squandered energy, to understand them and at times to defend them.

He'd never been a joiner, he disliked labels. Being outside of Sarah's faith had permitted him to accept it without pressure, and therefore to support it. Her convictions hadn't necessarily reflected his, and because he wasn't required to champion them out of any unexamined loyalty he'd always been comfortable with them.

Since Sarah's death he had tried to keep their past free from wear and distortion by not living in it. He had made lists of things to try not to think of again, posting these areas with off-limits signs. His warnings included certain beaches, the colors of the hills above the place they lived in Spain, and some streets in New York and a bar on Samson Street in Philadelphia where they had gone when they were first married . . .

But now everything was baited with hurtful memories, even Shana's troubled voice on the tapes . . . "a time to serve and to sin . . ."

That was from the Bible, he'd thought, but it wasn't in the hymn of Ecclesiastes he checked that began, "To everything there is a season, and a time to every purpose under the sun. A time to be born and a time to die, a time to plant and a time to pluck up which is planted . . ."

". . . a time to serve and to sin" wasn't in those lines, but reading the verses reminded him of proverbs that Sarah had quoted with teasing gravity to Davey and Shana. ". . . her children rise up and call her blessed, for in her tongue is the law of kindness."

In searching for the source of "Hell is alone . . ." and "I am . . . more barbarous in revenge . . ." he had gone through Sarah's college notebooks, finding not what he was looking for but only a memory of her straight shoulders at a typewriter and the frowns and smiles that accompanied the clatter of her thoughts being put on paper.

He knocked on Shana's door and heard a whispered rush of words. Then she raised her voice and asked him to come in.

She sat on the side of her bed, one bare foot resting on top of the other, and a robe pulled loosely over her pajamas. She said, "I know I'm not supposed to be talking to anybody. But what difference does it make?"

He said, "Dr. Kerr wants you to rest as much as possible."

"Rest for what? I'm not in class, I don't even have homework to do."

Her room needed tidying up; an empty glass and a half-eaten sandwich were on a tray on the floor; her wastebasket was full of crumpled tissues.

The bruise on her cheek had swollen; her whole face was now disfigured and discolored. They had used to tease her about her enthusiasm for showers and shampoos, her shelves of talcum and cologne, the closets with the separate racks for sweaters and rows of jeans with horseshoes stitched in daisies on the pockets. But now her hair was tangled in coarse strands, and it looked as if she had been picking at the bandage on her hand—the gauze strips were shredded and soiled.

But her small face looked vulnerable and troubled. Her pitiful girlishness seemed to be asking him for some kind of trust, or sympathy. Still, she wouldn't let him touch her. She stiffened if he came near her, or put out a hand to her.

Selby could feel the rebuke in her tense shoulders and tightly locked hands. Since the night he had carried her from Barby Kane's trailer there had been this barrier between them.

"There were a couple of things we should talk about, Shana. You feel up to it?"

"Sure, it's okay. That's what everybody's doing now, talking and *talking* about it. Charlotte told me Josey said I rode my bike on Fairless only because I like to hear the mushroom workers in the trucks whistling at me." Her voice was low, but the words came so fast they nearly blurred together. "The detectives asked everybody at school if I smoked grass and cut classes. Even Charlotte keeps hinting about what it was like and was he *handsome*. So we might as well talk about it too. What's the difference?"

97

"Well, to make an obvious point, I'm your father and that isn't going to change. So you're stuck with that, which is one way to look at it, if you want to."

He tried to keep his tone calm but he didn't quite understand her resentment and her seeming distrust of him. He knew what pain was, and he guessed he wanted her at least to give him credit for that.

Right now he only knew what Dr. Kerr had told him, and what he had learned from Nurse Redden and the detectives. Shana had been driven to a house in the country, over roads she wasn't familiar with, and there—in a room with a water-stained ceiling and a stone fireplace with a deer's head hung above it— she had been bound to a cot and beaten and repeatedly raped.

But Dr. Kerr had advised him not to press her for details.

Selby told her what he'd heard that afternoon at the switching yards near Buck Run, but she shrugged and said, "I've told you, I don't know *where* I was, daddy. Maybe I heard some things, but maybe I just imagined them."

"When you got out of the car at Pyle's Corners, do you remember what you did?"

"I'm not sure. Just part of it."

"Do you recall buying a candy bar at the Mobil station?"

"Did I do that?"

"A woman who lives across from the church saw you. You walked to the gas station. It was raining, but there was light enough for her to see you."

"I remember eating something sweet. So I guess I did buy a candy bar. What difference does that make?"

"The woman told the police it was ten o'clock. But you didn't get to Barby's for another three hours. Sergeant Wilger suggested we talk about it, and see if we could fill in that gap."

She was staring down at her clenched hands. "It was raining. I know that. But I'm not sure about anything else. I just walked up Fairlee to Barby's."

"But that wouldn't take three hours."

"Maybe I stopped, rested. I don't know."

"Did you go somewhere else before you went to Barby's? Were you with anybody else?"

He saw a flash of anger in her face. Her eyes had narrowed. "If you believe that, I can't help it."

"Shana, I'm trying to help you. I know a little about how you felt that night, try and believe me. If we talk it over maybe we can find some answers. You say it was raining. Did you try to find someplace that was dry? Did you go inside anywhere?"

She nodded slowly. "I was in a car. I remember the sound of the rain on the roof."

He said quietly, "Who was driving, Shana?"

"Nobody was driving. It was on the side of the road and I got into it to get out of the rain."

"And you sat all alone in an empty car on Fairlee Road for three hours?"

"It wasn't on Fairlee Road. It was parked off the road in some kind of clearing."

"You sat there for three hours?"

"Didn't you hear me?"

"Okay, okay, I heard you. There's no reason to shout, Shana. But I don't understand it."

"I tell you everything I know, then you look mad and say you don't understand. So what's the point of talking?"

"I'm sorry if I upset you. But I still don't understand. Why didn't you come home after it happened?"

She swung around and stared at him. Her eyes were bright with tears. "I wanted to *think,* can't you understand *that?* As long as I stayed in that car alone, what happened belonged to *me* and nobody else. I wanted to be sure of every thought I had, everything he did to me and why he did it, and why he hated me so much he needed to hurt me."

"Why are you wasting your sympathy on that damn psychopath?"

"Because he was part of it," she shouted. "There were two of us that night. I know what I did and what *I* felt, but *I've got to understand why he did it, what it meant for him.*"

"Shana, Dr. Kerr wants you to forget that part of it, for now anyway."

"Does he? Well, it didn't happen to *him.* I don't want to forget it. I don't ever want to wonder about it. That's why I stayed in that car. Because after I called you, I knew it wouldn't belong to me anymore. It would belong to everybody, to Dr. Kerr and the police and all my friends at school. They could make up their own stories about what happened and it wouldn't be mine anymore, and there would never be the one single truth ever again."

She was crying but her face was tight with anger. "But I know what happened. I'll never be afraid to think about it. No matter what anybody says, I'll know the truth. You can't help me, and nobody else can either."

After dinner Selby returned Jerry Goldbirn's call. A secretary at the casino told him Mr. Goldbirn was in Aspen but would be back in his office the following afternoon. Would he care to leave a message?

Davey came in with the county map and spread it on the coffee table near the fire.

"I heard Shana shouting when you were in her room." Davey looked at him, the flames reflected on his soft wavy hair. "Is she going to kill herself or something?"

Selby said sharply, "Where'd you get that idea? Did she say something to you?"

"Not about killing herself, dad, but she's mad all the time." He sighed. "Everything's my fault, no matter what I do. Yesterday she cut a picture out of the sports page, the whole top of the page, and when I asked her about it, she blew up and told me to mind my own business." He sighed again. "When I asked her if she wanted to shoot some baskets with Normie and me, she started crying and said she never wanted to see him again, or me either." He said gloomily, "People who act . . . well, who act like that . . ."

Selby patted his son's shoulder. "We've just got to be patient with her." He paused. "What kind of picture did she cut out of the paper?"

"It was something about a sports car show, that's all I saw . . . Did she remember anything about those diesels and railroad cars, dad?"

"No."

"Well, if she'd ever cool off"—Davey pointed to the map—"we could ask her about this." Davey traced a line on the map. "The Embryville road turns off at the Stoneville grade school. The night it happened, Stoneville had a soccer game with Upland Country. I know a guy there, Jimmy Cox, he's in fifth grade, that's how I know. I mean, I called him."

"Yes?"

"Well, those kids playing soccer would have been yelling and screaming. It could've sounded like birds or something, couldn't it, dad?"

"*Sure.* At a distance, it might have sounded like flocks of shrill birds. It's worth checking . . ."

"Dad, do you really think Shana will be okay?"

"Of course I do, Davey."

But the truth was that Selby wasn't sure of anything now. He knew Shana was deeply afraid, deeply upset. He knew that, and not much else. And he didn't know where to look for help, for the truth. And worse, he didn't know where to turn his eyes to avoid it.

The next morning Selby put his father's diaries in the car and drove to Muhlenburg and picked up the information Miss Culpepper had collected for him. A spinster with white hair and a straight back, Miss Culpepper and Sarah had been close friends. Selby had asked her to check the library for material relating to Harlequin Chemicals. Taking the request as a starting point, Miss Culpepper had put together a package of magazine articles (from *Fortune* and *Time* and *Commentary* and others) which embraced not only Harlequin and the Correll Group but touched on various publicly reported aspects of their relationship with the U.S. military and Congress.

Selby stacked the material on the rear seat of his station wagon and drove north out of Muhlenburg into the network of secondary roads leading toward Buck Run.

At the Stoneville school, three miles from the switching yards, he drove around the hockey and soccer fields. He traveled in widening circles then until he came at last to a road that cut through pasturelands and dead-ended on the White Clay Creek.

Twice that morning he spotted a dusty gray Ford on the road behind him. At a market outside Buck Run he bought a baked ham sandwich, a bunch of grapes and two cans of beer. The girl at the counter gave him some homemade horseradish in a twist of waxed paper. She recommended the barrel pickles her father put up. Selby said next time.

There were no cars at the gas pumps. A young man in jeans and a red wool shirt sat reading a paperback beside a rack of new tires.

"Not much business today," Selby commented.

"Well, it's early, truckers'll be stopping by pretty soon for gas and lunch."

"You do lube jobs?"

"Not much call for that, sir."

"Take care," Selby said and got into the station wagon and drove off. The gray Ford had been parked in the service garage beside the market, but Selby hadn't been able to get a good look at the driver. It was a man with a newspaper in front of his face.

Selby stopped on the Buck Run road in the shade of a big maple tree and ate the ham sandwich with horseradish and drank one of the beers. The breezes stirred the leaves and blew them against his windshield where they stuck in yellow and brown patterns. A herd of Holsteins, black and white like huge dominoes, huddled together in the lee of a barn.

Selby watched the road behind him in the rear-view mirror. It was flat and empty and curved out of sight through a grove of black locusts.

Selby opened his father's diaries and glanced through them. It was frustrating to study the cramped handwriting and not be able to wring some truth or significance from it.

The diaries were in three parts: the time in Korea, the time in the army stockade and hospital, and the time in California with his wife and Jarrell.

Three names were prominent in the Korean period: the chief, the major and a lieutenant named Kraager, all with the 916th Counter-Intelligence Section, a unit attached to the 7th Division. In the Chinese spring offensive, Jonas Selby mentioned the Kwach-on Reservoir, the retreat to Munsan-ni—the battle of the hills, the 1st Marines on Bunker Hill and the 3rd Division with Belgian and Greek Allied units on Big Nori and Kelly Hill . . . the 7th on the Triangle and a ROK Division on Whitehorse Hill.

It seemed unreal to drink beer on a dusty country road in Pennsylvania and read about those distant battles and to realize that the people living there now, farmers working the soil, children bicycling to school, had probably never heard of those place names coined by PR officers and war correspondents for American radio networks and newspapers. Arrowhead Hill and Heartbreak Ridge and Old Baldy—what did Koreans call them today?

In that phase there was evidence of a young man who had looked at the world in a wistful, innocent way. His father had listed the names of railroads and trains he must have ridden or seen or heard about—the Monon and the Nickel Plate, the Wabash and Southern Pacific, the Santa Fe, the Pennsy's Broadway and the New York Central's Twentieth Century. The "Q" (the Chicago, Burlington and Quincy) and the Boston and Maine's Owl, the Baltimore and Ohio and the Erie and the Soo . . .

Jonas Selby had written down the words to *The Legend of John Henry*—"I'll die with my hammer in my hand . . ." And John Henry's shout of defiance to the steam drill—"How *are* you, Mr. Steam Drill? I'm talking to *you.* "

There were notes about cattle drives and railroad corrals—laments of young men—"The hills are all climbed, the creeks are all past . . ."

It seemed of a piece. Except why had his father copied out the words of *The Bonnie Earl of Murray?* "Ye Highlands and ye Lawlands / Oh where hae ye been? / They hae slain the Earl of Murray / And hae laid him on the green."

But one thing was clear . . . Jonas Selby had been involved in something that frightened him. It was scattered throughout the entries over a period of several months. "I'll pay for it—we all will."

Then came Jonas Selby's court-martial. And a one-word entry that read: "Nailed!"

The diary stopped there for almost five years. It resumed in the army hospital in Colorado, where he met his wife, Rita—Jarrell's mother . . .

The Holsteins were drifting out from the shelter of the sprawling barn; the wind had eased off. Some were lumbering across the field toward Selby's station wagon. Others were drifting down to the locust trees where the road curved out of sight.

That's where the gray Ford must be parked, he guessed, just out of sight around the bend.

Having played violent games much of his adult life, Selby's protective instincts had become honed to a fine, reflexive edge;

103

his peripheral vision was automatic, and his awareness of his terrain was near-reflexive.

On offense or defense the rules were the same: if you didn't have a healthy built-in paranoia you stood an excellent chance of winding up in a basket typing your memoirs with your nose, since it was computed that the energy created by a pair of two-hundred-pound men running into each other at full speed (coaches liked to mention this) could overcome the inertia of a twenty-ton block of steel and jolt it one full inch from the point of impact.

If you were blind-sided by that crunch, the physical penalties would be extreme, and they didn't usually get you any sympathy. No one was sorry for fools, and if you weren't paranoid about protecting yourself, that's what you were, a damned fool . . .

He checked the rear-view mirror, started the car and drove away from the staring cows. At the first curve he floored the accelerator. The station wagon picked up speed rapidly and the tires raised a screen of dust behind it. At the first curve he cut the motor and coasted off the road into a hedge of beech trees. He could hear the sound of an approaching car in the country silence. When the gray Ford shot past, there was too much dust for him to see the driver, but he got what he wanted—the car's license number. Thanks to that old acute football-field vision.

In Buck Run he stopped at a drugstore and called the insurance man Jay Mooney's office. Mooney's secretary told him Jay was at lunch but asked if she could help. Selby explained that someone had nicked his fender in a supermarket lot in East Chester but left only a license number on a piece of paper under his windshield wiper. No name or address. He asked her if she would find out who the driver was.

Mooney's secretary said she would be glad to take care of it.

That evening Selby looked through the material he had collected from Miss Culpepper, trying to find the connection between Harlequin Chemicals and his father and brother. George Thomson (Tomaso) had started a garbage and waste recycling plant on the Schuylkill River years ago, but had sold the controlling interest to a conglomerate called the Correll Group. George Thomson had served in Korea. That was mentioned in several of the articles.

Harlequin Chemicals had grown and prospered enormously after its takeover by the Correll Group.

There were profiles of Simon Correll in *Fortune* and several other periodicals, detailing his wealth and entrepreneurial genius.

The Correll Group had offices in a dozen major cities and extensive ties to the major sources of power throughout the world, the military, of course, and energy, science and industry. A story in *Newsweek* mentioned that Correll often cited an incident in London involving a stricken dog and a blind woman as turning his energies to the world's needs for more tranquil, more *safe* living spaces, more rational and sustaining human environmental systems, free of abhorrent and perverse chance.

None of it meant a damn thing to Selby, or related to what he was concerned with. At least so far as he could see . . .

He made himself a drink and stirred the fire. There'd been a fireplace in the house where Shana had been taken, a deer's head over the mantel. The man had played loud music on a record player, he'd shouted at her and some of it seemed like poetry. She'd told the nurse that much . . .

The phone rang. It was Jay Mooney. "Dammit, Harry, why are you trying to screw me up? Don't you know I can't mess with those people at City Hall? I depend on those cops . . . every insurance man does . . . for accident reports, hit-runs, makes on plates, like you asked Annie for. That bull about getting your fender nicked could've got my ass nailed to the floor. Your story's a crock. They wanted to know why I'm checking up on one of their own people, Lieutenant Gus Eberle. Harry? You still there?"

"Sure, Jay." Mooney was a bit drunk, his words were slurred together, fused with righteous anger and whiskey. "So it was Lieutenant Eberle tailing me around," Selby said.

"Didn't you hear me? Eberle and Slocum run that shop, close, I can't afford a hassle with them. Annie called the Motor Bureau with that plate number. I got a call back from Slocum, that's right, the captain himself. He wants to know who's running checks on Eberle and *why*. I lied, Harry. Told him Annie'd got a digit misplaced, that it was a mistake. You got to cover for me. Forget you asked us to check out that plate. Okay?"

"Sure, Jay. But I'd appreciate some background on Captain Slocum and Eberle first."

"Some of it's common knowledge, Harry. Slocum's a mean sonofabitch. He's rich, which should tell you something. Owns condos over in Avalon and a high-rise in Atlantic City. But look, Harry, I can't get involved. You understand? Those people are real sons of bitches—"

Davey came in from the foyer with a large book that Selby recognized as a volume produced by the County Historical Society. As Davey knelt beside the coffee table and opened the book Selby said to Mooney, "Could we have lunch tomorrow?"

"I told you, Harry, I can't get mixed up in this. You're either a team player or a fink at the Hall. Oh, hell, know a place called the Bluebonnet on the Mercer Pike? Say around one o'clock?

When Selby hung up, Davey said, "Can I show you something?"

He opened the book and flipped the pages. "I got to thinking while I was trying to sleep, dad. About tunnels. I figured a tunnel had to go *under* something, like the railroad tunnel near Doylestown, or under something like maybe sewers or something. But everything around here is wells. I mean, that's where the water comes from, wells and those water rams. Right?"

Selby watched Davey turning the pages of the book. Smart boy. Only nine . . . "So, what did you find out, Davey?"

"A tunnel doesn't always go under something. It could go *over* something, too. And then I remembered the bridge over the White Clay Creek. Look, dad . . ." He pointed to a faded black-and-white photograph. "It's about five miles from the Stoneville school and it's on the same road as the switching yards in Buck Run. I bet that's the tunnel Shana's trying to tell us about. What do you think, dad?"

"I think, Davey, I've got myself one smart kid. We'll check it out."

CHAPTER NINE

The Rakestraw Bridge had been designed by a local architect, Charles Rakestraw, in 1885. Construction was completed by the Union Iron Company two years later. A sturdy fifty-foot span, it was built with iron rails and locust logs and covered with an arch of curved and seasoned planks which had weathered gray over the decades.

The Buck Run Road crossed the Rakestraw Bridge and dead-ended on the opposite side of the creek against Dade Road, a wide, two-lane blacktop.

Selby's station wagon made a rumbling noise as he drove onto the bridge. It's high roof cut off most of the early morning light, and for an instant he traveled through a long, dark cylinder with a glowing circle of light at its end.

Shana's tunnel, no doubt, he thought as he came into the daylight. But where from here?

About a quarter of a mile to his right was the Brandywine Lakes Country Club, a complex of houses and sports facilities, private and expensive. The community was known locally as The Lakes.

At the entrance to The Lakes a large billboard displayed aerial photographs of the fairways and swimming pools. The string of pools was like a blue necklace strung among the dark lawns and green belts. Selby noticed a name in the corner of the photographic display: "Creative Photography, J. D. Parks, East Chester."

In the opposite direction on Dade Road heavy woods stretched for miles with homes set back on lots screened by trees. A cemetery sloped down to the creek, slate-colored headstones glinting in the morning sun. Further on the countryside opened up and the meadows were bordered by thick stands of timber. The land was as yet untouched by the construction boom churning up the countryside.

He parked beside the cemetery and looked at the headstones stretching down to the water, some slanted with age, the letters and dates worn smooth as moss.

So far this morning he had seen nothing of Eberle's gray Ford. He waited beside the White Clay Creek for an hour or so, occasionally checking the rear-view mirror, then drove on home.

Shana was lying on her bed in the dark. Her radio was turned so low that the music almost faded out when occasional winds struck the house. In the glow from the dial Selby saw that she was staring at the ceiling, her arms crossed on her narrow chest.

He had the historical society's book with him. "Can I turn on a light, Shana? I want to show you something."

"All right, just a minute."

She went into her bathroom and closed the door. Water ran in her hand basin. Her room had been straightened up and smelled of talcum powder.

When Shana came out he saw that she had combed her hair. There were damp grooves in the blond waves. She had changed the bandage on her right hand; the strips of gauze and adhesive tapes were white against her tanned skin. A heavy lock of hair was combed to slant sideways and cover a pink welt on her forehead.

Her mood had changed from the day before; the anger and hostility seemed to have faded somewhat.

Selby showed her the picture of the Rakestraw Bridge. "This is probably the tunnel you talked about. It might help if you remembered which way you went when you crossed it. If you turned right, you'd have been heading for Brandywine

Lakes. To the left is a different stretch of country."

"That must've been the way then."

"Are you sure?"

"Not really." She shrugged. "I'm not sure of anything. You've got everything I let hang out on those tapes. What else do you want?"

"I'd like to know what you're afraid of and why you get your back up when I try to talk to you. Please try to understand we're trying to help—"

"Why am I supposed to understand?" Her voice was tight and angry again. "People do what they're strong enough and grown up enough to do, and then they expect me to understand it. Why should I? I can't make people do what I want, so why should I be expected to understand them?"

She turned and stared at him. "Why didn't you come home from San Francisco that summer? Because you didn't want to, that's why, but you expected me and Davey to understand, didn't you? Her name was Angela, wasn't it?"

Selby felt as if he'd been hit by a blockingback. "Yes, I think it was," he said, conscious of the inanity of his response.

"Well, I'm *sure* it was," Shana said. "I wrote her name fifty times on a piece of paper . . . Angela, Angela, Angela, over and over till my hand was tired and then I burned the paper and buried the ashes down at the pond and told Davey, because he was so little then, that that would make you come back."

"Shana, listen to me, those two weeks had nothing to do with you and Davey. I didn't even know you *knew*."

"How could we help it? We heard mommy on the phone and heard her crying after you hung up. Davey thought you'd never come home, he thought you were dead. He sat on my bed every night, with that spelling game you bought him one Christmas. He'd spell out the time he'd hope your car would come into the drive. Eight o'clock, nine o'clock, ten o'clock, till he couldn't stay awake anymore—"

"Your mother and I had an argument, Shana. There happened to be an Angela around afterward."

"It doesn't matter now." She had begun to cry, the tears bright under the hair that had fallen across her swollen face. "For a long time I thought what was important was somewhere outside of me. Where Tishie's mother and father died in Germany. Or how you had to work on a railroad and make teams to get through school, and that big Frenchman, Claud, you hated." She pushed her hair back and let her breath out slowly. There was a catch in her voice as she said, too wise for her years, "Life isn't outside you. What's outside is just what *changes*. But nobody tells you that. You hear about sex and not getting fat on the pill or anything. When I had my first period mommy said it was like opening a wonderful new book, but I think she was thinking about knitting things and grandchildren."

She looked out the window. "Your own bedroom, funny kittens, even poor old Blazer, the feeling that everybody will be at breakfast and dinner in their same places forever and ever—they tell you that's yours, that it belongs to you, but they can take it away any time they want to, except you don't know that until way later. Davey still doesn't know it."

The phone began to ring. "I'm sorry, daddy. Give me a handkerchief, please."

He gave her a handkerchief and she wiped her eyes. "Want me to get it, Shana?"

"Sure, go ahead."

"I'll take it in my bedroom," Selby said. "Will you try to remember I love you? I know what I mean by that. Remember that, too, okay?"

It was Casper Gideen. "Harry, I think you ought to know. There's talk going around Little Tenn about Goldie Boy Jessup and Coralee, Barby Kane's ma. They been meeting with some stranger, not here but once near the old Cooper Mill, another time at Pyle's Corners. I was watching, Harry. Coralee's mighty jumpy now. I figure they got to be hiding something. And it touches you, Harry—some way I can't figure yet. So I'll keep watching 'em."

"Casper, you could be letting yourself in for trouble."

"That could go two ways, I expect. Trouble for somebody else. I won't call next time, Harry, we'll meet somewhere. I don't want my wife and boys knowing about this. Goodbye to you, Harry."

Selby tried to concentrate on what Gideen had told him, but the scene with Shana had splintered his thoughts.

What was he supposed to tell her? How could he explain away her fears. Goddammit, Selby thought, and slammed his fist

110

down on the desk. The bell at the phone base sounded in tinny vibrations. The Israeli athletes on the wall . . . was there truth and comfort there? Or where Tishie's parents had died, or where he had hoisted creosote-soaked railroad ties onto a railway bed, or swung a spike maul in the heat? Did any of that make a little more sense than the words on Shana's T-shirts? "Reagan for Rex," "Sky Lab Missed Me," "Uppity Women Unite!" and "Miss Piggy Is a Pet Rock"?

Selby drove back to Dade Road and studied the terrain on both sides of the bridge again, the sprawling elegance of The Lakes, and the stretch of blacktop cutting through deep woods and past lonely houses.

He didn't see Eberle's gray Ford but he wasn't worried about that now. Something else was bothering Selby. He felt he had missed something. A big, simple truth was staring him in the face, but he couldn't make out its details and patterns.

He stopped half a dozen times to copy down names from signs and mailboxes, some of them barely visible through the underbrush—Sorenson, Windfall, Vinegar Hill, Ratcroft, R. J. Rose . . .

He drove back to Muhlenburg and picked up Davey. In the fading light they returned to Dade Road. "You were right," Selby told him as the station wagon rattled across the shadowed bridge. "I'm proud of you."

"But where'd he take her from here?" Davey asked, all but ignoring the compliment.

"Let's keep looking."

Selby drove first toward The Lakes, the creek shining on one side, a stretch of fairways and sand traps on the other. A wind had come up and the pennants at the entrance to The Lakes were pointing stiffly into the low, gray skies. The guard's kiosk was centered between red-and-white traffic standards. A man in uniform stepped from the booth when Selby stopped at the traffic barrier.

"Help you, sir?"

The uniform was smart and military, gray twill with epaulets and shining metal buttons. The guard's hair was white, but there was a capable look to his ruddy face and big hands.

"I was admiring the photographs," Selby said.

"I saw you drive by earlier, didn't I, sir?"

"That's right. I brought my son back for a look."

"You're sure welcome. We've got a fine place here, the pictures don't tell half of it."

The photographs were mounted on a billboard whose wooden supports were painted in black-and-white stripes. The large photographs were of swimming pools, homes and fairways. Smaller photos presented views of tennis courts and riding stables.

Selby smiled at the white-haired guard. "How long have the pictures been up?"

"Couldn't say for sure," the guard told him. "A few weeks anyway."

Selby backed out of the entrance and drove on for a few miles. Then he pulled off the road near the cemetery. When he rolled his window down, a cold wind blew around them. Birds were crying in the trees.

Selby said, "Shana's afraid of something. Something she won't talk to me about." He paused. "You have any idea what it is?"

"No, dad, I don't. But I wouldn't know anyway." Davey sighed. "She won't talk to me either—about what happened that night. Everything's different now. We used to talk all the time. We'd pretend we lived together and had our own house. Shana would be an airline pilot and I'd be the navigator and we'd fly through storms sometimes or so low we could see Blazer barking up at us . . . Or I'd be the steward, getting everybody Cokes. One time we were captains on a Mars shot. We talked about that every night one winter, figuring out how one of us would get lost and how we'd look for each other, or get hit by asteroids or something . . ." Davey nervously moistened his lips and looked at his father, his face a pale blur in the shadows. "She's afraid of you, dad. That's part of it, I think."

"You told me she hadn't been talking to you."

"It's not what happened that night, dad. It happened a long time ago, something about her playing a jukebox. She says I was there but I don't remember."

"Did she tell you this in secret?"

"Well, she didn't make me swear not to tell."

"Then we can talk about it, okay?"

"I guess so. She said she was playing records, putting dimes

112

or quarters in a jukebox and something made you mad. You and mommy were there. I was too but I don't remember it. It was in some kind of restaurant or a bar. An argument started not with you and mommy but with some men. That's all she'd ever tell me. Maybe that's all she remembers. But whatever you did, I guess it scared her . . ."

How old had she been? Selby had to think about it. Eight, nine maybe. The details were vague, but he remembered . . . Shana in shorts and a halter, dancing by herself, snapping her fingers like adults she'd seen on TV. But where? Philadelphia, or New York? And two young men drinking beer and calling out something to Shana.

"Do you remember what scared her, dad?"

"Some character said something unpleasant to her. I told mommy and Shana and you to go outside. Then I tried to explain to a pair of morons that their language was out of line. They had friends with them and didn't want to back down. But finally they heard me out. They hadn't realized Shana was so young. They were sorry they'd embarrassed her. That's the whole story, Davey. But Shana may have added some imagined details over the years."

"Maybe so," Davey said. "Maybe that's it, dad."

There had been one other thing, Selby recalled, as he turned the station wagon around and drove back to the bridge. She hadn't been wearing shorts and a halter, it had been a fancy skirt, and she'd been sick on the sidewalk outside the bar and grill off Sansom Street when she saw the flecks of blood on his knuckles.

As they drove back to the bridge, Selby tried to isolate a thought that had been puzzling him all that day. "Davey, what was it you told me about you and Shana being lost in space?"

"About getting hit by asteroids?"

"No, something else."

"Flying so low we could see Blazer staring up at us?"

Selby struck the steering wheel with his fist. "Right. Those aerial photographs in front of The Lakes were all taken at *night*. You could tell from the lights in the houses and swimming pools. Which means they were taken by a low-flying helicopter. The pictures have been on display a couple of weeks, the guard said. So the helicopter could have been flying around the night

Shana . . . if she was somewhere near Dade Road *that* could have been the hornets she heard."

At the drugstore in Buck Run, Selby checked a phone directory. Then after leaving Davey off at home he drove into East Chester.

The J. D. Parks photographic studio was in the business district of the old Quaker town. Parks himself was an energetic young man with high color and thinning but long, black hair which he had allowed to spread untidily over his forehead and ears. He wore a canvas windbreaker with slanted marks on the sleeves where chevrons had been removed, a yellow kerchief, boots and jeans.

Selby had caught him as he was leaving his studio on assignment, a folded tripod under one arm and a bulging leather camera bag slung over his shoulder.

"I remember the Lakes job, sure, but I can't check the negatives now. I'm running late." Parks put the tripod down, fumbled in his pocket, pulled out a wallet and gave Selby a business card. "How about you calling my answering service in a couple of days, give 'em the date and I'll check my files when I get back to town. Brandywine Lakes, you wouldn't believe the prices out there. There's nothing for sale, but I hustled the management into a layout. Image. Eat your heart out, you peasants. First time I worked out of a chopper since 'Nam. I must've shot a dozen rolls each night. What was it you wanted to check on, Mr. Selby?"

"A car on Dade Road, a red sports car. Probably parked in a driveway."

"I got it, you got it, pal—fair exchange? Call the service, okay? I'll be in Marcus Hook, underwater shots of a ship with a busted hull. Insurance stuff. Her name's Jenny, the answering service. Peace."

A delivery truck was parked in Selby's drive, the lights on and the motor running. The white door panels were decorated with smiling faces drawn inside fat doughnuts. As Selby got out of his car Normie Bride came hurrying along the flagged walk from the house.

"Evening, Mr. Selby. I stopped by to drop off some chocolate rolls for Shana. She likes them for breakfast sometimes."

"Did you talk to her, Normie?"

"No, sir, she's resting, Mrs. Cranston told me."

Norman Bride was seventeen, almost as tall as Selby but thin as a fence post. His long, gangling arms and big hands, along with good reflexes, had earned him a starting slot on Muhlenburg's varsity basketball team. Nights and weekends he made deliveries for the Dandy Doughnut Shop in Muhlenburg. His unformed boyish face became solemn as he said, "I wish you'd tell Shana, sir, that I don't mean to bother her by coming around. But I know she likes those chocolate rolls."

"I'm sure she understands."

"If I ever meet that guy who hurt her, he'll be sorry. I can sure tell you that, Mr. Selby."

"I understand how you feel. But finding who did it and punishing him is a job for the police and the courts. Remember that, Normie."

"Yes, sir. But it would be a temptation, if I ever saw him."

Something occurred to Selby then and he asked Normie if there had been anything in the sports section of last night's paper that might have been of particular interest to Shana.

"Well, she's not really into sports, sir. Basketball scores at school, maybe. But I usually tell her about them. I used to, anyway. Let's see. There was a story about field trials for gun dogs, and some pictures of old classic cars they're showing out at Longwood." He added, "I could call and ask her, Mr. Selby."

"No, don't mention it to her, Norm. I was just curious."

Selby wondered later at his injunctions to Norman Bride about the perils of private justice and the necessity for leaving retribution to the community's cops and judges. And other truisms and bullshit.

It was bullshit, or an excessive "tolerance," attitudes that had been as natural to Sarah as breathing. She would even be worrying about the man who had tortured and violated her fourteen-year-old daughter . . . Just like her daughter . . .

Selby was working off his frustrations by splitting up the sectioned tree trunks that Gideen had brought down from the meadow. A light at the corner of the garage gave him a pale illumination to work by. Yes, Sarah would have said, "Think how dreadful his *sickness* must be for *him*. Because it is a *sickness* —you can't send lynch mobs after him for *that.*"

He tapped wedges into place with the butt of an axe, battered them into the tree trunks with a twelve-pound sledgehammer, slugging their steel flanges until sparks flew in a stream and the apple wood cracked and sheared off into slick white staves that sharpened the cold air with the smell of wild fruit. Turn the other cheek, that beautiful, all-embracing absolution for everyone . . . even himself. Like hell . . . Turn the other cheek and feel noble all the way to the goddamn ovens . . .

Of Angela he remembered only the argument with Sarah about something or other on a bad connection from Pennsylvania to California, and then the Mark Hopkins Top-of-the-Mark bar and the girl with a gin drink in front of her. Of Big Sur and Angela he recalled most clearly that a stopper had worked itself out of a bottle of perfume in her luggage and that all her clothes, even her hairbrushes, smelled of violets. Why in Christ's name had he needed to be forgiven for any of that?

He was sweating heavily by then, his bare hands aching with each blow of the sledge. At last he was tired enough to bring the argument with his dead wife to an end. Let her alone, for God's sake. Forget it. All of it . . . her apartment with the picture of Judge Learned Hand and Satchmo and loving everybody and lost causes, and snapping back at racists and bullies because you loved them too and couldn't stand to condemn them for their ignorance . . .

She had gone into that curve too fast, that was all, or struck a patch of slick oil in the rain. Forgive her an instant of panic, for hitting the brakes too hard, forgive her for leaving them that night in Spain without a goodbye. . . .

Selby sat on a log, breathing slowly. The backs of his hands were pale and damp with sweat in the bright light. A fleck of blood where he'd nicked himself stood out clearly.

He had spent too much time this way, he thought, wondering about himself, judging himself . . .

In a magazine article he had read: "What your father made of himself may have little relation to the hereditary factors he passed on to you. He gave you, remember, only *half* his chromosomes. And those he gave you depended entirely on chance. You

116

can only guess what came to you by studying any *unusual* traits that you and your father shared . . ."

Without a father to study he had been forced to study himself. Once in a supermarket in Davenport he had asked his hands to make their own choices. Without looking at the shelves he had grabbed products at random, squandering a week's wages in an attempt to find some revealing pattern in these unbidden choices. Jars of pickles and cocktail onions, work gloves, powdered milk, breakfast foods, shoe polish, a corkscrew, paper napkins, cans of vegetables, he remembered the look of them when he spread them out on his bed in the dorm at St. Ambrose, and how anxiously he searched them for clues to his father's character and his own, as hopeful and credulous (he'd known later) as some bare-assed savage looking for auguries in monkey dung and cloud patterns.

From the back door, Mrs. Cranston called to him. "Mr. Selby? Mr. Selby, there was a call from your brother just now. He left a number."

Jarrell had called from a motel called the Greentree in Quinton, New Jersey. He had told Mrs. Cranston that he was using a pay phone but he would be back in his room, 119, in a few minutes and that he'd appreciate it if his brother would call him.

Selby dialed the number. A clerk connected him to room 119. The phone rang three times. A click. A voice Selby didn't recognize said, "Yes?"

"My name's Selby, Harry Selby. I'd like to talk to my brother. Is he there?"

"Jarrell? No, he's not. His brother, you say?"

"Yes. Who is this?"

"Me? I'm Johnny Cole. I expect him back pretty soon."

"You a friend of Jarrell's?"

"Well, you could say that. We've had some drinks in the bar here, hit it off pretty good. We're both looking for work, and we got to talking about prospects, that sort of thing. He asked me to come by tonight for a drink, a welcome notion, like the fella says."

"When will Jarrell be back, Mr. Cole?"

"Can't say for sure. I came by just a couple of minutes ago. His door was open and the phone was ringing. So I answered it. He must have went out to do some shopping."

"I'll call back in about a half hour. Would you tell him that, please, Mr. Cole?"

"I sure will, Harry."

Selby made himself a mild drink, walked aimlessly about the study. On the hearth, his head between his paws, Blazer followed him. Checking his watch, Selby experienced a flash of memories. Summitt and the girl and the sergeant with the brown and rigidly sculpted features . . .

A clerk with a high, nasal voice answered his second call to the Greentree Motel. He was sorry, he told Selby, but the gent in room 119, Jarrell Selby, had just checked out without leaving a forwarding address.

No, the clerk said in answer to Selby's questions, he couldn't tell him anything about a Mr. Cole. There was nobody registered at the Greentree Motel by that name.

CHAPTER TEN

Sergeant Wilger called the following morning and told Selby he'd like to see him as soon as possible. Selby asked if there was a development in the investigation, but Wilger said, "No, it's not that. It's something Captain Slocum wants to check out."

East Chester's City Hall housed courtrooms, various municipal agencies, District Attorney Jonathan Lamb's offices, police headquarters and Captain Walter Slocum's detective division.

Under fluorescent lighting the division's main squad room looked to Selby like a huge marine tank with shining green walls, smoke-blue air and weak sunlight filtered through dust-grimed windows. Computers, calculators and a bank of closed circuit TV monitors stood on wall shelving beside double doors, with Slocum's name printed across them in black letters.

Half a dozen detectives sat at metal desks. A bald-headed man in a leather jacket was taking a statement from an elderly couple. Another detective listened with a bored but courteous expression to a young woman speaking rapidly in Spanish.

At a counter that separated the squad room from a small reception area a black woman in uniform turned the pages of a loose-leaf folder and pounded them with a rubber stamp.

"Help you, sir?" she asked without looking up.

"My name is Selby. Sergeant Wilger asked—"

"Yellow form, Mr. Selby. End of the counter." She pointed her elbow at a metal box filled with Xeroxed sheets. "Print your name, address and don't forget the zip code."

Several of the detectives looked up when they heard Selby's name. The deputy DA he had met earlier stood at a desk making notes on a legal pad. A phone was cocked between her chin and shoulder. She held a cigarette in her free hand.

Sergeant Wilger walked to the counter. "Come in, Mr. Selby. It's an open file, Ellie," he added as the black lady looked at him. "You can skip signing in, Mr. Selby."

The sergeant raised a hinged section of the counter and Selby followed him to his desk, which was at the end of the room.

The deputy DA gave Selby an impersonal smile. She wore a gray denim suit. Her shoulder-length hair was dark.

Brett, he recalled, Dorcas Brett or Kelly Brett. She hadn't recognized him; her smile was a quick reflex, but Selby nodded to her as Wilger waved him to a chair. Traffic noises sounded from the street, faint and remote in the brightly lit, overheated office. It had been clear and sunny when Selby left home, but erratic bursts of rain now streaked the dusty windows.

Wilger leaned back and clasped his hands behind his head. The armpits of his beige sports shirt were dark with sweat. "The captain will be with us in a couple of minutes, Mr. Selby. So far there's nothing to tell you about your daughter's case. We need the kind of lead the computers just don't cough up. Somebody in a bar hears something, we get an anonymous phone call, that's the break we're waiting for."

Wilger removed a bulky file from his desk drawer. Nodding at the typed reports and handwritten notes, he said, "See, we've already logged better than a hundred man-hours on it. Checked the weirdo files in a dozen counties, but so far we got zilch."

The sergeant removed his glasses and began polishing them with a square of felt he picked out of a paper clip receptacle. He said, "You talk to your daughter about what happened when she left Muhlenburg that night, Mr. Selby? Remember . . . I asked you about that gap in her story?"

"I talked to her, sergeant, yes. She stopped to rest for a while, that's all she remembers."

Wilger's expression was politely quizzical. "That's all?

120

Three hours, and she draws a blank?"

His phone rang. The sergeant answered it, picked up a sheaf of papers, and began reading off pawnbroker numbers.

Selby glanced about. The view through the windows was bleak, yellow lights from office buildings across the street gleaming dully on the wet panes.

The deputy DA was gone. The young woman was still chattering to the detective who, Selby noticed, wasn't writing any of it down; his ballpoint pen was motionless on the note pad. Except for the lady's outbursts the big room was silent.

His presence had created a strain, Selby realized.

The door to the private office opened and Slocum walked into the squad room. Tall, heavily built, the captain was turned out in a three-piece gray mohair suit, polished black loafers with metal clasps shining on the insteps and a crimson tie flecked with tiny blue dots. His blond-gray hair was thinning, and he wore it in loose but carefully arched waves.

The captain fixed a good-humored but challenging smile on Selby. "I'm Walter Slocum, Mr. Selby, Captain Walter Slocum. Now let's start without any bullshitting," he said pleasantly enough, and pulled a chair up and straddled it, his prominent jaw tilted back, his eyes measuring Selby. "We know you've been looking for something this last week or so, driving all over the country around Buck Run and The Lakes. A farmer spotted you parked for an hour or more on a road near his place. He called the sheriff and gave him a description of your car and the plate number. It doesn't take too many smarts to figure out what you were looking for. You're trying to find a lead to that psycho who grabbed your daughter. But that tells us something else, Selby, which is that you don't trust us, or you're trying to find something before we do."

"Captain, I think you've been misinformed—"

"How's that?"

"Somebody must have told you I'm pretty damned patient. I've taken two shots since I came in to find out what you wanted. That's my limit, captain. The sergeant is more interested in where my daughter was that night than where the bastard who raped her was."

Wilger said, "We're checking every angle, Mr. Selby. You can't get touchy because—"

121

Slocum raised his hand. "Let him finish, Burt. Go on, Selby, speak up. I told you we don't want any bullshit."

He was good, Selby thought, the captain was good.

"*Then* you tell me," Selby said, "that I'm trying to cover something up. Let's get rid of *that* bullshit, all right?"

"Fair enough. But you missed my meaning. I was telling you how things look to us, as plain old ordinary cops. That's not necessarily the way they *are*, but I was giving you credit for understanding that." The captain's tone was pleasant; he seemed to be enjoying the conversation. "Let me just make a couple of general points now," he said. "Times are we lose a witness, somebody like you who can help us, lose his confidence, his cooperation. A cop says something that pisses him off, or he gets tired of telling his story over and over to a dozen detectives and clerks. Or maybe he figures we're incompetent or stupid or crooked, but whatever the reason, we lose him. I don't want that to happen with you, Selby, because frankly we need your help to find the scumbag who worked your daughter over. But I know something's bothering you. That's why I asked you to come in. Let's start with your daughter's bike. Your boy thought he saw some red paint on it. Maybe that's what's bothering you. You figure we screwed up from the start. But I've got the lab report in my office, and you're welcome to look at it. There wasn't any red paint on her bike, Selby, not a speck. I'll grant you this much, it would have been better if Lieutenant Eberle told you he was bringing it in for a lab check, but damn it, even so, I've got to back him, Selby. I've *got* to because time was the most important thing going for us then." He tapped a finger sharply for emphasis on Wilger's desk. "Getting a lead to that psycho took the top priority. Be honest, for Christ's sake, Selby. You got to realize that."

"I can see your point."

"Well, goddammit then," Slocum said, "we got that cleared up at least. Is anything else bothering you?"

"No, not exactly." He managed a smile; he understood the tension now. It was a feeling he'd known in locker rooms after games when key blocks had been missed, passes dropped, punts fumbled . . .

"Well, what's the rest of it then?" Slocum asked him.

"It's . . . well, I'm sort of curious why that farmer didn't ask me what my business was. I might have been a county surveyor, a salesman on a lunch break—or else"—Selby was still smiling —"just some character with a full bladder."

"Who knows, Mr. Selby? But I can give you a good guess. There's been a lot of timber cut illegally around that area, and . . ."

In a more expansive mood now Slocum told Selby of logging poachers up from the south in flatbed rigs, hillbillies, pineys, rough-as-a-cob woodsmen who used winches and powersaws in nighttime forays to take down poplar and buttonwood and even oak, working by flashlight, someone standing on guard with a shotgun . . .

"Naturally," Slocum concluded, "with that kind of trouble around his farm, he wasn't about to investigate anything on his own. Now if we're going to work together, Selby, supposing you begin by telling us what you were looking for out around Buck Run."

"I didn't have anything solid to go on."

"Let us be the judge of that. We're the pros, we got the equipment, the manpower, plus that's what we're paid for." Slocum laughed. "You amateurs wouldn't want to put us on welfare, I hope." There was a general laugh at that; everyone was relaxing now.

Selby said, "Dr. Kerr told me to humor my daughter and pay attention to anything she told me."

"Good advice, damn good advice." Slocum nodded. "So she told you something and you decided to check it out?"

"That's right. She mentioned something about seeing reflections of light in the sky. I wasn't sure what it meant. That's why I didn't bother reporting it. I thought it might have been a glare from a farm pond that caught her eye."

Slocum watched Selby thoughtfully. "Did you get a bearing on these reflections . . . or whatever they were?"

"No, I didn't. But the fact that I'd looked for them calmed her down a bit."

"Well, Mr. Selby," Slocum said, relaxing, "kids your daughter's age never make very reliable witnesses. They're restless and fidgety with the business of growing up, and you try to catch 'em, pin 'em down"—he closed his big hand suddenly— "they slip through your fingers like quicksilver."

123

He placed a glossy loafer against Wilger's desk, and took his time about removing the wrapper from a slim, gold-flecked cigar and lighting it from a match the sergeant held for him.

"I'm talking from experience," Slocum said then. "I've got a daughter of my own, she's a grown-up young lady now but when she was about eight or nine, I guess it was, she was always begging me to buy her a ballet outfit, the little dress, the slippers, the whole works. That was all she wanted in life, she told me, cute as could be then, so damned if I didn't do just that one weekend when I was in New York at a police convention. Found an old Jewish lady on Eighth Avenue and got her to make me up a costume, and you better believe she wanted an arm and a leg for it, but within a month my little girl quit ballet school and entered a pony class and she was out of her mind for me to buy her . . ."

The Bluebonnet Bar was tucked into a shopping mall on the Mercer Pike between a men's store and a Radio Shack. Jay Mooney was waiting for Selby in a rear booth with a double whiskey sour in front of him. A plump man with ruddy cheeks and wisps of gray hair, Mooney greeted Selby with a nervous smile.

"I ordered for both of us," he said, as Selby settled into the booth. "What're you drinking, Harry?"

Selby declined but Mooney finished his whiskey sour in one long gulp and signaled their waitress for another. "Slocum's a mean sonofabitch," he said, and leaned closer to Selby. "If I was a real friend, Harry, I'd tell you to fuck off. That would be smart for both of us."

"Did Slocum get rich fixing parking tickets?"

The waitress brought Mooney's drink and their lunch, soft-shelled crabs, french fries and coleslaw, and returned later with a pitcher of beer and tall frosted glasses.

"Shit no, it's not parking tickets." Mooney glanced at the crowded tables near them. "Slocum has a part-time job, you could say, with Harlequin Chemicals. He reports to a man name of Dom Lorso. Lorso's close to the president of Harlequin, George Thomson, a.k.a. Giorgio Tomaso, so close in fact that when Thomson unzips his fly Lorso pisses. A big company like

Harlequin needs a friendly face at the local lock-up. A cop with a white cane, that's what they're called. Someone who doesn't see certain things, or if he does, he looks at them with—let's say —a charitable eye. A hit-run becomes a speeding ticket, an executive in a motel room with a Moroccan sailor off a tanker, that's part of some company exchange-training. You name it. Things have to be taken care of, Harry, that's the way it is. You understand what I'm telling you?"

"I understand," Selby said. "And a rape could be viewed with, what was your phrase—'a charitable eye'—and a sports car could disappear into the blue with an assist from a cop with a white cane. That's what you're telling me, Jay. But I want to know *why*. What's the connection between the psycho who raped Shana and Harlequin Chemicals?"

Mooney pushed his coleslaw around his plate and finished off his drink. He looked around for the waitress, holding up his empty glass. There were dark, wrinkled pouches under his eyes. "I'm not sure, Harry." With obvious difficulty he looked at Selby. "How's Shana? How is she, Harry? That's why I called the other day."

"About as you'd expect, but you didn't answer my question."

Mooney drummed his fingers on the table. "I'm afraid of those people, I'll admit it." He laughed nervously. "Big deal, I admit it. What the hell else can I do? Deny it?"

"Did Slocum give you the speech about buying the ballet outfit for his kid, the flounced pink dress, and the cute little slippers? It figures," he went on, "he enjoys that number. Before *Miranda*, Slocum used to tell that story to suspects in the basement of the division and when they were blinking back their tears at how sweet it was, Slocum would slip behind them and bust their heads wide open with a nightstick."

The waitress put his fresh drink on the table, and Mooney took a long pull from it. "Don't bother counseling moderation, Harry. Stouter hearts than yours have never prevailed."

His speech was becoming drunkenly straitjacketed, overly controlled and precise. "Of course you got to realize the captain has come a long way. He talks about coddling criminals to Rotary and Kiwanis, he's a big draw at police conventions and" —Mooney drank and smacked his lips—"and wouldn't be

125

offended if the party offered him a run at the State Assembly in a year or two."

"The voters are lucky," Selby said. "They're to be congratulated." He took out his wallet and dropped a bill on the table.

"Harry, I'd like to help, but there's not a goddamn thing I can do."

"I understand, Jay."

"The hell you do. You think I'm a gutless lush. Which isn't too wide of the mark, my boy."

"Don't put yourself down. You kept this lunch date, you told me Slocum's a thief, and Lorso pisses when Thomson runs his zipper down. And you made the courtesy call to ask about Shana."

"Ah, shit." Mooney rubbed his mouth. "There *is* something else, Harry, but it's just gossip, might not mean a thing. A good while back, six maybe seven years ago, Thomson's son got his ass in a crack over in Jersey. It was near his school, and a girl was mixed up in it. She was hurt bad. It took some heavy pressure to clean it up. According to the talk, Slocum was involved."

"What was the name of the school?"

"It's a military college, Rockland Military. Near Jefferson."

"You know who the girl was?"

"I never heard her name, as God is my witness and my judge. Now will you sit there a minute and finish that beer with me?"

"All right, Jay." Selby picked up his glass. "To better days."

When Selby got home Mrs. Cranston told him that there was no call from his brother, Jarrell, and that Shana had gone out for a ride with Normie Bride.

"He came by about an hour ago in that funny truck of his, and I said it was all right. She's been moping around and I thought it would do her good. She wore that sweater she likes, the gray one with the red trim at the wrists. She even asked me to press a hair ribbon for her. It was good seeing her looking pretty again."

Selby turned on the early news. A live interview was in progress with Senator Dixon Lester from his Washington office. The senator faced a group of reporters and TV cameramen.

126

Middle-aged and of medium height, the senator's face was long and narrow with eyes set back in shadowed hollows beneath thick eyebrows. A wave of black hair fell in a practiced manner over his forehead, adding a mildly raffish touch to his conservative dark-suited-and-vested appearance.

Flat midwestern accents . . . "Our responsibility is to the American people, period. No one else, within our borders or outside them, commands my loyalty. We are investigating the Harlequin Chemical Corporation and certain divisions of the Correll Group, along with diverse suppliers to our military forces—not, *not*, I repeat, because we are attacking conglomerates *per se*, but only that aspect of conglomerate philosophy which holds that they can't be restrained by national interest or anything at all like old-fashioned patriotism."

"Senator Lester," a reporter asked, "would you say that Senator Rowan and his committee have been protecting the Correll Group?"

Senator Lester replied, "To that I can only say *de mortui nil nisi bonum.*"

Standing beside the senator was a tall Oriental woman with black hair and wide, startlingly made-up eyes. The network director cued back to the local anchorman, who looked into the camera and said solemnly, "Senator Mark Rowan, dead today at sixty-eight."

Selby turned off the set. The interview raised the same kind of questions he had put to Jay Mooney, and which Mooney wouldn't or couldn't answer. There was no help anywhere, especially not from a cop who wore shining loafers and owned high-rises on the Jersey shore.

Coming to a decision, Selby called Casper Gideen. His wife, Lori, told him Casper was out back but to hold on, she'd get him. Lori Gideen reminded Selby of dust bowls and crop failures, faded photographs from Depression days. Actually Casper's wife was just a few years into her thirties, although she had teenaged sons. Too gaunt to be considered pretty, Lori usually had a smile for everyone, and managed a dogged sort of serenity in spite of money worries and the emotional upset stirred by Casper's tempers.

When Gideen answered, Selby told him he'd like to come

by as soon as possible. Whenever you want, Gideen said. . . .

The rain had eased off, but drops still fell in sudden, noisy rattles from the trees whenever a wind came up. Gideen was seated in the shelter of an open shed he had built alongside his kennel run.

Selby joined him, ducking to clear the low roof. The red-bone hounds raced about in their narrow run, howling at Selby because they associated him with guns and open woods. Gideen spoke a command and the hounds loped away and settled down in their shelter.

"I may need some dogs, Casper."

Gideen grunted with surprise. "You want to go coon hunting, them redbones is ready."

"I don't need redbones for what I'm after."

Gideen was silent a moment, then said, "You got some notion where she was taken that night?"

"I think so. A stretch of country on Dade Road past the Rakestraw Bridge."

"How big a stretch?"

"I'm not sure. Six, eight miles."

"More we narrow it down, the better. You planning to ask anybody else to help out?"

"No, I'm not."

"Good. I don't think you ought. I ain't got no bloodhounds and there's nary one in the county. Cousin of mine in Lancaster has a pack. Keeps 'em for old times. Still calls 'em buck hounds, like my granddaddy did."

Gideen took out a big silver watch. After studying it he said, "I can be back a couple of hours after supper. You and me, we'll meet at the bridge, Harry, one or two in the morning." He was thoughtful for a moment, then went on, "My granddaddy taught me houndin'. He was a prison guard. Told us how they used to watch the stores of turpentine and black pepper. If the cons stole 'em they was planning to run. Put black pepper in their boots and turpentine all over themselves, no hound this side of hell-fire could nose out their stink." Gideen was still staring at his watch. "We got to meet late, Harry, and work fast. They'll be singing, them hounds."

"You got to do what you're thinking, Harry, because something ain't right. First Goldie Boy and the Kane woman. Then I saw a black car the other day cruising slow past Tenn and Pyle's Corners. Saw it twice. A Lincoln car, a Connie. Strangers in it. Fella with some red in his sideburns, I seen that much."

He put his watch away and pointed to a twisted pear tree. "See that fruit tree, Harry? It's dead now, dead as a hammer nail. Last spring it had a death crop—know about that? One last suck at the earth, a million white blossoms, and more fruit all summer than Lori could put up. Then it died, said goodbye like, plain died. Well, that's how I look at Ollie Jessup and the cops and strangers nosing around here, Harry, like a death crop, things busy and green and blooming, but something's coming to an end."

Gideen threw a stick into the run and watched the redbones scramble to fight for it. "Don't know why I'm talking about a dead tree this way. Let's get to business, Harry. We need two points tonight, one to stir the hounds up, the second to make 'em hunt. We push the second point into their noses and hit 'em around the ears with it, and that tells 'em what we're hunting for. So you get two things of your daughter's, gloves, boots, a sweater, a skirt. Okay, Harry?"

"How about a pillow she sleeps on?"

Casper looked at him and nodded. "Do fine, Harry. Do fine."

A few minutes after midnight Selby went down the hallway to his daughter's room. He wore a windbreaker and leather boots. Shana's room was dark, with only a faint spread of moonlight glowing on surfaces.

She was sleeping on her side, the bandaged hand touching her swollen cheek. Her breathing was soft, shallow. He picked up the sweater she had worn that day, the gray pullover with red trim.

Slowly and gently he pulled the warm pillow from beneath her head and replaced it with its mate. She murmured something, pushing at her hair, but didn't wake.

* * *

Crossing the Rakestraw Bridge, Selby parked near the cemetery. He waited in the silence and darkness until he saw the light of Gideen's pickup coming toward him on the road from Buck Run. As he stepped from his car he could already hear the eager bugling of the buck hounds.

CHAPTER ELEVEN

That same night George Thomson paced his office in Harlequin Chemicals headquarters, a glass-and-steel structure which rose in tiers from a ten-acre concrete slab softened by fountains and graveled walks.

Through his windows he could make out the bridges above the shining curve of Delaware Bay and the flaming grids of oil-cracking towers.

A buzzer sounded on his desk and a moment later his door clicked open and Dom Lorso came in. Lighting a cigarette from the stub he was smoking, Lorso said, "George, we better talk straight now. Like this was any other business problem. Let me explain something first. I'm worried about Earl's car—"

"Dom, I've just been talking to Mr. Correll. He's in New York. You know that Senator Rowan died?"

"I heard something about it on the news. But I want to finish this other thing, Giorgio."

Thomson frowned but nodded and turned from the windows. "All right, let's have it, Dom."

"The car," Dom Lorso said, "a forty-thousand-dollar set of wheels don't disappear like some goddamn magician clapped his hands. A professional thief wouldn't touch it. A chrome-and-red Porsche comes off an APB like a Roman candle. Every traffic cop in a dozen states is hoping to eyeball it. Only a punk stoned out of his skull would rip it off in the first place, and he'd dump it the minute he got his head straight." Lorso inhaled deeply, began coughing. "Number two, Earl's whole story hangs on Santos and—"

Thomson stopped him. "Dom, you've got your priorities screwed up. You're talking about details Slocum is taking care of. And everything you're saying is based on some half-assed assumption that Earl might be lying. Why are you assuming that? I want Earl to use his brains and balls without any hang-ups. I've got more than my share, and so have you, Dom. You still make the sign of the cross when you're in a bind, so let Earl alone, don't worry about him. There are two secrets—not being afraid of other people and not being afraid of yourself. I learned that much from Correll. You need worries, you can share mine. I taped the talk with Mr. Correll. He told me to.

"Listen to this, Dom, and you'll see what we *should* be worrying about."

Pressing the conference tab on his telephone console, Thomson looked expectantly at the webbed speakers. After a hum of static Simon Correll's amplified voice sounded through the office.

"—his death may be a serious inconvenience, Thomson. From private sources I know that Harlequin is close to the top of Senator Lester's hit list. Senator Rowan belongs to the ages now, as they say. The halls of Congress have been resounding all day with resolutions honoring his memory, his dedication and so forth. What that means, George, is that Rowan's no longer any use to us. Even while they're holding Air Force Two to fly him home, Lester was striking, before the old boy's flesh was hardly cold."

Dom Lorso coughed and pulled a face at the speakers, but Thomson held up a hand. "Get this . . ."

". . . immediately impounded Rowan's files and correspondence, which implemented a court order Miss Kim filed not more than minutes after Rowan's death. A district court judge has granted Lester broad subpoena powers to investigate—well, you heard him at his news conference, George."

Thomson's recorded voice sounded then. "That's the main thing he's after, Mr. Correll, if you ask me, prime-time news shows. If you want to make a reputation today, you've got to invent something raunchy or sensational to grab those TV dummies."

Lorso nodded, and lit another cigarette.

". . . could well be, George," Correll's voice continued, "but the practical and immediate results of this investigation will be these: government accountants and lawyers will be swarming over your office by next week. Cooperate with them. Tell your senior echelons to give Senator Lester's people whatever they want. Minutes of staff meetings, appointment books, schedules of company plane trips, communications between Dupree and Summit and your other plants.

"Another thing. The types you'll be dealing with are all on expense accounts. Provide them with office space for coffee breaks, plenty of snacks. And plenty of sandwiches and be sure they're wrapped so they can tuck them into their briefcases. Provide limos between your offices and their hotels. You'll find that these civil service types have no moral or intellectual perspective. They're fashioned by greed and equate superiority with unhampered elbowroom at the public trough. I want you to understand—"

Thomson's amplified voice interrupted him. "Mr. Correll, all I understand is that you're asking me to put my neck on the block and sharpen the axe for them."

"No, George, but I want you to understand the mentalities you're dealing with. Even if they knew that a child in Karachi is lucky to find edible insects to stretch its rice, it wouldn't concern them. But we'll survive them, George. Our work is too important to allow anything to deflect us. Everything is ready at Saliaris, thanks in good measure to you and to General Taggart."

The speakers hummed for an instant, then a click sounded and they were silent. Thomson said, "You see, Dom, what's on the *top* of the list to worry about?"

"I don't buy that, Giorgio. We've been together too long to be careful about what we say to each other." Lorso joined Thomson at the tinted windows and their reflected figures dominated even the glittering skyline.

Lorso said, "I don't give a damn about Correll and Senator Lester and those people starving in Karachi, wherever the hell that is. If they got maggots in their rice, fuck it. My world is here, with you, and Adele and Earl. That's family, and that's what I won't let anybody hurt."

It was impossible to ignore Lorso when he was in this mood, Thomson knew; he was at his most authentic and most valuable now. An early warning system and a first line of defense. "All right, Dom, let's have all of it."

"Okay. Go back to the car. Where is it? Who stole it? Why don't it show up somewhere? That's one thing. The second is, we've only got Santos and Adele to back Earl's story. It would be nice, of course, if those witnesses just didn't happen to be the boy's mother and a stuttering Puerto Rican refugee from a Miami massage parlor who happens to work for her."

Thomson said angrily, "Why are you talking about *witnesses?*"

Lorso drew a deep breath. "Last week Earl got a call from a girl, wouldn't give her name but accused him of hitting her with his car and then raping her, and she claims this all happened the same night that Selby kid got—"

"Why didn't you tell me this before?"

"You had your plate full with Correll. Earl was shaken up, naturally. He called, asked to see me. He'd already told Adele, which was a mistake but it was done by then. We all figured the same thing, some crackpot getting her kicks with a stiff phone.

"But then she called again today, Giorgio, the same one, bugging Earl about wanting to meet with him, to talk things over. Just the two of them, somewhere private—"

"Dom, *why* didn't you give this to Slocum? We've got nothing to cover up—"

"Easy, Giorgio."

"I don't want any damn weirdo hassling Earl."

"Relax a minute, will you? Slocum's people have stirred things up, questioned all kinds of crazies, kid-fuckers, whip-dicks, that kind. And the investigation's like a fever or something. Everybody gets heated up. So maybe some crazy broad gets a notion to lean on Earl. Maybe she's pressuring him for kicks or a payday, who knows? But if there's a frame in the works, I decided to damn well find who's behind it."

"You already set something up?"

"I didn't want to waste time trying to convince you I was right. I called Allan Davic in New York."

This news obviously disturbed Thomson. "We're not planning to sue anybody. You think that much firepower is necessary?"

"We need more than just a lawyer, Giorgio. If we wanted some klutz with a briefcase, we got twenty or thirty of them down on the eighth floor. But we need professional surveillance now and professional muscle, too."

Lorso put his hand on the desk, leaned toward Thomson, his small red features bunching in a frown. "I got hang-ups, you just said so. I smelled that garlic again, so I called Davic and told him we needed him."

"Hiring Allan Davic is like committing an army division to knock off a squad of toy soldiers," Thomson said. "I like Allan, Dom, don't misunderstand me. He can be smooth and pleasant, and very brutal." Lifting the lid of a humidor, Thomson removed a cigar and regarded it. "But I'm still not sure—"

"It's insurance, Giorgio. Slocum can take care of what's official, Davic will handle everything else. His people are here now, Davic will be down in a day or so. I don't give a damn about his reputation. He also gets the job done. At the end of every trial, he's smiling at the cameras on the courthouse steps and his client rides off free in a limousine. I only had one thing in mind hiring him. To protect all of us."

Lorso smiled suddenly, but there was a nervous tension in his narrow eyes. "Give me a break. It was the garlic . . . tell me I did right, Giorgio."

"Dom, you did fine. If I hadn't been so involved with—" He gestured irritably at the phone speakers.

"I understand, Giorgio. So I did it for you. Look, you want a drink or anything? If not, I think I'll drive into Philadelphia. Couple of Davic's men are staying at the Franklin and they asked me for club passes and where to find a good shore dinner."

After Lorso left Thomson sat in his dark office and looked at the distant bridges. A ship was moving and he could see the shifting reflections of its running lights in the water. Like Adele and Earl, he thought, who reflected one another in that way at times, except that it seemed that there was always a canny selectivity at work in whatever they chose to see of themselves. An uncritical, almost mindless love or fascination flowed between them, and with it the willing and sustaining dependence . . .

Yet before her accident . . . Thomson stood to make himself a drink, putting those thoughts of his wife aside.

Fortunately, he had other things to think about. Why hadn't Lorso talked to him first about bringing Davic in? Why had he moved so fast? Pure Sicilian reflex, a guard dog's automatic growl? Or was there something in that damned garlic after all? Lorso was acting like he *knew* they had something to worry about . . .

He sipped his whiskey. Lorso had been upset by the problems at Rockland, those undergraduate eruptions that Thomson knew were normal enough, and what you had to expect from high-spirited young studs. But for all his street-smart veneer and cynicism, the Sicilian was almost a Puritan in many ways. A girl had been hurt, true enough, but Thomson's thoughts were confused by a blur of images, and he realized he wasn't sure which girl he was thinking of, the one at Jefferson that Earl had gotten involved with, or the one with a bicycle flecked with red paint, or someone else, the girl at the club last week . . .

He decided he needed another drink. He also decided he might as well put Adele on that list too, don't forget her, put her right up at the top . . .

His phone rang. The lobby security guard told him his chauffeur was waiting for him at the plaza exit.

He might as well go home, he thought, why the hell not, but riding down in the express elevator Thomson felt a flick of envy for Lorso, over in Philadelphia somewhere, doing the clubs with Davic's people. Not so much, but face it, better than what he had to go home to . . .

CHAPTER TWELVE

A ringing phone waked Selby. His bedroom was in shadows, but the first sunlight was filtering dully through the frosted windows.

His dreams had been of hounds on leads, black and brown shapes with lolling tongues, and cemetery markers and objects in patterns he couldn't identify or make sense of . . .

The hounds had struck at the entrance to a small estate called Vinegar Hill. A lane from Dade Road led back through a hedge of locusts to a house and garage. After flashing his light through the windows, and seeing what he had both expected and dreaded, Selby had told Gideen to pack in the hounds and head back for Little Tenn.

No gas stations were open; Selby had driven home and called the sheriff's station on Route One. That had been two A.M.

He snapped on his bedside lamp and answered the phone.

"Sergeant Ritter here, Mr. Selby. Figured you'd better know this. Battalion Chief Quill and his unit at Coatesville got a brush-fire alarm a couple hours ago. Had to bring in the pumper from Odena to get it under control."

In some strange way, Selby knew with certainty what Sergeant Ritter was about to tell him. Last night, as Gideen had been loading the hounds into the truck, Selby had seen a red light like the dome of a police car flare briefly on a hill beyond White Clay Creek.

Sergeant Ritter was saying, "I logged your call around two-thirty and patched it straight through to Sergeant Wilger in East Chester. He said he'd get someone on it, check the county recorder, find out who's living there."

Selby let out his breath slowly. "Where did you say that fire was?"

"They tell me you could see the flames clear over to Quarryville. Kids probably, Chief Quill says, let a campfire get away from 'em, got scared and ran for it. No sign of 'em though. Fire took the old Vinegar Hill place except for the garage and some of the back trees around it."

A white Toyota Celica was parked on the shoulder of Dade Road at the entrance to Vinegar Hill. Behind it was a maroon sedan with East Chester police insignia on the door panels.

"This is obviously a waste of time." Shana stepped from the station wagon and stared at the blackened trees. The lane into the house had been churned into a glistening gridwork of mud by the fire apparatus. Water thick with soot and charred splinters foamed in the ruts.

"You can stay in the car if you want," Selby said.

"What difference does it make anyway?" Shana asked. "Sergeant Ritter told you the whole place was gone."

Her hair was in a loose ponytail and she wore Normie Bride's freshman letter jacket, compensating for the long sleeves by doubling the cuffs back over her wrists.

Burt Wilger came up the lane from the house, his boots and poncho wet and muddy, and his glasses smudged with soot.

Nodding to them, he said, "It's a tough break," and glanced behind at the layers of smoke drifting from the blackened house. "If you were right, Mr. Selby, we might have had something to go on."

"I was right," Selby told him. "Four hours ago, there was evidence here. Now we've got a fire sale."

"You're positive about that? Evidence, I mean?" Wilger looked at Shana and cleared his throat. "The DA's here, she'll want to talk to you. I've got to check the fence line, see if I can find out where those kids broke through it."

A patch of lawn had been trampled down by the firemen,

138

and churned into haphazard patterns by their hoses. Beyond the muddied grass stood what was left of the house, the beams and supports standing like a crooked black skeleton against the sky. The roof had burned completely away, and the bedroom and living room floors had collapsed into the basement. Only the fieldstone fireplace and chimney were undamaged; that and the garage, which had been protected from the flames by the thick crown of a maple tree which had toppled down around it.

Shana stopped on the sodden lawn and looked at the garage door, a tense frown shadowing her eyes. The whole place had a chilling look to Selby, a charnel house with black, twisted trees forming an arch above it.

Shana walked closer to the garage, but stopped, her arms, spindly looking in Normie's big, loose jacket, crossed across her slight breasts.

A woman came around the side of the house. As she lifted a dripping branch to duck under it, Dorcas Brett seemed taller than he remembered her, slim in a dark leather coat and copper-colored boots. The boots, flecked with water and mud now, were probably what made her seem taller, he thought; either that or the precise way she chose her footing, which gave a taut, controlled line to her body. In the morning light, drops of water glinted in her hair. Without gloves, her hands looked white as popcorn against the backdrop of charred trees.

She introduced herself and Selby said, "Yes, we've met, this is my daughter, Shana."

"I wasn't sure you'd remember, Mr. Selby." Dorcas Brett glanced at Shana, who was staring again at the garage doors. "Perhaps you'd rather talk somewhere else, Mr. Selby."

"What is there to talk about?"

"This place can't be very pleasant for your daughter."

"Then let's get it over with. This is where it happened. What else do you need to know?"

She hesitated and said, "Well, for one thing, Mr. Selby, the county recorder's office hasn't got back to us yet. We don't know who owns Vinegar Hill. We can't search the house or what's left of it until we have their permission or the evidentiary basis for a search warrant."

"I don't see any problem. Last night I saw what my daughter described to the police, specific things she saw inside this house the night she was raped. Doesn't my word count as evidence?"

"It's a sticky legal business, but I'll try to put it as clearly as I can. To satisfy the probable cause requirements, to prove to a magistrate that we have good and sufficient reasons for a search warrant, our evidence has to satisfy the same standards of admissibility that would be applied by a trial judge. The evidence has to be obtained legally, without violating anyone's civil rights. It can't be tainted. So it's not just a question of what you saw last night, but how and where you saw it."

"Because I was trespassing you mean?"

"Yes, and if you forced a door open and went inside you could be arrested for committing a felony. I can understand your frustration, but I didn't write the amendments to the Constitution that—"

He interrupted her. "Then let's try it this way. Supposing you claim you *overheard* me telling a bartender what I saw last night. You could act on that, couldn't you? Wouldn't that provide, what's the phrase—an 'evidentiary basis'?"

"Yes, but if we agreed to do something like that we'd both have to perjure ourselves."

"Let's go to a real bar then," Selby suggested. "I'll tell a real bartender all about it. You can listen if you want to. Wouldn't that soothe your legal conscience and protect your flanks from your bosses in East Chester?"

"No, listen. I don't have a particularly sensitive legal conscience, and I don't have any need to protect my flanks, as you put it. My only consideration was—"

She pushed her dark hair from her forehead. "Jesus, I'm sorry," she said unexpectedly. She was pale except for points of color on her high cheekbones. "I'm sorry about what happened to your daughter. I should have told you that first. It was rotten and vile and sickening and if any words of mine can help, if my sympathy and outrage means anything to you, you have them in full measure."

Selby said, "Yes, that means something, Miss Brett. Thank you."

From the lane, Wilger called, "Kelly, County Records just patched a message through to me. A caretaker checks this place out every week or so, but it's owned by an army officer stationed

140

down south somewhere, a General Taggart. He owns the property to the fence lines, sold off the rest to a developer."

"Have they notified the insurance carrier?"

"County's taking care of that. I've finished up here. I'll check the caretaker now."

Selby said, "It's a shame we can't make the next logical step, Miss Brett. I was trespassing, but I didn't kick in any doors. I looked through the windows with a flashlight. I saw the stone fireplace Shana told me about, and the deer's head hanging over it, and even the cot with ropes still hanging from the ends of it."

Wilger's car started up, the tires churning in the slick mud, losing traction with the crescendoing roar of the motor. As the sound whined in metallic blasts through the dripping trees, Shana screamed and stumbled toward them, her boots slipping on the muddy grass.

"No!" she shouted, "no!" and ran into Dorcas Brett's arms. The noise of the motor was all around them as the car bucked and rocked on the slick road.

"Dammit, Shana," Selby shouted. "What is it? What's the matter?"

Dorcas Brett pulled the crying girl close to her and stared at Selby. "Will you stop yelling at her, for God's sake! Why did you bring her here? Can't you imagine how she's feeling?" Her voice was rising, and her gray eyes looked nearly black. "Is this some exercise in dumb amateur therapy?"

An abrupt silence settled through the black woods; Wilger's car was moving, the sound of the motor fading.

"God," Dorcas Brett said, her arms falling to her sides. "I'm sorry, I shouldn't—" she began, but stopped suddenly and moistened her lips. A faint line of blue, like a surreal touch of lipstick, was forming a fine, dark edge about her mouth.

"Take it easy," Selby said to her.

With an arm around Shana, he walked with her out the muddy lane to their car.

"I'm all right, daddy."

"What was that all about?"

"I don't know. Give me a handkerchief, okay?"

"What frightened you back there?"

"It was the car, the noise. I wasn't expecting anything, it startled me."

"But you were staring at those garage doors. Why, Shana?"

"I told you, I wasn't thinking about anything. I was day-dreaming."

"Did he take you into the garage that night?"

"No . . . just the house."

Selby opened the door of the station wagon, and closed it when she slipped inside. "Turn on the radio," he suggested. "Get some music."

"What's the matter with that lady, daddy? She looked like she was going to faint."

"I'll check. You okay now?"

"Sure, but you better see what's wrong with her."

"Sit tight. I'll be right back."

The deputy DA was standing with her back to him. She turned and said, "That was very unprofessional. I had no right to come on that way—"

"You'd better stop talking for a while."

"The book says not to verbalize your feelings." She was speaking rapidly. "Remember the stats, not the people, don't get involved on a personal—"

"That's probably good advice," Selby said, "but you'd better get your breath back now. Don't say anything for a while."

"I wanted you to understand—"

"Dammit, shut up!" Selby held her shoulders and studied her face. Her eyes were distended with stress. An edge of blue had widened about her mouth. Her hands were clenched across her chest.

"Put your hands down," he told her. "Let them hang loose. Breathe deep and slow. Can you do that? Don't say anything. Just nod."

Lowering her hands, she swallowed with an effort and nodded. "I think I ought to—"

He tightened his grip on her shoulders. "Don't talk, you're overventilating, burning up oxygen faster than you're replacing it. Keep it up and you'll be out cold."

Holding her wrists, he elevated them until her arms were fully extended and level with the ground. "Breathe as deeply as possible, until you can feel it down to your stomach."

"I think I'm all right now."

"No, you're not. Something triggered a cyanosis jag. It's

142

like a muscular or emotional overdraft, tapping resources you don't have. I've seen it happen to athletes twice your size. Is it Dorcas or Kelly or what?" he added to distract her.

"Dorcas is a family name."

"And you're called Kelly? Just nod."

"Or Brett, it doesn't matter."

"Bodies have breaking points." He studied the line of blue about her lips. "Like machines. We're a complex of muscles and endocrines and feelings."

"I had a year of pre-med before—"

"Never mind that. Listen to me."

"It's good of you but—"

"Yes, I'm trying to distract you, but I'm obviously doing a lousy job of it. Keep quiet. Everything runs in harmony until there's an unexpected pressure against a vulnerable area. Then something breaks and we fall apart. You feeling better?"

"Yes, thanks."

"You feel up to driving?"

"I told you. I understand what—happened to me."

"How will that help you drive?"

"That isn't what I meant." She was still speaking rapidly, but color had returned to her face. "It's called hydroxia, a carbon dioxide depletion. It happened to me once in college. I didn't have breakfast this morning, only coffee, I was—" She paused and swallowed. "No, it was your daughter, her fear hit me in some way I wasn't prepared for." She glanced at her extended arms. "I'm all right now, thanks."

He released her wrists and she drew a deep breath as if experimenting with its effects. The blue line had faded from around her lips. She adjusted her scarf, and said, "Did you ask your daughter what upset her?"

"She told me she was frightened by the sound of the car."

As they walked out the lane he said, "If you don't feel like driving I'll stop in Buck Run and call a cab."

"Thanks, but that's not necessary." She glanced at him. "If there's anything else you think we should know, I'd like you to call us."

She took a business card from her handbag, and offered it to him. "My extension is on it," she said. "And my home phone."

"All right," he said.

"But you won't call, will you?"

"Does it matter?"

"I'm not sure. If you were put off by my attack I'm sorry. It's not part of my usual legal repertoire, but it's something else, isn't it?"

"Of course, Miss Brett."

He pointed back to the charred and smouldering house. "That's where some psychopath tortured and raped my daughter, but we can't even sift the ashes now because nobody at your shop seems to give a goddamn about finding him."

"You heard Sergeant Wilger, Mr. Selby, he's on his way to talk to the caretaker right now."

"I know. He'll log another hundred hours, and then sit around waiting for a tip from somebody in a bar. Meantime, he can listen to the captain talk about buying ballet clothes for his cute little kid. You better get yourself some breakfast, Miss Brett."

Hardly aware of what he was doing, Selby tore her card into pieces and scattered them over the muddy ground. "Sorry," he said, and walked away from her to join his daughter.

When they pulled into the driveway at their farm, Shana had her door open almost before Selby turned off the motor.

"Barby's got the homework assignments," she said, "and I told her I'd call her this morning."

"Can't that wait a minute?"

"What is it, daddy?"

Silence had settled, a quiltlike country silence, broken only by the stir of leaves and faint cries of birds. The sunlight drifted down through the tops of brilliant red and yellow buttonwoods and maples.

"Are you sure you didn't remember something back there that panicked you?"

"I told you it was the sound of that car. It scared her, too . . . the lady, didn't it?"

"I guess you're right, it did."

Shana pushed open the door and put a foot on the graveled drive.

144

"But there's another thing."

"Daddy, I *told* Barby I'd call her. Can't we talk about it some other time?"

"No, let's get it over with. Davey told me you were upset about something that happened a long time ago, something about a jukebox."

Shana settled back and crossed her arms. Staring through the windshield, she said, "I told him because I thought he deserved to know what was worrying me, what I was feeling. I didn't want him growing up with lots of mysterious things around him he couldn't understand, that he'd feel anxious and guilty about."

She looked skeptically at him. "It wasn't just the jukebox. Don't you remember anything about it?"

"We were in a booth having Cokes or something, I remember that much," Selby said. "Tell me the rest of it."

"I was wearing a white blouse and sweater, and a blue velvet skirt that Tishie made for me. Some men started laughing. They were having fun. I thought I was, too. When I started dancing, one of them said something and you told him to stop. It was a joke, I thought at first, but your face was mad, as if *you* were being threatened, not me. Outside I started crying, I couldn't help it."

"I told them to watch their language. You were pretty young, and I asked them to stop. That's all there was to it."

"But when you came out of the bar, there was blood on the back of your hands and you were laughing and that's what I always remembered, how you were laughing, and that's when I got sick all over Tishie's skirt. You were laughing because you were strong and because everyone else was so weak—"

"Shana, you've got the whole thing twisted—"

"Because you say so?"

"No, because maybe you're not seeing it exactly right . . . isn't that possible, honey—?"

"I don't care. Like this time . . . it was something happening to *me,* not to you, but before I could even try to understand it you took it away from me and turned it into something I could never be sure about. Daddy, you took over, but you left me out. That's not going to happen again . . . I know what happened that night in that house. Nobody can ever tell me I'm wrong about

145

that or didn't understand it or that there are always two sides to things. What happened, happened to *me*, daddy. Not you. If you find out who did it and knock him around in a parking lot or something, then it's yours . . . that might prove something to you, but it won't prove what I need to prove, what I've *got* to prove to myself before I can understand and feel all right with myself again."

"Shana, Shana," he said wearily. "What is there to understand? What is there to prove?"

She climbed quickly from the car and stared back at him through the open door. "Well, you never even knew what happened in your own life, you told us that a thousand times . . . about spending Christmas and holidays at college because there wasn't any home to go to after Davenport, and never knowing your father. . . . We grew up with your feelings, they got to be part of our lives. We were never sure what was you and what was us, or where the truth of anything was for *us*. Do you understand now what I'm trying to say? I mean, I don't want any doubts about what happened. I was raped. *I was raped*, and the man, whoever he is, has got to admit he did that to me. Not to you, daddy. Me. I didn't want it, or look for it, or like it and nobody is going to twist that around and say it was anything else, not now and not ever. I mean . . . I belong to *me*, the *truth* belongs to me . . ."

She slammed the car door and ran to the house, running from him, Selby knew, her hair streaming behind her under a drift of leaves.

Selby sat behind the wheel looking after her. "*I belong to me, the truth belongs to me . . .*" It wasn't a reasonable statement, it wasn't a logical or sensible one. Only the passion and the touching, high candor of someone very young could have found such words to frame them.

In the study, he called Gideen, who had heard a report of the fire on the radio and had already driven out to Vinegar Hill.

"Saw your car there, and the police, so I went on by, Harry. But I picked up a tail coming back through Buck Run. Them fellas in the black Connie again. New York plates, but I didn't get the numbers. Talk around here now is that Ollie Jessup might move his Tabernacle church over to Atlantic City, or somewhere on the shore. Except for them things, Harry, I'd got to say we wasted them buck hounds last night."

Selby changed into a sweat suit and jogged from the top of the meadow down a trail to their pond, which was like a flat, oval slate in the clear sunlight. When he was worried, as he was now, a workout sometimes burned away his restlessness.

Shana's bicycle, he thought, start there. Red paint on it, according to Davey. Not so, according to the police. Or start with Jarrell at Summitt City. And the girl who hadn't known where the coffee was. And the sergeant with a chiseled Indian profile. Someone tailing Gideen.

The grass was slick and brittle with the morning's frost, snapping like glass under his feet.

The ducks swam urgently from the sound of his running footsteps. Selby shook beads of perspiration from his eyelashes, and everything around him was refracted crazily by those tiny drops of water, the pond shot through with shards of light and the trees distorted and shimmering in surreal patterns.

Vinegar Hill. Bloodstains, ropes, fingerprints, any other physical evidence, burned to ashes, flooded under tons of water . . .

On the trail he and Davey had cut parallel to the logging road, Selby thought of the man in a car watching their house the night he had been at Summitt City. A man in a red sports car . . .

At last he rested under a shattered oak tree, a relic of an electrical storm that had struck the county during the summer Sarah's mother had lived with them.

"Pay the two dollars," had always been Tishie's advice about anything in life you couldn't budge or change—accept, don't argue, don't aggravate yourself, pay the fine, who can fight City Hall? Who wins? Don't break your head over what can't be helped, the will or whim of authority, the hem that couldn't be lowered because "there was nothing to work with," rain on wedding days, the undertaker, the tax collector, live with it. Pay . . .

Selby looked up at the dead tree, limbs gray and leafless, and remembered that she hadn't been so philosophical about thunder and lightning; they scared her out of her wits and she would invent any excuse to stay with Shana during electric storms, reading to her and Davey, or mending things that didn't need mending, anything so she wouldn't be alone in her room when thunder sent Blazer with his tail between his legs into the basement and lightning cracked like a big, bright whip over the meadows.

Tishie's husband had been Joseph Sager, "assistant to the concertmaster" of the Manhattan Symphony Orchestra, a man of shy dignity and manners—few faults and fewer words, Tishie had always said of him. Starting at the Manhattan as a janitor, a refugee from Germany, he had been eager for anything to turn his hand to. Mopping floors, sweeping out dressing rooms, loading instruments into cabs or vans when the orchestra traveled. Over the years he became the concertmaster's valet and personal chauffeur; in Tishie's view this had only confirmed the title she had bestowed on him from the start—"assistant to the concertmaster." With strangers and an extra glass of sherry, she might slur a word or two and smilingly elevate her husband to the post of "assistant concertmaster."

It was harmless conceit, in Selby's view. It fooled no one and wasn't meant to. But it was a private source of strength for Tishie, an affirmation of what might or could have been, if her parents had sold their shop and left Germany in time.

She had been afraid of much in life, and with good reason; you couldn't call all her fears groundless. But she hadn't been afraid of dying. At that kind of thunder and lightning she had shrugged and paid the two dollars.

Selby wondered why he had been thinking of Tishie so often lately, and now he knew why. Sarah's mother had been certain there was something dark and terrifying on the very edge of life, just beyond her straining, frightened eyes, a creature, a Leviathan, swimming soundlessly through the depths to destroy her. And Selby felt that same fear now. Something complex and dangerous, but completely silent and invisible, was threatening him and everything and everyone important and precious to him.

Tishie had at least known at last the name and shape of her fears.

As Selby started back toward the house, Davey came running down the meadow to join him, tossing a football in the air and occasionally fumbling it, and stopping to pick it up. He threw the ball in a wobbly pass to his father, but it fell short and bounced end over end on the slick grass.

"A man called, dad," Davey shouted. "A photographer, Mr. Parks, J. D. Parks, he said. He wants you to call him back—not today, but tomorrow. He's in Philadelphia shooting some pictures of a circus, he told me."

"Did he say what he wanted?"

"He thinks he's got something you want, dad, what you talked about. That's all he told me."

Davey scooped up the football and tossed it to his father. "Throw me a pass, will you? A real long one, okay?"

"All right, Davey," Selby said and waited while his son ran down the meadow, looking over his shoulder, waving his hands over his head. There was a touching urgency in the look of his stout, churning legs . . .

Cocking his arm, Selby let the ball fly in a high arcing spiral, and watched his son running to get under it, remembering with the sweat drying on his face another moment like this, a football in flight at dusk near a lake and youngsters racing after it, laughing with buoyant energy and exhilaration. A troubled memory, worrisome and disturbing. Boys, two little black boys . . . who hadn't remembered where they lived . . .

CHAPTER THIRTEEN

Camp Saliaris (in General Adam Taggart's original and highly classified précis) was described to the projects board of the U.S. Chemical Corps as a "locus for experiments in synthetic behavioral concepts," experiments to be independent of standard civilian or military overview.

A rubber stamp from the relevant congressional committee (Senator Mark Rowan's) had approved these conditions and appropriated the camouflaged funding to implement them.

Camp Saliaris was twenty miles from Summitt City. Much of its hundred-odd acres was in sandy soil. Stunted pines and tangled bracken bordered the camp's parade ground and playing fields where members of the post stood formations and engaged in various athletic activities.

In this closely guarded inner area were air-conditioned mess halls, officers' quarters, laboratories, auditoriums and classrooms.

The table of organization at Saliaris was top-heavy with brass, field grade officers (majors, colonels) and general officers (one to three stars). The camp's name had been chosen by General Taggart in honor of the Roman celebration of *Coena Saliaris*. Taggart had first learned of this ancient feast as a cadet at Virginia Military Institute, and had pondered the legend of the holy shields during his tours of duty in Europe and Korea. The fate of Rome, according to legend, depended on the veneration and safekeeping of these sacred shields, the *ancilia,* dropped from the sky by the gods in answer to that eternal city's prayers. These myths appealed to the general's imagination, coupled as it was to a highly practical view of world affairs.

On a chill morning, a Correll Group four-engine jet landed at Camp Saliaris, having cleared customs at New Orleans en route from Portugal. The passengers, sixteen men and five women, were delivered by limousines to the general officers' mess hall, where breakfast was waiting, foods and beverages chosen to respect and satisfy ethnic backgrounds and religions: yoghurts, semolina cakes, Turkish coffee with chocolate almonds, lamb savory with rice, pita breads, rashers and grilled tomatoes, kola nuts as big as tulip bulbs, roast okra, sausage puddings and fragrant kedgerees of smoked fish and cream requested by the Lord Conestain party. Also on the sideboard were Darjeeling and gunshot teas, bottled soda and palm-wine beers.

Later the group was conducted to the auditorium, a sound-proofed room with overhead lighting, and a high ceiling of patterned acoustical tiles.

The rows of spectator seats were separated by a single aisle, the chairs made of chrome frames and leather slings. The double doors were guarded by post soldiers wearing side arms.

The passengers from the Lisbon flight filed past these guards after breakfast and selected seats, their common mood subdued but expectant.

They had come here from Pakistan, Taiwan, the Philippines, Zimbabwe, Argentina and Sri Lanka. From Great Britain, Yugoslavia, Italy and Algeria.

At the Correll Group's headquarters near Escorial, each had received final briefings on the financial responsibilities his (or her) government would assume as participants in the Correll Group program.

Individually, the delegates were hardly known outside their own countries. Even within their particular departments and ministries, most were virtually anonymous. Their names—Feisal Bonahan, Niles Smythe, Jomo N'kruma, Morris Plumb and the others—were familiar, however, to geopolitical specialists who studied the international scene and made it their business to keep watch on these seemingly inconspicuous men and women who shaped, decided and carried out their governments' policies.

When the house lights were turned down, General Taggart and George Thomson entered through side doors and took their seats.

Simon Correll's security chief, Marvin Quade, appeared in the stage wings and stood studying the dimmed theater. After a moment of silence, broken only by someone with a nervous cough, Simon Correll walked from the wings to the speaker's stand. His body was almost lost in the shadows, but his deeply tanned face was outlined by the thin spotlight from the proscenium arch. Characteristically, he began speaking without introduction or greeting.

"What we will presently show you on film may outrage some of you. You may be disposed to deny that the past history of the world has ordained this experiment, and therefore deserves it. But we have learned by now that optimism in human affairs is nonsense."

As the audience stirred, Correll said, "I'm pleased you are paying attention. You can wake people who are sleeping, Gandhi observed. But if they are only *pretending* to sleep, you will have no effect on them."

Turning to the control panel beside the speaker's rostrum, Simon Correll depressed a tab on the keyboard. A white light illuminated the screen, twin beams flooding it from a projection booth.

Pictures appeared without sound: homes, apartment buildings, lakes and green belts. Children playing baseball. Men in golf carts. A crowded shopping mall. Industrial buildings with antiseptically clean windows.

As the camera panned slowly over these scenes, picking out smiling faces, gardens of shrubs and flower beds, running youngsters, a flag at full staff, Correll pressed a tab which froze the frame in a long, high angle shot of the city, its industrial plants, homes and recreational facilities spread out under sunny skies.

"This is the town of Summitt City, Tennessee," Correll said. "To aid in your orientation, the state of Tennessee, whose hospitality we are presently enjoying, is in the southeastern section of the United States. Neighboring states you may be familiar with are Georgia, Arkansas, Alabama and the Carolinas.

"Summitt City, as you can see for yourselves, is a pleasant place. It supports a prosperous chemical industry, and other congenial amenities. But before I tell you more of Summitt City, let me digress for a moment to talk to you about freedom.

"We might all agree that freedom is a desirable condition for human beings," Correll continued, "but it is unlikely we would agree on a definition of that condition. Army officers regard freedom of behavior as an aberration harmless in children but dangerous license in the case of, say, rebels and students. Novelists tend to think of freedom as a character's striving for transcendence or epiphany, the obligatory climax of a work of fiction—a break with tradition, a defiance of family loyalty or religious tradition.

"But to social engineers, Marxists and their religious counterparts, freedom is always an act of basic and disruptive anarchy. Now while such distinctions may be intellectually diverting," Correll went on, "they seldom if ever result in any reasonable consensus. That problem, that ageless semantic squabble, is a luxury none of us can any longer afford. *Because it is not a luxury anymore, it is a death sentence.*

"Therefore my colleagues and I—General Taggart, Mr. Thomson and Lord Conestain—decided it was essential that we cut our way out of that philosophical labyrinth while there was still precious time left, and create a *truly* free society to meet our generation's desperate, last-ditch needs.

"The fact is, we had no choice, because everything in our world today is at risk. Our equities, our birthrights, our privileges, our very lives, can be extinguished in a finger-snap. The old palliatives and restraints no longer work. The placebos, sedatives and titillations which either made life bearable or purported to give it meaning are useless. Religion, Marxism, sex, art, science and all the other therapeutic abstractions have turned out to be nothing but excess baggage.

"Because we live on a razor's edge in a time when any fool or madman, a despot with terminal cancer or a simple soldier neurotically ambitious or impatient with peace, can totally destroy this world of ours. Any border clash could activate a decision that could turn this planet into a speck of lifeless dust floating in space for the next few million years. Perhaps time would start things up again, a microbe in a rock eventually creating sonnets and cathedrals but *we saw no reason to chance that. Instead we created Summitt City.*"

Correll pointed to the screen. "What you are looking at is a community free from most of the social viruses that infect modern society—crime, pollution, terrorism, racial injustice, discrimination by color, religion or sex, unemployment, energy shortages, bankruptcy, mental illness, divorce, alcoholism, sexual dysfunction."

Correll turned back to his audience. "But most importantly, Summitt City is a community without fear. That is what we have built, a pilot social organism which works together in harmony for the advantage of all parts, a society that is contented and without disruptive curiosity, a society, in fact, incapable of analyzing and therefore criticizing itself, and needless to say, incapable of revolt or civil disobedience, a society of men and women as orderly and productive as a beehive.

"We have accomplished this vision with drugs. Our systemic revolution has been chemical. As I've warned, the film you will presently see may upset some of you. But view it with your *own* best interests in mind.

"There is nothing artificial in confronting and testing our problems with chemical modifiers, with synthetic opiates and stimulants. Because we have to change the way men think before we can change the way they act. And to change their thinking means breaking destructive mental habits, to alter their memories of themselves and refine their concepts of the world around them.

"Our true enemy was and is invisible, of course. The terrors of the world stem inevitably from the memory of man, the rage of flogged slaves, the arrogance of kings, shame and horrors men have always both inflicted and lusted after, fantasies of sexual and physical domination over their brother and sister human beings, the avenging and restoring of so-called national honor and so forth.

"These poisons, lesions, must be cut away as selectively as possible by employing chemical rather than surgical lobotomies. There is a nice justice, symmetry, in using drugs to *save* ourselves, because we have been using them in a suicidal form for

154

decades. We are, in fact, already a drugged society.

"We have lived in a world surrounded by chemical compounds since the end of World War II. It is illusory but comforting, of course, to polarize our concern in the ghettos of America's decaying cities, or on the docks of France, or the narcotic production fields of South America and Turkey and Pakistan and the Far and Middle East. We can thus relegate the drug problem to the trinity of the supplier, the dealer and the user —corrupt entrepreneurs, inhuman pushers and helpless addicts —the last condemned to steal and murder to supply their habits. That is a grim picture, and accurate as far as it goes. But it is in truth only a smokescreen that hides the true dimension of our chemical dependence and addiction.

"The facts are even worse than what the staggering police statistics tell us: millions of doses of powerful tranquilizers are routinely prescribed for pregnant women; a typical standing antepartum order for nearly every woman awaiting delivery includes Nembutal, Demarol, Scapolamine, Largon, Deladumone, Riger's lactate—notwithstanding the medically proven fact that the fetus is vulnerable to brain damage. The drug generation is a helplessly programmed entity; people of this group turn not *to* drugs but, in a real sense, *back* to them, finding again the first essential mood of their existence—the experience of being drugged at birth.

"From infancy on, chemical toxins reach all of us through the air we breathe, the water we drink, oil and asbestos, millions of square miles of crops dusted every season by poisonous contaminants, the vinyl chlorides, which are related to various cancers, including those of the scrotum and the reproductive organs.

"Brain cancer is now the second leading cause of death among children under fourteen in this country, and in addition these chemical cripples are tragically susceptible to cleft palates, severe thinking impairments and tendency to suicide—the last increasingly common when the child is old enough to prefer oblivion to pain, depression and chronic insomnia. And for those who survive the rigors of a chemical childhood, it is enough to tell you that one out of four Americans living today will spend a portion of his life in a mental institution.

"It is virtually impossible to plan a diet free of cancer-inducing agents. DDT is linked to liver tumors. Heart disorders and birth defects are the price we pay for the contamination of plastic garbage bags, bread wrappers and nylon clothing. Nitrites preserve meats, chlorine purifies drinking water. They both contribute to intestinal cancer. Great freshwater lakes around the world have become so layered with flammable vegetation and chemical debris that they are becoming both health and fire hazards.

"We are killing off the world and everything that inhabits it. There are approximately five million species on the earth at present—humans, animals, insects, plants and mosses. They are dying off at the rate of *one species per hour*—lost forever to pollutants in the air and soil and water and by our destruction of forest and sea habitats.

"A dozen years ago my associates and I decided to try to stop this mindless genocide and urbicide. Our problem was where to begin. We choose the United States, specifically Summitt City, rejecting France, Japan, Sweden, Brazil and certain smaller nations.

"In America, or rather in the peculiarities of the American character—stubbornness, a prickly independence, deep-down patriotism—here we decided would be the fairest test of our program. If we could chemically curb and modify these characteristics, we believed it would reflect a more significant success than a similar one in a starving or already subjugated population sample in—say—Asia or Latin America. If that is chauvinism, so be it."

Correll pressed the keyboard and pictures flowed across the screen. Workers entering a plant. Ball games, fishermen and golfers, children laughing under lawn sprinklers. People chatting on the steps of a church. Men and women strolling through nighttime streets and parks.

"The irony, of course," Correll observed, "is how little *surface* difference there is between Summitt City and communities regulated by other artificial stimulants. Religion, socialism, art and patriotism—yes, and television—tend to grind out citizens as uniform as sausage links."

Correll paused to study the scenes on the screen. "The difference here," he continued then, "is simple but profound. This is a social group that cannot be aroused to endanger its neighbors or itself. The emotional climate at Summitt City is permanently programmed and controlled.

"As you know from your indoctrination"—again Correll froze the frame—"we are prepared to produce and license the use of Ancilia Four, *franchise* is a more exact term since we will retain both the formula and the manufacturing rights. We will function as *suppliers* to those client-states who agree to all our conditions and, more importantly, who can *afford* them.

"The emphasis in the contracts is on *money.* You may wonder why I talk of mutual survival, and those sonnets and cathedrals in one breath and money in the next. That is because *money* is the quickest and most effective way to convince you that we are serious. Money is the only medium of exchange I know of which will ensure without question your respect and cooperation in the use of Ancilia Four.

"A word now from General Taggart. The general and I are not in philosophical agreement in certain areas. Perhaps I can illustrate that by the phenomenon among insects known as 'stigmergy.' A Greek coinage, it means roughly, incitement to work.

"It has been observed that three or four termites in a group are harmless. In a human reference, they are 'peaceful.' In small numbers, they *know* nothing and more importantly, they *do* nothing. But when you increase the termite population, competitive urges and instinctive compulsions cause them to build furiously. Prodded by genetic anxiety, these formerly peaceful insects become agitated and industrious. They collect one another's fecal pellets and stack them in perfect heaps, construct towering structures to support and enclose their *termitarium.* They do this though they are, by nature, blind. A mass of termites becomes a single entity, a flawless architect, cunning, driven, tireless. But the result of their robotic labor is always chaos. In their fearful zeal they destroy everything. Columns and arches collapse, they are crushed and smother, their world ends.

"To me there is an analogy between those termites and the human race on this crowded earth. The Russians and Americans are building nuclear weapons in a mindless compulsion. Statistics have become meaningless. Each can destroy the other ten times over, fifty times, a hundred. The same instinctual fears

157

have driven other nations to join the frenzied competition. To create 'peaceful' nuclear energy, Iraq, for example, used a French reactor, Italian processing equipment and Portuguese uranium. I believe they could as easily have gone to South Korea, Cuba, Pakistan or various countries in South America.

"The formula exists. Nuclear arms are now as uncontrollable as unregistered handguns. The growth is as mindless as that in a termite castle. The result will be identical. Our house will crumble and collapse about us, our world will end.

"I come to the heart of my difference with General Taggart. He has infinite faith in the capacity of the universe to repopulate itself. Edward Teller, the father of the hydrogen bomb, is convinced that a nuclear war can be won. If fifty Americans and only five Russians survived, they would both consider that a strategic victory.

"I, on the other hand, believe that man's fate, his continuing existence, can be protected. Even from himself.

"After an intermission, and a briefing by General Taggart, we will show the film which demonstrates exactly what we have accomplished here at Summitt City."

At Camp Saliaris's communication center, a captain processed George Thomson's call to Dom Lorso in an office humming with air-conditioning units. At various stations, sergeants monitored switchboards and radar screens. Windows gave on the parade ground and playing fields.

Thomson looked out at the exercise fields. Soldiers, men and women in shorts and tank tops, were playing volleyball. Joggers trotted by the obstacle course, weaving around the quilted stocks of a bayonet range.

The captain said, "We've got to tape this, Mr. Thomson. I'm required to tell you, sir."

"I understand that, soldier. But let's get with it."

"Should be about five minutes, sir. We're sweeping the Pennsylvania terminals for electronic surveillance. That's SOP during alerts, sir."

Everything looked so normal outside, the joggers, the young people playing volleyball, but circling the perimeters of the camp were chain-link fences with sound sensors, heat and pressure alarms. And jeeps with armed soldiers and guard dogs.

The legs of the women players were slim and white, fragile compared to the men's, and when they leaped for the ball their longer hair swirled and tumbled about their faces and shoulders. Like a college campus, Thomson thought, except for the radar screens and monitoring helicopters and the orders that had sealed off the air space above Saliaris for the last twenty-four hours to all civilian and military overflights, except one.

Thomson drew a deep breath to relieve a cold ache in his stomach. That pain had been with him since he had got Dom Lorso's message, telling him that Earl was missing. Gone, without a word to anyone . . .

Thomson's nerves were stretched tight, and he found himself envying the stolid composure of the soldiers around him. Strong impassive faces, steady hands, army regulars with stomachs and bowels in fine working order, no need of drink or pills to put them to sleep nights. They were people Thomson knew well, the "three hots and a cot" types who had served under him in Korea, as easy to control as well-trained dogs.

That had certainly been Taggart's view of them in those days, the "Chief" as he had been called then, because of his intense preoccupation with Rome and Spartacus's gladiators and those old legends.

The general had the ideal soldierly characteristics, complacently adjusted to male bonding; he had been relieved, Thomson felt, when his wife died and he had been able to settle again into the spartan luxuries of post life—squash rackets and polo, card games and bachelor dinners and solitary officer's quarters.

Taggart had a son, Thomson remembered, who had been at Rockland with Earl and was now a captain or a major somewhere in Germany. His name was Derek but for some reason he'd been called Ace by his classmates.

They weren't close, Taggart and his son, Ace, which would be the Chief's preference, no intimacies, the son posted overseas to make sure that problems, if any, could be cut in triplicate and sent through proper channels to the chaplain's office.

Maybe there was something in that, Thomson thought, thinking of Earl and Dom Lorso's call. Not to care, to be free from that . . . Maybe you shouldn't try to stay close to people, maybe your own needs were more important than those traps of responsibility and guilt. Any sensation, even pain of a certain kind, had become a surrogate to Thomson for sensual arousal, and now the ache in his stomach from Lorso's call had settled disturbingly but also pleasurably to his loins as he watched the girls playing volleyball.

"We have your call, sir."

Thomson took the phone and said, "Dom, I want the rest of it now. This line is hot, but say what you have to say, go ahead."

"Okay, then. It's this. They had dinner last night, Earl and Adele. This morning he was gone. It's the call from that girl that's bugging him, if you want my guess."

Thomson heard a tiny click; Lorso had snapped his lighter to light a cigarette. "A cop stopped by yesterday to talk to Earl, a sergeant name of Wilger, some questions on the missing Porsche. That could've upset him too."

"Did you talk to Slocum about that?"

Lorso hesitated. Thomson heard his labored breathing. "No, I asked the captain to check out Earl, make some inquiries. I don't want him to roadblock a routine investigation. That could just draw attention to the car. You agree, Mr. Thomson?"

"Yes, of course." The ache intensified in his stomach, the sensation pure tension and pain now, with no suggestion of distracting sexual excitement.

"The thing is," Lorso continued, "when Earl gets in certain moods he doesn't trust anybody, not even Uncle Dom."

"Then you'd better find him. Slocum might talk to some of his friends around the state."

"We'll do that. But there's one other thing. Adele isn't leveling with us. I think she knows where he is. Earl's one thing but Earl and Adele together—like they are now—that's something else. Take care, now."

When Lorso rang off, Thomson gave the phone to the captain and listened dully to the heavy stroke of his heart. Rain had started and the players were hurrying from the field, but they meant nothing to him now; the long-legged girls were little stiltlike figures running across the parade ground under low, gray skies.

CHAPTER FOURTEEN

The silver stars were as much a part of General
Adam Taggart as his big raw-knuckled hands and
narrowed eyes and sun-browned, weathered features. The proscenium spots glinted on those stars of rank and on his para-
trooper boots and four rows of decorations, and on the wide
balding head which narrowed sharply above the forehead, somewhat like an artillery projectile.

The general stared out across the unstirring audience, his
flaring smile revealing strong, clean teeth.

"South Korea is probably as good a place to start as any,"
General Taggart said, "because there was a kernel of something
inside those North Korean slopeheads we couldn't crack."

Oblivious to a hostile stir in his audience, the general continued with a cool smile. "Starve 'em, freeze 'em, take away their
privileges, none of that meant shit to them. On the other hand,
give 'em cigarettes, booze or even a kinky Red Cross chick to
sack out with, you still couldn't touch 'em. They were soldiers,
by God, sons of the army, and they'd stick a bayonet in you if
they got the chance, and die happy with the guards pounding
their asses into the mud.

"So we tried drugs on 'em, a mixture of barbiturate and
euphoric agents we hardly had names for then." The general
paused there, loose-limbed and as comfortable with his rank as
royalty. Taggart was seldom inclined to amuse or defer to his

audiences, or excite them with dramatic narrative effects, but he enjoyed the shock he could generate by figuratively changing intellectual gears.

He did that now. "This might be the proper place," the general observed, "to discuss certain moral issues that were involved in our decision. That was almost thirty years ago, remember. The North Korean POWs had information vital to our security. More than that, we needed that information to protect the lives of American soldiers.

"I am a soldier first, a scientist second, and according to my morality, which is the morality of the battlefield, I believed we had a right to secure that information any way we could.

"So, we began to shoot them full of drugs, experimenting with various combinations until we secured the necessary breakthrough.

"I called that first product developed in our battle-front laboratories a 'shield,' because that metaphor seemed to best describe its effects. A *shield*—the Latin word is *ancile*—*a shield against memory.* Ancilia One, our first breakthrough, lowered certain levels of resistance in POWs. Their angers and resolves, the adversary constructs that gave a cohesiveness to their character, even nostalgic thoughts of home and family, all that became shadowed and indistinct, less real and important. Under drugs, they lost their grip on things we could never get at to smash, that kernel of pride rooted in what their country expected of them.

"It was a selective, chemically controlled amnesia which permitted and encouraged those enemy soldiers to cooperate with us. But only up to a certain point. Their reactions to the drug were erratic, we couldn't predict their responses as accurately as we needed to.

"Ancilia Two, our next breakthrough drug, was, however, a disappointment. Which is a classic understatement because, the sad fact is, it killed thirteen Korean POWs and left a lot of others with permanent brain damage. Unfortunately that fiasco leaked out to the inspector general at headquarters.

"A court-martial was convened in Seoul but we were able to confine its impact and control adverse stateside publicity. The charges ultimately were reduced to theft and insubordination and manslaughter and were limited to a handful of enlisted men and medics.

"Yet what we were up to in Korea only reflected what was happening everywhere else in the world.

"As you're all aware, intelligence and chemical warfare branches of every major nation have been on crash programs for three decades to find some reliable method of controlling behavior. Call it what you like—brainwashing, mood manipulation, mental straitjacketing, induced chemical delusions, anything else in the way of sensory regimentation they could profit from. Everybody knew what they wanted to *do,* and they were determined to find a way *to do* it.

"A man or woman, as you know, no matter how strong or adjusted, no matter how deep the fundamental perceptions and most cherished values—right and wrong, time and space, what is possible and what isn't—all that can be distorted by even a speck of LSD.

"The Russians are years ahead of the pack, at least judging from their funding and programs, and they're drooling in anticipation of results.

"Since the Stalin era they've been selecting healthy people to send off to labor camps and hospitals to cure their religious and political problems with drugs and electric convulsive therapy. We never needed double agents to winkle that information out. Solzhenitsyn was our Baedeker there.

"At the same time, our own people, CIA, that is, seemed to be doing their asinine best to *destroy* whatever chance the U.S. Army Chemical Corps had to bridge the generation gap between Ancilia Two and Ancilia Three. They got a dose of publicity about as welcome as a turd in a punch bowl by turning some GIs in France into permanent epileptics with lysergic acid. And compounded that mess by using drugs on draft resisters, civil rights activists, college agitators and even on convicts and enlisted troops in 'Nam and Europe.

"Of course, those same assholes," the general continued with good-humored scorn, "also wasted tons of money trying to train seals and dolphins to attack enemy subs and coaching plants to talk to each other. In addition, they pumped nerve gas into the Holland and Lincoln tunnels in New York City at rush

163

hour to see how it worked on commuters, and figured out a simple way to kill enemy agents by locking them in airtight rooms with blocks of dry ice. No ice, no evidence. Carbon dioxide did the job.

"Most of these experiments were directed at the young, and that helped spread the use of drugs through every economic level of society and in my judgment was responsible to an important degree for the anarchic counterculture of the sixties.

"But one good thing came out of those freaked-out programs. They clearly demonstrated to Mr. Correll, and to me, that *something* was crying out for attention everywhere in the world.

"The need was there, the time was right, because a vacuum had been created by a promise of chemical salvation, a promise that in turn had eroded the traditional foundations of psychoanalysis. Patients no longer wanted to spend half their lifetimes talking about why they despised their parents or why they got into sexual rut at the sight of clergymen or booted women or telephone poles or whatever. They were looking desperately for alternative therapy. So they turned to drugs—the new and available drugs—to relieve their anxieties and depressions and mental aberrations.

"A blind, lemminglike rush was on—into primal scream therapy, Rolfing, eastern cults, mantra chanting and drugs of every description. Which told Mr. Correll that the world was not only *ready*, but *eager* for the programs of Summitt City. A vacuum existed and it was screaming for somebody and something to fill it.

"We—the Correll Group—heard those cries and began trying to determine *exactly* what it might be that vacuum was demanding—what it *craved*. Which led us in turn to take a closer look at how our human brains interpret sensations and regulate our responses to them."

General Taggart tapped his forehead. "Here we have a brain weighing about three pounds, with a volume of roughly one and a half quarts. It contains more than a hundred billion nerve cells or neurons. But unlike other cells, neurons cannot grow and divide because their physical area is bounded by our skulls. In spite of this immense concentration, neurons—except for a few exceptions—have no physical contact. The space between them is submicroscopic—thousands side by side wouldn't equal the thickness of an onion skin.

"Chemicals bridge these gaps, carrying messages, alarms, pleasure signals and so forth. For a long time, scientists thought of the brain as an exquisitely tuned and proportioned electrical-chemical instrument or machine, a fabulous computer, in fact. But the brain isn't a computer, it's a gland; not electronic circuitry, but endocrine tissue through which the traffic of nerves and impulses are ruled in a not always benign tyranny by bio-chemical activators and their suppressors.

"These are the neuro-transmitters, the endorphins and the enkephalins, which pop science magazines are now touting hysterically as passports to a chemical Garden of Eden. But they regulate everything we do, in fact, whether we feel happy, excited or ready to blow our brains out. The illusion of free will is probably only an interplay of chemicals in the brain. Anybody using massive doses of tranquilizers knows that. Valium and the rest of them make you unable to express your anger, and if you can't feel and do anything about rage, you sure as shit can't change anything else in your life.

"These endorphin transmitters operate on specific receptor sites in the brain and spinal cord—like keys fitting into locks. We've used poppies for thousands of years without a clue how they worked. It wasn't until the discovery of endorphins that we found out that these pretty flowers that poets loved to write about were simply mimics of the brain's own morphia.

"These internal opiates, the endorphins, are there to monitor and screen out ambiguous, unbearable or destructive information. We've used opium, cocaine and alcohol for the same reason and with the same hope since we came down out of the trees. Now we're learning that the human brain may be a god-damn natural warehouse full of chemicals designed to protect us not only from ourselves but from all the terrors of human experience. It's just a question of finding the right synthetic chemical to fit the right receptor—the specific key for the specific lock—and releasing substances to create euphoria and guard us against fears and depressions."

The general bared his strong teeth. "Very neat and tidy, one might assume. But there are contradictions along the way. Information about pain is processed in receptors, call them pain

165

centers or agony switchboards, if you like, that are paradoxically loaded with opiate 'locks.'

"Other sensory structures, chockablock with opiate clusters, deadening suppressors, remember, are part of the brain's liveliest pleasure centers. Go figure."

The general paused to remove a cigar from his olive-drab jacket and strip off the wrapper. After inspecting the green-flecked leaf, he applied a flame to the slender tip with a silver lighter whose sides were studded with miniaturized insignia of units he had commanded.

"The plain fact," Taggart continued, "is that we simply don't know how whatever it is we call 'the mind' relates to those hundred billion or so neurons that make up our brain. The mind may be an electrical field generated by the brain's operation. We don't know.

"But scientists are trying to map the roots of human nature by creating synthetic endorphins that can be fired like magic bullets at specific brain receptors.

"What kind of behavior do we expect those chemicals to activate? What sort of behavior do we *want* and *need* from human beings? We can eliminate pain and alcoholism and drug addiction. That's a plus, certainly. And we know the sites of clinical anxiety and depression, and we're zeroing in on dozens of new receptors. So good, you say. But once we find them and duplicate their triggering mechanism, we still don't have any clear idea of what we want or what we've accomplished.

"Because we don't have the slightest notion why those hundreds of unused receptors were plugged into our brains in the first place. Or what they're there for. Sentinels guarding us from terrors outside this planet? Or further horrors from inside ourselves? I tell you, ladies and gentlemen, I wish to God I knew."

Blowing smoke toward the ceiling, Taggart smiled at the rows of intent faces below him, brown and white and dusky ovals, eyes glowing with reflected light from the stage.

"Nevertheless, at Summitt City," he went on, "we're searching for keys to unlock as many neural receptors as we can find. We haven't created what you'd expect from lurid magazines, charging bulls brought to a dead stop by somebody throwing a switch in their heads, cats running in terror from mice, men and women driven into sexual frenzies by chemicals tick-ing their pleasure centers. We haven't done anything like that. Neither have we created a chemical wonderland. In some Utopia, chemical compounds may control our genetic codes and eliminate most pathology, prolong or shorten memory, eliminate pain, increase pleasure, moderate our aggressive thoughts, just like we use deodorants now. But Ancilia Four only produces manageable and functional human beings. They don't need Moses and Jesus and Buddha. They'll never preach brotherhood or go around spreading equality and liberty and freedom. But none of that's going to be enough, which is why I don't think a scientific solution to the world's problems is possible.

"Because with all that input and theory, we still don't have a good idea what we're playing around with, which is why I trust my soldier's instincts first, because they're programmed to *function*, not to understand, which is also nature's way of going about things. Nature creates blindly and without apparent purpose. It kills in the same fashion. The people who frustrate and obstruct nature aren't soldiers—soldiers do nature's work without any thought of kindness or cruelty or fairness or justice. Ulysses S. Grant and Stonewall Jackson did more for this country than Abe Lincoln and whoever the hell wrote *Uncle Tom's Cabin.* One Napoleon or Wellington is worth a whole passel of Pascals and Newmans."

The general snapped a switch on the control panel and lighted the screen. Life at Summitt City flowed before the audience.

Taggart said, "I'm not convinced there's time left for gradual adaptation. Mr. Correll hopes there is. As a good soldier, I'm doing my best to prove he's right."

The general nodded to the screen. "Initially at Summitt City we created situations which powerfully stimulated defensive mental responses, and then identified and synthesized the chemical shields secreted by our test subjects.

"Our experiments proved the brain is capable of producing chemicals to defend the host organism against damn near *anything*—the pain of injustice and discrimination, the shock of violent stimuli, hunger, torture and even death.

"To these natural opiates, we added a synthesis of the brain's natural chemical, serotonin, which is located in the raphe nucleus, buried protectively within the brain system, be-

167

tween the nexus of the corpus brain and the spinal cord.

"Serotonin neurons are the messengers that bring instructions and warnings to the areas of the brain that control vision and the affective emotions—pity, terror, anger and so forth. While we're awake, as I stand here blowing smoke at you, and you sit out there looking up at me, those serotonin neurons—automatic sentries—send out chemical signals at the rate of twenty-four per second to tell us that this is happening, *that we are not imagining it.*

"Serotonin is a reality signal. It validates the evidence of sensory perceptions, certifies that we aren't dreaming or imagining. If we witness a violent automobile accident, serotonin neurons authenticate the screams of the injured and the flames melting down steel and glass. Police sirens, the stench of smoke —serotonin permits us to react logically to experience. We may run like cowards, or drag the trapped people to safety, but we know goddamn well we are in a real-life situation and can respond accordingly.

"But the exact opposite occurs when we sleep. The flow of serotonin stops and the absence of that reality signal allows us to endure the experience of nightmares. We may be troubled and restless, flail at our bed partners, even have a succubus attend us if we're lucky, but because the reality signal isn't ringing, we can get back to sleep.

"Of course," the general remarked, after blowing a stream of smoke over his audience, "if we thought for one second those nightmare monsters from our unconscious were really *real*"— he smiled—"insomnia would then become our dearest luxury. Who could sleep if it meant encountering *that* kind of reality?

"But that consideration led us to the ultimate refinement of Ancilia Four, because what we needed was an element to make our *waking* horrors as bearable as the absence of serotonin renders the sleep-time monsters.

"In short, Ancilia Four deceives perception by turning off the reality signal when *real life* threatens to become unendurable.

"For how long?" The general shrugged. "That brings us back to how much time we've got left, doesn't it? Which means it's up to you people. Ancilia Four is a control mechanism that can keep people in line more effectively than cattle prods and guard dogs or prayer wheels and muezzins and church bells.

"This might be our best and our last chance to take the lunatic's hand off the nuclear plunger, put a steel bell over Soweto and Lebanon and Belfast and Haifa and Harlem, and squirt it full of an element that will muffle the sounds of the reality signals—for a time.

"But right now," the general said, his voice suddenly becoming quiet and cold, "as we anticipate a pleasant lunch and a briefing on further details of our program, half the world is starving to death. In India cows and rats are stuffed and fattened while infants die of hunger. In Uganda, life expectancy is under eleven years. On the banks of the Chari, for hundreds of miles, mothers, mere children themselves, live in slime and pollution without milk in their breasts for their dying babies. In South America and Cambodia, there is even a shortage of garbage for the starving. And yet millions of more disadvantaged and unwanted children are born every day. No scientist can solve that problem, nor can any priest or rabbi or shaman.

"All across black Africa, food production is decreasing at the same rate the population is growing. A half billion people in the sub-Sahara regions are facing starvation. The only hunger being satisfied is that for power—by the military and privileged.

"These problems don't stem only from the Third World. Or from those people that in our good-humored way we call gooks and wogs and slopes and ragheads. No, the western alliance, with America in the van, has chosen to make greed not only a national policy but a national ethic. Every man, woman and child in the United States needs a support system of forty thousand pounds of minerals per year. One hundred thousand gallons of water is required to make one deliberately inefficient automobile. While we escalate the use of energy, the gulags are doing the same thing with human misery. And those forces are now creating a mix of crisis flashpoints all over the world.

"Ancilia Four will control those flashpoints and defuse them for a while. But unless we seize this opportunity to establish some order and sanity, then we'll hand the job over to the soldiers by default. It's the work they're trained and suited for, and by God, they're eager to get on with it.

"Give me—give any soldier—control of the headwaters of the Kiang, the Niger, the Congo and the Amazon, and with a few hundred thousand pounds of explosives, I'd turn half the world back to sand and gravel and reduce the number of people on earth to decent proportions. That's one way to do it. Pave Africa, maybe that's another, from the Med right on down to the Cape.

"Elephants and lions and brilliant spotted snakes would be gone forever, of course, with all those unwanted humans. But we have pictures of lions and cages full of monkeys.

"The solution to a disastrous oversufficiency is one of textbook clarity to the military. Destroy the surplus. That's the orderly and soldierly way to handle it. Sounds terrible, but the scientists don't offer us a thing better. Here's what Andrei Sakharov had to say. After a first military strike by either side and the inevitable response spasm, Comrade Sakharov predicts at the very least the complete destruction of major cities throughout the world. I'll give you a little chapter and verse in his own words."

The general removed a sheet of paper from an inside pocket, thrust it before him at arm's length and began reading: "—an end to all systems of education and industry, a poisoning of fields, water and air everywhere by radioactivity, poverty, barbarism, a return to savagery and a genetic degeneracy of survivors under the impact of radiation, a destruction of the ultimate basics of civilization—"

The general tossed the paper onto the desk of the control panel. "That's the genius who created the Russians' thermonuclear weapons system, telling us in horrified tones what we can expect from the megabombs. Didn't he *know* what he was doing in his laboratory? Can we *believe* he was stricken with terror at the results of his work? What the hell did that clever man *think* would happen when he flipped those switches and loosed the equivalent of lightning bolts inside his test tubes?

"So much for scientists and soldiers, and the governments who jerk them around like puppets.

"You people were selected by Simon Correll and the associates of the Correll Group—Eric Van Pelt, Lord Conestain and Mies Kraager—to implement an alternative to the collision course we're on with oblivion. Your areas of influence are strategically pivotal, because they spread across the world's most dangerous social fault lines. Your states are classic amalgams of the modern disastrous mix—right-wing military juntas, left-wing rebels, massive poverty and overpopulation, crime, disease and all the other contemporary ingredients of terminal eruptions—torture, terrorism, genocide. Which is exactly why you're qualified to receive a franchise for Ancilia Four. I like the irony of that, by God, I do."

The general was interrupted by a series of delicate chimes from his wristwatch.

"When you control the emotions of your people," he went on, clicking off the timing device, *"you will control everything else they do.* That is what our film will demonstrate to you. But before that, ladies and gentlemen, we're going to break for a glass of something or other and some lunch."

During Taggart's briefing, Jennifer and Simon Correll waited in a conference room adjoining the general's office. Quade brought them coffee and a bottle of Spanish brandy. Logs burned evenly in a corner fireplace and reflections glinted on the wooden frames of parchment maps on the paneled walls. With the rain came the throb of coursing helicopters.

Jennifer said, "Why did you insist I come along, Simon?" The reasonableness in her tone emphasized her exasperation. "I hate places like this, guards and fences and gates. The soldiers are like animals in cages. They're polite and docile with their ma'ams and heel snapping but their eyes give them away."

"They probably resent you because you're out of reach. That's normal enough."

"I have the feeling nobody's been laid around here since, God, I can't imagine."

She was seated in a leather chair with wide arms. Her slender legs were crossed on a suede ottoman. The chair was huge, the leather against her shoulders and hips was cold and unyielding. She uncrossed her legs and twisted about to make herself comfortable.

"I just don't understand, Simon. Are we going to be here long?"

Correll stood looking out at the playing fields, at the gray and misting rains. "Yesterday morning Bishop Waring called me in New York." He walked to Jennifer and put his hands on her slim shoulders.

171

She looked up at him. "Is that unusual?"

"My mother isn't well. That was one reason he called."

"Simon, I'm sorry."

"Don't worry, she has the best of care." Correll gently but expertly massaged her neck and shoulders. His probing fingers felt her muscles relax.

Maps glowing in the firelight showed German attack lines in Belgium marked with black-and-red arrows. Others routed ancient Roman marches in England. The cold, spare room depressed her, he knew, that and the rain and the menacing sound of the searching helicopters.

"His Excellency also wanted to tell me," Correll said, "that one of Lester's investigators, a Victoria Kim, was at Mount Olivet yesterday. She had a subpoena for my appointment books, correspondence and so forth."

"Haven't you been expecting that?"

"Yes, but Senator Lester is moving faster than I thought." He suddenly pressed his thumbs hard against her neck muscles. "There, that should do it."

"Oh, yes, *yes*. Thanks, that marvelous. I don't know why I'm so jumpy."

Correll absently stroked her pale, smooth hair, his thoughts turning back to his own problems.

Someone with sensitive information was briefing Lester's people. The senator had a competent staff, was wealthy, and could afford to buy every variety of "deep throat" that infested Washington and most other world capitals. He could enlist undercover agents if he wanted or needed them, police officials, aides to other committees, spies tucked away deep in opposition offices. But it was more than that, Correll suspected; the penetration and pressure against the Correll Group here and abroad suggested higher echelons. The White House or State, possibly one of their all-purpose so-called advisers.

Last night he had tried to pump Bishop Waring. His Excellency was politically sophisticated, catnip for Washington hostesses, much like the late, charismatic Bishop Fulton Sheen, and with wide government contacts, on easy terms with Ferdinand Bittermank, who worked in low profile for both the Oval Office and State.

172

But the bishop was no help. He'd been in his most apostolic mood last evening, on a plane far above the trivial and mundane. His concern was only for Correll's mother's spiritual welfare. The old woman was probably dying; the trip to eternity must be attended to, forms stamped, bookings confirmed; all of which occupied the bishop's total attention.

Correll paced in front of the fire and said to Jennifer, "One thing worries me about Miss Kim's subpoena. Can you guess what?"

She was wearing smoked glasses that were like black mirrors in the firelight. "I haven't a clue."

"Her search warrant included your rooms. Any idea what she was looking for?"

Jennifer quickly removed the glasses and looked up at him. "Can they do things like that?"

"Of course they can."

"But supposing I'd left something personal around. A . . . gift I'd wanted to surprise you with?"

"Who knows what they're after? It could be bureaucratic make-work, or a scare tactic. But that's why I brought you here with me. Even a United States senator couldn't serve a warrant on you now. I don't want you surprised by Miss Kim before we have a chance to talk."

"But what's there to talk about? It's unfair to put it like that, I don't know anything. You're accusing me of something, whether you realize it or not."

"I'm sorry. Would you like a brandy?"

"No. Just tell me why you think the senator's people wanted to search my rooms, and why they'd want to talk to me."

"Have you ever kept any notes of our conversations?"

"Why would I do that?"

"But have you?"

"Of course not."

"What about a diary? Shopping lists, phone calls, notes about what to pack for trips?"

"What harm would there be if I had?"

"None at all. But they might be interested in whether you were packing for a ski trip or a vacation in Cape Town, let's say."

"I see. The itinerary. But I never know when we're leaving

173

Olivet, or anywhere else for that matter. Quade usually lets me know the night before."

"Did you say anything to Harry Selby at Summitt that might connect you with me? Anything that would tell him where to contact you?"

She sat up. "You're making me nervous, Simon. What's Harry Selby got to do with a search warrant?"

"You said you tried to impress him, told him more than you should have—"

"That's *not* what I told you. I talked too much, that's true. But I didn't say *anything* I shouldn't have. I was nervous because I didn't feel comfortable with him."

"If you're questioned by Miss Kim or the senator's people, what will you tell them?"

She hesitated and Correll forced himself to be patient because he knew there was still another ordeal in store for her this morning. Which was difficult, because he had been distracted by Bishop Waring's news... "Your mother was restless at supper, I knew something was wrong when she refused the fruited chocolates she likes so much. I noticed her manner at Vespers too. Usually the music calms her . . ." The senator's investigation and Miss Kim's court order were of trifling importance compared to the old lady's refusal to be calmed by chocolates or the solemn filigree of the old Latin hymns, *Cibabit Illos* and *Ecce Sacerdos Magnum* . . .

Jennifer was saying, "I'd tell Miss Kim or anybody else, that I don't know anything about your business. What else would I say? That I like Houston and London and some of those old tapes by Duke Ellington? Or that at Olivet I prefer to sun myself and walk by the river and . . ."

Correll watched rain slanting under a heavy sky . . . "I gave your mother conditional absolution after the rosary last night," the bishop had told him. "She had difficulty breathing. I took the liberty of telling her you'd be coming soon. That brought a light to her eyes. There's a precious bond between the souls of a mother and son. We needn't look beyond Calvary and the Pietas of Michelangelo . . ."

A knock sounded and after a moment Marvin Quade admitted himself and told Correll that General Taggart was ready now with the Summitt City film.

174

"You go along with Quade, Jennifer," Correll told her. "I'll join you at the theater in a few minutes."

"Simon, do I have to? I'm very tired."

"I'm sorry, but yes. It's a short film, twenty or twenty-five minutes. It was shot the day after you left Summitt City and there's something in it I particularly want you to see."

When Jennifer and Quade went out, Correll poured himself a brandy. A moment later General Taggart knocked on the open door and came in.

"Well, everything's going fine, I'd say." The general put out his big, knuckled hands to the fire. "It's damned strange how hooked people are by the Apocalyptic vision. The real banality of evil is that it's always such a letdown. Why'd you want that little lady of yours to see the film? She won't like it, you know."

"I need her, General. I want her to be just as involved as I am."

"Well, she sure as hell will be. You have any additional poop on what that Lester's up to?"

"I don't think he's a problem. If it weren't for the diversion of someone named Harry Selby, and possibly Ferdinand Bittermank, I'd be very optimistic. But that can't be helped. I want you to be prepared to neutralize Summitt City if it turns out we have to."

"Whatever you say, sir. But we still need that input."

"Summitt may be compromised. We'd better be prepared for that. It's time for Phase Two. We can profit from our blueprint here and activate another on-line unit. But where they least expect it, where the logical connections make it unlikely. The obvious is always the best camouflage."

"But I'd suggest," General Taggart said, "that we utilize overseas personnel now."

"I'll leave that to you. Van Pelt tells me he has a cadre he's satisfied with."

"For that matter," Taggart said, "so has Mies Kraager. We discussed it in Cape Town only a week ago. Security, lab people, administrators, the lot."

"If you prefer Kraager's team, fine." Correll looked at his watch and put his glass aside. "I think we'd better go in. Frankly, I hope this is the last time I have to sit through this thing."

CHAPTER FIFTEEN

J. D. Parks's darkroom was a converted closet in the rear of his office suite. It smelled of acid and was eerily illuminated by a green "safe" light.

Harry Selby stood in that cramped space with Parks, watching pictures forming on sheets immersed in shallow developing pans.

They had been at this for several hours, since Parks returned that afternoon from an assignment in Marcus Hook, struggling from the elevator with a pipe in his mouth, a yellow scarf about his neck, burdened down with two leather sacks of gear and a tripod, and full of apologies for having kept Selby waiting. "Don't worry," he said, unlocking his office. "I got most of the stuff on the Brandywine Lakes job enlarged, must be a ton of it. I think what you want is buried in there someplace. You're a big fella, Selby. Want a beer or anything?"

Much of the film, even those shots featuring cars, Selby had been able to dismiss with a glance; aerial views of Brandywine Lakes homes and fairways, the cemetery near the development, a drive-in theater and high school stadium, rows of houses with lighted windows.

They stopped at last for beers and sandwiches, which Parks brought out from a refrigerator which doubled as a support for developing frame racks.

"I was using Tri-X film that night, f-14 at 60," Parks told

him, as he unwrapped a pastrami on rye. "Shooting with a Hasselblad, a Graflex, a Kodak Extar lens. Pretty sensitive stuff. But maybe we didn't fly close enough to the place you're looking for."

Selby doubled the beer can with a snap of his fingers before tossing it into a wastebasket.

Parks went on. "We might have turned back to Brandywine Lakes before we got to Vinegar Hill." In the same tone, he added, "I saw you play once. It was back in Philadelphia. I remember, I guess, because you got hurt. It was third down, and it looked like a pass play coming up. That's when you got that scar on your cheek. You could hear it clear up in the press box when the helmet bar broke. But it was a long time ago. You might not remember."

"I remember it pretty well," Selby said.

"I'll bet." Parks wrapped the crusts of their sandwiches in a waxed bag and stowed that behind a window plant. "For the birds in the morning," he explained. "The super tells me it attracts ants, but everybody's got to live. I got a kind of Buddhist slant on things in 'Nam. Let's get back to work, okay?"

They found what they were looking for about a half hour later, the images swirling in the suffused light, Vinegar Hill's short driveway leading away to the house and garage. When Selby leaned forward, straining to see through the trembling emulsion, he could make out the silhouette of an automobile.

"That's it. There it is," he said, surprised that the tension building in him didn't sound in his voice. "How much closer can you get?"

"More details? Let's see. This is as much enlargement as I can get with any real clarity from the four by fours. I'll have to cut the negatives into thirty-five-millimeter frames and change the lens in the enlarger. That'll take time."

Selby used Parks's phone and called Shana. "I should be home in an hour or so," he told her. "But don't you and Davey wait dinner. Is everything okay?"

"Yes, everything's fine. We're all right." Her impersonal tone, the one he was accustomed to, changed slightly. "But Miss Brett, she called a few minutes ago. She's with that sergeant. They wanted to talk to me. I said okay."

"You're sure you feel up to it?"

"I told you, daddy, I'm fine."

"Did she—did Miss Brett say what she wanted to talk to you about?"

"No, she didn't."

Parks glanced at Selby, held up a strip of film and pointed to the darkroom. Selby nodded and said to Shana, "Okay, honey. I'll see you at home."

Parks took the new enlargement sheets from the developing pans, washed them and clipped the wet proofs to the frames above the refrigerator. After inspecting them, he said, "Take a look," and handed Selby a magnifying glass.

The postage-stamp-sized pictures expanded magically under Selby's artificially strengthened vision; through a tangle of trees flecked with streaks of moonlight, he saw the metallic glint of a bumper, and the oblong shape of the license plate. He couldn't make out the letters or numbers; they reproduced only as separate black squares.

"We could try a reducer," Parks suggested. "The film is blocking up now, it's too thick to let the light through. There's a computer process, electronic gadgets that could do this faster, but I can try for a finer gradation and see if that helps."

He worked on sheet after sheet, experimenting with reducing mixtures and attenuating the emulsion's density, talking to himself while he studied the results, in arcane references to exposure lines, light values, Farmer's Reducer, ASA ratings . . .

"About how long will this take?" Selby asked.

"Twenty minutes, maybe half an hour. But I got a different slant on *how long* in 'Nam, Selby. Buddhists think babies are as old as God because they're complete. That's a heavy idea. You better make that forty-five minutes."

"I'll be back," Selby said.

He walked from Parks's studio to the offices of the Brandywine *Standard*. Buying a back issue, he went through the paper until he came to the photograph Shana had cut out of their copy, a four-column picture taken at Longwood Gardens. A group of people stood near a four-door sedan that was identified in the caption as a Maserati Quattroporta. In the background were other antique cars, cordoned off by ropes in front of a greenhouse.

An elderly couple in bulky tweeds was prominent in the photograph. Behind them stood three young men. Two wore crew cuts and military school uniforms. The third young man was taller than his companions and wore a cardigan jacket and a long scarf. A thin chain glittered at his throat. His head was bare, his thick, dark hair blown about by the breezes.

Selby cut out the picture, folded it and put it in his wallet. Discarding the *Standard* in a trash receptacle, he returned to Parks's studio and joined him in the darkroom.

"Pay dirt, geronimo, eureka and other sundry shit," Parks announced cheerfully. "Take a look, pal."

Selby wiped a bead of sweat from his forehead and stared closely at the surface of the shimmering developing solution. Mag wheels gleamed dully through the liquid, and the details of the license plate were coming into a trembling focus. Selby saw a letter emerging, clearly and sharply, the letter "N," and after that, two numbers, "9" and "6" . . .

The other numbers remained lost in smudged shadows.

By the time Selby left Parks's studio, the streets were empty. Shop windows were slick and white with frost, and some had Christmas decorations up, holly wreaths and strings of colored lights.

The uniformed black lady at the counter of the detective division didn't remember Selby. She asked his name and pointed to a stack of forms.

"Write it on one of them, and your business."

"The name's Selby, Harry Selby. I was here before. Would you tell Captain Slocum I need to see him? It's important."

She regarded him dubiously. "You got to write your name down anyway, but I'll tell him. You better take yourself a seat. Captain's on the phone. They got a homicide downtown." The floor of the narrow reception room was covered with brown linoleum, patterned randomly with cigarette burns. A framed photograph of a smiling uniformed policeman hung on the wall. A caption told anyone interested that Patrolman Anthony Vito had died in the line of duty 11/13/1972.

Selby didn't recognize the detectives on this shift. A constant clatter sounded as they typed reports, answered phones, talked to witnesses and/or victims. A woman was crying; someone had struck her in the face; her jaw was round and shiny as a big, red apple. A shabbily dressed black man with blood dripping from his hand responded to a detective's questions with exaggerated, head-bobbing smiles. In whining, righteous tones, a drunken white man was reporting the theft of a blanket by a teenager he had given a lift to. A white hooker complained that a trick had cut her leg with his belt buckle and hadn't paid her for—

The black clerk said, "Captain says he'll see you soon as he can, Mr. Selby."

He stretched his legs and rested his head against the wall beneath Patrolman Vito's smiling picture. Take a number, wait your turn. . . . Pay the two dollars . . . He thought of the night he had taken Sarah's mother to the hospital for the last time.

Her pain had become constant by then, but it wasn't particularly worrisome. It was just an inconvenience, so pay the two dollars.

"The bad thing about being sick," Tishie said on the way to the hospital, "is that you think you got squatter's rights on what's real. You stop believing other people are buying and selling things, cooking and putting food on the table. Sick people think their world is the only one that's real."

Her eyes were bright when she came out of the doctor's office.

"She never liked bad news at night, my Sarah," she told him on the way home. "We won't spoil the evening for the children. We'll have a nice dinner and I'll tell Sarah when they're off to school in the morning."

Shana and Davey had never known their grandmother was sick and in pain. Tishie could handle that kind of thunder and lightning. She was slim and small under her bed covers the next morning, the pink of her best nightgown showing against the blankets, the empty bottle of Demarol on her night table . . .

Selby's number came up. "Captain'll see you now, Mr. Selby."

Slocum was at his desk, his thinning hair and broad face shining under strong fluorescent lighting. His tie was pulled down and a day's beard smudged his wide jaw. Glancing up, he

180

said, "We're pretty busy tonight, Mr. Selby. What's on your mind?"

Selby dropped the stack of photographs on his desk. "Captain, those are pictures of a parked car. It's parked in the driveway of a place called Vinegar Hill over on Dade Road. That's where my daughter was taken and raped. The pictures were taken that same night. What you're looking at, Captain Slocum, is the car the rapist used to drive her there. It's a Porsche Turbo 924, a distinctive, customized job. One letter and two digits of the license are visible. *That's* what's on my mind, Captain."

Slocum looked steadily at him, patches of red darkening his cheekbones. "Maybe you better come around and sit down at my desk, Selby. Maybe you better take over the whole job."

After flipping quickly through the photographs, he punched a button on the base of his phone. A pulse leaped in his throat, a pounding rhythmically under his carotid artery.

"I thought we had an understanding, Selby, about who was the cop and who was the civilian." His voice was thick, hard with anger. "Remember our talk? I told you not to go off on your own. I told you it was our responsibility to investigate your daughter's kidnapping and rape."

"I remember that," Selby said. "But I've been getting the impression you're too busy around here to pay much attention to that. There's a room full of cops and detectives outside spending time on hookers and winos. Somebody's typing up a report about a teenager who stole a blanket from a car."

Slocum said, "So you figured we were too busy, is that it, Selby? Figured that gave you a green light to handle things yourself? Well, this probably hasn't occurred to you, but when you go off chasing shadows with bloodhounds, or horsing around with local photographers, you could be destroying leads we're already working on. You want to play the outraged citizen who thinks the local police are a bunch of fuck-ups, be my guest, Selby. I'm used to it. I get priests in here with long hair and windbreakers, complaining we're too hard on faggots, that they're God's chilluns just like the rest of us. Every time a drunk falls down a flight of stairs into the basement, we get screams of police brutality from the ACLU Jew boys. Last week, a professor of African studies—"

His office door opened and the noisy clatter from the outer

181

office spilled in. A detective sauntered to Slocum's desk, glancing curiously at Selby.

"Where the hell's Wilger?" Slocum asked him.

"He's not back yet, Captain. Took a ride over to Muhlenburg a couple of hours ago."

Slocum waved irritably from the detective to Selby. "Lieutenant Eberle, Mr. Selby."

Eberle nodded. "Selby, sure. That kidnapping out on Fairlee Road."

The lieutenant could have been anywhere from thirty-five to fifty; his face was fat and pale, his eyes appearing as little more than slits of blue light set deep in pouches of gray flesh. Strands of black hair were combed across his scalp. His brown suit was a size too large for him, and his heavy hands were tracked with veins as thick as lead pencils. He wore a wide red tie.

"What we have here, Eberle," Slocum said, "are some pictures that could help us in that Selby case." He handed them to the lieutenant. "Check out the photographer, but call Harrisburg first and get a make on this Porsche. Tell them to put their computers on it."

When Eberle went out, Slocum stood and leaned over his desk, supporting his weight on his clenched fists. The pulse in his throat seemed to be trying to jerk itself free from the tight flesh around it.

"Like I was saying, I had this educated darky in here the other day, Selby. Wearing a turban and one of them African bathrobes. He didn't like how we treated his brother boogies. He told me they had cities of ivory and gold in Africa ten thousand years ago, libraries, museums, hospitals and were doing eye surgery and things like that while we were still learning to count our fingers and toes. I asked him what happened to all those beautiful African cities, and he told me they were the victims of floods and disease, historical cycles and so on. Know what I told him? I said the same thing happened right here in beautiful America. To Detroit and New York and Cleveland and what's left of Newark, New Jersey. And the people who destroyed civilization in Africa are the same people who are doing it here and now in America. He said that was an unfair comparison and I told him the only thing his people know about fair or unfair is that it rhymes with *welfare* . . . so we get all kinds here and I'm pretty fucking thick-skinned. We're the pros, we got the troops and we're paid to do the job."

He jabbed a button on his phone. "Now I got a couple of homicides and some other shit coming down, Selby, so would you mind letting me get back to work? You heard what I told Eberle. When we get a make on that car, we'll be in touch."

Selby nodded. "You obviously needed to make that speech, captain. Naturally, I'm wondering why, since the lost cities of Africa don't have a goddamn thing to do with checking out that plate number. As a pro, I imagine you know that . . . I'll hear from you, Captain, or I'll be back," Selby said, and walked out of the office.

When Selby got home, everyone was in bed except Blazer. He made himself a sandwich, poured a beer and went through the notes he had made of Shana's outbursts under sedation. He had checked what she had said, *Bartlett's Quotations* and Sarah's college books and reading guides.

The list now read:

1. Hornets—(The helicopters).

2. Waves—(Diesel locomotives and freight cars. Noise from the switching yard).

3. Birds crying, singing.—(The children playing at Stoneville grade school).

4. Mommy, I'll kill it—hand hurts—hate it, mommy. (Shana says she doesn't remember saying this. But there was a cut on her right palm that night.)

5. A time to serve and to sin.—(S. said this twice, I think. Not in "Ecclesiastes.")

6. Tunnel or tunnels.—(The Rakestraw covered bridge).

7. Hell is alone.—(A lot of hells in Bartlett's, a couple of dozen or more. Still checking).

Selby took Blazer for a walk to the top of the meadow. From there he thought he saw a car slow down, then make a turn on Fairlee Road, its headlights flickering through the trees. But when he got back to the house with Blazer, the lights were gone and the woods were dark again.

Before turning in for the night, Selby slipped the photograph from the *Standard* under Shana's bedroom door. They could discuss that tomorrow.

Captain Slocum called the next morning, before Selby had a chance to talk to Shana. The captain's voice was cheerful and expansive.

"Well, we're finally making some progress . . . sorry if I rubbed you the wrong way last night. But we had those homicides and a string of burglaries going off like goddamn firecrackers around here. So let's forget the other shit, okay? The important thing is, we got a lead. You know the old saying, Selby, nothing cheers a cop like overtime and a break in the case he's working on."

Selby was in his bedroom, still in his robe. "Glad to hear it, Captain. Who did that plate lead you to?"

"Just a second. I'll get my notes sorted out." Selby heard papers rustling. "Okay now," Slocum said. "Here's where we are. Lieutenant Eberle got a reply from Harrisburg, the Motor Bureau, around one-thirty this A.M. Computers kicked out the whole plate number. It's N4796, issued this year to a 1978 Porsche registered to an Earl Thomson in Wahasset.

"Late as it was, Eberle and I drove out to his house and got him out of bed. That's always best, don't give 'em time to think. It was Earl Thomson's Porsche at Vinegar Hill, no doubt about it.

"Thomson told us he was in Muhlenburg that afternoon at a bar called The Green Lantern. Around five-thirty. After a few beers, he went out and found his car gone. He'd left the keys in the ignition like a damn fool. Two things struck us kind of funny. One, he didn't report his car stolen until the next morning. Second, The Green Lantern's a colored joint. You know the old saying, a redbird don't sit on a blackbird's nest. Thomson's white, comes from a wealthy family, went to good schools, doesn't have a police record. So we shook his story pretty goddamn hard to see if something else funny might fall out of it."

Selby said, "Is this the Thomson family that owns the Harlequin Chemical Company?"

Slocum hesitated. Selby heard him grunt. "Yeah, I think it

is. His father's George Thomson. But I got news for you, Selby. A stud walks into my office with a smoking gun, I don't give a shit about his Dun and Bradstreet rating. It doesn't matter who Earl Thomson's father is. He's got nothing to do with this, understand?"

"I hear what you're saying."

"Okay. Thomson told us he'd been to The Green Lantern to look at a shotgun some colored boy wanted to sell. Boy name of Charlie Lee. I sent Eberle and two other men out to Muhlenburg to check that out. They also talked to a waitress at The Green Lantern—" Again Selby heard a rustle of paper. "Here it is, a colored chick, Ellie Mae Cluny. It all checks out. Thomson was at The Green Lantern, no question about it. After he found his car gone, he called home for a lift. Miguel Santos, he works for the Thomsons, picked him up around six-thirty and Thomson was home for dinner with his mother a half hour later. We checked them out, too, Selby, the Puerto and Thomson's mother. Thomson's in the clear, Selby. No doubt of it. But eliminating suspects is ninety percent of a cop's work.

"So we eliminated Earl Thomson, Selby. That's for sure. We taped everything he said to Lieutenant Eberle and me, so that's part of the case record now. The Thomson kid was never at Vinegar Hill. He told us that. Told us he had a vague idea where Dade Road was, but he'd never been to anyplace out there. Never heard of you or your daughter either, by the way. On the plus side, Selby—thanks to you, we've got a positive make on the stolen car the rapist used, license, engine number, all the other specs. When the bastard tries to sell it or trade it, we'll have his ass. An APB went out on it early this A.M. If that heap's still on the Atlantic seaboard, we can expect a report any time. Like I told you last night, the minute I had news, I'd be in touch. Anything else comes in, same thing holds."

Selby said, "Why didn't Thomson report his car stolen when he found it missing?"

"Well, who the fuck knows? You and me, we'd report it for sure. But maybe we weren't born with a rich old man who'd buy us another one without thinking twice about it. But what Thomson told me sounded reasonable. Said he figured some friend might have borrowed it as a gag. There's an antique car show in town and quite a few of his pals are here for it. But the theft was reported the next morning. We checked that. Selby, I'll keep in touch." What, what the hell, Slocum thought, it was what Lorso had told him Earl had said. It just happened at a different time. And he had gone through the motions of interrogating Earl and hearing it all once again . . .

After hanging up, Selby stood for a moment or so looking out at the meadow. The surface of the pond was flat and bright. A crow flew through the cold, heavy air and settled in a bare locust.

Selby showered, put on slacks and a flannel shirt, and lit the logs in the small corner fireplace.

Davey came in later with the Sunday papers and a tray of orange juice and coffee. Mrs. Cranston had gone to church, his son told him, but had left breakfast in the warming oven.

Davey was in an animated, excited mood, eager to talk about Miss Brett and Sergeant Wilger. "I did something dumb, really stupid, dad. I asked him if he'd show me his gun."

"He's probably used to that. Where's Shana?"

"I don't know. She helped Mrs. Cranston with breakfast, and then went down to the pond, I guess."

Davey squatted on a three-legged stool beside the fireplace. The flames glinted in his light, silky hair. "But the detective, the sergeant, showed me his gun, dad. He didn't take it out of the holster, but he pulled his coat back so I could see it."

"Well, that's something," Selby said. "Did you talk to Shana this morning?"

"About what, dad?"

"I left a photograph from the newspaper in her room. I wondered if she'd mentioned it."

"She was pretty busy with Mrs. Cranston. The lady's first name is Dorcas." Davey was speaking very quickly now. "Dorcas was the last name of one of her father's best friends, that's what Miss Brett told Shana."

"How long were they here?"

"About an hour, I guess. Then they went for a drive. I wanted to go, too, but—" Davey sighed. "They had fun, I guess. Shana thought there was a car following them, but it wasn't. I'd of known what kind it was, all Shana knows is whether they're new and shiny. But Sergeant Wilger told me I'd better stay here and hold the fort. He really said that, dad. 'Hold the fort.' "

186

"You're even then," Selby said. "You asked for a look at his gun, he said 'hold the fort.' Where did they go from here?"

"They drove into Muhlenburg. They stopped at Goldie Boy's church. Then they drove over to Dade Road."

Selby poured himself coffee. "What were they looking for?"

"Shana didn't say. But she told me about Miss Brett. She's got a niece and two nephews. She's twenty-eight, and she's divorced. Shana asked her, which I thought was kind of nosy. Her father and mother lived in Florida and he's retired. Her sisters are both older than she is, they live in Maine."

Selby watched the meadow and pond while Davey informed him that Dorcas Brett had been a deputy district attorney for almost a year, had been to college at Bryn Mawr and at Yale.

Miss Brett told Shana, Davey went on, enthused now, about some of the scary things she'd been afraid of when she was young . . . She had been locked in the gym at Bryn Mawr one night alone in the swimming pool. The janitor forgot her and turned off the lights and locked all the doors.

There was no movement at the pond. Blazer was in the high meadow barking at a squirrel. Davey was saying, "Then, dad, *then* Miss Brett got the feeling there was someone else in the pool with her—or *something* was. It was dark and she couldn't see anything, the water was *black,* and she was afraid she'd brush against it, or it would reach out and brush against *her*—she told Shana it was just her imagination working overtime—"

"Davey, hold it a minute."

"Miss Brett said that when people are too frightened, they can forget what really happened—"

"Davey, where's Shana now?"

"Don't be made at me, dad." Davey's voice trembled. "She did find the picture this morning, and called Normie . . . She made me promise not to say anything . . ."

Selby put an arm around his son's shoulders. "Level with me, Davey."

"Normie picked her up about an hour ago. She waited for him out at the driveway."

"Where were they going?"

"There's a car show at Longwood Gardens."

"Are they looking for someone in that newspaper picture?"

"I don't know, dad. But she didn't want you to go out there. I brought up your coffee and just tried to make everything normal. I didn't know what else to do."

"You did fine," Selby said.

They went down to the foyer then, Selby keeping an arm about the boy's shoulder. Davey watched him pull on a duffel coat and gloves.

"Can I go with you?"

"No, you and Blazer stay here." Without smiling, Selby added, "Hold the fort."

"Yes, sir." Davey used this formal response only when his father's expression told him further discussion would be pointless. At such times, which were infrequent but easily recognizable, his father's emotional temperature was as obvious as the heat from a furnace.

Longwood Gardens had been funded by the late Pierre Du Pont in an attempt to preserve a particular variety of estate garden that was to be found decades earlier in wealthy regions of the eastern United States.

Each season was celebrated for its distinctive features. In the summer, brilliant outdoor flower beds and shaded paths, views of malls and playing fountains—sounds of water mixing naturally with the songbirds. Hyacinths, daffodils and other spring bulbs were to bloom in greenhouses through the winter months. Thousands of chrysanthemums grown under glass for Thanksgiving, and Christmas to blaze with poinsettias, and miles of tiny lights in fir trees glittering like swarms of strange polar fireflies.

On this morning that Harry Selby drove to the gardens, the Grand Concours Automobile Club of Chester County had scheduled its all-class exposition in Longwood's flag mall, taking advantage of what was likely to be the last decent weather before winter set in.

The rain clouds had blown away, the sky was clear and white. A brilliant sun spread a pale light over the tweedy crowds strolling through the wide green mall past the standards of fluttering flags.

Protected by squares of velvet rope were Ferraris, fifty-year-old Packards, Daimlers, Jaguars and Cords. The prize of the show, standing out among famed Lamborghinis and Royces, was a Mercedes roadster built in 1933 in France, where it had remained through World War II. Its immaculate tires had never touched German soil, its engine had never drawn deeply from the air of the Fatherland, and these facts together with the owner's name—Robert "Beetle" Burkholder of San Francisco—were displayed on a placard in front of the car.

As to what exactly occurred that frosty morning at Longwood Gardens, there was considerable disagreement, even among those who witnessed the events, but the most complete and reliable account was provided by a security guard named Clarence Summerall.

A retired policeman, Summerall made careful notes on what he was told, and what he personally saw and heard, and incorporated them into a report which was delivered later by a sheriff's trooper to Captain Walter Slocum of the East Chester Detective Division.

In his report, Summerall wrote:

The girl was with a youngster wearing a letter sweater from Muhlenburg High. Her name was Shana Selby. His name was Norman Bride. According to various witnesses, they arrived at the flag mall around ten o'clock. From there, they walked to the line of display cars and stopped in front of a black 1924 Packard touring sedan. A dozen people were standing there. Most of these spectators did not figure in what happened. I will list the names of those involved in the subsequent action. They were three young men, identified to me later as Earl Thomson of Wahasset, Pennsylvania, and his friends, Willie Joe Bast and Richard Knarl, both from New Jersey. These two young men, of good size, were wearing uniforms. On the yellow shoulder patches of the two cadets was the name of a school—Rockland Military College.

The girl, Shana Selby, walked up to Earl Thomson and pointed at him—this is according to the statement of witnesses—and accused him of running her down in his automobile sometime in the past (no exact date at this writing) and then taking her somewhere and assaulting her. The girl was angry and speaking rapidly. Witnesses did not get all

189

she said. But the above is the substance of her charges against Earl Thomson.

After these accusations, Earl Thomson told her to stop bothering him. He stated he did not know who she was, or what her "hustle" was. Thomson's friends, the Bast and Knarl boys, told her that if she was joking, or if this was some sorority initiation stunt, that she could get herself into trouble. One of them, Knarl it was, asked her if she thought they were a bunch of "goddamn Hell's Angels or something." (I should mention here that they had motorcycles parked outside the roped-off place where the Packard was —bikes painted yellow and black like the shoulder patches with the Rockland school name on them.) At this point, the young man with Shana Selby intervened. Norman Bride said something to one of the cadets. He spoke to Willie Joe Bast. That young man became angry and struck Norman Bride in the body, a severe blow, according to reports. Bast hit him again, in the face. Norman Bride fell to his knees. The other cadet, Knarl, told the Selby girl to "get your dirty little c—— out of here." What the girl replied is not known. She was trying to help her companion, Norman Bride, to his feet, according to spectators.

By this time, I had the news that something was going on, and was at the scene. I can testify to what else occurred. The other man showed up before I did. I saw him coming through the flag mall toward the cars. He wasn't running, but he was hurrying. His name, I learned later, was Harry Selby. It was when Willie Joe Bast grabbed the girl and shoved her toward the exit area—it was just then that Harry Selby arrived there.

Harry Selby is the girl's father. Selby pushed Willie Joe Bast and Knarl away from his daughter. Earl Thomson ran around behind the Packard automobile, climbed on one of the motorcycles and started it. When I say Mr. Selby pushed those two cadets, that is not all of it. He put a hand against their faces and shoved them hard. They stumbled back and fell across their motorbikes and rolled onto the ground.

Earl Thomson rode off on a motorcycle. In looking back, he lost control and ran into the side of a greenhouse. I took no action because it was not an unprovoked, disorderly incident, as I understand such matters. Mr. Selby gave me his name and address of his own accord, and offered to

190

wait for police. I told him that was not necessary. He left with his daughter and N. Bride.

I called for an ambulance from Chester General and collected various names and addresses from witnesses.

Completed this date, 11:35 A.M. Submitted by hand to Trooper Milt Karec, Sheriff's Station, Highway One, Muhlenburg.

Guard Clarence Summerall (signed)

CHAPTER SIXTEEN

The rain that had threatened most of the day was coming down hard by the time Selby arrived at George Thomson's home. Dom Lorso opened the door, introduced himself and said abruptly, "Mr. Thomson's waiting. It's this way."

The lights in the study shone on leather furniture and the black surfaces of wet windows. Thomson was at his desk, with his back to French doors and the illuminated terraces. Tubs of box cedars glistened there, and beyond them were dark lawns and trees.

Thomson said, "You can sit down if you want, Mr. Selby. I asked you here because we've got some things to straighten out. I'm not your friend or your enemy. You can take that on faith or dismiss it as bullshit. I don't care. What happened at Longwood today could have been a misunderstanding, a mistake on your daughter's part, an overreaction on yours. That's how I figure it. Obviously, you've got other ideas. I think we should talk it over, try to put a lid on before something gets out of hand. You want a cigar, or a drink?"

Selby shook his head and took a chair facing Thomson's desk. Dom Lorso stood watching him, a cigarette between his lips.

Thomson lit a cigar with a desk lighter. "You mind if I lead off, Selby?"

"Go ahead."

"If my son hurt or raped any young girl, I'd still get him the best lawyer I could, not to help him weasel his way out of it but to make sure he had a chance to get the kind of therapy he needed, at some institution that would treat him until he was cured, if that took his whole lifetime. But I'd stand behind him and try to help him. That's what I'd do if I thought he was *guilty.* So you can be sure I don't intend to let him be hounded and framed for something he didn't have a goddamn thing to do with. That's all the explaining I intend to do, Selby. The doctor at Chester General said Earl's lucky he didn't lose an eye. A splinter of glass came close to going straight through it when he hit that greenhouse. His mother's under sedation—she got hysterical when they brought him home. He's upstairs now. In my view, Selby, you and your daughter have a goddamn heavy tab to pick up. I hope you can handle it. But I asked you here to talk. If you've got anything to say, I'll listen."

Selby said, "My daughter has twenty-twenty vision, Thomson. She had a long look at the man who raped her. She says it was your son."

Thomson shrugged. "If that's all you got to say, we don't have anything to talk about. But you better understand one thing, Selby. You're never going to hurt my boy again. I want you to understand that. It's really why I asked you here, to make sure you got that through your head."

Selby said, "I'll make the same speech, Thomson. Your son will never lay a hand on my daughter again. Believe it."

Thomson waved smoke from his face, as if trying to see Selby more clearly. "You think this is a tennis game we're playing, some tit-for-tat horseshit? You think I'm putting on an act for your benefit, or that I'm lying, or my son is?"

"That's occurred to me," Selby said.

Dom Lorso moved closer. "Don't press your luck, big man. We're being gents for the time being."

A red light flared against the terrace windows. Thomson said, "This will be Captain Slocum. My attorney Allan Davic is already here. You have any objection to them joining us?"

Dom Lorso blew a stream of smoke down at Selby. He said, "I don't see what the shit we're being so polite about. He'll talk

193

to 'em now, Giorgio, or in jail later. I'd just as soon make it later."

Lorso's face was flushed. A bristling, attack-dog ferocity was running in currents through the little Sicilian. He looked ready to explode.

Selby said quietly, "Mr. Lorso, don't blow smoke at me again, and don't press me. Mr. Thomson, I don't mind talking to Captain Slocum. He's a good storyteller. Now go open the door."

Lorso's flush deepened, but Thomson raised a hand. "Let it go, Dom."

Lorso walked out. Thomson stared at the darkness beyond the terrace windows, ignoring Selby. From the foyer a doorbell sounded, its echoes trembling through the big study.

Allan Davic entered with Captain Slocum and Dom Lorso. There were no introductions, only a hostile silence in which the attorney removed a silver pencil from his pocket and wrote the date on a yellow legal pad.

Davic was in his forties, with a stocky body neatly compacted within a well-cut three-piece suit. His hair was dark and streaked with gray. Deep grooves lined the sides of his nose.

His thick glasses were coated by reflections from Thomson's desk lamp. It was impossible for Selby to guess who or what the lawyer was looking at.

Captain Slocum broke the silence. "Selby, I told you this morning Earl Thomson wasn't involved with what happened to your daughter. I told you we'd checked out every move he'd made, established where he was every minute of the time. Are you going to sit there and pretend you weren't informed *personally* by me that our investigation cleared Earl Thomson?"

Selby said, "I didn't come here to talk to you, Captain. Or to Mr. Davic. For the record, if this conversation is being taped, I haven't been informed of it. I came here at Thomson's invitation because he said he wanted to talk to *me*. Then he asked me if I'd mind if you people joined us. So far I haven't heard anything that makes my coming out in the rain worth it."

Davic adjusted his glasses. "Perhaps I can justify your braving the elements, Mr. Selby. I'm not sure you appreciate the gravity of your situation. As yet I don't represent Earl Thomson against you or your daughter, so it isn't improper for me to give you advice. Listen carefully to what Mr. Thomson and Captain Slocum have to say. They can put you to a great deal of expense, and trouble, if you force them to take legal action. Those are facts, Mr. Selby."

"If you want *my* advice," Selby said, "you'd better listen to a few more facts. Earl Thomson's car was photographed at the place my daughter was raped, the same night it happened. His car is a red Porsche. My daughter was knocked from her bicycle earlier that same afternoon by a red car. There was red paint on her bike. But after Lieutenant Eberle came to my home like a common thief and walked off with the evidence, the red paint disappeared in the police lab."

Pointing at Selby, Slocum said, "Eberle was acting under *my* orders. The lab found no red paint on that bicycle and you know it."

"I suggest we keep our tempers, gentlemen." Davic made a note on his pad. Glancing up, he said, "Mr. Selby, it's obvious you intend to take an adversary stance. I'd prefer to settle this some other way. You were informed by Captain Slocum that Earl Thomson was not a suspect in your daughter's case. Told that the testimony of disinterested witnesses placed Mr. Earl Thomson here in his own home at the time that the assault occurred. But you obviously didn't bother to tell your daughter that. This morning, in front of witnesses, she accused Earl Thomson of committing a series of felonious attacks on her person, accusations which leave her open to charges of malicious slander. And you, Mr. Selby, committed physical assault and battery against"—Davic checked his legal pad—"one Richard Knarl and one Willie Joe Bast, friends of Earl Thomson, who were trying to dissuade your daughter from making a public nuisance of herself. The Bast and Knarl boys come from outstanding families. Their parents are outraged."

"I'm sorry they're upset," Selby said, not bothering to check his anger. "If it helps, you can tell them that their goon sons got off lucky."

Davic folded his hands. "I've given you good advice, Mr. Selby, but you're obviously not about to take it. I have no alternative but to ask the county magistrate to place you and your daughter under sizable peace bonds, to restrain you both from any further harassment of Earl Thomson.

"Such court orders," the lawyer continued, "are restrictive and punitive. A peace bond will enjoin you and your daughter from any personal contact whatsoever with Earl Thomson. You will not speak to him, write to him, or approach him within certain proscribed distances. If you drive your car past his house, or accost him in a public place, you will be subject to arrest and fines, and possibly a jail sentence. Further, the principal of your daughter's school will be instructed to monitor her conversations with classmates to make sure that none of these slanders are repeated. As for you, Mr. Selby, if you make any more threatening gestures toward Earl Thomson, physically or verbally, you'll pay a high price for it."

"We'll have your ass, Selby, if you ever think about bothering these people again," Captain Slocum said.

Davic frowned at the crimson glare on his glasses. Another red light was flashing across the terrace, and over the wet branches of the tubbed cedars.

Slocum went on: "I spelled everything out for you, Selby."

"Hold it, Walter." Thomson nodded to Dom Lorso.

"Mr. Thomson, I was trying to explain that—"

"I understand, Captain, but that can wait. Dom, see who it is."

A revolving dome-light splintered the darkness beyond the study windows.

Voices sounded from the foyer, Lorso's first, then a man's. From somewhere behind the house, dogs were barking, their howls carrying above the rain.

Lorso's voice rose angrily. Thomson stood and walked from the study, Slocum got up and followed him. When the door closed behind them, the voices in the foyer subsided into murmurs.

Davic studied Selby. "I'm glad to have a chance for a few words in private," he said. "Do you smoke, by the way?"

Good cop, bad cop, Selby thought. A cigarette, the understanding smile . . . "I don't smoke," he said.

Davic nodded. "Good. It's counterproductive to jog for miles, eat sensibly and then have to do business in smog-alert conditions."

He removed his glasses. His eyes were hard and brown and expressionless. "Don't think I'm being presumptuous, Mr. Selby, if I say I understand how you feel. I don't have children of my own, but I do have a niece who is very dear to me. I know how I'd feel if she were hurt in any way. So I do have an idea what you and your daughter have been through. Even the most familiar sights and sounds must seem frightening and threatening to her. Speeding automobiles, dark roads, a stranger asking directions, they can only heighten her feelings of terror, depression, even what I believe is called cognitive dysfunction. She's got to overcome all that. But if you persist in ignoring the facts of the police investigation you'll only add to her insecurity. Wouldn't it be more helpful to explain to her that she simply made a mistake today? I know your circumstances, I know that the child's mother is deceased." Davic's expression was understanding. "Actually, Mr. Selby, a vacation might be the best therapy now, a pleasant trip to distract her from these painful associations. Otherwise your daughter may see the man who assaulted her every time she steps from your house—delivery boys, truck drivers, construction workers, even teachers. If you can't convince her to trust the police, she'll be living in a nightmare of terrified fantasies, imagining him stalking her, chasing her down streets, sitting beside her in buses." He shrugged. "She could be making these same accusations about other people, conceivably for the rest of her life."

Selby studied the windows shimmering with the flare of the police lights.

Davic said, "What do you think of my suggestion, Mr. Selby?"

"A vacation for Shana? It's worth considering."

There were pieces that didn't fit together, Selby thought, a puzzle whose outlines he couldn't define, whose very existence might be the work of his nerves or imagination.

"But you're not considering it, are you, Mr. Selby?"

"No, I'm not."

"I didn't think so. All right, let's cut out the bullshit. You're ass-deep in trouble. You're dealing with rich, powerful people. There's nothing to negotiate here. You've got no options. No, I'll amend that. You *can* determine to some extent just how badly you and your daughter will be hurt."

197

"How do we go about that?"

"First, we want a letter from your daughter admitting she was mistaken in every detail and particular of her charges against Earl Thomson."

"That's for starters?"

"Correct. Then I'll need a sworn statement from you, Selby, repudiating your daughter's accusations and expressing your regret at the distress her malicious actions caused Earl Thomson and his family. Also—"

"Save your breath, Davic. You're bluffing. You said too much."

Davic tried to recover. "Don't bank on that, Selby. I told you these people are rich *and* powerful. That's a distinction even smart people aren't always aware of. Money can influence things. Power can destroy them. Let me give you a historical example. Adolf Hitler stipulated certain conditions to Neville Chamberlain. In a meeting at Munich he told the prime minister of Great Britain that the issues of Poland, Poland itself, in fact, were not negotiable, could not and would not be placed on the agenda. Chamberlain agreed. Poland was *not* negotiable. Now *that's* power, Selby, and it has nothing to do with money. A country centuries old, with an empire of forests and lakes and mountains, a country of soldiers and artists, scientists, great traditions, Copernicus, Pulaski, millions of human beings—and one man, not a god or a conqueror from a distant planet but one human being who might have been pulling up his pants after defecating, or poking a bit of rotting meat with a toothpick, that man announced that Poland was not subject to negotiations— couldn't be discussed, mentioned, talked about in any way at all because he'd made up his mind and that was the end of it—for Poland, for Chamberlain and damn near for the rest of the world . . . We're not all the same . . . I've no talent for power, I decided to become rich. What was your choice, Selby?"

"I never had your problem."

"Mr. Thomson told me you were a professional athlete, a jock was his word. Wasn't there a kind of power in that? Millions of people watch those games and millions of dollars are bet on them. I recall reading about a teammate of yours—Goldbirn, I believe it was." Davic nodded thoughtfully. "Yes, Goldbirn,

Jerry Goldbirn, that was his name. Wasn't he involved in some dubious financial deals?"

"I wouldn't know anything about that," Selby said untruthfully.

"I thought he'd agreed to throw some games for people in Chicago and Las Vegas. Of course, it might have been just rumors. But if they were true, it was fortunate Goldbirn was injured in practice before he could compromise himself."

Selby watched the red lights on the windows and thought about how this lawyer with the masked eyes had checked on Sarah and Jerry Goldbirn . . .

Selby remembered Jerry going up for the pass on a spring afternoon in dummy scrimmage, his hands reaching for the ball with lazy precision. And he remembered lowering his head and hitting Goldbirn—a tap would have told the backfield coach he'd beaten the play—but Selby had hit Jerry at full speed with his legs driving, a blind-side shot that had broken Goldbirn's collarbone and four of his ribs and put him out for the rest of the season . . .

Davic said, "Well, it ended happily enough for Mr. Goldbirn, didn't it? Virtue enforced by accident, one might say. Or was that how it was, Mr. Selby? An accident?"

"It was a mix-up in the defensive signals," Selby again replied untruthfully. "I had a play contact sign. Goldbirn wasn't expecting it."

"So he sat out the season," Davic said, "and never had the chance to throw a game, even if he'd wanted to."

"Rumors, Mr. Davic."

"Then in a circuitous fashion," Davic said, "you saved Goldbirn's ass, didn't you, Selby? Was he grateful?"

"What you're asking, Davic, is whether I was involved in a payoff."

"You're a hostile person, Selby."

"Maybe. What happened to Goldbirn was an accident. But when people get in each other's way, even accidentally, they can get hurt."

"In professional football, you mean?"

"That's what you're talking about, isn't it?"

"Tell me, were you expecting that second police car?"

"What matters," Selby said, "is that *you* weren't, Mr. Davic. And neither was Thomson."

A scream sounded somewhere above them, cutting the tension like a falling knife. The lawyer stood so quickly that his legal pad fell to the floor. The doors from the foyer were pushed open and Thomson walked into the study, his face scored with anger. A sheet of parchment paper with a black seal attached to it was crushed in his hand.

"It's a warrant," he told Davic, and shoved the paper at him. "You hear me? There's a DA here and one of Slocum's cops, a detective named Wilger. They're actually trying to hang it on Earl . . . the rape, kidnapping—"

Davic took the warrant and scanned it. "It's in order, Mr. Thomson. But I can't accept service. Bail has been waived."

"They're *lying*. Earl's fingerprints . . . they say they're all over the garage at Vinegar Hill, that's what they're tying to tell me."

Davic said, "The preliminary hearing is set for nine tomorrow in Magistrate Teague's court in Muhlenburg. We can reserve any plea until—"

"I sent Slocum over there already. My son's not going to line up with a bunch of winos and vagrants."

The screaming upstairs had stopped; the only sound in the study was Thomson's heavy breathing.

"Your son has to honor this warrant. He'll be a fugitive from justice if—"

Dom Lorso had begun to raise his voice at someone in the foyer and Selby heard a familiar voice, a lighter one, trying to interrupt the outbursts.

The front doors of Thomson's house were opened, and the wind and rain swept around Dorcas Brett. When Selby entered the foyer he was struck by Lorso's rage and by the whiteness of her face.

Lorso turned around when he heard Selby, but his eyes went past him to the second floor landing where a woman in the shadows watched from a wheelchair. A stocky man in white trousers and a white shirt stood behind her.

Thomson and Davic came in then, the lawyer holding Thomson's arm. "As your attorney," he said insistently, "I don't want you to say another word, George. Not one word."

200

Thomson shook off Davic's hand. "I'll say what I want. Selby, you get out of my house. Your daughter is lying, you *hear?*"

"Listen to your lawyer—"

"I told you to get out of here. I'll make you *and* her regret you ever started this."

Selby said, "You're making it easier for me to do something I'm trying hard not to. You'd better understand that."

"George," Davic said tensely. "Don't say anything else."

"If you do," Selby said, "if you say one more word, Thomson, I'll do what I'm trying not to. I'll go up those stairs and kick in doors until I find him."

For an instant the atmosphere was volatile; any sudden movement could have touched it off.

Dorcas Brett put a hand tightly on Selby's arm. "We have work to do, I think we'd better go."

"Okay," he said, "okay." But his voice sounded strange to him, thick and hoarse with the effort he made to control it.

They were in the driveway beside her car before the white anger faded and Selby saw things clearly again, the rain slanting around them and the worried look in her eyes.

"Are you all right, Mr. Selby?"

"Yes," he said, and touched her arm. Her raincoat was slick and wet. Her presence steadied him.

"There's a diner on the pike," she said. "On the left-hand side before Golden Road. I'll wait for you there, all right?"

"Yes, sure."

Selby stood staring at Thomson's sprawling house as she drove off, listening to the barking dogs in the kennels and wondering from which of those many dark windows Earl Thomson might be watching him . . .

Dom Lorso's emotions were in check, his tone matter-of-fact as he said, "If we don't pay them back for this, Davic, we lose Earl. If you don't show him the kind of loyalty he understands and needs, you might as well forget what you're over here for. They dragged that filth into his home, they shamed him in front of his mother. I know what that did to Earl. I know better than his father. So we don't take it Mr. Counselor. We can't."

201

"Let's be clear about this," Davic said, leaving the window. "If you want peace officers hit, Mr. Lorso, I imagine you have the necessary phone numbers. If you don't, I'll lend you mine. But that would be a miscalculation, I assure you."

"Respect never hurt anybody," Lorso said. "She could've let us know what was coming down, spared him and his mother the humiliation. Screw the miscalculation shit. Call those characters I fixed up the other night in Philadelphia. The Cadles. I'm not talking about a contract, I'm talking respect, fear of God."

Davic was silent a moment and then shrugged indifferently. "Where's the DA likely to be tonight?"

"Her office probably. But I'll check Eberle at the district to make sure."

Davic picked up Thomson's phone and dialed a number. After speaking briefly to a man named Ben, he broke the connection. "Your decision, Mr. Lorso," he said. "Remember that."

Dom Lorso lit a cigarette and blew a stream of smoke at him. "So fucking *what,* Counselor? That kind of decision makes itself."

George Thomson came downstairs as Davic was leaving. His face was pale and strained, but he had recovered his composure; his eyes were hard with a disciplined angry anticipation.

"Hold it a minute," he said to Davic. "I got something for you before you go."

Opening a wall safe behind a framed hunting print, Thomson removed a bulky cardboard file with metal-tipped corners. He presented it to Davic who read aloud the stenciled information on its front cover. U.S. ARMY. K/S-36663864. O.C. CONFIDENTIAL.

"A court-martial transcript," Thomson told him, "a trial that took place in South Korea. I want you to study it and use it. Harry Selby's father was in my outfit. A fuck-up named Jonas Selby. We nailed his ass with charges just this side of murder. You want my guess, Harry Selby is after me and my son now. That's why he's concocted the shit about Earl raping his daughter—I was the senior officer who presided on the court-martial. I sent that sonofabitch, Jonas Selby, to the stockade for five years."

The attorney studied the classification on the file: O.C. CONFI-DENTIAL. "A question occurs, of course," he said.

"You mean where I got hold of that transcript?"

Davic smiled faintly. "No, I understand things like that. You paid for it. But how does Harry Selby know of your connection to his father? He couldn't have seen the transcript. He couldn't get a look at anything classified O.C."

"You're right." Thomson's tone was hard and complacent. "He tried though, a few years ago, and struck out. So did the DA just recently. My guess is Harry Selby got a lead from his brother."

"Let me explain something," Davic said. "If I included this material in a court trial, and it's premature to think this business will ever go that far, but if I *do,* the People can cross-examine and tear into every point and issue I raise. Do you understand that?"

"You've done your job, Davic. I understand what you're saying."

Thomson went to the bar and poured himself a half glass of Scotch. "But when I get hit, I hit back. Harry Selby and his cunt daughter are going to find that out."

CHAPTER SEVENTEEN

When Selby returned home, Shana was in the study watching television, sitting cross-legged on the leather sofa. A bowl of popcorn was on the table beside her. Blazer was stretched in front of the fireplace.

"Can we turn the TV off for a while?"

"Sure, daddy." Shana hurried in her bare feet to snap the set off.

Selby had phoned her after talking to Dorcas Brett. As Shana sat down again, Selby said, "I'm not blaming you, but it's time we get things out in the open. Miss Brett filled me in on what you told her. I'll start with two questions: when did you know it was Earl Thomson and why didn't you tell me about it?"

"It wasn't until I saw the picture in the paper, but I still wasn't sure so I didn't want to tell you or anybody."

"And that's why you phoned him?"

"Yes, I told Miss Brett, I had to hear his voice. Can't you understand, daddy? I had to hear him talking. I called him from here, from my room, and hung up the minute he answered. Then I called him from a pay phone when Normie and I were out driving around. I pretended I had a wrong number that time. But seeing him at Longwood, I was sure."

"It seems you've been doing a lot of pretending lately, Shana. That's what we've got to get straightened out."

He made himself a drink at the bar, a converted marble-topped table with carved legs. "You want a Coke or anything?"

"I'll get myself a glass of milk. But Mrs. Cranston made some sandwiches for you. You want me to bring them in? They're salamis on rye with tomatoes and pickles."

"No, no, thanks, honey." He watched her walk quickly through the front hallway, looking small and vulnerable in her bare feet. Her penny-loafers were lined up beside the old sofa . . .

Dorcas Brett hadn't bothered to remove her raincoat at the diner, only opening the collar and pulling it back from her shoulders. She had explained over a cup of coffee and with an occasional glance at her watch that ". . . Burt Wilger and I knew something was odd about Shana's reaction at Vinegar Hill. The garage, the look of it, obviously terrified her. Burt and I went back and checked the driveway. Some of the ruts had been packed with wooden slats and underbrush—what a driver would use if his tires were spinning in mud. The fire trucks and water had covered most of it, but we found enough to give us the picture. His car was stuck, and our guess was that he'd gone into the garage to get an axe and to try to find some wooden slats or pieces of kindling to jam under his tires. But guesses don't meet probable cause requirements. The statute is explicit—*probable cause may not be created after the fact, not by a successful search or seizure, nor by an arrest.* But when Shana remembered what happened, and pointed to the garage and said, 'The man who raped me went in there that night. *I saw him,*' that gave us sufficient reason to go to Teague for the warrant."

Buttoning the collar of her coat, she added, "It took twenty-four hours to process the prints and get the confirmation from Washington. When we called you late this afternoon, you were on your way to the Thomsons'. Excuse me now, but I've got to get back to the office . . ."

Shana put her glass of milk on the coffee table. Sitting on the sofa, she wrapped her arms about her knees, locked away in her own private thoughts.

Pulling his chair around to face her, Selby said, "I'd like to say this first, Shana. We're still a family and that means telling each other the truth and trusting each other. I'm your father and I always will be. I said that before and I know it sounds obvious, but it's important to emphasize because . . . well, you still don't seem to understand what it means. It's not whether I'm a good or bad father, wise and smart, or dumb and insensitive. But it's my job to take care of you and help you when you need it. That's the way I am. I taught you to use a compass, I taught you to swim, I raised hell with you for playing with matches in the hay barn, and I raised hell with those idiot grooms at Harvey Nelson's farm for putting you up on a green hunter when you were still in pony class."

"I fell off that hunter, daddy," she corrected him quickly.

"What difference does that make?"

"Well, that's what really happened. It was my fault because I kept begging them to let me ride that big chestnut."

"Shana, please, let's stick to the point. Whether you fell off or got thrown off isn't the issue. You could have broken your neck. My job is to protect you from things like that until you can take care of yourself. Like that time when you were playing the jukebox. You insisted that was your own private experience and that I sort of intruded on it but—"

"I didn't say that, daddy."

"Let me finish, okay? That jukebox and the scene at Longwood this morning . . . honey, they belong to me too, because what happens to you happens to me . . . is my responsibility—"

"But when I found his picture under my door this morning . . ." Shana drew a trembling breath. "I knew you were going to try to go out there."

"Well, dammit, aren't you glad I did?"

"Why are you getting mad?"

"I'm sorry, Shana."

"You want me to say I'm glad you helped me and Normie and shoved those bullies down—well, sure, I *am*, daddy. Except that turned it into a family fight—"

"Dammit, Shana, I'll never stand by and let *anybody* put a hand on you against your will. Can't you understand *that?*"

"I can see that, honestly, I can, daddy. But you're my father and that's the only reason you believe me. Davey believes me because he's my little brother, and Miss Brett believes me because she's paid to, but I want it to be different, can't *you* see that, daddy?"

"Miss Brett isn't paid to believe anybody, Shana. Her job is to prosecute the defendants by presenting the facts to a jury."

"I know that much." In profile to him, his daughter's fore-head was smooth in the firelight, her blond hair layered in moving shadows. "I took civics and history. I knew how things are *supposed* to work, but there are two sides now, mine and his." Her voice had become tense. "But it can't be just a family thing with everybody feeling they're right. I want *his* family and *his* friends to know the truth. I want to hear *him* admit it, I want them *all* to admit it. I don't want people wondering why I was wearing such tight shorts, or what I was doing down on Fairlee Road when it was almost dark, and what I was *looking* for or *waiting* for—"

She swung around to stare at him then, the movement so coiled and tense that it startled Blazer, who raised his head and growled softly.

"Earl Thomson did this *to* me. Not *because* of me. Not *with* me. That's what I want the judge and jury *to tell the whole world.*"

Selby said quietly, "All right, let's settle down, Shana. Let's see if we can't try to understand each other. I don't think you used good judgment going out to Longwood. Not just because you didn't confide in me, but because it's foolish to think a man who did what he did to you would admit it simply because you accused him of it."

Shana slumped back in the sofa. "I guess you're right, but yesterday it all seemed simple. When Miss Brett and I went back to Vinegar Hill she told me some people have memories that are so painful they're afraid to remember them, that they can't until they feel secure and safe enough to. Something like that happened to her in college, she got locked in the gym in Bryn Mawr one night and—"

"Yes, the swimming pool. Davey told me about that."

"Well, anyway . . ." Shana leaned forward and moved a finger slowly around the edge of the milk glass. "We drove into the driveway, and stood looking at the garage. Miss Brett and Sergeant Wilger didn't say anything, but I felt safe. Then I remembered. After it was all over that night . . ." Her voice became soft, flat. "He couldn't get the car moving. The motor made that awful whining noise, like screaming. That's why I was so scared when you were there. I remembered he went into the garage to get something. But"—she frowned—"it wasn't clear . . ."

Her finger was still moving in slow circles around the glass. "It was like when I walked up Fairlee Road in the rain. There's a vacant lot where people dump some old cars. I sat in one of those cars a long time that night but I didn't remember anything about it till later. Things are still coming back in pieces."

"Well, as rough as that is," Selby said, "wouldn't it be better if you'd come to me whenever something comes back to you?"

She laughed sharply. "God, daddy, how can anything be *better?* I've got to be examined by a psychiatrist during the trial. Not by a doctor like Dr. Kerr but someone who's going to get into my head because of what *he* did to me . . ."

"Did Miss Brett tell you that?"

"Yes, and she said she can't do anything about it because that's the law. I'm the crazy loon who has to explain everything. Why don't they make *him* talk to a psychiatrist? Make *him* explain why he wants to run people down with his car and everything? But he'd just lie his way out of it. Maybe in some crazy way he thinks he's telling the truth . . . I'm still not *sure* where I was for three hours that night. I don't know what's the truth about that."

She turned away quickly but he saw a flash of tears in her eyes. "Part of the truth is, I was ashamed to come home, because I didn't want to see you and tell you about it. You said you taught me how to swim and everything. When I was afraid of the hoot owls when we first moved here, you took me out wrapped up in a blanket one night and there was one hooting in the old apple tree we were sitting under. You turned your flashlight on him. He was only about four inches tall and he had puffy little feathers around his eyes."

Her voice was rising, beginning to break. "Don't you think I liked doing things like that with you? Can't you see why I didn't want to come home and tell you I'd been *raped?* That he'd done things to me that I didn't even know men wanted to do to girls? I just sat in that car listening to the rain and thinking that with mommy gone, I was all you had left. And that I could never be what you wanted me to be."

"Please don't say that," Selby said. "Please don't even think that, Shana. We've talked enough for now."

She nodded gratefully. "I better put this milk away then,"

208

she said. "I want to shampoo my hair and get my clothes ready. If you're not going to walk Blazer, I'll take him up to my room."

Selby kissed her good night. She hugged him tightly and he drew her into his arms and gently rubbed her thin shoulders.

And then she pulled away from him and brushed her eyes and said, "Come on, Blazer."

East Chester was a Quaker town of twelve thousand, its business district lined with eighteenth-century red brick and white clapboard shops. A highschool and open-air theater bordered the southern end of the village. A shantytown with tar-paper roofs lay to the north on the Brandywine. The city's parking mall ran the length of the commercial area, between City Hall and St. Christopher's white, steepled church.

A uniformed guard in the lobby of the hall signed Selby into the building. He had called ahead and there was a pass for him. The corridor on the DA's floor was dark except for a rectangle of light from the open door of her outer office.

Selby heard someone shouting, "You may know about those goddamn lawbooks of yours . . ." A string of profanity followed, and then the heavy, growling voice rose again. "But you got a lot to learn about *team* work. You don't know *shit* about loyalty . . ."

As Selby walked into the reception room, Lieutenant Eberle came out of Dorcas Brett's office, almost colliding with him.

"Watch it, for Christ's sake." The detective's breath was sweet with mints and whiskey. Recognizing Selby, he looked him up and down, a grin touching his lips. "She's all yours, pal. And you're welcome to her."

Selby turned his back on him and went into Brett's office. She was opening a pack of cigarettes, picking nervously at the foil wrapping. She wore a denim suit with a yellow scarf. Her raincoat was over a chair.

"Captain Slocum called the Detective Division," she said with an uneasy smile. "He wanted our notes on Earl Thomson, and that touched some macho nerves around here, as you probably just heard."

"They probably heard it all the way down to the river."

209

Selby looked at her fumbling hands. "Would you like some help?"

She looked in surprise at the cigarettes. She said, "No, thanks. I'm not supposed to be smoking now anyway."

Selby said, "I called because I had a talk with Shana. It occurred to me then I could use some help from you."

When he told her his worries, Brett said, "As far as the psychiatrist is concerned, that's a defense privilege, guaranteed by statute. On the other point, I agree. Shana's probably not telling us everything, but I think she's *trying* to."

"I don't want her hurt anymore, Miss Brett. I can't save what's been lost. But I can try to prevent her going through anything else. So I want to *be sure* you can nail Earl Thomson."

She picked up the cigarettes, shrugged and dropped them back on her desk. "A conviction is a risky assumption in any trial. But we have three solid props—Shana's identification of Earl Thomson, and the presence of Thomson's fingerprints and car at Vinegar Hill. Plus the conclusively damaging fact that he denied he'd ever been there. He lied to Captain Slocum and Eberle about that, and we have the taped interrogations to prove it."

"But you said a conviction is a risky assumption," Selby reminded her. "What's the problem? The fact that Shana phoned him afterward?"

"No, those calls are legally irrelevant. Her identification isn't based on the sound of his voice. It's based on his physical appearance."

Selby said impatiently, "What *is* bothering you? The psychiatrist?"

"That's part of it. But a cultural preconception about rape will also be working against us. If Shana had been murdered, or mugged and robbed, as ghastly as that sounds, we'd have fewer problems. But in a rape trial, the plaintiff can be humiliated and emotionally scarred, and I can't promise I'll be able to protect Shana from that.

"Allan Davic, for starters, will insist on the psychiatric examination. That's his right under the judicially sanctioned notion that a young girl who accuses a man of rape may simply be fantasizing a wishful, biological urge. So it's got to be *proved* she's not a sexual hysteric. It's this thinking that debases rape

210

victims, particularly children. Their young age and ignorance of sexual terminology can be used to impeach their testimony. In rape trials the sexual habits of the *victims* can be hung out for speculation. If the female is 'unchaste,' in the legal term, unclean is the implication, that's considered relevant. 'What's been used can't be abused'—as old common law has it. But Earl Thomson's sexual activities can't be hinted at, they're cloaked in privilege. His kinks might influence the jury—the same jury that may be told the *victim* is unreliable because she had the carelessness, the stupidity or sheer bloody gall to *lose* her virginity. That's the sexual bias available to the defense. In most felonies victims are presumed honest unless competent evidence proves they're not. But in rape cases and reports of child molestation there's an *a priori* suspicion of the injured party, which is why rape is probably the single most unreported major crime in the country. In spite of that," she said, beginning to pace, "a *reported* rape takes place every ten minutes around the clock in the United States, and forty percent of those attacks are committed against girls like Shana, from ten to fifteen years old. And those figures represent just the literal definition of rape—penile-vaginal assault by force, committed on a female against her will. The stats don't include oral or anal sodomy and God knows how many gang-rapes. The sad fact, Mr. Selby," she said, returning to her desk for her cigarettes, "is that sexual aggression against young females is actually considered *normal* by many highly publicized psychologists and anthropologists, their point being, I guess, that such behavior isn't pathological because it's typical of many animals, particularly *monkeys.*" Moistening her lips, she said, "Forgive me, Mr. Selby, but I burn at the notion that the abused and raped child is left with the solace that the gravity of her condition has been overstated, that what's good enough for young monkeys can't be all that bad for her."

Selby said, "Miss Brett, I'm glad you're on our side, but you've been angry since we first met. I had a feeling some of it was toward me—"

"You're right," she said, "I *was* angry when I met you and your daughter at Vinegar Hill. The whole damn scene had such an air of . . . biblical vengeance and righteousness about it. You brought *her* back to the place where she'd been raped and forced her to witness and relive all that terror again. *You* weren't frightened by that place. *You* had some thoughts of revenge and reprisal going for you, pumping you up. But Shana, the abused female of the piece, had to stand there until her memories drove her into a screaming hysteria—"

"*Hold* it, goddammit." Selby raised a hand. "You're forgetting something. I was there trying to find out who raped Shana because nobody on the official payroll here seemed to give a good goddamn about that. There's been a cover-up since it happened, and don't bother telling me you don't know that. As for biblical righteousness and the rest of it, the Bible is just as often in the eye of the beholder as anything else."

"Well, if that's true, I'm sorry but—"

"Let me finish, will you?"

"If I've been wrong I want the chance to say so." And she meant it.

"Never mind, just hear me out. Shana may have lost a kind of trust she can't recover. She's known pain and loss before, her mother died recently. But that happened in a framework she could adapt to. This thing has turned her life upside down. That's what she's lost, that's what's gone."

"Good . . . I just hope we can put my outburst at you behind us and get to work. We do have to trust each other, you realize."

Selby said, "What about Captain Slocum and his people?"

"Sergeant Wilger was detailed to the DA's section by Slocum," Brett said, "even before we knew we were going to trial. But the Commonwealth is in charge of this prosecution, which means the captain reports to this office. If he doesn't do his job we have the authority to suspend him."

"Tell me, how did you happen to be assigned to this case?"

"It didn't happen, Mr. Selby. I was in line for it. The other deputies are on trial duty and our staff back-up, Bill Corum, is out with a flare-up of diabetes." She smiled tightly. "Is that what's bothering you? That I might not be any good because I'm not wearing a beard and a jockstrap?"

"Come on, Miss Brett, I said I was glad we're on the same side. But I can't help wondering about other things."

"Such as?"

"Mr. Davic ran a check on me, even before you served the warrant on Thomson. He'd learned my wife was dead, among other things."

"What's your question then?"

"How did he know in advance that Earl Thomson was involved? Or that a warrant might be served?"

"There's an obvious answer to that. Which is that I *told* him. Is that what you think?"

"No, but I have to wonder about it."

She shrugged and turned back to the windows. The lights glinted in her hair, which was damp from the rain. Something distracted her, because she moved closer to the slotted blinds, her eyes traveling along the parking mall. He noticed a tremor in her hand as she loosened her scarf.

"Well, if you're wondering about Mr. Davic," she said, "you must also be wondering about Lieutenant Eberle. Do you think we staged that scene in my outer office for your benefit? That we waited until we heard the elevator door close, heard your footsteps in the corridor and then went into an act to convince you I'm one of the good guys?"

"No, that didn't occur to me," Selby said truthfully.

"But you're thinking about it now."

Selby said, "It was the second scene tonight, wasn't it?"

"What do you mean by that?"

Her phone rang. She crossed to her desk and lifted the receiver. "Dorcas Brett," she said sharply, then, "all right, just a minute." She lowered the phone to her side.

She looked suddenly tired, and angry again. "You meant Mr. Lorso reading me out. That was the other scene you imply might have been staged, right?"

He shrugged. "Miss Brett, I'm her father, I can't take any more chances. I'm dependent on you, but I can't afford to overlook anything. I've had one hell of a runaround since this started, as you know . . ."

Sighing wearily, she nodded at the phone. "Sergeant Wilger's finished the paperwork at Magistrate Teague's. He wants to know if you'd like him to pick you up in the morning. We're due in court around eight-thirty."

"Tell him no thanks, I guess we'll meet you there."

"Fine . . . then I'll say good night, Mr. Selby."

He had the feeling she wanted to add something to that, but he couldn't be sure because her expression was masked by the overhead lights shadowing her eyes.

CHAPTER EIGHTEEN

Selby signed the lobby check-out register and pushed through the revolving doors. The streets and sidewalks were slick with rain that reflected the red and green Christmas lights.

The parking mall was several hundred yards long, a broad avenue that ran from City Hall to the church, and was divided by a green belt with graveled crosswalks and playing fountains. The big square was dark except for the Christmas lights and a flashing neon bar sign. A young couple walked past the bar, their arms linking them together in a single, swaying unit.

Turning his collar up against the wind, he walked toward the dark bulk of the church. His footsteps sounded above the leaves rustling in the gutters. Something had distracted Brett, he knew. He looked back at City Hall, and saw that her office lights were still on. He wondered what had caught her attention in the mall. Her face had been worried when she turned from the window. But Selby saw nothing unusual—water splashing in the fountains, a shimmer of neon on parked cars . . .

He passed the church and turned into the narrow street where he was parked. Another sound mingled then with the wind stirring the trees. A car had started up. Glancing the length of the mall, Selby saw exhaust fumes rising from a sedan facing City Hall.

There was a strength about her, he thought, a sense of

conviction that impressed him. People could fake those heated responses, but they couldn't fake the fire he sensed in her.

The Italian, Dom Lorso, had been furious with her. So had Eberle. Had that been an act? Or had she enraged them by ignoring the local power structure? Was that what made her a lightning rod for their attacks? If that was true, she wasn't alone . . . Shana had been a target, and now he was in Slocum's and Thomson's sights too.

The sedan, a black Lincoln, turned on its headlights. For some reason, he thought of Gideen and his son . . .

Dorcas Brett came through the doors of City Hall, belting her raincoat as she walked toward St. Christopher's, her high heels sounding sharply in the silence.

The grassy divider and fountains glittered in the lights of the moving Lincoln. Selby thought of Gideen again, and the black Connie that had tailed him around Muhlenburg and Buck Run . . .

Turning into an access lane, the Continental swung into the street behind Brett, the powerful lights outlining her slim figure. And Davey . . . Davey had told him about the car following Shana and Brett yesterday.

She was fifty yards from him. The Lincoln was about the same distance behind her, but gathering speed, the sound of the motor rising sharply.

Selby ran through the mall and between the trees along the divider, waving desperately at her. But she was blinded by headlights; his warning shouts were lost in the motor's roar.

There was only an instant to consider the angle and to judge his speed and the car's. The angle was wrong, he didn't have the edge, but that was his last reasoned thought; adrenaline swept aside everything then but his instincts and reflexes.

Breaking from the shadow of the trees. Selby threw himself in a headlong dive in front of the car, and just managed to roll out of the way of its wheels and glaring headlights.

His swinging arm struck Brett at the knees. They tumbled across the sidewalk and against a storefront at the same instant the car's fender struck at the flying hem of Selby's raincoat.

Twisted rubber sounded as the Lincoln bounced off the curb. In moments its tail light had flashed from sight beyond the big church.

A man in a leather jacket appeared from the bar. "Up to me, them hit-run assholes get life. You people okay? Saw the whole thing, crazy goddamn fools. You okay?"

"I guess so," Selby called across the mall. He held Brett close to him; she was shaking. "You get a license number?"

"Saw the whole thing, man. They shouldn't be allowed behind a wheel, crazy bastards. Bunch of drunken Puertos or freaked-out kids. The lady all right?"

"Call the cops," Selby shouted at him.

"That's another thing," the man said. "Where's a *cop* when you want him? On their butts in a parked squad somewhere . . ."

He rubbed his face and returned unsteadily to the bar, the closing door cutting off a wail of country music.

Selby helped Dorcas Brett to her feet. He found her handbag and put it in her hands. "Can you walk?"

"I dropped my purse." She was trembling. "My keys are in it."

"It's all right, I found it."

He put an arm around her shoulders and she sagged against him. "I'll take you in my car. Walk slow. Do you feel any pain anywhere?"

"Where did they go?"

"Never mind, they're gone. Lean against me."

Her eyes were unfocused. She put both hands on his arm and clung to him. Selby steadied her and helped her into his station wagon. Climbing in beside her, he saw that the mall was empty, the streets and sidewalks shining in the reflected Christmas lights.

"This isn't my car, Mr. Selby." Her voice was like a worried child's.

"If you feel any pain, tell me," he said.

He stretched her legs slowly, lifting them onto the seat. Her stockings were torn, her kneecaps scraped raw and smudged with dirt. "Okay?" he asked gently.

"I've got to find my car."

"I know where it is, Brett. There's nothing to worry about." He moved her kneecaps gently with his fingertips and watched her face and eyes.

216

"Does that hurt?" She didn't answer. He squeezed her hands. "Can you hear me, Brett?"

"I can't leave my car here." She had begun to stutter slightly.

"Your car is fine. You took a fall, Brett. Try to listen. You fell on the sidewalk, but you're all right. You're not hurt."

He took her wallet from her handbag and checked the address on her driver's license. "I'll drive you home. We can get your car tomorrow, don't worry about it. Just sit back and relax."

"I left my cigarettes in my office," she told him in a plaintive helpless voice. "Goddammit . . ."

"We'll stop on the way and buy a pack."

"They're on my desk, I left them there."

"That's okay. They'll be there tomorrow. Now relax."

She stared through the windshield, her eyes wide and vacant as he pulled away from the curb and drove out of the mall. It seemed he, not she, was the lightning rod for violence. Right from the first, from his visit to his brother, his questions about their father . . .

She lived near the river in a fieldstone house with narrow windows. Her street fronted a park on the Brandywine where the waters forked at the site of an old powder mill. One branch flowed smoothly toward Delaware Bay. The other frothed in a white turbulence beneath the rows of unused milling sheds.

The wind came up noisily when he cut the motor, whistling and snapping through the bare trees. Lights showed from only a few windows.

She said abruptly, "May I have a cigarette now? I'm trying to stop but so far I've only managed to stop carrying them."

He gave her the package of Salems he had bought in an all-night market. "You've seen that Lincoln Continental before, right? You were watching it from your office . . ."

"The book I'm reading," she said, "the one on how to quit smoking, it says that it's a therapeutic"—she stuttered again—"humiliation to ask for something so bad for you . . ."

"Let me help you into your house."

"What did you say? About the car?"

"You've seen it before, right?"

She stiffened suddenly. Her hands tightened in a spasm on the pack of cigarettes, crushing them. She shuddered so that her teeth chattered. An after-shock, he knew from his own game injuries, a recoil, a whiplash of memory . . . .

"Take it easy now," he said. "You're home, it's all right."

"The car hit you, I heard it."

"It didn't hit either of us. We're safe. Can you hear what I'm saying?"

"I couldn't see anything. The lights were in my eyes." She started to cry. "I knew it was going to hit me and I couldn't do anything. It hit you and I don't know where anything is . . ."

Selby put his arm around her and held her close. The car smelled of her perfume and the crushed cigarettes. She was still shaking.

"Okay, okay," he said, and stroked her hair. "We're parked in front of your house, the street is quiet, everything's fine."

He held her until her body relaxed and her breath lost its edge of panic. At last her eyes cleared. She lay against him without moving . . .

"I've seen it before," she said then. "So has Burt. He didn't get a license number."

"I think you'd better forget it for now. You need a compress on your knees and a sleeping pill. Do you want me to go in and turn on the lights? Take a look around?"

"No, thanks, that's all right, Mr. Selby." She straightened up and pushed her hair back from her shoulders. "There are dead-bolts on the doors."

A wind whistled high in the trees and a shudder went through her. "Of course I'd like you to come in. I'm scared silly. I'd appreciate it, Mr. Selby. Thanks." . . .

Her living room ceiling was low and beamed. A fireplace was framed with fieldstone panels and a dark wood mantelpiece. The rear windows looked out on a walled garden, where lamps glowed under a pair of dwarf boxwoods.

He lit the fire while she went upstairs to change. When she came down she asked him if he'd like a drink or a cup of coffee.

"Coffee would be fine."

"It won't take a minute." She went into the kitchen and

Selby looked around at the bookshelves and prints and the miniature rolltop desk at the foot of the stairs. An appointment book
and phone were on the desk. She brought in a tray and put it
on the table at the fireplace and poured two cups of coffee. She
was limping slightly.

"You feel okay?"

"A little stiff but that's all. I'm very grateful to you, Mr.
Selby. What about cream and sugar?"

"Just black, thanks."

She handed him his cup and sat down and crossed her legs.
She had put tape and bandages on her knees. "Sergeant Wilger
noticed that Lincoln following me the day we took Shana back
to Vinegar Hill. I saw it parked in the mall tonight when you
were in my office."

"Why didn't you mention it?"

She shrugged. "It didn't really register, I didn't make a
connection."

"Who besides Lieutenant Eberle knew you'd be working
late tonight?"

"There was no secret about it. I'm usually there when I
have a hearing the next morning."

"Do you know who was in that car?"

"I don't have a clue."

"A friend of mine," Selby said, "spotted a black Lincoln
cruising around Muhlenburg a few days ago. He noticed two
men in it, one had red hair or red sideburns. Does that help you
any?"

"No, I'm afraid it doesn't."

"Does Sergeant Wilger have any ideas?"

She sipped her coffee. "I'm not holding out on you, Mr.
Selby. I hope you believe that, but if you don't there's not much
I can do about it. I understand your anxiety about Shana can
make you suspicious of everyone, but . . . well, we're due in court
at eight A.M. Thanks again for what you did tonight. I'm very
grateful—"

"Do you live here alone?"

She looked surprised. "Yes, why?"

"Just curiosity, I guess. I'd like to know you better."

"In what way?"

"The usual way, I suppose. I've got to trust somebody, you know."

She looked at him with a skeptical smile. "Knowing people doesn't always mean you can trust them. It's just the opposite sometimes."

"I don't want to argue with you, because I don't have anything logical to argue about. I do know I like you. I like you because you were the only person in this goddamn business who bothered to say you were sorry about what happened to Shana." He held up a hand. "Just a minute. I know something about moving objects and getting hit by them. So not even Superwoman could have staged that scene in the mall. But I *don't* trust Slocum and Eberle, and you're working with them, I guess you have to . . . but I know there's something strange about the pressure coming from Thomson . . . It's all the same package, and I guess liking you isn't enough to make me accept it—"

She said angrily, "Goddammit, I don't need a seal of approval from you."

"You were as frightened as Shana about something that morning out at Vinegar Hill. Why, Brett? Why?"

"I was moved and outraged and showed it, I cracked a little. Are you still holding that against me, along with the fact you'd probably prefer a man on this case?"

"That's not it at all." Selby stood and picked up his raincoat.

"Then what the hell *are* you trying to tell me?"

"I've been trying to tell you that I need help, and need it badly."

Her phone rang. She started and looked at her wristwatch. It was after midnight. "Excuse me," she said. She picked up the receiver and said hello twice and waited for a few seconds. "Who's this?" she asked and said hello again.

Shrugging, she put down the phone. "Whoever it was hung up."

Limping slightly, she moved back to the coffee table, poured two more cups of coffee. "How about my calling you Harry to save time?"

"That's fine."

"I think maybe we both need help, Harry," she said.

"Then let's talk." Selby put a small log on the fire and told her about the letter he'd received from Breck, the attorney in Truckee. "Everything that's happened to me and Shana seemed to start with that trip to Summitt to see my brother. . . ."

When he left he drove twice around her block before he started home, slowing down to check the side streets and alleys. An elderly couple was walking a dachshund, but as far as Selby could tell the neighborhood was peaceful and quiet, nothing stirring but the breezes rising from the river.

When he drove by her house the second time, all the windows were dark.

CHAPTER NINETEEN

In the case of the People of the Commonwealth of Pennsylvania against Earl Thomson, sufficient evidence was presented by Deputy District Attorney Brett to fulfill the two basic requirements—that a crime had been committed and that there was reason to believe the defendant, Earl Thomson, had committed the crime.

The fingerprints of the accused at the place of the assault and plaintiff's identification of the accused satisfied those conditions.

The test at this hearing was not whether there was reasonable doubt concerning the complaints. Given the Commonwealth's statutes of criminal procedure, Magistrate Teague was required to entertain only a reasonable belief in the accused's probable guilt.

Counselor Allan Davic was not obliged to enter a plea of any sort—either guilty, not guilty or *nolo contendere.* As a result, Earl Thomson was automatically bound over for further action by the Commonwealth's judiciary system. The defendant was released on his own recognizance.

The trial judge was appointed at a later date by the district's president-judge, J. Matthew Eames.

The Superior Court's current rotation and schedules indicated that the assignment would probably go to Judge Nathan Karr. But President-Judge Eames bypassed Karr and appointed

Judge Desmond Flood to try the Thomson-Selby case.

Judge Flood was surprised by the assignment. He had been a respected jurist in the Superior branch for almost two decades, but since the death of his wife—she had been killed in a private plane crash six years earlier—since then, the judge's attention span had narrowed, and his performance on the bench had steadily deteriorated. His courtroom—Superior Court Nine in East Chester's City Hall—was often referred to as Appellate Nine by exasperated attorneys, an allusion to the frequency with which his decisions were reversed in the higher courts. Flood was amused by his court's nickname, and a local paper's comment that "the State Appellate Division seems forever awash in a Flood of appeals."

A tidily built man with gray hair and still keenly alert eyes, Judge Flood lived with a divorcee named Millie Haynes, twenty years his junior. In her youth Millie had been an accomplished gymnast and drum majorette. The judge's study was now lined with old glossy photographs of his still agile companion on parallel bars and swings, and in white boots and spangled skirts at the head of marching bands.

After his wife's death Flood had got into financial problems as a result of impulsive speculations. Because of this and because of his intermittent drinking and sick leaves, President-Judge Eames had placed him on a reduced schedule; for the past few years, Flood had been given little court work and then only in relatively unimportant cases.

To Flood's relief, Millie Haynes seemed to possess sound financial instincts. After consulting with experts, she had consolidated the judge's debts into one large sum, which was being reduced by monthly payments to a management firm in Camden, New Jersey.

With free time and no financial distractions, Flood busied himself preparing for his retirement. He shopped for the waterfront condo in San Diego that Millie had put a down payment on. To surprise her, the judge bought a yachting cap and a blazer with silver buttons for the Chris-Craft which would be delivered to their marina slip at the end of this court term.

The Commonwealth against Earl Thomson would be Desmond Flood's last trial. On being notified of his assignment,

Judge Flood had instructed his clerk to begin preparations for Thomson's arraignment and to advise counsel for the People and the Defense that His Honor would be available to consider motions at their earliest convenience. He'd go out in a blaze of glory. So to speak.

Several weeks after the preliminary hearing, Earl Thomson was arraigned for a second time in the presence of Superior Court Judge Desmond Flood, where he pleaded not guilty to Commonwealth charges of sundry crimes against the person of the plaintiff, Shana Selby. The full indictment read: "assault and battery by automobile, assault with intent to do great bodily harm, kidnapping, unlawful confinement of a minor, statutory rape, sodomy and oral copulation."

After arguments from both sides, bail was set by Judge Flood at ten thousand dollars, a significant victory for Counselor Davic. The judge ruled against the People's motion for bail of one hundred thousand dollars, holding that this amount would be excessive and inappropriate in consideration of the defendant's good family background and substantial personal financial assets and since Earl Thomson had no prior criminal record. Also, the higher sum could have an inflammatory effect on the jurors—the larger the bail, Judge Flood felt, the worse the criminal might appear in the public eye.

Discovery proceedings were routinely expedited. Medical reports, X-rays, records of conversations between the plaintiff, Nurse Edith Redden and Dr. Merwin Kerr, Trooper Milt Karec's reports and time logs—all these were ordered to be made immediately available to the defense. Names and addresses of witnesses, photographs shown to them, statements of intended prosecution witnesses, police officers' (Slocum, Eberle) taped conversations with Earl Thomson—all conceivably relevant information, had been included in Counselor Davic's discovery motions.

It was ruled by Judge Flood that a psychiatrist, to be defined as a defense "expert witness," would be allowed to examine the plaintiff, under a schedule and circumstances agreeable to the People, but that such inquiries by the "expert witness" be consistent and in accord with the regulations of the Commonwealth statutes.

A panel of jurors would be drawn for the consideration of counsel for the Defense and for the People. After consultation with both attorneys, His Honor set a trial date toward the end of the following month in that Year of Our Lord.

Soon after this, Judge Flood met by appointment with an officer from the Camden management firm which handled his business affairs. Over an excellent lunch the officer informed Flood that, as a result of escalating interest rates, and certain improvement "levies" on his properties, his affairs were not in as good shape as the finance company would like them to be. Certain balloon payments had come due on his condominium and motor launch at the San Diego Conquistador Marina. In response to His Honor's protests, the adviser told him that while Miss Haynes's financial planning had been blameless, it might now be necessary for Judge Flood to meet in person with an officer of the company, the president himself perhaps, to appeal for an extension of his now-due notes and monies.

One night that week, Jerry Goldbirn phoned Harry Selby again from Las Vegas.

"Why didn't you get back to me, for Christ's sake, Harry? I called you weeks ago."

"I tried to, but your secretary said you were out of town or something and wouldn't be free until—"

"Oh, crap, you haven't learned anything. Left your brains scattered around the artificial turf. If you'd told her you were a lawyer with a paternity rap, or an IRS auditor—"

They hadn't talked for several years, not since the memorial service for Sarah, but Goldbirn's voice was as Selby remembered it—accusing and threaded with suspicion.

Selby's deliberate blind-side shot some years ago had done more than put Goldbirn out for the season; it had . . . as Davic suspected . . . saved his reputation and quite probably his life.

Goldbirn was a second-year man out of the Southeastern Conference that season, with an honest flair for case aces and marked decks. But playing poker with professionals on credit had got him into serious debt. They had wanted their money and when Goldbirn couldn't come up with it, they wanted his help in shaving points. Goldbirn had been forced to consider their suggestion, because he believed that a deliberately dropped pass or two was preferable to having his legs broken in an alley.

Selby had solved Goldbirn's problems by putting him on the bench for the year. If he couldn't play, he couldn't affect the score.

With time to maneuver, Goldbirn solved his problems by lending his name as a front for a small casino in Reno and ultimately becoming partnered with his creditors.

"What a rotten, goddamn business," he was saying now, not bothering to mark the transition in mood or subject. "I remember Shana when she was learning to walk. Sarah brought her out to practice once, looked like she'd scooped her out of the bulrushes. Wrapped up in so many clothes that we rolled her around like a practice ball. They got the sonofabitch, right, Harry? Thomson something or other?"

"Earl Thomson, yes. They've got him, but whether they'll *get* him is another matter."

"I was afraid of that. I heard about it before it was in the papers, just some talk in Atlantic City. A radio report on a missing kid. It got back to a friend. He can't swear where he heard it, a pit boss, a stiff on a comp flight, maybe a hooker. But it worried me. They remembered her name, how do you figure that? Who's talking in a gambling casino about a teenaged kid missing a few hours? It don't figure. You know how I keep the roses in my cheeks? I stay away from jai-alai games with Mexican partners, anybody in the Teamsters without callouses . . . anything that don't figure, female impersonators, Irish Catholics voting Republican. What do you need, Harry?"

Selby said, "I'd like you to check out some names, get me a reading on them. There's no reason why a case like this shouldn't have top priority with the cops, right?"

"Something screwy going on, is that it?"

Selby gave him the names. After reading them back Goldbirn said, "One of them turns the tilt light on. The others are John Does to me . . . Slocum, Eberle, the Jesus freak, what'd you say his name was?"

"Oliver Jessup."

"No, but I heard of Lorso. A tough little fucker. If he was in a jai-alai pool, I'd get out of it. Whether he's legitimate, who knows. Because he's got a vowel on the end of his name, don't prove he's not. Remember that stud, Ziggy Carlotto with the Forty-niners? He's a bald-headed Hare Krishna, hangs around the L.A. Airport now, it's a goddamn embarrassment to meet him. Lemme think. Lorso's got an interest in some management hustle in New Jersey that's a country cousin to loan sharking. I know that much. What else?"

Selby told him about Jennifer.

"No address, no last name? What do I do? Put personals up over big cities with sky-writers?"

"Here's the only lead. Jennifer rented a car at the Memphis Airport to drive to Summitt City. That was back in October, the fourteenth or fifteenth. She told me she got a speeding ticket on the way over to Summitt. You could check that, Jerry."

"Yeah, she'd need a driver's license for a renter. Then she'd have to show it to the state trooper. I can check the rental agencies at the airport and the Tennessee State Police. You know that crazy bastard played tackle one season for the Eagles? Baby Joe Minton? His relatives came to all the games, Christers, and the uncles would crowd into the locker room to check out our bladder stems?"

"Vaguely," Selby said.

"Baby Joe's a state senator now in Tennessee. Listen, how's Shana taking this? Shit, what a dumb question. Would it help if I sent her some flowers or alligator boots or something?"

"I'll tell her you asked for her, Jerry."

"Sure, she probably wouldn't remember me anyway. Next time, tell that dumb secretary of mine who you are. If she puts you on hold again, I'll sell her to a guy I know in Morocco who's got a thing for whipped cream and feathers."

There was another call for Selby later that night from Sergeant Ritter at the sheriff's substation.

"I called his wife first, of course, and she thought you should know right away, Mr. Selby," the sergeant said. "They found Casper Gideen's body up in the woods behind Muhlenburg a few hours ago, head half blown away by his own shotgun.

227

Looks like it went off when he was trying to climb a fence or something."

Captain Slocum left City Hall after dark and drove to a public park on the Brandywine. The snack bar was closed for the season, the barbecue pits covered with canvas tarps, but one bundled-up group sat around a redwood table with sandwiches and coffee and beer. A young girl in a ski sweater played a guitar with her mittens on and laughed at the muffled music she was making.

Slocum took a drink from a flask in his glove compartment, popped a mint in his mouth and strolled past the picnic tables and down a slope to the river bank. He waited there until he saw the headlights of a Cadillac turn into the park and stop beside his car. When the lights went off, Slocum walked back and joined Allan Davic.

They greeted one another casually. Standing between their two cars, they were concealed in shadows. From a distance they could hear the guitar's smothered chords.

"You understand," Davic said, "this is just a formality," and proceeded to pat down the policeman carefully and expertly, even checking his crotch and running a hand under his shirt and over his hairy chest and stomach.

Davic then opened his overcoat and unbuttoned his vest and allowed the captain to frisk him with equal care for microphones and wires.

They got into the front seat of the attorney's Cadillac and Davic said, "We won't meet again, Captain, or phone each other. I'll have to tear you apart on the stand, because of the defendant's taped meeting with you and Eberle, but that's the last time I'll talk to you in person. When you have information, get it to me through George Thomson."

"I don't like that," Slocum shook his head with deliberate emphasis. "That brings it too close to Earl. I know Earl, you see. Know him better than you ever will 'cause he's an actor and he'll play a part for you. But I pulled his ass out of a crack over in New Jersey a while back. He was in college, a military school full of imitation grunts to my mind, fake soldier boys. Earl worked over some black cunt who'd apparently asked for it.

228

There was some fuss, didn't amount to piss-ants, but I had to lean hard on some characters. Afterward Earl suggested we shake 'em down because they'd saved his fucking ass but left themselves vulnerable. He's a greedy bastard . . . When I've got something, I'll park my blue Olds in Eberle's slot at the Hall. You watch for that. Then you'll get a call. No names. I'll set up the drop."

Davic said, "You've already earned my gratitude, Captain. What you've told me about Earl is very significant."

"That he wanted to shaft the people who'd bailed him out?"

"That's important to know, Captain. If we save him, he's likely to do the same to us . . . we'll want to keep that in mind . . . But that's not the immediate problem. Thomson and Dom Lorso are too complacent. Winning is a habit with them. They have money, power and a friend in need on the bench. They figure that's enough. Usually they'd be right. But in a rape case, with a stormy character like Selby and an unreliable defendant, there's always the chance of a live grenade rolling into the court-room. We need all the insurance we can get."

Slocum chewed on another mint, filling the warm interior of the car with its fragrance. Someone with a transistor radio blaring walked behind their cars and on toward the shuttered snack bar.

"That brings us to the point, sir," Slocum said. "The insurance you want to buy.

"You can depend on us, Captain."

"I also depend on Ex-Lax and antifreeze in the winter. But not to pay my bills."

"I think you know we'll take care of you. Thomson's a generous man."

"He can afford to be, can't he?"

Davic removed an envelope from his briefcase and handed it to the captain. "That's a down payment. Money isn't our problem, and it won't be yours. I guarantee that. Any other help you want or need, now or in the future, will also be available."

Slocum didn't count the money. He put the envelope away and took out a notebook which he opened under the dash light.

"I can't find anything more on Selby's connection with Goldbirn," he told Davic. "Could be he simply did the Jew boy a favor. No evidence he got paid off for it. The house and farm

229

is clear, but Selby used money his mother-in-law left, and a couple of pro-bowl bonuses. About the prosecutor, she went to school at Bryn Mawr, got her law degree at Yale. Big deal. She was married for a year or so, then divorced. Her ex-husband lives in Cleveland, designs furniture. He remarried. Her father's a retired accountant, lives in Florida. She's got two sisters in Maine."

"How long since her divorce?"

"Five years."

"She didn't remarry?"

"No."

"She lives alone?"

Slocum nodded. "Nice place over near the river."

"Any men in her life?"

"I get your drift, or what you're looking for. She dates guys occasionally. They could be beards, but there's no obvious butch pals."

"No Commie causes, radical affiliations, that sort of thing?"

Slocum put his notebook away. "No, but something funny hit me when I was checking out her schools. I checked around St. David's and Bryn Mawr on the Main Line, cops and newspapers, gave 'em a bullshit story about looking for who assaulted Shana Selby. I found a local story going back nine years about our lady DA. She was beat up one night. Happened in the college gym. She was swimming late all alone in the pool. Some stud sneaked into the locker room and waited for her. Guy name of Toby Clark. He was slated the next morning on an assault charge. Clark worked at the school, a handyman. I smelled something." Slocum looked at the lawyer, the dark light flickering on his smile. "There was no follow-up story in the papers. I checked records. The charges were dropped. But Clark got fired."

"What interested you about that?"

"Hard to say. Call it my cop's nose at work. But maybe there was some kind of shit going on with her and that classy ladies' school."

"I'll put my people on it," Davic said. "They're from New York. They're brothers, Ben and Aron Cadle. Very discreet but effective. If you need anything from them, don't hesitate."

"Tell 'em to find that Toby Clark character to start with."

230

Slocum patted the money envelope in his pocket. "Good talking to you, but from now on wait till you see my car in Eberle's slot."

Stepping from the car, Slocum closed the door respectfully. Crossing behind the Cadillac, he waited beside his Olds until Davic drove off, then lit a cigar and listened to guitar music drifting on the frosty air. The girl was playing "Red River Valley." Her friends were singing too. Slocum loved that song . . . "The maiden who loved you sooo true . . ." Damn . . .

From the darkness of the shuttered snack bar Eberle joined him. "Nice night," the lieutenant said. "Good, healthy weather."

"Cold, too cold for me." Slocum blew on the tip of his cigar. "You get it all?"

"Every word." Eberle patted the wireless receiver bulging below his holstered police special. Slocum nodded and gave him the suction-mike he had removed from the rear bumper of Davic's Cadillac.

"Big city lawyer," Eberle said. "Big fucking deal."

Slocum said: "Big cities, bigger buildings, bigger problems, bigger jackasses. Erase my voice from that tape and bring it by tomorrow night when you pick me up for bowling. Good night to you, Gus."

"One thing, Captain." Eberle rubbed a hand across his wet lips. "It got out of hand. I only meant to scare the piss and wind out of that piney—"

"I didn't even hear that, Gus," Slocum said, and got in his car. "Pick me up around seven tomorrow. League title's up for grabs and them Knights of Pythias are tough. We better be lucky. I shit you not, Gus."

CHAPTER TWENTY

Neighbors in Little Tenn brought covered dishes to Casper Gideen's trailer, noodle and hamburger casseroles, meat loaves and pans of biscuits. A man whose left hand had been ground to a stump in a sawmill accident forty years ago came by to dicker for the coon hounds.

Gideen's sons were in the kitchen of the trailer with a TV glowing silently. A sleeting rain struck the windows. In the kennel run, the redbones were barking.

Lori Gideen sat in the front room near a squat iron stove backed by aluminum panels. Rows of brick formed a hearthstone. Maple logs were stacked beside it, short and thick and tinder-dry. It was the careful way Casper had done everything, Selby thought, the logs cut to fit the stove exactly, and aged so long that starting a fire was no more trouble for Lori than striking the match.

She had called after Sergeant Ritter. "State Police claim it was an accident," she told him. "Gun wasn't on safe, and went off under his chin. He must have tripped on something in the dark."

Lori Gideen was tall and thin with a solemn girlish face and red-knuckled hands now lying open on her knees.

She said, "Casper set a store by you, Mr. Selby. He'd be pleased you'd come by."

"I tried to get in touch with him these past few days."

"I know. He wasn't here."

"When did you talk to him last?"

She hesitated and wiped her flushed cheeks. Her eyes were dry but strangely enlarged, as if she were straining to see everything very clearly. "I talked to him yesterday, Mr. Selby, after breakfast, it was. Casper called from a gas station."

"He wasn't staying here?"

"Stayed where he pleased, you know that."

"Lori, your husband and I were friends. Can you tell me what he was worried about?"

"That was his business. Didn't do to ask. You know how Casper was, you better'n most maybe. Didn't believe in explaining."

One of Gideen's sons came into the living room, Eli, who was sixteen, with wide shoulders and thick blond hair. "My ma is worn out now, Mr. Selby." Selby remembered that Shana had once made Eli a woolen skating cap for Christmas. "We'd just as soon be with our own selves now."

"I understand, I'll be going, Eli. But your father didn't trip over a shotgun like some goddamn fool out with a gun for the first time. Anybody who says he wouldn't put his gun on safe before climbing a fence is a liar. His death wasn't an accident, Eli."

Lori's hands were locked together now, the knuckles strained and white.

Eli Gideen said, "We're obliged to you for coming by, Mr. Selby."

"Mrs. Gideen," Selby said, "if I can be of any help at all . . ."

"Thank you kindly for that."

"I flooded my car," Selby said, "so I'll have to let the engine dry out for a while. I'm parked on Fairlee. If I can't get it started, I'd appreciate it if I could come back and use the phone."

"Phone is here," Eli said.

The station wagon was cold, the windows steamed, and the sleeting rain making a metallic clatter on the roof and fenders. Selby started the car and turned on the heater and wipers. The blacktop materialized as the rubber blades swept the windshield

233

clean. The road curved through ground mists toward Pyle's Corners and Muhlenburg.

"Casper's boys won't talk to anyone." Selby turned and looked at Dorcas Brett. She wore a brown wool coat with caped shoulders. Her face was white with the cold except for sharp points of color in her cheeks.

"Will Mrs. Gideen talk to us?"

"She knows I'm waiting. Maybe she's angry enough and hurt enough to tell us whatever she knows."

The hum of the motor mingled with the slap of the windshield wipers. The white scar on Selby's cheek caught a reflected light as he glanced at the rear-view mirror.

They had made progress during the last ten days, finding links that raised further questions. General Taggart who owned Vinegar Hill also commanded Camp Saliaris, the chemical corps installation near Summitt City. Lieutenant General Adam Taggart, from an old Pennsylvania family, had once owned the hundreds of acres along the river which had been developed into the exclusive community known as Brandywine Lakes. The general had sold the land to a holding company a dozen years before.

Sergeant Burt Wilger had got hold of several curricula programs and relevant yearbooks from Rockland College. (He had persuaded a local librarian to request the material from the school as an "aid to the library's educational reference program.") Derek Taggart's class photograph was on the same page as Earl Thomson's. A handsome young man, nineteen or twenty then, young Taggart had a challenging, mocking smile. Derek was the general's son. He had been an editor of the school paper, and nicknamed "Ace" during his years at Rockland.

They waited for ten or fifteen minutes in the station wagon. Occasionally, Selby glanced at the rear-view mirror.

"That wasn't easy for you, was it?" Brett said.

"It wasn't easy for Lori Gideen, either."

"I understand that . . . I was thinking of you."

Selby shrugged and rubbed the steam from the rear-view mirror. He remembered Gideen when they'd been together at the kennel run, Casper talking about this dying pear tree, its last extravagant death crop and then the swift, final decline . . .

Selby said, "If Casper trusted you and thought he owed

234

you, he'd cut off his arm for you before you could ask. He wanted to help me." He rubbed the mirror again. "Yes, it was hard, talking to Lori and Casper's sons."

She pulled off her glove and put a hand against his face, then traced the scar on his cheek. "That hurt badly when it happened, Harry. You told me it did . . ."

Selby moved her hand away from his face.

"Do you mind that?"

"No, but I think you've got a point to make."

"It healed over, Harry, it doesn't hurt anymore. That happens."

"And has everything in your past healed over?" he asked her. "We all go through things, marriages, break-ups with friends, the ice cream cone falling in the gutter."

"I'm all right, I think."

"That scene at the college swimming pool, that must have stuck with you over the years. If I'm saying something you don't want me to, I'll shut up. But it was more than imagining piranha fish in the water that night. That's what Davey thinks, by the way."

"It was a long time ago," she said carefully. "I was frightened, all right, but I'm over it. I'd just as soon leave it at that, Harry."

"Okay. We'll leave it at that."

Lori Gideen appeared in the rear-view mirror then, hurrying toward them with one of Casper's old hunting jackets pulled around her shoulders. She climbed into the rear of the station wagon and when Selby introduced her to Brett, nodded shyly.

"The boys is worse than Casper ever was . . ." Her voice was low, impersonal. "Casper was my husband, ma'am. He and Mr. Selby went hunting a lot. They was good friends. He used to say that Mr. Selby here had enough sense to listen."

Looking steadily at Selby, the rain on her girlish face mingled with her tears. "The boys don't want me to talk to anybody, they think any stranger could be the devil, just like Casper did. But I'm going to talk 'cause you'll listen, Mr. Selby. Casper knew Goldie Boy and Barby Kane's momma was together that night your little girl got hurt. That's what started the talk. Others knew about it but wasn't saying, him being a preacher."

"Did Casper know where they were?"

235

"It was what he was trying to find out. But two nights ago, Barby Kane and her momma, Coralee, they up and left Little Tenn. A big car came for them in the middle of the night. Two in the morning, didn't even take all their clothes, and Barby's cat, it's whining around everywhere for food."

"Casper knew where they went?"

"The car took 'em to the airport in Philadelphia. He found out that much. The same night they left, Casper packed some food and his shotgun in the truck and drove off. Told me not to pay any mind if anybody came around asking for him. Just to say he'd gone hunting, even if it was the police. He wasn't afraid, you know Casper, Mr. Selby, but he didn't want anyone bothering me or his boys."

She pushed open the door, letting in a spray of wind and rain. "He's gone, but he set a store by you, and he'd want me to tell you all this, never mind the boys. I thank you again for coming around, Mr. Selby."

Lori Gideen ran clumsily through the mud toward the entrance to Little Tenn, slipping occasionally in her heavy rubber boots. The trailers had their lights, the small windows gleaming with forlorn cheer through the gathering darkness.

Selby drove on through the rain into Muhlenburg. Turning at Pyle's Corners, he parked a half block from Goldie Boy Jessup's storefront church. The name was spelled out in gilt letters on the glass window—"Tabernacle of the Golden Flame." A large room beyond the ornate sign was brightly illuminated, crowded with men and women huddled on benches facing Goldie Boy, who stood above them gesturing and shouting from a raised platform. Speakers carried his voice to an adjoining parking lot. Cars and trucks lined up there, dogs in the rear of pickups, howling at the pounding rain and Goldie's amplified voice.

A spotlight glowed behind his head, framing him in a yellow haze. The preacher wore a blue shirt with a buttoned-up collar and khaki work trousers.

His eyes were large and clear with tiny blue pupils and whites as milky and soft-looking as the whites of eggs. When Goldie Boy preached, shouting and swinging his arms around his head, the eyes became blank and glazed, like empty globes in his pale face.

Selby rolled down his window; it was like turning on a blaring radio. Goldie Boy's voice surged around them.

"Do you know what the Lord Jesus wants from us?" What our Lord Jesus wants from you and me? Tell me you know what Jesus, the Lamb of God, *wants!*"

In the trucks and cars, the drivers leaned on their horns. The dogs barked furiously.

"You *know* what He wants! The Lord Jesus wants us to *share* His sweet, holy spirit, *share* His love—He doesn't want us to keep His blessed love only for *ourselves*—He wants us to *share* that love with even the worst sinners—with whores and thieves and jades, even the bitch in red with her fragrant thighs clasped in lust about the flanks of the white beast of the Apocalypse. . . ."

Goldie Boy's voice rose with the pure anger of conviction. "The lewd, the immoral, the perverted—we must share the Lord Jesus with *them*. Jezebels, devil's whores with painted faces, seductive women and yes, *children*, thrusting themselves at God-fearing family men, inflaming them with their exposed and perfumed flesh . . ."

Selby cranked up the window, but they could still hear the horns and dogs.

"Praise the good Lord," Brett said wearily, "for saving those nice men from those little fiends." She lit a cigarette. "Do you know Freud's phrase, the polymorphic perverse?"

Selby studied the buildings on all sides of Pyle's Corners. "No," he said. "Afraid it wasn't in our play book."

"What? . . . oh, I get it . . . well, anyway, Sigmund believed and wrote that women have a genetic tendency toward victimization, that their universal desire is to be roughly and forcefully handled in, you should forgive the expression, acts of sexual congress. I'm quoting Freud, Harry. I'm *quoting*." She ground out her cigarette in the dashboard ashtray. "End of speech. His and mine. Let's get a cup of coffee."

"I heard you . . . I also noticed something." He pointed to the Tabernacle of the Golden Flame. "Anyone at those windows would have a clear view of Earl Thomson and Shana that night."

"But the church was dark," she reminded him. "There were no services. The only witness was Mrs. Swabel across the street and she only saw Shana."

237

"I know," Selby said, "but the preacher's church is the best seat in the house. Casper Gideen was checking out the preacher. And Casper's got his head blown off."

Later that night, Selby looked again through his father's pictures and diaries, the familiar yellowing pages and snapshots. "The chief and the major," his father had written, "they run things, they say *jump*. But we'll pay for it." He felt a fresh pang at the look of his father in his army uniform, tall and strong, a powerful, scowling young man, so very damn young at the beginning . . .

Selby heard Blazer barking in the pen beside his doghouse. He picked up a leather lead and went outside. As he walked toward Blazer's barking, he thought of Claud Lissard. He wondered why. Maybe because Brett had touched his scarred cheek, except she did it as a reminder that things healed, that pain diminished, in time. Coincidentally Selby paid off the Frenchman the same summer evening the long distance phone call had come in from the recruiters at Penn. ("You cut it, son, or *they* cut you. It's as simple as that. You get four years of the best coaching anywhere, pro sets and game plans, a shot at the national championship, then post-season bowl games.") That call triggered the explosion, which in turn made Selby realize how much his grandfather had needed someone like Claud Lissard to discipline—no, to punish and humiliate his daughter's bastard son . . .

Blazer stood stiff-legged and bristling, barking at something beyond the trees that bordered Fairlee Road. Snapping the lead to the big shepherd's collar, Selby started down the trail toward the fence line.

As Blazer jerked and pulled him along, the strain on Selby's arm reminded him again of Lissard . . . The Frenchman was round and fat, but his big, sagging stomach was deceptive; it was, in fact, hard as a board. The challenge Claud offered Harry, and which his grandfather always put aside his newspaper to watch, was simple enough; the Frenchman would order Harry to take a two-handed grip on his wide belt, after which Claud would swell his stomach muscles until Harry's hands were clamped helplessly between hard leather and muscled flesh. The object was to pull free, but while a young Harry Selby struggled, the Frenchman would dance about the room, hopping from one foot to the other like a trained bear, swinging the boy from side to side until his arms were almost jerked from their sockets. There was no humor in this game, and never had been, in spite of the booming laughter that filled out Claud's cheeks. The last time they played, Harry had tried to settle for a stand-off; Claud was older then, almost forty, and not as powerful as he had been in his younger days. But he muttered under his breath about Selby's leaving for college, saying, "You think you're too good for us, but I'll show you, like I always . . ."

Selby's own anger, which was deeper than he realized, began to rise as he thought of the hot sun on the spur track and the fight he'd had to keep the name Selby and the way his grandfather stressed the name when he had to use it with strangers—*Sel-by*, two spaced syllables, the last one emphasized and always attended by a mildly sardonic question mark. "And here's little Harry—Harry Sel-*by* . . . ?" . . .

Harry had spun Claud Lissard around in dizzying circles that last night, finally hurling him into the adjoining parlor, where Lissard crashed into the ancient upright piano. That ended it forever with the Frenchman, and with his life in Davenport, Selby realized, because his grandfather had stared down at his own pale, freckled hands for a moment, his expression oddly wistful, withdrawn, and then had deliberately returned to his paper without another glance at his tall grandson. In those moments Harry had looked at his own hands, young, strong, and suddenly felt he could take care of himself with the bullies of the world. He had never before loved his father so much. It was a damn good feeling. . . .

There were two cars parked on Fairlee Road, and Selby saw their lights and heard men's voices through the trees. He walked through the woods to the fence, but they must have heard Blazer's growling challenge because the cars started up and drove off, leaving behind only the acrid smell of exhaust fumes.

Selby examined the shoulders of Fairlee Road with his flashlight. This was where Shana had been struck by Thomson's car, and someone had been at work with a rake; the heavy grass was combed for dozens of yards on both sides of the road and deep grooves furrowed the hard ground.

239

Selby stood with a hand on the panting dog's collar, wondering who it was who'd been searching around here in the dark at the scene of Shana's accident. Which wasn't the important question, he decided, walking back through the woods. The real question was—what had they been looking for?

CHAPTER TWENTY-ONE

The night before Earl Thomson's trial, George Thomson and Dom Lorso took an electronically monitored elevator to the penthouse in one of Philadelphia's tallest and newest high-rise apartment buildings.

Marvin Quade escorted them into a drawing room where modern paintings and tall lamps were framed by an electric glitter of the skyline beyond glassed-in terraces.

In a dress the color of ivory, Jennifer Easton stood at a bar, adding white mint to a pitcher of brandy and cracked ice. Above her blond hair hung an arrangement of shining discs and triangles, swaying in balanced patterns. Behind the bar a checkerboard mural was illuminated in chiseled precision by gallery lights which sparkled on her bare shoulders.

She greeted the men with a pleasantly vague smile and poured herself a drink. Quade stood in front of the glass-walled terrace where his bulk partially blocked out the city's lights.

Simon Correll came in from the adjoining study, and Jennifer excused herself and took her pitcher of brandy stingers upstairs.

"Sit down, gentlemen, sit down." Correll's expression was tight as he watched Jennifer stroll along the railed balcony above the drawing room.

Thomson and Dom Lorso settled themselves in leather chairs at a mirrored coffee table. Lorso lit a cigarette and looked for an ashtray. He caught Quade's eye, but Quade frowned and shook his head. Lorso dropped the match on the carpet.

Correll poured himself a whiskey and added a splash of Evian water. "Would you gentlemen like a drink?"

"Not for me, thanks." Thomson glanced at his watch. "Perhaps we should get right down to it, Mr. Correll."

Correll said, "I wouldn't have asked you here, Thomson, if I didn't plan to get right down to it. I'm sorry if this meeting has inconvenienced you."

Lorso tapped a length of ash onto the coffee table. "We got some considerations with the trial, Mr. Correll. Mr. Thomson meant we've still got things to arrange. The way Davic wants it set up—"

"Excuse me, Mr. Lorso," Correll said, "but I understand exactly what Mr. Davic requires. I intend to tell you how to satisfy those requirements, considering certain other priorities. The trial is important, yes. Clearing Mr. Earl Thomson of those charges is a first order of business. But that has to be done within the legal framework. There can be no question of outside pressures. We are—I speak of Harlequin, Summitt City, the Correll Group—a goldfish bowl that is not made of bulletproof glass. We are vulnerable and can be hurt, by public opinion and by the government."

A phone in the study rang and Quade went to answer it. Correll looked at his watch, knowing from the special chiming alert that it was Mount Olivet. A Snow Virgin was on the bar beside a bottle of Fundador. Correll picked up the globe and rocked it gently. The motion caused a miniature storm of white flakes to fly about the blue and gold figure of the Madonna.

Quade returned and said, "It's Brother Fabius, Mr. Correll. He's talking to Miss Jennifer on her extension."

Correll put his drink down, excused himself and went into his study. Dom Lorso moved closer to Thomson, lowered his voice and said, "This is bullshit, Giorgio. Listen to me. He says leave it to a jury. But who knows what a goddamn jury's going to do? Get a fucking bunch of coloreds, they might stick it to Earl because he's wearing a clean shirt. I know how to protect him, and you do, too, Giorgio."

"No, forget that."

"Shit, you know I'm talking sense."

"And I'm telling you, *forget* it."

Lorso sat roiling with frustration. Giorgio hadn't been himself since the warrant was served on Earl, he'd lost either his
guts or his nerve or his brains, maybe all three. His skin was
gray, the usual healthy brown color washed out of it. Lorso
knew what they had to do, but he couldn't force Giorgio to face
it. There was no foolproof safety for Earl, and even more important, no satisfaction for any of them as long as Selby and his
bitch daughter were walking around with lies on their lips. One
of their family had been called a rapist, a torturer, an animal
who'd tear a girl to pieces, do sick, filthy things to her, not able
to screw her like a man should . . .

Correll returned and continued the discussion where he
had left it. "Senator Lester's investigation is confined to Harlequin Chemicals and I *don't* intend to give him the opportunity
to expand it."

"If you'll excuse me," Lorso said, "I don't see the connection. What I see is that somebody has Earl Thomson's balls in
his fist and is about to bust them wide open. My idea is to stop
that from happening. You mind explaining what that's got to do
with the senator?"

Correll said, "Mr. Lorso, a computer study by our people
in Switzerland projected that if I explained all my decisions, it
would cost our companies about half a million dollars a day in
wasted time alone. So I'll tell you only this. An orderly trial is
what I intend to have. I will not tolerate any irrelevant publicity. Do you understand what I'm telling you?"

Spots of color flared up in Lorso's gray cheeks. He lit another cigarette. "Sure, I understand you, the words are clear
enough and I'm no dummy, Mr. Correll, but maybe I don't
happen to see it that way."

Thomson said, "Let it go, Dom, let it go."

"Mr. Lorso," Correll said quietly, "I didn't ask you here to
debate these issues. This meeting isn't intended to be an exercise
in democracy."

"Then what's the point of me saying anything?"

"None whatsoever. I want you to *listen*. Democracy em-
braces moral indulgence, a tolerance of wasteful eccentric diver-

sity in human activity. Such is largely responsible for the condition we see around us in the world today. I lecture, I'm sorry . . . but you must understand. Violence is not a solution, it is a symptom of the disease that brings feelings of shame, futility, helplessness. Violence is a reaction to personal inadequacy, Mr. Lorso, an explosion of personal impotence. *We* won't resort to violence of any sort, because we are *not* helpless, we are *not* impotent. We'll proceed as I've outlined, *within* the legal system."

"But what if worst comes to worst? Supposing those assholes on the jury decide to nail the boy. What's the good then of this stuff about the legal system?"

Correll picked up the Snow Virgin, his eyes narrowing as he studied the swirling flakes. His mother had painted the eyes a dark blue, with streaks of pale gold at the centers. At certain angles the figurine's expression was solemn; in others, the Virgin smiled at him. The second Snow Virgin she'd made was having some finishing touches. It was at Mount Olivet; his mother kept it in her room there . . .

"The legal system," he said to Dom Lorso, "will work for us, you can *depend* on it."

Lorso shrugged. "Maybe, but what's wrong with a little insurance?"

Correll slammed the Snow Virgin down on the bar. "Dammit, will you please shut up and *listen?*"

Quade moved forward, his body tense, like an attack dog reacting to the anger in Correll's voice.

Thomson's face was a sickly gray. Even Lorso's little monkey fingers, yellow with nicotine, shook slightly as he sucked on his cigarette.

Correll said, "The worst cannot and *will* not come to the worst. But that requires care and discretion from all of us. *In seriatim*, there will be irrefutable contradictions of each and every piece of alleged evidence the prosecution presents. I'm aware of the role Judge Flood will play. I know to the dollar his indebtedness to you, Mr. Lorso. I'm also aware of the conclusions that will be reached by Dr. Leslie Clemens. But one more stupid act of violence—I will refer once and only once to the death of a man named Gideen—one more such mistake could compromise the trial, and everything the Correll Group has been attempting to accomplish for years."

When he stopped speaking the silence deepened in the large, glowing room. He stared out at the city's lights flashing beyond the terraces, his fingers stroking the globe embracing the Snow Virgin.

Lorso thought with relief that Correll knew nothing about Aron and Ben Cadle, Davic's "investigators" from New York. There had been no police report on the attempted hit-run in the East Chester mall. Slocum had assured him of that. Which meant the DA and Selby had figured it was a drunk behind the wheel, or some pot-head kid . . .

Lorso also had an uneasy feeling about Quade. He had heard things about the bodyguard he didn't quite believe. Which was why he tested him by lighting a cigarette and dropping a match on the carpet, because that was the kind of thing you had to do, not just challenge your enemies but challenge your fears about them.

After a moment Correll shrugged and said, "Perhaps I'm at fault for not advising you gentlemen of the complexity of our problems." His tone was almost amiable; it was apparent that the flashpoint of his anger had cooled. His glance at his watch was a gesture of courteous dismissal.

After they had gone Correll went upstairs to Jennifer's bedroom. The walls and furniture were done in red, the bed scattered with tasseled black pillows.

The doors leading to the terraces were open and Jennifer stood outside in the fine rain, arms held in a graceful circle above her head, pirouetting with a slow, deliberate elegance. She had changed into gray leotards and tied her long hair back with a dark ribbon, and was smiling dreamily, eyes closed against the misting winds.

When she became aware of Correll watching her, she lost her concentration and balance and stumbled slightly, catching herself with a quick hand on the terrace railing.

She smiled at him and her eyes were as blank and merry as a doll's.

Correll led her back into the warm bedroom. After a dizzying glance at the balconies below Jennifer's room, and the sheer
drop beyond them to the street and sidewalk, he closed and
locked the terrace doors.

He helped her out of her soaking jersey and gently eased
her onto the bed, straightened her legs and smoothed her tangled hair on the pillow.

"I don't like you out on the terrace at night, and I don't like
you talking to the good brother when you've been drinking," he
said. "What did Fabius want?"

She laughed at him. "You were listening, Simon. I heard
you pick up the phone. I could hear you breathing. The way
some people breathe is . . . like fingerprints, Simon." She
laughed again, her eyes closing, the lashes dark and wet on her
pale cheeks.

"I listened, Jennifer, because I thought there might be news
of my mother. I have a notion Bishop Waring would prefer you
to tell me if her condition is worsening."

"No, Simon, it wasn't that. Your mother is sleeping very
quietly. Everybody is asleep now."

"What did Fabius want to talk to you about?"

"Like little mice, that's what you told me, and I thought
that was rather dear. Little laboratory mice." She moved her
head restlessly. "Fabius has some shells, Simon, tiny pink and
blue shells from Portugal. He's making a rosary for your
mother. He wanted to know if the first and last decades should
be made with the pink shells . . ."

She was breathing slowly and deeply, the muscles of her flat
stomach rising and falling in gentle contractions.

"Or what, Jennifer?" Correll asked her.

"Or the blue shells, of course, darling."

"What does it matter? Did Fabius tell you what in the name
of Christ difference it makes?"

"I forget, Simon."

Correll took off her slippers, the thin leather soles damp and
slick from the rain. She murmured drowsily as he untied her
cord belt and slowly slipped the tight, clinging leotards from her
legs, which were white and slack and vulnerable against the
flaming red covers.

As he lay beside her slim, warm body, and studied her face

for a moment, Correll was moved by the stillness in Jennifer's expression and her lack of awareness of him, of everything around them, of everything in the world. He was grateful for the promise of oblivion she offered him, that welcoming and sustaining darkness. Reaching across her quiet body, he turned off the lights.

CHAPTER TWENTY-TWO

The day of the trial was bitterly cold. The first shoots of spring, spiky tips of skunk cabbage, were buried under a foot of snow in the bottoms of drained quarries and mica pits. The weather had been unsettling, gray days with clouds like torn and dirty curtains, followed by drenching rain and then sunlight glistening in the trees.

Casper Gideen's body was shipped back to his hometown of Ahashie, South Carolina. East Chester police had accepted a coroner's verdict that the deceased met his death "as the result of accidentally self-inflicted gunshot wounds."

The Selby family attended the service at the Muhlenburg Baptist Church. They sat in the pew behind Lori Gideen and her sons. The Selbys' floral wreath of field daisies and violets and pussy willows had been chosen by Shana.

On the morning of the trial, Shana was in the foyer when her father came downstairs. She wore a blue sweater, a gray flannel skirt and polished brown loafers. He kissed her cheek and thought that her hair smelled like flowers left in a cold room. She pulled on a coat and gloves while Selby drank a cup of coffee.

"I know Miss Brett filled you in on everything," he told her, "but remember, the jury is just a group of ordinary, everyday citizens."

"She told me how normal they were," Shana said, "except for two of those big women wearing the born-again buttons."

The jury consisted of seven whites, three blacks and two Puerto Ricans, eight men and four women. Three of the group were on welfare. All but one, at Mr. Kahn, said they believed in a Supreme Being. Their average age was thirty-four and their mean educational level that of eleventh grade.

"The important thing," Selby said, as they went out to the car, "is to keep in mind there's nothing to be afraid of."

"You must think there is," she said, "because you keep telling me that. I know Earl Thomson's going to swear I'm lying, daddy. And I know Miss Brett is worried about Dr. Clemens, but I think he's an old *fool.* "

She had spent a total of three hours with the psychiatrist, meeting with him in Dorcas Brett's office. According to a court ruling, no tapes had been made of their conversations, and the defense expert's notes were subject to review by both Dorcas Brett and the Selbys' doctor, Merwin Kerr.

After the charges were read into the record, Dorcas Brett opened for the People.

In Selby's opinion, her opening statement had an inconclusive effect. Or at least an ambivalent one. She presented her arguments logically enough, but as far as Selby could tell they failed to generate much sympathy among the jurors. Maybe it was because her manner and appearance were so at variance with the decor, the atmosphere, of Judge Flood's courtroom, which was colonial in tone—high-ceilinged, spacious, with tall narrow windows, white plastered walls and random-width pine floors. On those shining planks, Brett's high heels sounded with a light but insistent clatter, an almost irreverent or impertinent sound in a male atmosphere suggested by brass inkwells, rugged beams and a large mural depicting Quaker merchants and Indian chiefs greeting one another with upraised arms on the banks of the Brandywine. Cornfields and turkeys in flight stretched off beyond them to infinite blue skies.

Brett wore a dark skirt with a pale, pleated blouse, wooden bracelets and strings of gold chains. Worse perhaps, to judge from the glances Selby noticed from a large woman in the jury box, Dorcas's body was trim, her legs shapely and she had what Tishie always referred to with resignation as "Gentile bones," by which the old lady meant narrow hips and slim wrists and ankles.

The courtroom was crowded, with marshals posted at the exists. Near the witness stand was a roped-off section for the press and TV cameras. A spray of ferns, a crystal carafe and drinking glass stood on Judge Flood's high bench. His bailiff, a thin black man in uniform, shared a desk below with the court stenographer, a middle-aged woman who wore a green eyeshade.

Shana sat alone at the People's table, facing the jurors and Judge Flood. At the Defense table were Earl Thomson, Allan Davic and two of his associate attorneys. Behind them in the spectators' gallery were George Thomson and Dom Lorso.

Earl Thomson leaned comfortably back in his chair, tilting the front legs an inch or so from the floor. His clothes were conservatively informal, a dark sports jacket and a white shirt with a maroon tie. He seemed gravely interested, observing the jurors with courteous attention.

Selby glanced once at Earl Thomson's hands, but decided it would be easier to concentrate on the proceedings if he ignored those powerful wrists and fingers and the burning images he associated with them.

Allan Davic listened to Dorcas Brett with an intensity that Selby recognized and understood—a player studying an opponent for evidence of tension or nerves.

But there was no uncertainty in Brett's attitude, which was Selby thought; her manner was perhaps too confident to gain sympathy from the jurors. Who knew?

She spoke rapidly, and at least used no speaker's tricks, no "charming" mannerisms, framing well-crafted sentences, which were seldom relieved by the simple errors of common speech, broken rhythms, fumblings for words, or any other folksy lapses.

After listening a while, Selby began to see that her formality and crispness came not from overconfidence but from something just the opposite. She was simply nervous.

Brett drew a precise outline of the Commonwealth's case

against Earl Thomson, which included his fingerprints in the garage at Vinegar Hill, and the presence of his car in the driveway there. These facts, together with the defendant's "as we will show, outright lies to Detective Captain Walter Slocum," formed the circumstantial basis of the People's case.

"But this is only the physical evidence," Brett added. "This evidence is weighable, measurable, but there is still a more conclusive kind of evidence, that of an eyewitness. The plaintiff is that witness. Shana Selby has identified Earl Thomson—without reservation or qualification—as the man who assaulted her, held her against her will and raped her. That young girl had five agonizing hours to memorize every feature of his face, his coloring, his physique."

In a low voice which carried with arresting clarity throughout the silent courtroom, Dorcas Brett then asked the jurors to return a verdict of guilty as charged on all counts of the indictment against the defendant.

Shana attempted to ignore Earl Thomson, who was staring at her with a seemingly puzzled smile. But a rise of color in her face seemed to betray her awareness of him. Thomson nodded slightly and looked again at the jurors, his manner once more respectful, attentive.

Davic stood up and said, "Your Honor, with the court's permission, I would like to preface my opening statement to the jury with a general comment." Without waiting for approval or even an acknowledgment from the bench, Davic went on, "As the court is aware, I haven't moved that these hearings be closed to the media and public. I'm not presuming Your Honor would have ruled in favor of such a motion, but I want to explain why I didn't file that motion. While it might have been to my client's advantage to be spared the inevitable notoriety that accompanies such a public trial, I believe in this instance his interests and the interests of justice will be best served by giving the widest possible publicity to every facet of this case, by turning the most searching spotlight I can on what the prosecution chooses to call evidence. But I would also like to make it clear that I am opposed in principle to invoking those precedents which encourage the exclusion of the public and press from criminal trials. Such precedents take us in a perilous direction—the issue is the asserted conflict between two constitutional rights: the First

Amendment's guarantee of press freedom and the Sixth Amendment's guarantee of a fair trial, although, as the court is aware, the Constitution nowhere mentions any public right of access to a criminal trial. That notwithstanding, it remains my deepest conviction that the rights of all the people are best served by open hearings and trials."

During this stretch of self-serving *dicta,* Davic fixed each individual juror in turn with his eyes, trying to establish his authority over them, each practiced gesture and intonation asserting his claim to their attention and respect.

Davic then walked to the jurors' box and said in a conversational tone, "We've met before, of course, during the selection process. You were good enough to answer our questions and tell us something about yourselves and something about your personal experiences with rapes and assaults, and whether such violations had ever touched anyone in your immediate family or anyone close to you. I want to thank you again for your help in these areas and for contributing your valuable time to serve on this jury.

"I'm not sure I mentioned that I'm a New York lawyer. I am indeed, but I'm also privileged by license to practice here in Pennsylvania. My associates, Mr. Royce and Mr. Kilroy, are members of my firm.

"Let me point out now, as we begin the trial, the People's attorney has not as yet presented you with any *evidence.* Her opening statements were only what she *hopes* to prove. Her charges do not constitute evidence of any kind whatsoever, although she tried to make them sound as if they did. I will refute those charges in due course. But first I want to tell you openly and candidly what I need from you as a jury, and, indeed, what I expect. I need, ladies and gentlemen, a complete and unqualified exoneration and vindication of Earl Thomson. I will not call him the defendant. I'll dispense with that legalism. My client's name is Earl Thomson. He is twenty-seven, he has been employed by the Harlequin Chemical Company in a responsible position for more than three years. He graduated with top honors from Rockland Military College in Jefferson, New Jersey. Earl Thomson has, of course, no prior criminal record." Davic shrugged. "But since his hobby is high-powered cars, I suppose there might be a traffic violation or two that I am not aware of. But that's it."

Davic moved closer to the jury box and placed his hands on its burnished wooden ledge. For a moment he silently studied the jurors. "Let me explain," he said then, "why in this particular case Earl Thomson so desperately needs your unqualified exoneration. In other cases, both *civil* and *criminal*, a unanimous and unequivocal verdict isn't always essential. A hung jury, for instance, is often as good as a not guilty verdict. Because a hung jury simply means that men and women of good character and intelligence couldn't reach an agreement on the facts. A mistrial may serve the defendant in the same manner, whether it results from a technical error on the part of the prosecutor, or some other irregularity. A reversal of a guilty verdict on appeal—for whatever reason, trifling or significant—also represents a victory for the defense. These inconclusive results tell a person who reads about them in the newspaper or hears about them on television that the issues were so confused and complicated, the so-called facts so contradictory that jurors, with the best will in the world, *still* found it impossible to say who was right and who was wrong.

"But . . . in a trial of rape where the charges include kidnapping, torture and other bestial acts, the exact opposite is true."

Davic slammed his hand down on the ledge of the jury box. "You cannot *partially* clear Earl Thompson of such charges. You cannot *partially* cleanse the stains from his reputation and good name. A hung jury, a mistrial, appeals, reversals, another trial with a new judge and a new jury—those will have the effect of branding Earl Thomson just as if you had, in fact, found him guilty on every charge and specification in the indictment. In the gossip and rumor mills of offices and shops and barrooms, people will say . . . 'That Thomson character got away with it, beat the rap on some technicality . . .' "

Davic turned and pointed to Earl Thomson. "That young man—and remember, his worst offense is a speeding ticket, he has no prior convictions—that young man will be marked for the rest of his life as a sadist and rapist by any verdict *less* than a full and complete acquittal on all charges. No halfway measure will suffice. Now you may be saying to yourself, that's all very well, Mr. Davic, but you can't just tell us that Earl Thomson *needs* an unqualified verdict of not guilty. No, Mr. Davic, you've got to prove that he deserves it. Well, that is exactly what I intend to do, ladies and gentlemen, just as surely as I stand here before you.

"Consider the People's attorney's so-called evidence—fingerprints, photographs, taped interrogations and the like—I will expose that *evidence* for what it is. A smokescreen to obscure the fact that the Commonwealth in fact has only one piece of evidence to place before you, which is the unsupported identification of Earl Thomson by the plaintiff, Miss Shana Selby.

"So, it is time to consider that young woman. While it is true that she is *young*, it is also true that she is a *woman*, with all that suggests emotionally and biologically.

"Now"—Davic turned from the jurors and regarded Shana thoughtfully—"we don't intend to deny for an instant that this young woman was physically mistreated. Whether she was a voluntary or involuntary participant in that mistreatment is *totally irrelevant to our defense*. We will stipulate Miss Selby's physical injuries. Stipulate, as all of you probably know, is a legalism that means 'admit and concede.' So in this instance we admit and concede in advance the extent and severity of Miss Selby's injuries, though I'm sure every bruise and welt on this young woman's body will be dramatically described and demonstrated to you for maximum shock effect.

"Well, that's the People's privilege, if they really want to exercise it. But I ask you to remember, as you listen to testimony describing the physical abuse Miss Selby suffered, I want you to please keep in mind that we have never *denied* those injuries. We have no reason to. No reason whatsoever. Because our contention, which we will prove beyond any doubt, is that while Shana Selby was injured—and we regret that she was, needless to say —*Earl Thomson was not the man who inflicted those injuries on her.* It follows, therefore, that Miss Selby is *mistaken*, or that she is deliberately *lying.*"

Davic walked to the defense table. "If she is mistaken, it is our hope to convince her of her error in the course of this trial. If Miss Selby will admit she has made a mistake, I can assure her we will accept her word for that and extend our forgiveness and even our understanding. But if she is *lying*, and persists in those untruths, that is another matter. Because it will be obvious that she is lying for personal reasons or out of deep psychopathic compulsions—*or* because she is being *forced* to lie by someone who has an ulterior motive to destroy Earl Thomson's character and reputation by these malicious accusations . . .

"Therefore—to protect Earl Thomson from the possibility of such a conspiracy—I will ask the court's permission in these hearings to broaden the areas that normally define the parameters of permissible inquiry." Davic placed a hand on Earl's shoulder, "When I have completed my defense, I honestly believe you will find it not only your duty to clear this young man's name and character—but also your privilege to do so. Thank you very much for your attention."

After rapping his gavel to silence a murmur in the courtroom, Judge Flood settled back in his chair and glanced at the jurors.

"Mr. Davic was correct in advising you that opening statements do not constitute *evidence*. In such statements the attorneys have the opportunity to tell you in narrative form the basis of the case they will present. Such expositions—and they will occur again at the close of the case—are only promises of forthcoming evidence and exhortations for you to believe that evidence."

After a glance at his writing pad, Judge Flood said, "I would like now to amend a statement I made during the process of jury selection. In the *voir dire* process I examined several of you as to what you might have heard or read about this case. I told you we would all be greatly surprised by a prospective juror who claimed he knew *nothing* of this case—such an admission would suggest that said juror never looked at a newspaper or television, never made small talk at work or on lunch breaks. We were not looking for jurors who are blind and deaf to the world around them, but for men and women who might preserve a reasonable impartiality despite pretrial publicity."

After pausing, the judge continued with a smile. "I don't think justice and a little humor are mutually exclusive. When I advised you that a stupid, careless jury, a negligent one, even, might be considered a defendants's best ally, I was, of course, indulging in exaggeration. But the Appellate Division might consider those comments unwise . . . those high justices are notoriously solemn. What I meant was this: in criminal cases, conviction is based on proof of guilt beyond any reasonable doubt. This is to guarantee—as far as is humanly possible—that any mistakes made by the jury will not harm the defendant but will, in fact—as is appropriate and *fair*—benefit him. I want to be certain that what I said was not misconstrued, I want it understood that it had as its intent to make the serious point I have just described."

Judge Flood then nodded to his bailiff, who stood and called for the People Sergeant Remus Ritter of the Muhlenburg sheriff's station.

Dorcas Brett's first series of witnesses, including Ritter, developed the chronological, factual foundation of the People's case against Earl Thomson. Sergeant Ritter was followed to the stand by Harry Selby, who recounted—in answer to Brett's questions—the action he had taken on learning that his daughter had been kidnapped, and his subsequent attempts to find where she had been taken that night. Trooper Milt Karec then gave his account of the sheriff's investigation, the times of the various procedures and so forth. Counselor Davic waived cross-examination but reserved his rights to question both witnesses later.

The People then called, in order, Nurse Edith Redden and Dr. Merwin Kerr.

The restless sounds in the courtroom died away as the nurse responded to Brett's questions. "I removed her clothes, yes. They were bloody and her shoes were wet and dirty with mud. I didn't handle them any more than necessary because I knew the pathology lab would be going over them for evidence.

"Miss Selby had tried to clean herself up before I got there, yes. She had splashed some water on her face. But it was so beaten and swollen, it was almost black in places . . . and her right hand, it had a deep cut in it. She was crying so hard, I couldn't talk to her. She was bleeding from between her legs, but I knew Dr. Kerr was on the way, so I just got her into a clean nightgown and into bed. And I cleaned the wound in her hand and put a dressing on it.

"—no, she didn't say anything about who had done this to her. I made her as comfortable as I could and then Dr. Kerr asked her about what had happened and she told us about the car hitting her and the man . . . the alleged rapist. I gave all that information to Milt, to Trooper Karec."

Dr. Merwin Kerr's testimony was clinical and impersonal, his delivery restrained as he spoke of Shana's loosened teeth, the "penile assault" that had ruptured her hymen and the membranes of her vaginal orifice, the blows that contused her cheekbones, the rope burns on her wrists and ankles, the presence of semen in her anal aperture. The cold, detached tones only emphasized the horrors.

Davic listened thoughtfully but again deferred cross-examination. But when Dr. Kerr was excused, he called Trooper Milt Karec.

"Trooper Karec, there are a few points you might clarify for us. Specifically, a clearer understanding of the *time* certain things happened. The Selby girl was first reported missing around six or six-thirty on that October afternoon. Correct?"

"Yes, sir."

"Her bicycle was discovered on Fairlee Road about two hours later. Is that right?"

"Yes, sir, we thought that—"

"Forgive me, Trooper Karec, but I'd prefer to ask these questions in my own way. I'd like you to bear with me, please. You assumed that Miss Selby might have been struck by a car and driven by the motorist to a nearby hospital, is that it?"

"Yes, sir, that's what we were hoping had happened."

"Much later that night," Davic went on, "early the following morning rather, the Selby girl was brought home by her father from a housing park known locally as Little Tennessee or Little Tenn. Is that correct, Trooper?"

"Yes, sir. But meantime we'd had our squads out checking back roads and school parking lots and—"

"Forgive me again, Trooper. Were you notified immediately when the Selby girl was returned home?"

"No, sir, we didn't know anything about that for almost an hour."

"How *were* you advised of that fact?"

"Sergeant Ritter had been checking the Selby place every half hour or so to see if they'd got a call or anything. Around one-thirty, Mrs. Cranston told him the kid was back, had been

257

for an hour or more. Said with all the excitement, they'd forgot to call us."

"What did you do then?"

"Trooper Jimson and I drove over to question her."

"That was routine procedure?"

"You better believe it, sir. Sergeant Ritter gave us the call direct, didn't patch it through Central. Told us to roll on a Code Three, red lights and siren."

"When you got to the Selbys', did you question Miss Selby?"

"No, sir. Mr. Selby wouldn't let us talk to his daughter, wouldn't even let us see her."

"Did he tell you *why?*"

"He said he didn't want any cops talking to her . . . he meant any *men,* I believe."

"Did you explain to Mr. Selby why it was essential that you speak with his daughter?"

"You're damned—sorry, sir, you better believe we did. Told him we needed a description of the perpetrator and the car to put out APBs and set up roadblocks."

"Did Mr. Selby then change his mind?"

"No, sir. He called Sergeant Ritter and told him he wanted a nurse to look at his daughter. Wouldn't let me or Jimson go near her, never mind we're both family men."

Karec then explained that he had waited with Trooper Jimson in the Selby driveway until the nurse and the doctor had treated and questioned the plaintiff. Nurse Redden then provided them with a description of the car and the assailant.

"Trooper Karec, is Nurse Redden a trained police investigator?"

"She's a fine nurse, sir, a fine woman."

"That wasn't my question. The nurse's description of the alleged perpetrator and vehicle—were they as exact and helpful as you would expect from a trained police officer?"

"I object, Your Honor."

"Overruled. Witness will answer."

Karec was eager. "No, sir. The Selby girl was scared out of her wits. Nobody can blame her, but she told Edith things like the man was tall and dark and that the car was shiny and that it was warm and quiet inside it. She should have asked the kid

258

if by dark she meant he was a black guy or a Puerto, and tried to get some—"

"Objection, Your Honor!"

"Sustained. We can't speculate on what facts might have been developed in a hypothetical interrogation."

"Yes, Your Honor . . . Trooper Karec, from the time you arrived at the Selbys' home, from that moment until you finally put Nurse Redden's sketchy descriptions of the alleged rapist and his car on the police network—how much time had been lost by then?"

"I'd say more than three hours, sir."

"In addition, you weren't notified immediately when the girl was returned home?"

"That's right, sir."

"Trooper Karec, even if this alleged rapist had obeyed every posted speed limit to the letter, couldn't he have driven hundreds of miles from the scene of the crime during those four hours?"

"Objection, Your Honor."

"Sustained. We won't admit that speculation."

Davic nodded deferentially to the bench, but he was pleased the jury had heard the question. "Tell me this then, Trooper. Wouldn't you say, as a professional, that *someone*—or let's just say *circumstances*—conspired, unintentionally or otherwise, to give that alleged and vaguely described criminal a long headstart on you and your fellow police officers?"

"Objection, Your Honor!"

"Sustained."

"Thank you, Trooper Karec. I have no more questions."

Brett said, "Just one thing, Trooper. When Mr. Selby told you he didn't want you to interrogate his daughter, do you remember *all* the reasons he gave?"

"Like I testified, ma'am, he told us he didn't want policemen talking to her. He wanted a woman, a nurse for that."

"Mr. Selby had still another reason, I believe." Brett paused. "Do you remember what it was?"

"Well, I think Mr. Selby told us his daughter wouldn't even talk to *him*. Maybe he figured we couldn't do any better but—"

"Thank you, Trooper Karec. No further questions."

259

"The witness is excused."

At the defense table, Davic briefly nodded to Brett, with an accompanying smile that he made certain the jury saw. A gracious gentleman, this fellow . . . even if he was from New York . . .

After the luncheon recess Dorcas introduced the Commonwealth's physical evidence against Earl Thomson. The defendant's fingerprints from the garage at Vinegar Hill were presented as People's exhibits, together with photographs of his red Porsche. After dates and times had been corroborated, and the authenticity of the fingerprints established, Captain Slocum was called to the stand to identify the taped interrogations of Earl Thomson. The tapes were played in open court and the exchanges between Slocum, Lieutenant Gus Eberle and the defendant, Earl Thomson, were linked to the People's chain of evidence.

Captain Slocum made an excellent witness, forceful, assured and professional. His expensive clothing enhanced that image, adding to an overall impression of poise and authority.

Counselor Davic did not defer his cross-examination of Slocum. His impatient manner—more than impatience, it was closer to a caged ferocity—made it clear he could hardly wait to get at this smoothly plausible detective. But he was careful to begin in a disarmingly courteous manner.

"You've been a police officer how long, Captain?"

"Twenty-three years and nine months, sir."

"And your associate, Lieutenant Gus Eberle, has an almost equal amount of experience, I understand?"

"Yes, sir, the lieutenant's been with my division for fourteen or fifteen years at least, came right up through the ranks."

"Then in the course of a routine investigation involving a stolen car, it could be assumed that you and the lieutenant, would know what you're doing. Is that a fair assumption, Captain?"

Davic's tone had abruptly turned caustic. Slocum seemed puzzled by it.

"When you put it that way, sir, it sounds like you're damning us with pretty faint praise. Yes, we know what we're doing, sir."

"Good, excellent. Now we're going to replay the section of the tapes that were introduced in evidence by the prosecution. After that, I'll have more questions about you and your lieutenant."

The bailiff turned on the machine and Earl Thomson's recorded and metallic voice sounded in the courtroom.

". . . no, Captain, I'm sure I've never been there. I'm positive. Vinegar Hill, you say?"

"That's right, Earl" The voice was Slocum's. "It's a farm, a small one, a dozen acres maybe. It's on Dade Road, near Brandywine Lakes."

"I've never heard of it, Captain."

"How about the Rakestraw Bridge?" This was Lieutenant Eberle's voice, low and rasping. "You know that bridge, Earl? It's covered, got one of them old-style wooden roofs over it."

"Maybe, I don't know—"

"So your statement," Captain Slocum interrupted, "is that you don't know anything about Vinegar Hill, and that you've never been there. Is that it, Earl?"

"That's what I've been telling you, Captain. I don't know the place, I was never there and I don't know how my car got there. Whoever stole it probably—"

"Hold it." Eberle's growling voice broke in. "We'll get to that later. You know some people who live near Fairlee Road named Selby?"

"Selby? No, Lieutenant, I don't."

"You know where Fairlee Road is?"

"I have an idea. Near Muhlenburg, isn't it?"

"You ever drive over Fairlee Road, Earl, around Little Tenn or Mill Lane?"

"I don't believe so. My car was stolen in Muhlenburg, though, if that means anything, but—"

The captain interrupted him again. "Earl, do you know a young lady named Shana Selby?"

"Shana Selby? No, should I?"

"No reason you should, Earl, but on the other hand, there's no reason you shouldn't. We have good cause to believe that girl was taken to Vinegar Hill in your car and very seriously assaulted."

"Hell, Captain, my car was reported stolen. I was having a beer in a bar called The Green Lantern when it happened. It was late in the afternoon. But I was home a half hour later having dinner right here with my mother. Look, late as it is, you can wake her up and talk to her if you want. But when you find out who ripped off the Porsche, maybe they can tell you about that girl—what'd you say her name was?"

Davic snapped off the tape machine. He clenched his hands and stared at Slocum. "Tell me this, Captain. Why did you and Lieutenant Eberle go to Earl Thomson's home in the middle of the night and attempt to intimidate him with those irrelevant and slanderous insinuations—?"

Brett instantly objected and Judge Flood sustained her.

Listening to the subsequent charges, countercharges and legal rulings, Selby couldn't help believing that he was witnessing the trappings of a charade . . . He hoped not, but the judge and Davic did seem somehow mannered, rehearsed . . . He wanted not to believe that. But . . .

"You gave Earl Thomson no advance warning, Captain?" Davic was now pressing. "Not even the courtesy of a phone call before getting him out of bed—when was it, one-thirty in the morning?"

"No, sir, we decided that—"

"I know what you decided, Captain. You just *decided* to scrap any paragraph of the Constitution that didn't meet with your—"

"Objection!"

"Sustained."

Davic drew a deep breath. "Captain, Earl Thomson's car was stolen several months ago, correct?"

"Yes."

"The theft was duly reported at that time. Correct?"

"Yes."

"Then why—*why*, Captain Slocum, did you and your lieutenant seize on the pretext of a stolen car investigation to interrogate my client about a rape case and an alleged victim named Shana Selby?"

"We were exercising"—Slocum paused and wiped his forehead with a handkerchief—"what I'd term a discretionary caution—"

"In regard to *what*, Captain? A car had been stolen. You had news of that fact. You then interrogated Earl Thomson about the details and the locale of a *rape* case, did you not?"

"Yes, sir."

"Was he a suspect in that case?"

"No, sir."

"Then why, Captain, did you ask him about Vinegar Hill? Or about Shana Selby?"

"We were looking for . . . links."

"Captain, will you agree you have violated my client's civil rights?"

"No, because—"

"Will you admit"—Davic was raising his voice—"that you have abused your authority?"

"Your *Honor!*" Brett raised her voice too. "It isn't my place to remind Mr. Davic that this isn't a playpen for his tantrums. This is a court of law and—"

"Sustained. Mr. Davic, you will observe the proprieties and . . . and not badger the witness."

"I apologize, Your Honor, I apologize to the court and to the jury. It is my sincere intention to conduct myself with decorum. But at the risk of your displeasure, I must state that I am here in your courtroom for one purpose, and that is to fight for justice for my client . . ." Davic turned from the witness stand and dismissed Slocum with a gesture, saying, "I have no further questions, Your Honor."

The jury, it seemed to Selby, was favorably impressed by Davic's defiant and emotional attitude. Glancing at Brett, he saw a tension in her face as she spoke quietly to Shana, touching her arm, a quick gesture to reassure her.

Selby now decided what he'd suspected all along—the scales of justice in this old courtroom, with its solid pine floor smelling so cleanly of good, rubbed-in linseed oil, had been carefully tipped from the start against his daughter.

He decided to do something about it.

*　　*　　*

The insurance agent, Jay Mooney, lived on a residential street near East Chester's slums, the stretch of ancient row houses and tar-paper shacks that bordered the Brandywine.

"They're not bad neighbors," Mooney said, leading Selby into his overheated living room. A twenty-four-inch color TV glowed from a corner, coughing out bursts of canned laughter and applause. An upright typewriter rested on a card table surrounded by a clutter of dusty business stationery and insurance forms. What was left of Mooney's dinner, crusts of pizza and several empty beer cans, were on a coffee table. A single fly walked around on the flakes of tomato-flecked dough.

"We do just fine here with our dusky friends along the river." Mooney snapped off the TV set. "Sit down, Harry. Failure creates sympathy, and we're all failures at this end of town. Can I get you a drink?"

"No, thanks, but you go ahead."

"Well," Mooney said, "since you insist."

He returned from the kitchen with a large glass filled with whiskey and water. Seating himself at the coffee table, he waved at the fly crawling around the pizza crumbs. "I can guess why you're here, Harry, so maybe I can save us both some time. I was in court this afternoon, heard Slocum's testimony. Nice little gavotte the pair of them danced, wasn't it? Not subtle, but effective. So you're back for some more help from the old lush, is that it?"

"That's right, Jay."

Mooney took a long pull from his drink without taking his eyes from Selby. The soft paunches under his eyes were the color of oysters. From the street sounded motorcycles and children shouting. After another long drink Mooney set the glass down. His eyes, glinting in deep rolls of fat, were not friendly.

"You want a name now, is that it, Harry? You want to involve me up to my ass, right?"

"Just tell me where I can start checking," Selby said. "I won't mention you, Jay, that's a promise."

"You obviously feel I should help you because it's the decent thing to do." The whiskey had made Mooney's speech deliberate. "Which means you don't think my life is worth much of a shit one way or the other. Therefore, I'm pleased to tell you I don't know one goddamn thing more than I've already told you. Earl Thomson got in some trouble with a girl when he was at school over in New Jersey. Some other students were mixed up in it. Captain Slocum rode like a knight errant to the rescue."

With the flat of his hand, Mooney struck at the fly crawling around the pizza tray. The blow shook the table and shattered a few soggy crusts, but the fly flew off and alighted on the dark television screen.

"I'm not getting involved," Mooney said, "and that's final. In a few hours, kids outside will be playing transistors and there'll be a dozen motorcycles racing up and down in front of my house. My agency in East Chester is being phased out of business by the home office in Dayton, Ohio. You won't believe it, but I still want to go on living. If I talk to you, the odds on that could go way down. So do me a favor and get the hell out of here, Harry. You'll get no more help here."

"Okay, I'll forget this conversation." Selby stood and walked to the door. "And I'm trusting you'll forget it, too, Jay."

"You're a damned fool," Mooney said. "I could score points by picking up the phone and getting to the right people before you're halfway down the steps."

"Good night, Jay. If you were thinking about doing that, you wouldn't have mentioned it."

Selby left Mooney's house and walked along the noisy street to his station wagon. Mooney stood in his open door and called after him, "Don't do this, Harry. You know I'm no good. Don't *trust* me, for Christ's sake, you sonofabitch . . ."

CHAPTER TWENTY-THREE

Allan Davic began his deferred cross-examination of Harry Selby with the question: "Mr. Selby, do you *fully* understand the meaning of the oath you took yesterday morning?"

"Yes, I fully do."

"You understand that you are still bound by that oath?"

"Yes."

"Do you believe in God, Mr. Selby?"

"I believe in a prime mover, a superior being or consciousness."

"That wasn't my question. You did not swear to a being or consciousness. You swore to *God*. My question was and is: do you believe in God, Mr. Selby, the God you asked to help you give truthful and responsive answers to my questions?"

A large female juror was watching him with sudden fascination, and Selby was relieved when Brett stood and said, "Objection, Your Honor. As the court is, of course, aware, the use of the divine appellation in our procedures has been expanded —by the ruling of numerous higher courts—to embrace the beliefs that prevail in various faiths and religions. Muslims are permitted to seek help from Allah, American Indians from their tribal spirits and so forth."

". . . Sustained."

Davic said, "May I comment on the court's ruling?"

"You are noting an exception?"

"No, Your Honor, but I'd like to expand my remark."

"Very well. You may make your statement on the ruling."

"I did not mean or intend to be combative on a semantic issue," Davic said to the jury. "But the fact of the matter is, the heart of my defense rests in truth. The truth of the plaintiff's charges, and the truth behind those charges. I don't believe my question was irrelevant. I wanted to establish that God is the author of all truth and to find out if the witness and I are in agreement on that fundamental fact."

"I object, Your Honor. You have ruled on this question."

"Yes, I did, Miss Brett. Now I'm as religious as the next man, which isn't saying too much, perhaps. I once asked a witness if he knew who God was. He was either ignorant or very smart, depending on one's viewpoint. Because his reply was: 'God? Is his last name *damn,* your honor?' "

Judge Flood tapped his gavel; the murmur of laughter faded away. "So let's presume," he went on then, "that none of us is either too dumb or too smart to know what's meant when we refer to God, or a Supreme Being, or whatever force it is that directs human affairs. Please continue, Mr. Davic."

Davic, Selby thought, was obviously glad to. He had made his point with the jury, which was what counted. And the judge had given an impression of fairly witty impartiality. These people weren't just venal . . . they were also clever . . .

"Thank you, Your Honor. Now, Mr. Selby, in reference to the story you told the court yesterday about how you discovered where your daughter had been taken that night and so forth. Did your daughter accompany you on those excursions about the countryside?"

"No, she didn't."

"I find that strange. Since you were following her clues— those bread crumbs she dropped along the way—didn't you ask her to help you find those various landmarks? The school, the covered bridge and so forth?"

"No, I didn't."

"Did you ask her for any help at all?"

Selby hesitated. "I asked her what she meant by some things she said under sedation—"

"Ah, the bread crumbs she dropped in the forest—"

"Objection."

"Sustained. Never mind the colorful asides, Mr. Davic."

"I beg the court's pardon. Mr. Selby, did your daughter explain to you what she meant by her reference to 'tunnels' and 'screaming birds' and 'hornets' and the like?"

"Some of those references," Selby said, "were unconsciously self-protective. She'd been through hell. Who wants to face that without some protection. The unconscious helps. She didn't tell me what they meant, because she couldn't."

"But you had no trouble following those unconscious, self-protective clues straight to the mark, right, Mr. Selby? Didn't they lead you directly, even miraculously, straight to Vinegar Hill?"

"Objection, Your Honor, to counsel's sarcasm."

"Sarcasm, Miss Brett, is in the ear of the listener. Overruled."

"The question then," Davic continued, "is this, Mr. Selby. While those sedated mutterings meant nothing to your daughter, you were able to follow them like a compass directly to Vinegar Hill. Isn't that correct?"

"I used a good deal of trial and error."

"Please answer the question. Did you not follow that abracadabra *straight* to the house where your daughter was allegedly raped?"

"Yes, but only after—"

"Good. We've got that much cleared up."

"Objection, Your Honor."

"Sustained."

"Mr. Selby, in the course of that search, you had a conversation with Captain Walter Slocum. Would you tell the court the substance of that conversation?"

Selby briefly retold the details of his meeting with the captain and Sergeant Wilger in the office of the detective division.

Davic then shifted to the testimony of Trooper Karec. He took Selby back to the night Shana had been kidnapped and raped, emphasizing again for the jury that Selby's "delaying" tactics had impeded the start of the police investigation by a full four hours.

Brett objected forcefully to the use of the word "delaying," and the bench ordered it struck. The jury, of course, heard it.

Davic shifted again. "Isn't it true, Mr. Selby, that Captain Slocum told you to bring any further information about your daughter's alleged rapist directly to him?"

"Yes."

"But isn't it a fact that you ignored those orders? That you continued to look for him on your own?"

"That's right."

"Specifically, didn't you acquire tracking dogs from a Casper Gideen to search an area along Dade Road?"

"Yes."

"Without notifying Captain Slocum or anyone else in his division?"

"Yes."

"According to testimony elicited by the People's attorney, you gave the photograph of a certain license plate to Captain Slocum. Later—the following morning—you had another conversation with Captain Slocum. Would you tell the court the substance of *that* conversation?"

"The captain said he talked with Earl Thomson and that Thomson had an alibi for the night my daughter was raped."

"I submit the captain put it much more emphatically. Didn't he tell you there was *no conceivable way* that Mr. Thomson could have been involved in those attacks on your daughter? That he was, in fact, dining with his mother at the time they occurred? And that he was *not a suspect in any way whatsoever?* Didn't he tell you those specific things, Mr. Selby?"

"Yes."

"But you nonetheless permitted your daughter to go to Longwood Gardens and accuse Earl Thomson of raping her? Isn't *that* true, Mr. Selby?"

"She went on her own, but—"

"Do you seriously expect the court to believe that?"

"Objection. The question implies a contemplation of perjury."

"Sustained."

Davic shrugged. "Mr. Selby, after Vinegar Hill burned down, after the house had been gutted by flames, soaked with tons of water by county firemen—then, and *only then*, did you take your daughter there. Correct?"

"Yes, that's right."

"What did you expect her to find in that soaking heap of charred rubble?"

"I wasn't sure. Something to jar her memory . . ."

"You weren't sure? May I suggest a reason? You went there *after* the house had been gutted by fire because then you could claim that all evidence against any alleged rapist had been lost in the flames. If your suspicions were anything but delusions, I suggest you would have taken your daughter there *before* the fire. Isn't that true, Mr. Selby?"

"Your Honor, may I instruct Mr. Selby not to answer that question?"

"Yes, Miss Brett. The word 'delusions' will be struck from the transcript."

Ignoring these exchanges, Davic abruptly directed his examination to the statement from the security officer at Longwood Gardens.

"In Officer Summerall's words," Davic said, "you shoved Earl Thomson's friends so violently that they fell backward over their motorcycles. Is that a fair statement, Mr. Selby?"

"Yes, I'd say it is."

"You're aware that both of these young men were treated for abrasions and contusions at Chester General Hospital?"

"I heard something about that."

"Were you concerned for their welfare?"

"No, not particularly."

"I trust the jury will note your casual attitude toward the young men's injuries. You are also aware then, that Earl Thomson, trying to get away from you, crashed into the glass of a greenhouse and as a result very nearly lost the sight of an eye?"

"I was told that by his father, and by *you*, Mr. Davic, just before the warrant was served on Earl Thomson for raping my daughter."

"Your Honor, I ask that you warn the witness about these gratuitous responses."

"Mr. Selby, when a yes or a no is sufficient, you will spare us embellishments."

Davic said, "You admit you are aware that Earl Thomson suffered an injury to his eye? Yes or no?"

"Yes."

"And isn't it a fact, Mr. Selby, that these attacks on Earl

Thomson and his friends occurred many hours *after* you had been informed by Captain Slocum that Earl Thomson could not *possibly* have been responsible for the harm done to your daughter? Aren't those the indisputable *facts*, Mr. Selby?"

"Yes . . . after he said those things . . ."

"Then let me ask you this, Mr. Selby. And my question goes to the heart of the matter. Outside the issues at trial in this court, do you have a personal or emotional bias against the defendant?"

"No, I don't."

"Against his father, George Thomson?"

"No."

"Prior to the issues at trial, did you have any reason to believe either of them had wronged you or your family?"

"No."

"You had no information about them whatsoever?"

"No, I didn't."

Davic asked the court's permission to confer with his associates. As he spoke to the other attorneys, Earl Thomson leaned close to follow the exchanges.

Earlier Selby had told Brett what he'd learned the night before, without mentioning Mooney's name. But she had explained that Earl Thomson's prior sexual assault convictions, however violent or numerous, couldn't be introduced at this trial. "Priors," as they were known, could only be admitted if the defendant were found *guilty*, and then only as an aid to the jury in determining sentence.

Judge Flood glanced up. "Mr. Davic, would this be a convenient place to recess for lunch?"

"Whatever is the pleasure of the court," Davic said.

"We will recess until two o'clock then."

Flood retired to chambers, the stenographer covered her machine and the spectators filed out past the marshals. It hadn't gone well, Selby knew. Davic seemed too confident. His manner suggested he'd got hold of something damaging, but Selby didn't have a clue what it could be.

The defense team went down the aisle, a TV crew following them to the corridor, where reporters and photographers waited. The media pack scenting the winner, Selby thought.

Collecting her papers, Brett said, "We've got some things to talk about, Harry. Could you stop by my office after lunch?"

"Sure." He smiled at Shana. "What're you in the mood for?"

"Anything, a Coke and hamburger, it doesn't matter."

Allan Davic and George Thomson lunched at a country club outside of Wilmington. Their corner table faced a duck pond and rows of forsythia and workmen repairing greens and fairways. Thomson ordered a double martini, the lawyer a glass of white wine. They both decided on the mixed grill.

Thomson said abruptly, "I was pretty goddamn uptight the night that warrant was served on my son."

"That's understandable. You were angry, which is natural."

"But it's not always the best time to make a decision. You've read the transcript?"

"Yes, of course. I laid the groundwork for Selby's motive this morning. This afternoon I'll introduce the transcript of his father's court-martial, and develop your relation to it. It won't be difficult to convince the jury that Selby lied under oath."

"Then the lady DA, she can cross-examine, right?"

"Yes, I've explained that. The People can move into any area I open up."

Thomson nodded and sipped his martini. The gin released softly and gently in his stomach. He hadn't eaten breakfast, just a cup of coffee, and he could feel the icy gin spreading pleasurably through him, dissolving his anxiety and warming his hands and face.

A young woman stood on the practice tee hitting orange-striped range balls. Thomson watched her through the window and bit into his olive. It tasted of the juniper. The woman was a small figure at this distance, but he could see the swell of her breasts against her sweater as she completed her swing, hands high, and her slender body uncoiling strongly. He ordered another drink.

Davic said, "Is something worrying you, Mr. Thomson? Something you'd like to discuss?"

"I'll answer that with another question. How's our case going so far? How does it look to you?"

"It will depend a great deal on the Selby girl's impression

272

on the jury and how your son handles himself. Miss Brett will try her best to impeach his testimony."

Thomson continued to stare at the woman hitting golf balls. "Earl doesn't take criticism too well. You'd better know that. Particularly from women. I'm not talking about girl friends, I'm talking about *women.* There's only been one in his life, and she idolizes him. That's his mother. And those honchos at Rockland taught those young studs the best defense was a good offense."

Davic sipped his wine. "That's may be good advice in a bar fight, but not in a courtroom. Tell me frankly, do you think your son can handle a direct and hostile attack from the People's attorney? Because if she can make him blow his cool, she might blow him right out of court."

Thomson said, "What do we know about her? Have your people checked her background?"

"Let me make a general comment first, Mr. Thomson. A man I respect but don't particularly admire told me something interesting the other night. He said nobody is clean. You can dismiss that as street cynicism or remember that it's a sentiment held by a good many respectable philosophers. If one believes in original sin, we're all evil and it's logical that we should start in prison and earn our way to freedom. Jonas Selby's court-martial can be used to strike a damaging blow against Harry Selby. About his self-interested vindictive motives against you in behalf of his father. But in reading that transcript, it's evident Jonas Selby made no defense against the charges. Neither did his military attorneys. Conclusion: he had no defense or he was too ignorant or confused to demand his rights." Davic sipped his wine. "If we introduce the court-martial, we will be going back three decades to a time of conflicting motives and relationships and guilts." He shrugged. "As to People's counsel, Miss Brett, I won't involve you in our investigation. I'll insist, in fact, that you know nothing about it. She's my responsibility and I'll handle that. But Jonas Selby's court-martial—that's up to you, Mr. Thomson. But as your lawyer, I strongly urge you not to open up ambiguous issues that go back in time to areas I may not be able to control."

Thomson sipped his drink and nibbled on the second olive. He was grateful for Davic's advice. The court-martial *could* open

up a lot of embarrassment . . . to him, to the general, to Correll
. . . "That lady's got a nice swing," he said. "It's all timing.
Doesn't weigh more than a hundred pounds, I'll bet, but she's
really powdering that ball."

Yes, the court-martial would touch General Taggart, and
those muddy pens in Korea, the off-limits barracks and POWs
under sedation, a trail that could lead back through all those
years, back to Summitt City . . .

"Don't go any farther, Counselor," Thomson began to cut
up his lamb chop and sausage. "You already made Selby look
bad. But don't press it. Forget the court-martial."

Davic said, "I think that's a wise decision. You know the
phrase, 'Beware the wrath of a patient man'? I have that feeling
about Harry Selby. He could be more trouble than we'd want."
Unfolding his napkin, he glanced at his plate. "Very nice, but
do you suppose we could ask for a little mint sauce? I prefer it
to the jelly."

Selby left Shana with a police matron after lunch and went up
to Brett's office. Sergeant Wilger was with her. He said to Brett,
"Want me to finish this up, or wait till later?"

"I'd like the rest of it, please. But you'd better start from the
beginning. Mr. Selby should hear this."

The sergeant removed his narrow glasses and polished
them with his handkerchief. "I was telling Miss Brett about
something that happened around the time Vinegar Hill was
torched. I didn't have any word on it. The captain and Eberle
made sure I didn't. I got the story last night from a detective on
Eberle's shift, a pal who owes me one."

After examining his glasses, Wilger carefully replaced
them. "Earl Thomson disappeared after that fire. A ton of pressure came down on Slocum to find him. The captain and Eberle
were on the phone all night checking airports, trains, bus stations. Talked to cops all over the state, up and down the Atlantic
seaboard, with Mr. Lorso blistering them for news."

Brett was pacing tensely as he talked.

"Thomson caught a plane in Philadelphia late one night,"
Wilger went on. "That's what Slocum found out. Flew down to
Memphis, rented a Hertz car and drove to Summitt City. He

stayed two nights. It sure as hell wasn't a casual trip, otherwise it wouldn't have blown up such a storm. Thomson worked at Summitt a couple of years ago. You'd expect he'd have some friends there. But he just turned the car in at Memphis, flew on home. So why the heat and pressure?" The sergeant shrugged. "Thought you should know, Miss Brett."

When Wilger left and the door closed, Selby said, "So why did Thomson go to Summitt?"

"You heard the sergeant. He doesn't know."

"Then what else are you uptight about?" Her responses, he'd learned, were at times oblique and apparently irrelevant. Sometimes he had to hunt for clues to what she was getting at.

She was saying, "We could have submitted Shana's written deposition, or filed a motion for closed hearings. That was what Davic wanted all along, never mind that pious bull to the jury. He was safe to champion open inquiry because he felt sure we'd file for a closed trial. The last thing the defense wants is an articulate, intelligent child like Shana with enough character to tell a crowded courtroom precisely what the"—she turned and put out her cigarette—"what the defendant did to her and how many times. I think closed trials in rape cases are an abomination. Is it cruel and unusual punishment to ask that an alleged rapist at least *hear* in public what was done to a victim? Whose feelings are we being so damned sensitive about? I explained the options to Shana. She told me she was willing to testify. But I'm not sure you realize what she'll face under Davic's cross-examination."

"Then will you spell it out, for Christ's sake?"

"All right, dammit, I will. Anything that hurts the case hurts Shana. What hurts you can hurt her." She picked up her cigarettes but dropped them nervously. "Don't you see what Davic is *doing?* He's establishing that you have some *need* to want to hurt Earl Thomson, or his father . . . a motive that has nothing to do with Shana."

"How the hell can he? I never even saw Earl Thomson before that morning at Longwood Gardens—"

"Davic is too shrewd to start anything he can't make pay off. He knows something I don't, which could mean you haven't leveled with me." She looked at him. "What about it, Harry?"

He shook his head, kept his temper. "I've told you every

275

sight and sound and smell that could conceivably relate to this business." He ticked items off on his fingers. "About my father, as much as we could get about him. About Jarrell, his girl, what I've asked Jerry Goldbirn to check out, the fact that somebody was on Fairlee the other night looking for something."

"Could it be something you're holding back . . . unconsciously? To protect Shana?"

"If it's unconscious, how the hell would I know?"

She sighed. "Dumb question, sorry."

Selby said then, "If Davic's got a bomb to explode, I'll be as surprised as you, if that's any consolation."

"It's not much, Harry."

A tap sounded on the office door. She said, "Yes?"

Flood's bailiff looked in on them. "Miss Brett, the judge is robing now. I'll be calling us to order in just a few minutes."

"Thank you, Thomas, we'll be there in good time for his entrance."

She put her arm through Selby's. "Let's go on down and see what they've got to blind-side you with."

But the afternoon session proved anticlimactic. Davic, as agreed between him and Thomson, dropped Selby's relationship to the Thomsons and directed his attention to other areas.

"You are a widower, Mr. Selby?"

"Yes."

"Would you describe your relationship with your daughter as trusting and confident? Does she confide openly and truthfully in you?"

"Objection, Your Honor. The questions are irrelevant."

"Sustained."

"Mr. Selby, isn't it a fact that your daughter called you at your motel in Memphis the day before the alleged attack on her?"

"That's right."

"To tell you a car was parked in the dark somewhere near your home?"

"Yes."

"Did she tell you she was frightened by the presence of that car?"

276

"No, she didn't."

"Were strange cars and vans, motorcycles perhaps, such a common event around your place?"

"Objection, Your Honor."

"Mr. Davic," Flood said, "what is the purpose of this question?"

"I want to pursue an inconsistency in the testimony of the witness."

"Overruled. Proceed."

"If your daughter wasn't frightened by the presence of that car, Mr. Selby, why did she place a long distance call to you to tell you about it?"

"Our housekeeper had called the police. Shana felt I ought to know that."

"Mr. Selby, when you talked to your daughter that night, did she seem her usual self?"

"I don't understand what you mean."

"Well, did you notice any undue excitement in her manner?"

"Objection, Your Honor. The question demands a subjective evaluation."

"Sustained."

"Your Honor, I was trying to find out if the young lady's call to her father might have been in the nature of a prank or a practical joke. Because it's a fact that Mr. Selby didn't respond seriously to that call. He didn't cut short his trip and return home. But I will accede to your ruling and ask no further questions along that line."

Davic excused himself to confer with his associates.

Brett made a series of question marks on her legal pad and underlined each one firmly. Whatever the defense attorney had been developing that morning obviously no longer interested him. Or presented some risk he'd decided not to take. Brett wasn't sure which. But his present questions, she felt sure, were designed only to provide a camouflage for, a diversion from, whatever he'd been digging into earlier . . .

Davic returned to the bench and told Judge Flood he had no further questions of the witness at that time but added, "If it pleases the court, we're expecting further information and would like to reserve the right to talk to Mr. Selby again."

                    *   *   *

That night Selby found the quotation, "Hell is alone . . ." in *Bartlett's*. It was from a play, "The Cocktail Party." The complete line read "Hell is alone, the other figures in it merely projections."

He called Brett, but her line was busy. Upstairs, Shana's shower was running. He took Blazer for a walk, and when he returned Shana's shower was off and her hair dryer was humming.

Brett's number was still busy.

Selby couldn't imagine what it was he had brought to Summitt City that could possibly threaten anyone. But why had the reaction to him been so peculiar? The sergeant, Ledge, he'd told Selby to put the past behind him and forget it. But whose past was he warning him about? His father's or Jarrell's or his own?

He dialed Brett again, but got another busy signal. Shana came in and sat cross-legged on the sofa, tipping her head sideways to brush out the damp ends of her hair.

"Honey, doesn't Brett ever get off the phone?"

"She's probably talking to one of her sisters," Shana said. "Kay's the oldest and she has dogs, a pair of standard poodles. Her other sister, Nancy, is married to a doctor. They have two little daughters. Miss Brett told me she talks to them almost every night, but I think she was showing five" . . . she looked at him shyly, her expression strangely remote. "Anyway, she said if I needed to talk to her I'd better call her in the mornings at her office. She gets in early."

"What do you mean, showing five?"

"It's a signal we use, like a code." Shana put her brush down and looked at the fire. A stillness smoothed her soft face. "When we first talked about it, about what happened to me, there were things I didn't want to tell her. So she said to hold up my hand then, you know, show five, like taking the Fifth. That meant I wanted to skip it, or talk about it later maybe."

"She's showing five about calling her sisters?"

"Not about that, but about being on the phone. She's been getting calls that bother her. Not just your neighborhood breather, even I've had a couple of those. But somebody's on her case, so she leaves the phone off the hook. I heard her telling

Sergeant Wilger about it. He's trying to trace whoever it is, but they don't stay on long enough."

Shana pushed Blazer away and stood to kiss her father good night. When she straightened up, he held her wrist lightly. She seemed fragile and small and tenderly young in her short night-gown, but her shoulder-length hair and the gravity in her eyes created a curious duality, the girlishness merging before him into a womanly maturity.

"Are you feeling all right about tomorrow?"

"I only have to tell what happened, and I'm not worried about that. Miss Brett will help. We've been over and over it."

"Do you mind that I'll be there when you're on the stand?"

"No . . ." She put a hand on Blazer's collar and shook her head. "That's all right, daddy."

"I don't have to be there. There's no law says so. I could go out and have some coffee or something."

"I told you it was all right." Her voice was higher. "I want to get it over with, okay?"

"Sure, honey. But I don't want you to be afraid of anything. I'll help you any way I can. I love you. I'll do anything for you. You can put that in your piggy bank."

She smiled and held his hand tightly against her face. "I love you, too, daddy, but the last piggy bank I had I lost at a show-and-tell in about third grade."

"Okay, okay, so time flies . . . good night, honey."

He dialed Brett after Shana went upstairs. Her line was still busy. He could imagine the receivers off the hook, one on the rolltop desk, the other beside her bed, the electronic beats growing louder as the house became still, humming faintly against window panes, mingling with the crack of the dying embers. His own phone rang then. He hoped it was Brett, but it was Jerry Goldbirn in Las Vegas.

"What time is it there, Harry?"

"A little after midnight. Why?"

"Why? Mine was a loser's question, Harry. Ever know a loser with a watch that wasn't either slow or fast or in hock? Nobody gives a damn about time in gambling joints. They have dinner at six or seven in the morning at the crap tables, steaks, banana cheesecakes, that's why they're losers."

"That's fascinating stuff, Jerry. If you want to know the

time on the east coast look at your watch and add three whole hours. That's why you never made all-conference, Jerry."

"A point, you got a point. Now listen." Goldbirn's tone changed to serious. "The girl's name is Jennifer, like she told you. Her last name is Easton. Lives on Sutton Place South, New York City. An unlisted phone. That's usually no problem, Harry, a cop or newspaperman can get it for us. But this time, no way. Jennifer Easton's number had a sealed code on it. That puts it out of reach."

"How about her address?"

"That won't help. Nobody's used that Sutton Place apartment for months. We checked that. I'd have to call in a big marker for that unlisted number."

"She's important, Jerry. Believe me."

"Okay, pal. A big deal vice-president of New York Bell kited checks in my place last year . . . would you believe it? Probably got his start robbing pay phones . . . and I covered for him. I'll call him tomorrow, Harry. I'll call him *collect.* The rest of it's like first down and goal to go on a sunny afternoon . . . they're in a motel in Fort Lauderdale, Florida, place called the Glades . . . Coralee Kane, the mother, and her kid, Barby. Some friendly cops checked 'em out for us. Two sets of wheels arrived the week the Kanes checked in. First a delivery van from the local liquor store. Coralee, it seems, likes a belt of gin with her ginger ale. Then a 450-SEL from Miami. Man name of Hank Swanson spent most of the day with the Kane woman. Swanson's with an outfit called H. and H. Rates and Escrow, Limited. H. and H. is an offshore bag company, Harry, operates out of the Bahamas, but it's owned by a firm in London. They launder real estate mortgages, cash, any commercial paper that needs a phony birth certificate. One of our cops spent his day off at the pool at the Glades. Had some drinks with your cracker tart. After a few off-duty slugs of gin, he got this. Mrs. Kane and her intended husband have just come into some oceanfront property around Avalon, New Jersey. That's why this Swanson came. The paperwork's been funneled from the Jersey shore out to Nassau and back to Miami. Which means the parentage of that property is about as kosher as an Easter ham."

"Did I miss something, Jerry? Who owns H. and H.?"

"I told you, it's a limey outfit in London. But here's what's interesting. The happy bridegroom is that Jesus freak you told me to check out, Oliver Jessup. He's leaving Pennsylvania. He's building himself a church over in Jersey. Lucky Jersey. Now they'll all be saved in the Garden State . . ."

Selby hung up and looked through the notes he'd made. With one or two assumptions, he had a fairly coherent picture . . . someone was paying off Goldie Boy and Coralee Kane.

The night he'd picked up Shana at Little Tenn, Barby Kane had shouted at her mother about the blanket Shana was wrapped in. "It's already been worse places tonight . . ."

Casper Gideen had been convinced the preacher and Coralee had been together that night . . .

Where? In the Tabernacle of the Golden Flame, it must have been there. And they could have seen Earl Thomson, could identify him . . .

Gideen had been shot and killed because he had suspected that and was trying to prove it . . .

"Someone" had sent Coralee Kane down to Florida, and was arranging through a British company to bribe Goldie Boy with land and a new church in New Jersey.

Selby called Brett a last time and got another busy signal. He settled down then with his father's diaries and sheaf of snapshots.

For the first time since they had come into his possession he felt the beginning of a sympathy for the tall, scowling young man in the cracked snapshots, some recognition and understanding of the voice that seemed to sound from the frayed old notebooks. "The hills are all climbed, the creeks are all passed . . ."

They were both up against something hidden and threatening, he thought. The same thing, perhaps, except a generation later . . .

It made Shana feel sad, even disloyal to wonder if it meant all that much to love people. Her father said, "I love you," and she knew he meant it. Loving was sort of easy . . . it always was for her. It was something you didn't really have to think about. She loved her father and she loved Davey and Mrs. Cranston and Blazer and lots of her friends and the kittens and flowers and biscuits in the morning and she'd loved her mother's wide smile. Even the tiny gap between her mother's front teeth, she'd loved that.

In school she'd read a poem that said, "Love loves to love love." She'd copied it out and passed it around to her friends, and they'd smiled at it because they knew what it meant too.

But *hating* was hard. She didn't really know how. She didn't even hate Earl Thomson, even though she realized he hated her. And tomorrow she'd have to say in court the shameful, hideous things he'd done to her that would make him hate her all over again and worse than ever. And she couldn't understand why he'd done them in the first place.

It had almost made her sick to tell Miss Brett what he'd done. She'd hardly known the words to describe it. She'd been surprised that there were actually words for it. Miss Brett had finally shown them to her in a dictionary.

Shana's tears were cold on her face. The shadows from the trees moved across the picture of the dead Olympic athletes. She wished she could talk to her mother even for a minute, or just touch her. Or pray to someone who could answer.

Tishie had prayed all the time. She told Shana she didn't expect the clouds to open and an old man to say nice things to her, but the answers to prayers were in the world around you, in rainbows, and in what was inside you. Shana didn't understand or believe in Tishie's rainbows that meant new life, as her grandmother claimed, or the songs she said she could sing again after Treblinka. But now Shana tried to pray. She spoke aloud in a clear voice, but softly so as not to wake Davey . . . "I wouldn't say those things about anyone unless I knew they were true. *Unless I knew* . . . It would be better to live with the hurt and pain inside me than take the chance of being wrong. It would be too terrible to hurt anybody else by making a mistake, or accusing someone who was innocent. . . ."

That was Shana's prayer.

Well, she'd told the truth. Nobody could take that away from her . . .

She had heard the cars on Fairlee Road and Blazer's barking, had seen the flashlight going through the woods that night . . .

She knew who it was and what he was looking for on the

road where his speeding red car had hit her. Earl Thomson would never find it there.

"Love loves to love love . . ."

That's what she'd thought. But she had heard a different truth in her own voice, a voice she hardly recognized, hoarse and bitter, on the tapes . . . "Mommy, I'll kill it, it's evil."

Shana lifted the picture of the dead Israeli athletes away from the wall. A tissue-wrapped object was Scotch-taped to the back of the frame. She unwrapped a layer of paper from the silver swastika she'd torn from his neck when he struggled with her that awful night in the farmhouse. She held up the square cross by links of chain still attached to it and let it swing back and forth in the moonlit shadows.

His initials, E.T., were on one side and MUNICH—11/9/38, on the other. Thin traces of dried blood streaked the edges that had pierced and cut the palm of her hand.

He knew he'd lost it. But he'd lie and say it was stolen, or that he'd given it away . . .

She wrapped the swastika and taped it in place, carefully straightening the picture. The leaves and vines that decorated it had turned dry and brittle, but the eyes of the young men were as joyously stern as when she had cut out their photographs and surrounded them with the flowers of love and honor and remembrance.

CHAPTER TWENTY-FOUR

Judge Flood's clerk said, "Place your left hand on the Bible and raise your right hand. Do you solemnly swear that the testimony you are about to give is the truth, the whole truth and nothing but the truth, so help you God?"

"Yes, I do."

"State your full name."

"Shana Teresa Selby."

"State your address."

"Mill Lane and Fairlee Road. Muhlenburg, R.D., Pennsylvania."

"Please be seated."

Shana removed her hand from the Bible and took the witness stand. Her face was pale. Tiny silver clips held back her long hair. As Brett approached the stand, Judge Flood rapped his gavel to quiet a stir in the courtroom, a murmuring tension, anticipation.

When the sounds faded, Flood said, "I don't want any disorder in this courtroom. The testimony to be given will be of an intimate and sensitive nature. Television coverage of these hearings has been suspended for the duration of plaintiff's testimony."

Flood raised his eyes to the crowded spectators' gallery. "If there is any unseemly reaction to these proceedings I will order the marshals to clear the court. Your presence here is a privilege, not a right."

Swinging around in his chair, the judge looked down at Shana. "Now, young lady, I don't want you to be nervous. I want you to be just as relaxed as possible. Take your time answering our questions. If there is anything you don't understand, feel perfectly free to ask the People's attorney or myself for clarification. You understand?"

Shana nodded yes, then blushed, realizing she would have to say yes out loud so the court stenographer could record it.

"Yes, sir."

The judge nodded to Brett. "The People may proceed."

"Thank you, Your Honor . . . Shana, I'd like to go back to October sixteenth of last year, a Friday. On that day, you rode your bicycle from your house down to Fairlee Road?"

"Yes."

Brett had positioned herself so that she could watch the judge and jury's reactions to Shana's responses.

"How far is it from your driveway on Mill Lane to Fairlee Road?"

"About a hundred yards, I think."

"What time of day was it?"

"It was just getting dark. It was around five o'clock."

"Do you ride down to Fairlee Road every afternoon?"

"No, not every afternoon. But when the weather was nice, I usually did."

"Did you usually go alone?"

"Sometimes my brother Davey went with me. Or I took our dog—"

"But on this afternoon, you were alone?"

"Yes."

"So what you were doing—riding your bike a hundred yards from your home—that was routine and casual after-school activity. Is that right?"

"Yes, that's right."

"Shana, will you tell the court in your own words what happened on that particular Friday afternoon?"

Shana began her recital in a firm voice, her eyes fixed on Brett's . . . "I heard a car coming, it was still a long way off, but I got over to the shoulder of the road. I couldn't see the car, there's a curve where Mill Lane and Fairlee come together. The car was on the other side of the curve. I could hear it. It was going the—opposite way I was—"

"Excuse me, young lady," Judge Flood said, "but I'm not sure I get the picture."

"Well, that's what I saw, sir."

"Yes, but we want to be sure the jury sees everything just as you did." Flood glanced at Brett. "A question or two might clarify the geography for us, Miss Brett."

"Yes, Your Honor. Shana, you were facing the sound of the approaching car, right?"

"Yes . . ."

"You rode onto the shoulder of the road when you heard it?"

"Yes."

"Did you get off your bike?"

"No, I just stopped and put my foot on the ground."

"You were in full control of your bicycle?"

"Yes, I wasn't moving at all."

"And the car was heading toward you? You saw it then?"

"Yes."

"Could you see the driver?"

"Yes. It was a man, he was alone. The car came around the curve and slowed down." Shana swallowed; the small dry sound traveled to the ends of the big room. "He headed straight for me then and I knew he was trying to kill me—"

Davic stood and said quietly, "Objection, Your Honor. There is no evidence to support that conclusion."

"Sustained. Young lady, I don't want these proceedings to confuse you. So let me explain something to you now. I'll try to be as clear as I can. We want you to tell us just what happened, and when it happened. But you mustn't get into the *why* of it. It's possible the driver fell asleep or was distracted by a flash of sunlight. I'm not saying that's what happened, you understand. It's just as an example. He could have driven onto the wrong side of the road for a number of reasons. But we can't admit your conclusion that he did so for the purpose of harming you. Is that clear?"

"Yes, I think so. Sir."

"Good. Please go ahead, Miss Selby."

"The car came over to my side of the road, heading straight to me. I tried to get out of the way, but the fender hit my bike. I heard a grinding kind of noise, and then I was in the gulley beside the road. A man got out of the car and ran over to me. I thought he wanted to help me . . . I'm sorry if that's a . . . a conclusion, but it's the only reason I could think of. Then he grabbed me and got me to my feet and pulled me toward his car. I started to try to get away from him and he hit me in the face. I tried to—"

"Tell me, young lady," Flood interrupted, "what did the alleged assailant hit you *with?*"

"His hand. His fist, I mean."

"Please go on."

"I hit him back and tried to get away from him too. I must have fallen down because he picked me up again and hit me in the neck and in the face. That's all I remember until we were inside his car somewhere, driving in the back country."

Judge Flood said, "How did you know you were in the country, Miss Selby?"

"I . . . I don't know. But I couldn't hear any other traffic, and the air smelled like meadows."

Brett said, "Shana, will you please tell the judge now if the man who forced you into his car that afternoon is present in this courtroom?"

"Yes . . . He's sitting next to his lawyer there, Mr. Davic."

"Will you point to him?"

A stir of excitement as Shana pointed to Earl Thomson.

"That's him, Miss Brett, right there."

"Let the record show that the plaintiff has pointed to and identified the accused, Mr. Earl Thomson."

Davic put a hand on Thomson's arm and said something in a whisper. A flush of color had come into Earl's face.

Brett said quietly, "Shana, tell us what happened then?"

"We drove through the . . . the darkness for a long time."

Judge Flood looked annoyed but said nothing.

"My face hurt where he hit me. I tried to watch the numbers on the . . . the odometer, I think it's called. I thought I could figure out the distance. But I was partially on the front seat beside him and partly on the floor. It was hard to look without moving my head and I was afraid he'd know I was conscious and could see . . . We turned into a driveway. He pulled me out of the car and made me go into a house with him. It was starting to rain. He was angry about something. He shouted at me, told me to sit on a chair. It was a living room with a fireplace and antlers. I saw that when he turned on a lamp. He tied one of my arms to the arm of the chair with a thin strip of leather like the kind we use on ice skates, square and hard. It was new, I think. I asked him what he was going to do with me. He didn't tell me, he didn't say anything, I mean. He went into the kitchen and closed something . . . shutters, I think, from the sound. He made a fire in the fireplace with paper and kindling. Then he turned on a record player and started shouting at me again, about how bad I was. The music was classical, I think, lots of horns and woodwinds. I didn't recognize it, though. He drank something in the kitchen. He filled a glass from a bottle and drank it and filled it again. It was whiskey, I could smell it. Then he came and stood where I was in the chair. There was a water stain on the ceiling just above me. He started shouting again. He told me I was a sinner, that I was evil, I would be sent to hell by myself. Everything seemed crazy then. I thought once I was having a terrible dream. I hadn't done anything wrong. I hadn't knocked anyone down with a car and tied them up. But he kept getting angrier, said I had to be punished."

Shana locked her hands in her lap and stared down at her whitening knuckles. A wall clock ticked stolidly in the silence, lights gleaming on the brass pendulum. In a low voice, Shana told how the man had knelt to take off her sandals, how a rivet had torn from the cloth while he jerked and pulled at her cut-off jeans, of the tearing of her cotton shirt . . . How after releasing her from the chair he had pushed her across to a canvas cot, forcing her to lie on her back, then had bound her wrists over her head to the wooden supports of the cot . . .

"And you were struggling all of this time?" the judge asked her.

"I was trying to talk to him," Shana said, "but I was kicking him too. He . . . he spread my legs and tied my ankles to the sides of the cot. It hurt, the leather was cutting me, and I got mad. Real mad. I asked him what I'd ever done to him, and what reason did he have to treat me this way, I told him he was going to get into trouble . . . He started . . . doing it to me then and

I don't know if I struggled anymore. I was screaming but wasn't sure it was really me screaming. The music was so loud. I thought if I'm not sure who's screaming, maybe this isn't happening, but he kept on doing it and I knew who was screaming then . . . it was like all of me . . . my whole body . . . was screaming."

Brett put a hand on her arm. "Just take your time, Shana."

"*No.* I'm all right."

Judge Flood said, "We can recess here for a few minutes—"

"No, I want to get it over with."

"I understand your feelings, but painful as it may be, you must tell us in detail"—Judge Flood looked sharply at the gallery; whispers had started among the spectators.

Earl Thomson spoke to Davic, his words softly blurred but carrying a tone of derision.

Flood rapped his gavel. "The court will be cleared if there is any disorder in the gallery. Miss Brett, you will elicit the testimony that is required of your witness."

"Yes, Your Honor. Shana, you have testified that the defendant, Earl Thomson, did something to you while your wrists and ankles were bound to the frame of the cot. Would you please describe his actions?"

"He got on top of me. He put his penis between my legs and forced it into my vagina. He was shouting something about women and squeezing my breasts hard. He hit me in the face when he got soft in me and fell out. His face was wet when he put his head between my legs. He licked me, between my legs, then started hitting me again. He got up and untied my hands. He went into the kitchen and filled his glass again. I hoped he'd get drunk and go to sleep. I'm not sure what I was thinking. I didn't know why he was shouting at me and hitting me. Everything inside my head was white. I had a feeling I could write words on it if I just knew how. I was frightened, but I was sad, because I knew he was going to kill me and I started to cry because nothing made any sense."

This time Davic did not object to Shana's conclusions.

"I must ask you one or two more questions," Brett said. "Then we'll be through with this. Did the defendant tie your hands to the cot a second time?"

"Yes, he untied my feet and made me turn over. After that, he tied me up again."

"Tied your wrists and your ankles to the frame of the cot?"

"Yes."

"You were then lying face down on the cot, is that right, Shana?"

Shana nodded, moistened her lips. Her face had become red.

"While you were in that position," Brett went on, "would you describe what the defendant did to you?"

"He got on top of me again—" Shana swallowed hard and looked at her hands.

Brett said, "May I lead the witness at this point, Your Honor?"

"Yes, Miss Brett."

"Shana, did the defendant force an entry into your anus, up your anal aperture, using his erect penis for that purpose? Is that what he did?"

"Yes, Miss Brett."

"Is there anything else?"

"I started screaming and he pushed my face against the mattress. It was hard. It hurt so. It was like something hot from a fire . . . then he was yelling, and then he suddenly stopped, was quiet. He stayed on top of me for a long time, just lying there. Then he moved around and put his . . . his penis in my mouth."

Judge Flood pinched the bridge of his nose between his thumb and forefinger. The pressure left white marks.

In a quiet, strangely distant voice, Shana told about leaving the farmhouse and sitting in the Porsche while Earl Thomson went into the garage. She told about his efforts to get the car out of the rutted driveway, using a shovel and shafts of wood and kindling.

When she finished, Brett turned to the bench and told Judge Flood she had no further questions.

"Mr. Davic?" Flood looked down at the defense table.

"No questions, Your Honor, not at this time."

Earl Thomson muttered, "What bullshit, what *bullshit* . . ."

Davic stood and said in an overriding voice, "Considering the painful nature of Miss Selby's testimony, I won't add to her ordeal at this point. But the Defense reserves the right to cross-examine."

Brett helped Shana down from the witness stand and led her to the People's table.

His daughter was pale, Selby saw, her lips dry and trembling a little.

As they walked past Judge Flood and the jurors, Brett squeezed Shana's arm and gave her a quick nod of encouragement.

When Shana was seated, Brett said, "Your Honor, the Commonwealth will call no other witnesses. The People rest, if it please the court."

A commotion then broke out at the defense table. Attorney Royce was trying to quiet Earl Thomson. Davic gripped Thomson's shoulders, but he knocked the lawyer's hands away.

"I don't give a *damn,*" Thomson said. "It's a phony setup and you know it, Davic." His face tight with anger, he stood so abruptly that he almost knocked over the defense table. Papers fell and scattered onto the floor. "It's a goddamn *lie,* it's all *lies* . . . how long do you expect me to sit here and take this—?"

Marshals moved quickly from their posts to converge on him. Judge Flood hammered his gavel and spectators stood, craning to follow the action.

Thomson shouldered Davic aside and took a step toward Brett and Shana. "Some con game . . . you bitches . . . not one word of truth in any of it . . ."

Selby jumped quickly over the gallery railing and put himself between Earl and his daughter. He swung his forearm against Earl's chest, checking his momentum and holding Thomson until the marshals surrounded him and led him, struggling and cursing, from the courtroom.

For an instant Earl Thomson's flushed face had been only inches from Selby's, so close that he could see the sweat on Earl's upper lip and smell his mint-scented after-shave lotion. He had felt the strength in Thomson's hard shoulders, and the thought of that power violating Shana's slender body made Selby devoutly wish that no officers were there to intervene . . .

Later, Selby helped his daughter through the crowded corridor, an arm tight around her shoulders as they passed the gauntlet of reporters and photographers and TV cameras.

291

A man unexpectedly joined them, a short, fat man falling into step beside Selby. His breath smelled of whiskey. "A terrible business, Harry, a terrible thing for the child, but your Shana's a gutsy little lady, God bless her."

It was Jay Mooney. He slipped a folded piece of paper into Selby's hand, patted Shana's shoulder and hurried off into the crowd lining the sidewalks.

That night Selby studied the information Jay Mooney had given him. Her name was Emma Green and she lived somewhere in or around Jefferson, New Jersey. She was black, twenty-six or twenty-seven, and once worked in a bar off-limits to the students of Rockland Military College. She had been sexually assaulted and grievously injured several years back by the then-Cadet Colonel Earl Thomson.

Captain Walter Slocum and Dom Lorso had personally prevailed upon the assault victim to drop charges against young Thomson.

Why Jay Mooney had changed his mind and decided to help him, Selby couldn't guess . . . maybe because he couldn't kill the fly sharing his pizza . . . futility might be as good a reason as any.

Selby called Burt Wilger at the sergeant's apartment in East Chester and asked him if he could help him find the address of a woman named Emma Green who lived somewhere in Jefferson, New Jersey.

When he explained why he wanted it, Wilger was silent a moment, then said, "You know you can't use it, Selby. Not in this trial."

"I understand. Brett explained that."

"Okay then, I'll check out where your Emma Green is living. But it could take time. She could've moved anywhere by now, you know."

The hall was dark but Shana's door was open and her light was on. She was sleeping on her side, an arm trailing over the side of the bed. The radio was still playing.

Selby eased himself carefully into the wicker armchair at

her worktable, but it creaked under his weight and she turned quickly to look at him.

"Is anything wrong, daddy?"

"No, I just wanted to look at you. I'm sorry I woke you up. Try to get back to sleep, honey."

She turned off the radio and pushed her hair from her forehead. Then she smiled uncertainly and he knew she was puzzled, and maybe embarrassed.

"Do I look okay?" she asked him.

"You look fine, you look perfect," he told her. "I like to look at you. It's one of the things about being a father that's fun. But after kids are about three or four, it's all over. They're always running up and down stairs, in and out of rooms, and they don't sit still long enough anymore. If you look at them while they're eating or watching TV, they get self-conscious and want to know if they've done something wrong or why you're staring at them. I thought you were asleep so I came in to look at you, okay?"

"Sure, it's fine. But I'm awake now. Does that spoil it?"

"No. I guess I was hoping you'd wake up. I wanted to talk to you. I wanted to tell you I've been sort of stupid about this whole business. I knew what happened, but I guess I never really absorbed it. I questioned you about it and asked for explanations, asked you to remember details and the times things happened, like it was . . . just an automobile accident, like which way you were going on your bike and what way the car was coming from. I want to tell you I felt proud of you in court today, what you were able to say, how you said it. I felt very glad we belonged to each other . . . But when this is over, and you go on with your life, I'd like you to try to understand that I loved you and cared about you and *still* didn't understand what you've been through . . ."

"I'm going to cry," she said, "unless you stop talking like that."

"Okay," he said quickly. "I won't say another word about it, I'll change the subject. What about this summer? What would you like to do? You tell me and we'll try to set it up."

"Well, I don't want to sound like some dumb kid or a kind of nut, but I'd really like to stay home and go to summer school. Miss Calder, all the teachers, are making it easy for me now. But

I know I've lost a lot of ground, regardless of grades." She propped herself up on her elbow. Her face was animated. "I'd like to cram in French and take a science minor, and then . . ." She regarded him doubtfully. "Does it matter if it's expensive?"

"Well, we'll see. What is it?"

"I've been reading about skiing in Switzerland, daddy, a little town in the Alps where the snow's so deep in the streets you can't even hear the cars or anything. People have hot chocolate and wear bright sweaters and ski all day. They have bunny slopes that Davey and I could practice on. I was thinking that we get a long vacation at Christmastime and maybe we could do it then. You could teach us, couldn't you?"

"We can sure check it out. We can start thinking about it."

She fell asleep soon afterward, and Selby watched her for a while and then kissed her on the forehead, gently, so as not to wake her.

CHAPTER TWENTY-FIVE

A Lebanese maid opened the door of the suite and told Thomson his wife was having her massage. Would he perhaps enjoy some tea or a drink while he was waiting for Mr. Santos to finish?

Thomson shook his head and sat down beside his wife's circular bed. Her quarters included therapy pools and a gymnasium that opened off the main room with its carefully controlled temperature and artificial sunlight.

Miguel Santos, brown and trim in white T-shirt and trousers, supervised Adele Thomson's water therapy and her sessions in the rhythmically pumping exercise machines. Their grueling regimen fulfilled Adele's desperate hopes of walking again one day, and perhaps even dressing herself and doing her own hair. It was a hope no doctor had ever given her the slightest chance of realizing. But Adele refused to consider their verdicts as long as the machines could twist her body into simulated contortions, and Santos's probing fingers could bring color and tone to her wasted flesh. . . .

The accident that paralyzed Adele Thomson had occurred when Earl was twelve. She had been on a shooting trip with her husband in Iran, at a Pahlavi "shooting box," a lodge on the Elburz mountains only a short flight from Tehran. . . .

Everything in Adele's bedroom, except for mirrors, was done in flat whites—draperies, furniture, carpets. But her wardrobe doors always stood open so that her clothes provided a colorful contrast to the relentlessly neutral walls, furs and dresses of purple and green and cool grays, tiny jewels gleaming on cashmere sweaters and edging the straps of evening sandals. Her golf and tennis footwear were also on display, the uppers plumped up tautly with slim wooden shoe trees.

Thomson couldn't get the Selby girl's testimony out of his mind, her quiet, deliberate voice, the awful words and images they created—he noticed a pair of headlights coming up the driveway. Davic. . . .

The Iranian guides had driven them into the hills where lemon and rose sunlight spread over the tallest peaks. Chairs were placed at strategic sites, guns loaded and distributed, certain thickets pointed out—it was like a stage set, animals caught in spotlights, deer or large cats, to be admired before being shot to death with grace and precision. The fields of fire were marked by whitewashed poles. If a gun barrel strayed beyond these limits, a sure brown hand would be there to move it firmly back into the firing zone. Flowers glistened on the ground, tiny blue flowers that grew around the rocks and through the scaly brush like delicate veins. . . .

Adele's hair was still blond. She had worn it long when she was young, but now it was cut short. Her maid washed it each day, and it stood up like a healthy crown, springing vibrantly from her bony, fragile forehead in a subtly ironic rebuke to her body, which was slack and useless . . . ever since she'd leaped up to pick a strange blue flower glinting in the last sunlight, and Thomson had fired at the movement, sending her body crashing into a ravine, broken and stained with blood. . . .

A knock sounded on the half-open door and Davic came in. Thomson said, "I'll see if my wife's ready."

Adele lay on the massage table, eyes covered with cotton pads. Her thin legs were a deep brown against the white sheet tucked around her hips. Santos was vigorously massaging her neck and shoulders. Adele heard her husband's footsteps.

"George?"

"Yes, Adele. Mr. Davic is here."

"Santos isn't through yet."

She wanted him to stay and watch, of course, to forgive her for the pleasure she took in Santos's hands, those oiled and sturdy fingers which manipulated her wasted muscles and forced contractions that created at least a memory of pleasures she had once known.

She'd always needed forgiveness. He had learned that early about her. That was why she had been disloyal to him, why she had taken lovers, only to be forgiven. That's what he had told himself for a long time. It had helped a little. Her last had been the American colonel in Tehran. Madsen, was that his name? Something like that.

They returned to the bedroom together—her massage table was electrically powered, the controls at her right hand—and Santos helped her under the coverlet.

The muscular Cuban smiled a good night and left the room silently on rubber-soled shoes.

Davic then said, "Judge Flood has agreed to take your testimony from here, Mrs. Thomson. A van from the TV station with a power pickup will relay your testimony to a screen in the courtroom. That screen faces the judge and jury. A TV camera crew will be here"—he glanced about—"probably in front of the closets, the camera shooting at you but including the bed, the books behind you and so forth. The deputy DA will ask you what time you and Earl had dinner that night. I would suggest you watch Miss Brett as she questions you. When you reply, shift your eyes from the monitor to the red light. Then you'll be looking directly at the judge and jury."

Davic paused and glanced at his notes. "There won't be anything in her questions for you to be concerned about. You know exactly when Earl got home, there's always a clock at your bedside. You took no medication, nothing that would make you sleepy or confused. The prosecution will know that you use prescription medicines for pain and insomnia. It's their business to find out such things. We won't sidestep it. We'll bring it out in direct examination. Now . . . Earl showered and changed, remember, before he joined you for dinner. That was his custom, what he did as a matter of course."

"Oh, I know what she's after, all right." Adele's one useful hand stroked the covers tensely. The mattress below her right hand concealed her security needs, a secret compartment installed by Santos, a steel box with her diary, a single pill and a small revolver. "She wants the jury to think I'm a poor excuse

297

for a mother, isn't that what she'll try to prove? That I'm crippled, that I can't push a child in a swing, paddle around a swimming pool—"

"Your relationship to your son is irrelevant, Mrs. Thomson. Miss Brett may inquire *only* into those areas that relate to my direct examination."

"Let her *inquire* then." Adele picked listlessly at threads in the coverlet, snapping them with the thin fingers which had unaccountably escaped the vise gripping the rest of her body. "She's never had a child, you know. She's never had that experience."

Her oiled face became slack, the flesh under her cheekbones sagging toward her mouth. She was like a wax figure beginning to melt, a decorative object carelessly left too close to a flame.

Thomson nodded to Davic and told him he would join him downstairs. The lawyer said good night to Adele and left.

"Today was the worst of it," Thomson said then.

"You promised there'd never *be* a trial."

"Earl will be cleared, Adele."

"But you let her make those obscene charges. That was too much for Earl. It shouldn't have been allowed to happen." Adele's face hardened. Her eyes were sharp again under the cap of lush blond hair. "You've talked with him, you know what he wants. You'd better explain that to Davic."

"Yes," he said. "I intend to."

"I suggest you do before he leaves."

A panel beside Adele's bed controlled a TV set mounted in the ceiling. Snapping it on, she watched a smiling game show host exuberantly addressing a panel of contestants. Her eyes remained fixed on the screen as her husband left the room.

Thomson had talked to his son Earl after the day's session in court, and its stormy conclusion. Earl had been in his room, his face flushed from jogging about the grounds. At first his mood had been ominously mild and reasonable, his emotions masked by an apparent indifference.

"I don't blame you for not understanding," he'd told his father. "But you can't realize what it's like to sit there and have to listen to the things she said. Facing that jury and hearing myself described as a degenerate and a sadist. It just got to me. I couldn't take it any longer. Sorry."

But then as he pulled off his sweat shirt, his voice began to quiver with anger. "A pervert, a sodomist, a goddamn unnatural animal, that's what she kept calling me, and those morons on the jury were licking their lips over it. I know what they're thinking, what fun it'll be to whip my privileged ass. But you don't care, none of you do, because you don't have any idea of loyalty . . ."

It was futile to try to reason with him. Earl had usurped the role of the victim. Now it was *Earl* who had been damaged and vilified and so it was his *right,* more, his *obligation,* to strike back at whatever had hurt and betrayed him.

"Even if I *did* fuck her," Earl had shouted, "even if I did every goddamn thing that bitch is whining about, I'd *still* be innocent in a way you can't appreciate because you don't understand about loyalty to truth, to *ideas* that are more real than any damned little piece of reality, so-called, of the moment. I'm taking the heat because I *believe* in something . . . in an elite society. Damn right . . . and *I* live what I believe in. There never should have been a trial. *I* shouldn't be crucified for trying to live up to something special, to what I believe in, to what, by God, is *right* and *true*—"

"Goddammit, Earl, *listen,*" Thomson had said. "We got problems enough already."

"Screw it. I've taken all the abuse I intend to. You're going to pay them back now, the lying bitch, her hypocrite lawyer and her goddamn righteous father. Did you see him slam me in the chest when the marshals were holding me?" Earl had stopped to draw a deep breath, trying to calm himself, but his neck and face were swollen and red with anger. "Tell that shyster you hired what I want him to do," he'd shouted. "You *tell* him."

Thomson went down the broad stairway from his wife's suite to the foyer, where Allan Davic waited for him. The lawyer had collected his hat and gloves.

"I have an appointment in Philadelphia," he told Thomson. "But I believe we've covered the events that could come up in regard to your wife's testimony. I'm sure she'll make an excellent witness."

"Just one thing," Thomson said. "Forget the talk we had at lunch yesterday."

"I don't understand."

"I'm telling you to use the court-martial material, use every goddamn thing you've got or can get on Selby and the DA. *And* that girl."

"Mr. Thomson, the testimony of the plaintiff today was devastating. Whether you believe her story or not, take it from me as your lawyer . . . those jurors did. She had the whole courtroom with her."

"Davic, I don't want to discuss—"

"May I finish?"

"Go ahead."

"Earl's emotional display in court today probably won't hurt him. That was a reaction people can relate to and even sympathize with. In fact, it might have been the smartest thing he could have done. But make no mistake, we're in a fight. My job is to defend your son, and I've got my work cut out for me. That jury—any jury—is an unpredictable beast. They're supposed to weigh the facts impartially. But too often they believe their job is to *punish* someone, to take revenge. Do you understand what I'm telling you? They *know* there's a victim. They've seen her. She sat before them today. They heard the doctor, those pictures showed the cuts in her hands, the welts on her face. They didn't have to *imagine* those rope burns. Now they're looking for a *culprit.* We *can't* risk creating additional sympathy for Shana Shelby. There's such a thing as legal overkill. We've got a case to make, our witnesses to call. But if we now drag her *father* into it . . . and with him drag the past into it . . . well, we may create results we can't foresee."

"Never mind all that . . . I'm doing what I have to do . . . I don't intend to explain myself any further. Take the wraps off. Use all you've got to hit them. That's the way it's got to be. Good night, Mr. Davic."

After the sound of the attorney's car faded from the drive, Thomson and Dom Lorso talked in the shadowed study.

300

"We can live with it, Giorgio." Dom Lorso studied his cigarette. "Earl wants to protect himself, that's normal. He's taken a lot of shit. But you and I, Giorgio, we gotta be clear about it. Very clear between you and me, okay?"

Thomson opened a bottle of wine and filled two glasses. He snapped on a lamp and was relieved to see the shadows leap away, the light revealing shelves of books and pictures of Adele in silver frames. On a beach with Earl, on a horse in an exercise ring . . .

"Earl should have satisfaction," Lorso was saying, "but we got to know what it could cost, right?"

"It won't cost you, Dom. That's a promise."

"If it hurts you, it hurts me." Lorso inhaled deeply. "Davic does what Earl wants, right? Earl calls the shots?"

Thomson nodded and sipped his wine.

Dom Lorso pointed his cigarette at him. "That's what we got to be clear about. Something could go wrong, Giorgio. You and me, we know Earl was involved with that girl—" He held up a hand. "Hear me out. You don't want to admit it and he probably considers himself innocent the way he looks at it. Maybe he does know more about loyalty than we do . . . except we must've been doing something right for thirty years."

Thomson nodded and drank some wine. It warmed him, was more comforting than whiskey. He'd never lived in a kitchen with melons and cheese hanging on the walls and peppers drying in the windows, but he missed it all the same. Bocci games on church lawns, old men and women sitting out on the stoop in the summer watching children play . . . it was all a world his grandfather Carmine had told him about, but still, he could hear echoes of those distant, safer days in Dom Lorso's doggedly blood-loyal defense of Earl . . .

"The Selby kid, hey, she could be as kinky as a fox, never mind those choir girl eyes. Maybe, once it started, she wanted him to do all that shit to her, threatened to blow a whistle if he *didn't*. I don't put anything past *any* of them. I knew a crazy cunt once liked electric shocks in places you wouldn't mention in front of your mother. I'm with Earl, but if things go wrong, can we handle it *our* way? That's what I got to know, Giorgio."

Thomson shook his head, more an act of despair than an

answer to Lorso's question. "You got your money, Dom, hell, you old guinea bastard, you could buy half of Miami, Palermo, if you want. You can get out now. I wouldn't mind if you did, that's the truth. You're the friend of my life and my heart, Dom. That sounds like a bullshit thing to say, but I heard my grandfather use those very words, and I couldn't have been more than six or eight at the time. Funny the things that stick in a kid's mind."

Lorso lit another cigarette and blew smoke at the ceiling. "How long's Earl had a gun at your head, Giorgio?"

Thomson poured more wine. He offered the bottle to Lorso, but the Sicilian waved it away.

"How long, for Christ's sake?"

Thomson finally said, "I heard Ledge's tapes on that call to Earl. Ledge told him we had a problem with Harry Selby about Summitt. I think Earl took a notion to help us out by scaring the Selby kid, creating a little accident that would get her father home and away from Summitt. He didn't mean to hurt her. Then it got out of hand . . . like that business at Rockland. He panicked when that DA made a case against him. He's got cracks like all of us, Dom. He's afraid, and who can blame him for that? He decided to protect himself. Nobody looks out for number one like number one. We taught him that, Dom." Thomson smiled ironically. "But he's also got other ideas . . . an office next to mine, a place near the center of the Group, a voice in decisions." He sighed. "Can't blame him for that either, I suppose. Once you get power, it's hard not to use it. Otherwise you're never sure you've still got it."

Lorso said, "How long's he had this gun at your head?"

Thomson looked directly at his old friend. "Since that fire at the general's place, since Slocum's people torched Vinegar Hill. That's how long, Dom. But it's not a gun like you mean." Thomson sighed. "It would be simpler if it was. Remember when Earl slipped off and flew from Philadelphia down to Summitt City? And you had Slocum and Eberle burning the wires trying to find out where he was? Well, that's where he found the pressure to use against us."

Thomson sipped his wine and looked out at the darkness beyond the terrace. "He knows we killed Jarrell Selby, and he can prove it. He also pretty well knows why we killed him, that he'd become a threat to our experiment at Summitt City. So you might as well go ahead and buy Sicily and plant the whole damned island in garlic, Dom."

CHAPTER TWENTY-SIX

Before opening for the defense, Davic apologized to the court for Earl Thomson's behavior of the day before.

"There are, Your Honor," he said, "no extenuating circumstances which can or will ever justify a violation of our judicial processes. No pressures are so heavy, no allegations, unfounded or otherwise, so provocative that they may be offered as an excuse for disrespect to the bench or to our legal traditions."

Judge Flood said, "Mr. Davic, the court notes your apology and the defendant's contrition. But I warn you, I will tolerate no further displays of temper from him." Judge Flood liked the sound of that.

"You have my word for that, Your Honor."

"Will you then call your witness?"

There was a stir of anticipation when the clerk stood and said, "The defense re-calls Mr. Harry Selby."

"You are still under oath," Davic reminded Selby after he had taken the stand. "I asked you yesterday what knowledge you had of the defendant or his father prior to the alleged attack on your daughter. I will ask you that again: what knowledge *did* you have, Mr. Selby?"

"None."

"You knew nothing of Earl Thomson, his family or his background?"

"That's right."

"Mr. Selby, is your conscience comfortable with the charges your daughter has brought against the defendant?"

Brett stood up. "I object, Your Honor. The question is pointlessly subjective—"

"Sustained," Flood said. "Please come to your point, Mr. Davic."

"The point, as I emphasized from the outset, is truth." Davic turned from the bench and studied the jurors. "Truth is the heart of this matter. At the heart of the truth, ladies and gentlemen, is the question of motive." Then in an almost conversational tone he said, "Mr. Selby, will you *now* tell us *why* you are attempting to destroy the good name of the defendant, Earl Thomson—?"

"Objection, Your Honor."

Davic quickly pursued his questioning. "What personal reasons have compelled you to inflict such pain and anguish on him and his family? Why are you attacking this young man who—"

"*Objection,* Your Honor! The question is haranguing, abusive and presumptive."

"Sustained."

"All right, Your Honor, but I intend to produce supportive evidence."

Davic turned to the defense table, where Royce handed him a cardboard filing case.

"Your Honor," Davic said, "I will ask the court to identify the following material as Defense Exhibit K.S. 36663864, the United States Army's referral number for this particular material."

"The court stenographer will so identify it."

Several inches thick and bound in a gray plastic, the front cover of the file was stamped with an identifying label. Davic gave each juror an opportunity to read the lettering:

Headquarters of the U.S. Army Office of the Adjutant-General Washington, D.C.

"This document," Davic then told them, "is the transcript of a U.S. Army court-martial, registered in the Office of the Adjutant-General."

305

"Your Honor!" Brett was standing.

"Miss Brett?"

"The prosecution, Your Honor, attempted to obtain the files Counselor Davic introduced. We were told by the Office of the Adjutant-General that the materials were classified and not available."

"Counselor Davic?"

"I don't understand. My request for these files was granted as a matter of course."

Brett said sharply, "Then the material has been mysteriously declassified since *our* request."

Flood said, "I will instruct the defense to provide the People with copies of this document. You may proceed, Mr. Davic."

Selby saw Earl Thomson smile briefly at his father.

"The proceedings of this court-martial," Davic informed the jury, "were recorded more than a quarter of a century ago in South Korea. The trial was ordered by the commanding officer of a counterintelligence unit of the Seventh Army.

"Specifically, a sergeant was charged with manslaughter and unlawfully administering drugs to enemy prisoners, drugs he obtained by theft. As a result, numerous prisoners died, others suffered permanent brain damage. That sergeant received a dishonorable discharge and was sentenced to five years in a military prison."

Davic studied each juror deliberately. "The sergeant who disgraced his country and his uniform was Jonas Harold Selby, the father of Harry Selby, who is seated before you now in the witness stand.

"The president of the court-martial that found Jonas Selby guilty of those charges is also present today"—Davic pointed to the gallery behind the defense table—"*he is George Thomson, formerly Major George Thomson, Sergeant Jonas Selby's commanding officer in Korea.* I asked Mr. Selby *why* he set out to persecute and defame Earl Thomson. I think the reasons are now transparently clear. Harry Selby is attempting to avenge his own father's disgrace and punishment by striking at George Thomson through his son, Earl—"

"Objection, Your Honor. Mr. Davic has made what amounts to a closing statement to the jury." Brett controlled her voice with an effort. "He is drawing conclusions from evidence the People have had no opportunity to examine. The issue at trial"—Brett raised her voice over Flood's gavel—"is not a court-martial convened in Korea thirty years ago. The issue at trial is the *current* violent abuse of a minor child. Is the accused guilty or not? *That* is the issue at—"

"Miss Brett, you will not tell me what issues are at trial. You will not instruct me on what is pertinent to these hearings. Don't press me in that fashion again . . . Mr. Davic?"

But Allan Davic was content to rest on the doubts he'd created. Brett attempted in her redirect to establish that Selby had had no information about the details of his father's court-martial, and no knowledge of George Thomson's part in it. But when she finished her examination it was obvious from the reactions among the jurors that certain sensitive scales had definitely tipped against the credibility of the People's case.

At the recess Selby walked to the underground parking lot where he'd left his car. A slender man with rimless glasses joined him a few minutes later.

"It's a small world, isn't it?" Burt Wilger said, and handed Selby a folded newspaper. "Emma Green's address is on a piece of notepaper clipped to the sports section. She probably won't talk about Earl Thomson. If she tells you to kiss off, I wouldn't crowd her. I'd say she's gun-shy."

"She learned that from Captain Slocum, I guess."

Wilger shrugged, put a toothpick in his mouth and chewed on it, then said, "Well, Selby, cops come in all shapes and sizes. All of them don't shit chocolate ice cream and spend their spare time teaching civics in ghettos."

"Who's leaning on Brett now? Is that Slocum, too?"

"She tell you about it?"

"My daughter did," Selby said. "She heard you talking."

"I don't think it's Slocum." Wilger spat the toothpick from his mouth. "It's some characters from New York, that's all I got. I picked up one of their calls to Brett. They mentioned somebody named Toby Clark. Brett clammed up on me, wouldn't talk about it. The name mean anything to you?"

"No. Who are the New York people working for?"

"Who knows? Davic maybe. Or Lorso, or Thomson himself. There're two of them. Brothers. Ben and Aron Cadle. Might've been that pair that tried to hit Brett the other night. Lucky you were there. If you wonder why I owe you, by the way, that's it. She's good people."

"Let me ask you something," Selby said. "Maybe you can't give a civilian a straight answer, but at least you can tell me if I'm wasting our time—"

"Stop being so damned hard-nosed. Try me."

"Do you believe my daughter's telling the truth?"

"Goddammit, I helped make Brett's case, didn't I?"

"Do you think she'll nail Thomson?"

"I got a very cracked crystal ball about things like that, Selby."

"Captain Slocum perjured himself, didn't he?"

"You said that. I still work for him, remember?"

"Somebody used a ton of pressure to get hold of my father's court-martial," Selby reminded him. "That's the kind of weight she's up against."

"You want it straight, I don't think Brett's got a prayer."

Selby opened the door of his station wagon and dropped the newspaper on the passenger seat. He hesitated a moment, and then said, "We're still in the game, Wilger. We're holding some cards. Goldie Boy Jessup is on the hook to perjure himself. They're paying him for it."

"How'd you find that out?"

Selby hesitated again, then told Wilger what Goldbirn had heard from the Florida police—that the preacher was being given title to land on the Jersey shore near Avalon.

Wilger whistled. "Pretty expensive real estate for saving sinners."

"Let me ask you another question," Selby said. "If you were going to lie under oath, to perjure yourself, what's the first condition you'd insist on?"

"If I was in a position to make demands, which I probably wouldn't be, I'd make sure I couldn't ever get caught. That's a bottom line."

"But somebody's got to lie about Thomson's fingerprints at Vinegar Hill."

"Right. Somebody's *got* to lie about those prints. Somebody *will* lie, Selby. Unless they come up with some bullshit explanation, Thomson's dead. Davic's got to prove to the jury those prints were in the garage at that farm either *before* or *after* your daughter was raped."

"Then somebody else has also got to lie—*will* lie—about the time Thomson came home that night."

"What's your point, Selby?"

"That whoever tells those lies under oath has got to be damn sure it's perfectly safe. That no other area of the case will blow up in his face. But it wouldn't be enough simply to *tell* a prospective perjurer he's got nothing to worry about"—Selby studied the detective—"you're the pro, Wilger. Am I right?"

"Sure . . . you'd have to *prove* it." Wilger shrugged; his expression had become deliberately neutral. "But you're talking about finding that proof, the heat the defense is using, and why they're scared shitless to let this trial take its legal course. It could mean a numbered account somewhere, any kind of blackmail material . . . that means running informants, digging into the sensitive places, surveillance in relays. So try to understand, Selby, I'm a working stiff. I sign in and out of Division, run a shift, fill out case sheets, daydream about a pension . . . Slocum can nail my ass to the floor if he wants to."

Wilger removed his glasses, then polished them with the end of his tie. "Good luck over in Jersey. I've gone as far as I can, Selby. Do me a favor and forget where you got Emma Green's address. Okay?"

Selby nodded and got into the car. Wilger closed the door for him with a soft click of finality.

"Thanks, Sergeant."

"Take care, friend. It's a cold world."

After turning off the old Baltimore Pike, Selby drove through Philadelphia and crossed the George Washington Bridge on his way to the town of Jefferson, New Jersey. . . .

In Superior Court Nine, Allan Davic prepared to continue his attack against the foundation of the People's case against Earl Thomson. He instructed Flood's clerk to call, in order, Ellie May Cluny, Charles Lee, Miguel Santos and finally the accused's mother, Mrs. George Thomson.

* * *

A waitress in The Green Lantern, Ellie May was in her twenties, solemnly pretty with a full bosom and attractive legs. She made a good witness.

Earl Thomson, she testified, had been in the Lantern around five o'clock that Friday afternoon back in October. Ellie May pointed to Earl and identified him; that was the man she'd served some beers to while he was waiting for Charlie Lee. Ellie May knew Charlie Lee; he worked at a mushroom house in Hockessin, over in Delaware.

On cross-examination, Brett asked how, after several months, Ellie May could identify Earl Thomson so positively. Very few white people came by the Lantern, Ellie May answered. Mr. Thomson naturally stood out. He was dressed cool, too, good jacket, nice sports shirt and a shiny kind of chain necklace and ring, and a watch he kept studying.

He'd talked to Ellie May about buying a gun from Charlie Lee. But Charlie Lee called and told her they'd had a flush—a "flush" was an overnight sprouting of mushrooms that had to be picked right away. She'd put Earl Thomson on the phone.

"Miss Cluny, did you know that Earl Thomson's car was stolen while he was in The Green Lantern?"

"No, ma'am, I didn't."

"After the call from Mr. Lee, what did Mr. Thomson do then?"

"He seemed kind of pouty."

" 'Pouty'?"

"Kind of mad, ma'am."

"But what did he do?"

"He just left, ma'am. Threw down some money, and went out."

"Miss Cluny, is The Green Lantern's phone private?"

"No, ma'am, it's a pay phone. Bartender answers it, calls for whoever it is."

"Anyone in The Green Lantern can use that phone, right?"

"Yes, ma'am."

"But Mr. Thomson did not return and use that phone?"

"No, ma'am, he didn't."

"Have you seen or talked with Mr. Thomson since that Friday afternoon last October?"

310

"No, ma'am, I haven't."

"Thank you, Miss Cluny."

Charlie Lee was a stocky, middle-aged black man, dressed in a blue suit with a denim shirt and black tie. His testimony was simple and direct: he owned a Parker shotgun and wanted to sell it. Mr. Earl Thomson answered his newspaper ad and they agreed to meet at The Green Lantern. But the mushrooms had flushed a day early, and he had to break the date. Ellie May told him the white man was there, called him to the phone. He'd explained about the flush to Mr. Thompson, told him he had to work.

"Mr. Lee, did Mr. Thomson make another appointment with you at that time?"

"No, ma'am, he didn't."

"Did you suggest one?"

"Sure, 'cause I wanted to sell the shotgun. But he told me to forget it, like he was disgusted, and hung up."

"You had no further contact with him since that time?"

"No, ma'am."

"Did you sell your shotgun to someone else, Mr. Lee?"

"No, ma'am. I still got it."

"Well, I hope you find a buyer, Mr. Lee. Thank you."

The attention of the jurors sharpened when Miguel Santos was called to the stand. The testimony of Adele Thomson's therapist was crucial to the defense structure and it was obvious Davic intended to shore it up as firmly as possible.

Santos was attentive, his voice determined, earnest, anxious. His eyes followed Davic with obedient interest. A film of sweat shone on his broad, smooth forehead.

The Cuban's nervousness seemed to stem from an immigrant's pride at participating in such important official proceedings, plus a fear of failing to live up to whatever was expected of him; his attempts to be responsive and cooperative were painful in their eagerness, but seemed to make a favorable impression on the jurors.

311

On cross, Brett asked, "Mr. Santos, do you have a valid United States driver's license?"

"No, miss, I don't."

"How long have you been in this country, Mr. Santos?"

"Objection, Your Honor."

"Sustained."

"Mr. Santos, are you a competent driver? A good driver?"

"Oh, yes, I drive all kinds of trucks, cars, in Cuba. Very good."

"Then when Mr. Thomson called you on that occasion we're talking about—early Friday evening, October sixteenth—you weren't worried about driving over to Muhlenburg to pick him up? Is that correct?"

"*Sí*, yes, correct."

"It didn't bother you to be asked to drive fifteen miles at night through rush-hour traffic? That didn't worry you at all?"

"No, miss. I drive very well."

"You were not concerned about not having a driver's license?"

Santos shrugged uncertainly. He looked for help to Davic, who stood and said, "Your Honor, many Cubans who fled the present regime there are political refugees. Naturally they don't have official papers. It's difficult for them to obtain U.S. drivers' licenses. That isn't Mr. Santos's fault."

"Your point is well taken, Mr. Davic. The question is irrelevant in any case. Go on, Miss Brett."

"Mr. Santos, how long have you worked for the Thomson family?"

"Seven years, ma'am."

"In that time were you ever asked to serve as a chauffeur for Earl Thomson?"

"No . . . I don't think so, miss."

"Do you mean 'yes' or 'no,' Mr. Santos?"

"I mean no, miss."

"Then you must have been surprised when Earl Thomson asked you to drive to Muhlenburg and pick him up. Were you surprised?"

"A little." Santos shrugged. "But I am there at the house to work, you know, miss. I do what work is there, what I'm asked."

"Then you were *not* surprised at Mr. Thomson's request?"

312

"Objection, Your Honor."

"Sustained."

"Judge Flood," Brett said, "I'm trying to establish that the actions Miguel Santos took that night were of an unusual nature, an *unprecedented* nature. Surely the jury is entitled to a clarification of these *unique* circumstances."

"Miss Brett, I have sustained defense counsel's objection. I'd appreciate it if you'd get on to something else now."

Brett again took the stocky Cuban over the events of that particular Friday night—a second time and a third. With each repetition, it became increasingly obvious that Santos's testimony had been carefully committed to memory; his answers were a word-for-word duplication of his testimony to Davic on direct examination.

Santos had been in his quarters above the garage when Thomson had phoned from Muhlenburg. This was five-thirty— "or maybe a little after." Mr. Thomson asked Santos to drive over to Muhlenburg. The chauffeur, Richard, was not home— he was in New Jersey with Mr. Thomson, Mr. *George* Thomson. Santos had left immediately in a family car. Santos described the route he'd taken that night with mechanical accuracy, listing without hesitation a stream of street names and route numbers. But Brett gained little by establishing that Santos's account seemed to be memorized; his methodical delivery strengthened his credibility with the jury because it appeared so in keeping with his character. The Cuban obviously was the sort of person who would have to be certain of his facts before he would put a hand on a Bible and swear to them.

"Mr. Santos, where did you pick up Mr. Thomson in Muhlenburg?"

"In front of a diner. He told me where he would be. The Bellflower diner."

"He was waiting outside?"

"Yes, miss."

"Who drove home then, Mr. Santos?"

"He did. Mr. Thomson."

"Did he tell you his car had been stolen?"

"No, miss."

"Did you ask him about it?"

"About what, miss?"

313

"About what happened to his Porsche Turbo 924?"

"No, miss."

"Weren't you curious?"

"Objection, Your Honor."

"Sustained."

"Mr. Santos, what time did you and Earl Thomson arrive at the Thomson home?"

"Seven o'clock, just about seven."

"What time did you go to bed that night?"

"Maybe ten, ten-thirty o'clock."

"Did you have dinner after you returned from Muhlenburg?"

"Yes."

"Did you eat alone?"

"In my room. Yes."

"You stayed alone in your room until you went to bed?"

"Yes."

"Thank you, Mr. Santos."

The defense then called Mrs. George Thomson, but Judge Flood ordered a half-hour recess to give the TV technicians time to set up and test their equipment and remote hook-up to her home.

Adele Thomson wore tiny pearl earrings and a blue bed jacket with a microphone clipped to a quilted lapel. Her maid had brushed her tight, vibrant curls into a soft crescent around her fragile forehead; they were like a small, shining halo against the white bedstead and pillows.

Her image was brought to the courtroom on a large screen set up beside Judge Flood's bench. It was immediately obvious that her appearance created a favorable and heightened emotional impact on the court and the jury; her motionless body provided a touching contrast to her resonant voice and lively, intelligent eyes. She seemed intent on testifying clearly and accurately, her manner suggested an eagerness to cooperate and, more important for its effect on the jurors, a gallant indifference to her physical helplessness.

Her account was simple and straightforward . . . Earl had stopped by her room around seven o'clock on the night in question. She was certain of the time. Two clocks, one electric, the other solar-powered, were in clear view of her bed.

314

Earl was dining with her that evening. After looking in to say hello, he'd gone off to shower and change. He returned fifteen minutes later. They had a glass of wine and watched the end of the news. Dinner had been prepared; Earl set up trays and served.

Davic asked if she could have been mistaken about the time. Had she taken any medication before Earl arrived? Was it possible she'd been drowsy or confused?

Adele Thomson replied firmly in the negative. She had taken no medicine, cough syrups or alcohol (except the single glass of wine) that night. She volunteered that she did take medication on occasion, both for pain and to help her sleep. Prescription drugs—five milligram Valium and Dalmane. Actually she hadn't taken anything that night. With a smile, she said, "Imagine taking a sleeping pill when you're expecting your son for dinner."

They had talked and watched television until ten-thirty or eleven o'clock. Then Earl went off to his own room.

"Then it's your sworn testimony, Mrs. Thomson," Davic said, "that your son was with you from seven o'clock until approximately eleven o'clock on that Friday night last October sixteenth?"

"Yes. That's what I've told you, Mr. Davic, that's right."

"Thank you very much, Mrs. Thomson. I know this has been an ordeal for you. I have no further questions, Your Honor."

Brett began her cross-examination by assuring Mrs. Thomson that if she wanted to pause or rest at any time, that would be satisfactory to the prosecution.

"Thank you, but I don't require any special consideration. I'm not a hothouse flower, Miss Brett, regardless of what you may think. I can be as strong as I need to be, particularly in circumstances like these."

"Mrs. Thomson, when your son stopped by your room for the first time on that night in question—before he showered and changed—did you notice what he was wearing?"

"No, I don't believe I did."

"Was his hair damp?"

315

"I think it was. Yes, I'm sure it was. It had started to rain, as I recall."

"Were his garments wet, Mrs. Thomson?"

"I suppose they were. Does it matter?"

"Did you notice if his shoes were muddy?"

"No, I would have noticed that." Adele's frail hand gestured to her carpets. "Everything here is white, you see. He would have tracked dirt all over the place."

"Mrs. Thomson, did your son always shower and change before dinner?"

"Well, I surely encouraged him to. Any mother would understand that, Miss Brett. I wasn't always successful, of course, particularly when he was young—"

"When your son returned to your room, what was he wearing, Mrs. Thomson?"

The question seemed to surprise Adele, her hand plucked at the cord of the microphone. "I'm not sure."

"You don't remember what he was wearing?"

Adele Thomson's voice rose. "Are you suggesting I was in no condition to know what he was wearing? That I wasn't even sure of the time. Is that what you're getting at?"

"Mrs. Thomson, you testified you had taken no medication that night. I have no reason or intention to question that."

"My son was wearing—" Adele was frowning. "He was wearing—I remember quite clearly—slacks, gray flannels, and a sports shirt with short sleeves. But he wasn't wearing his watch, or any jewelry. I do recall the details, you see. He'd taken a shower and hadn't bothered to put them back on. But there's no doubt about the time, my clocks are very dependable. You can have them checked if you wish."

"Mrs. Thomson, did your son tell you Miguel Santos had driven him home that night from Muhlenburg?"

"No."

"Did he tell you his car had been stolen?"

"Of course he didn't."

"Why do you say 'of course,' Mrs. Thomson?"

"You wouldn't understand, and it would probably be a waste of time explaining." Adele's voice was strained. "Earl would never worry me about such things."

"Forgive me, Mrs. Thomson, for laboring the point. When did you learn your son's car had been stolen?"

"I have no idea."

"He never mentioned it to you?"

"He's my son!" Adele's voice was rising again. "He would never frighten me, or worry me about such things. I'm his *mother.*"

"Forgive me again, but why would it frighten you to know his car had been stolen?"

"It would destroy a . . . mood. He would never upset me like that. He loves me, don't you see? Why are you trying to hurt him?"

Adele closed her eyes, but not before the camera lights caught the glitter of her tears. Davic gripped Earl Thomson's arm and forced him back into his chair.

Brett said, "Your Honor, I regret any distress I may have caused the witness. I have no further questions."

As she walked to the plaintiff's table, Brett's eyes fell on the empty chair in the gallery behind Shana. Harry Selby hadn't come back to the courtroom since testifying that morning. His absence was a reminder of his presence . . . of *him* . . . to her, she realized, as Judge Flood announced the lunch recess.

CHAPTER TWENTY–SEVEN

She was light-skinned with oddly flecked brown eyes and kinky red hair cut short above a broad face. Her expression was wearily impassive, but it suggested to Selby a childish petulance rather than mature reserve. The roots of Emma Green's bronze-colored hair were dark when the light touched them. A scar on her upper lip tended to pull her mouth into a grimace. Two of her upper front teeth were missing. She kept a hand close to her face when she talked.

An eight-year-old daughter, Libby, was studying at a table in the kitchen off the living room, but her agile little body was twisted around to watch Selby.

Emma Green wore jeans that were tight across her stomach, and a blue T-shirt with the words "Country Gal" stitched in white on the front. She was thirty-two and didn't want to talk about Earl Thomson.

"I had my fill of that big honky shit with his uniform and all. He fucked me over good. And no real cause for it, if you'd like to know the truth. But it was a long time back, mister, days long gone."

A church bell rang somewhere down the block. Emma Green lived in a white frame house on a dirt lot outside of Jefferson, New Jersey.

Rockland Military College—Selby had driven by there earlier—was twenty miles away, sprawled across neatly tended acres, with playing fields marked by white goal posts, tennis courts, an enclosed skating rink and a half-dozen fieldstone buildings standing about a rectangular quad—dormitories, classrooms and administration offices.

The entrance to Rockland was marked by stone columns topped by a rounded arch. On the face of this span, the school's motto was carved in Roman capitals: THY COUNTRY IS THINE HONOR.

"That Earl boy was such a mean fucker, he got up early and stayed up late just to work at it."

"Momma, don't you talk that way," her daughter called from the kitchen.

"Never you mind, Libby. Just study them books."

Libby came to the door between the two rooms. She wore a blue blouse and a tartan skirt. Her black hair was pulled into side braids and tied with white ribbons.

"She's *busing* now," Emma Green told Selby, and smiled derisively at her daughter.

Libby was embarrassed. She frowned and put her hands on her hips. "You keep your mouth off me, momma. Miss Keener says that kind of talk is common. She says it's how drunk women talk."

"Listen to her, mister. She's got little white friends and they go to their houses after school and cook things in the kitchen and make candy. They don't think nothing of the mess, them white mommies."

"You say his name when you asleep," Libby said. She looked seriously at Selby. "I'm not lying, mister. She used to say his name out, call out near *all* of 'em that she had . . . that's the truth."

"You a sweet child, Libby, but it's days long gone. Miss Keener, she's your friend. You listen to her. I love you, baby."

"You want something, you don't fool me."

"Just a touch, honey. It's my day off." Her voice was easy. "Don't be mad. I used to be pretty like you." She smiled at Selby, but hard defensive lines had formed around her mouth.

Libby went into the kitchen and brought back a pint of gin and a glass half-filled with water. "You sweet, you really are," her mother said, and smoothed the child's hair.

Emma Green was only an inch or so above five feet with

319

wide hips and large, firmly molded breasts. Her lips were full and handsome, even with the scar that pulled the mouth up into an expression of sly skeptical anger. Her skin was clear and smooth, and Selby could easily imagine how pretty she must have been.

Libby closed the door. Emma Green poured a little gin into the glass and sipped from it. "I do the check-out at Safeway market all week so a little drink on my day off don't hurt. I surely am sorry for your kid, mister, but I ain't writin' nothing down about what they done to me.

"They showed me I was still a nigger wench, that's what they did. Never mind Martin and JFK and that shit people got so excited about. I believed it, too, I guess." She covered her mouth and laughed. "'I *do* believe . . .' Thought black was beautiful, the colleges and good jobs and *everything* gonna bust wide open for us. You honky bastards shouldn't lie and fool us, 'cause we're so damned dumb . . ." She laughed and tapped her forehead. "—solid bone up here, solid ivory from Africa. What's the fun of it? But I was pretty and had me a nice-sounding laugh, if I say so myself. Low and easy, not like some dumb-ass darky screeching and showin' off. I could show you pictures of me laughing. You'd see how it was. How people liked to hear me laugh."

She sipped the gin and water. "I worked at a bar over near the college. The bar was named The Letter Drop. We was off limits, the soldier boys, they'd sneak in at night and go upstairs with the gals.

"The name Letter Drop, you see, was a joke. Let 'er drop . . . see? Get out of them drawers, boy. Earl, he was a boss man, the others minded him 'cause he could be wild and mean, see. One night a new soldier boy came for the first time. They called him AC-DC, he didn't want to go upstairs with any of us. They got on him, Earl mostly, yelling and teasing him. They was a kind of bet with him and Earl. They made him go up with me, 'cause they said I was the prettiest and laughed the most and if he couldn't make it with me, he'd better start looking for somethin' scusin' gash."

Shielding her mouth, Emma Green drank again and ran her tongue around her lips. "But the soldier boy couldn't do it. He got undressed and I could tell he was scared. It was all shriveled up, hiding from me. I was mad at first, I was so pretty, and I was clean, so what was he afraid of? What'd he come upstairs for anyway? I started touching him, rubbing him nice, but nothing could make that little thing of his stand up and look around. He was a nice built boy, too, strong and brown, kind of. He started crying when I told him we better go downstairs. I was still working see, and needed some more tricks, but he begged me not to. He was kind of nice. Said it wasn't because I was colored or anything. I felt good about him saying that, so I asked if there was anything he wanted me to do. Something he was ashamed to tell me . . . but he said no and went on crying, saying he couldn't do it with girls. They was calling him AC-DC, Ace for short, because they thought he could go *two* ways, but he couldn't go *no* way with me . . . I told him to shush crying. We'd dunce Earl. I told him to start laughing and pretending like we was carrying on. So that's what we did. Drank some wine and I started shrieking and making goosey noises and giggles. I'm calling him sweet names and moaning like he was driving me wild. We was standing close to the door so they'd hear us downstairs. I yelled—'slow down, boy, you're passing my *heart.*' And I called out real loud, 'My, my, you so big, you could lean over and give your *own* self a blow job, honey.' "

Emma Green sighed and drank some gin. "Didn't mean no harm, mister, just thought to help the kid. He was payin' good money. When we went down to the bar, well, lordy, they treated that hombre like a hero, pounding him on the back and buying him beers. Everybody was happy but Earl, 'cause he didn't like us fussing over AC-DC and having to pay off the bet."

The church bells sounded again. The small room was quiet. Small white paper napkins were spread on the arms and headrests of chairs. The tables and windowsills were clean and shiny with furniture polish; a lemon fragrance mingled with the tart, wild berry smell of the watered gin.

"All this busin' gonna lead to heartbreak, you watch." Emma Green's eyes were sad. She drank again, but didn't bother covering her mouth. She put the glass down and let her hands rest palms up in her lap, a weary gesture that reminded him of Lori Gideen.

"I thought nothing bad could happen to me because I was pretty. Men would just about die to get me in bed. They couldn't

321

get enough of me. My waist was so tiny, they could put their hands all the way around it. I got pictures I could show you, mister, but it don't matter no more."

Sighing, she picked up her glass. "I'll *tell* you about Earl, and that fucker from over in Pennsylvania, a cop, Slocum, his name was. But I ain't writing it down or signing it, see. One of the other girls heard me and that little ole AC-DC cadet talking about foolin' Earl. Girl called Rocio, she was part Mex. Heard us goin' on about pretending to screw up a storm. She told Earl. Don't know why. She's dead now, poor baby, got a cold and died of it. So one night a couple days later, I was walking home and it was dark. I lived with my daddy and he helped out with Libby. Earl stopped me in a car, almost ran me down. He had some of the other soldier boys with him. They pulled me into the car and Earl told me he knew about what me and the queer had done. I tried to pretend it was a joke, but Earl was in a crazy mood, said nobody could make a fool of him. Driving through the dark with them soldier boys holding me, I thought all right, gal, you gotta take your whippin'. You asked for it, you gonna get it. They drove me to an old place with a basement. Couldn't see too clear 'cause the only light was little bitty candles in bottles. They had that boy down there, three of them holding him down on a mattress. He was buck naked, all little goose pimples, and crying. The soldier boys was teasing him. They hollered when Earl brought me in. He made me take my clothes off and get on top of the boy. I could feel how scared he was. Then they rolled him on top of me and pulled my legs open. I don't know how long it went on, they shouting he'd better fuck me if he knew what was good for him.

"They pulled him off me. Earl made him watch while *he* fucked me. I was bleeding. It wasn't my time, but I started anyway. They rubbed it on that boy, on his stomach and chest, and made me watch while they messed around with him, played with him and teased him till his cock got stiff. He was crying and begging them to let him loose but they kept messing with him. He laid there real quiet after a bit, whimpering like a puppy. They all laughed like crazy folks then and jerked him off. After he came, they messed his jizz with my body blood and smeared it on his face, said maybe that would make a man out of him. They let him up then but they made him sign a long paper saying he couldn't fuck girls, that he was a queer and all. Everybody signed it, and Earl promised that he'd get everybody a copy. . . ." Selby remembered that a priest at St. Ambrose had once expounded the proposition to him that "the existence of hell was irrefutable proof of the compassionate nature of mankind's Heavenly Father." Earl Thomson could have been his disciple.

"There's not any more to tell," Emma said, "except what that fucker Earl did then. He tied me up and he beat me like he was afraid to stop. He kept telling me how bad *I* was. That sounds crazy, I know, mister, but it's true.

"I remember bein' in a car, and then a field. It was cold. Half my clothes was off and my hands was still tied. A white man and woman found me, took me to a hospital. I don't remember that part of it. Some doctor hadda pull my teeth out.

"The cops came and went to the school. But all them soldier boys was asleep in their bunks, nobody been anywhere that night. There was a little fuss. My daddy and the people who found me, the white folks, they thought something ought to be done. That's when Slocum came over to the house and talked to me. He had a little wop fucker with him . . . I think Dom something. They showed me how beautiful black was, mister. They said I better be careful. My boss at The Letter Drop, he told me to listen to 'em. That Slocum, he says Earl was just funnin' with me, nothing to cause trouble about. I wouldn't sign a paper they wanted me to. I told that bastard Slocum and that dago prick to fuck off. So I lost my job. Boss said nobody'd want to look at me no more. My daddy, he was a welder, *his* boss got the word to him. Slocum said if I didn't drop the charges, it would happen again, and my daddy would be watching. So then I signed what they wanted. Nobody cared I was pretty, I got pictures proving it, but that didn't matter. Nobody cared about this little nigger. You don't care, mister. What *you* doing here there, you big honky fucker, staring at me—?"

"Momma, stop. *Please* stop."

Emma Green had been shouting. She took a deep breath and smiled shakily at Selby. "She is sweet, my Libby. No real daddy, but they set a store by her at school. This ain't helping you, mister. That Earl's crazy. He wanted to mess up daddy's boss and the man owned The Letter Drop, never mind they lied and helped him. Tried to get that wop fucker to hurt them. You better go, hear?"

Selby nodded. He smiled a goodbye at Libby and turned to the door.

Emma Green said, "You ain't gonna ask to look at my picture? See I wasn't just braggin'?"

"I'll take your word for it."

"You ain't no hustler, are you, man? You kind of dumb too."

"Momma, stop talking that way."

"Well, it's the truth." Emma Green was near tears. "He know if he looks at the picture and says how nice I look that I'll be foolish crazy and write anything he wants. Don't you know that, mister?"

"I'm not going to add to your problems, Emma."

"Hey, I ain't got only a few teeth left to get knocked loose anyway. Sit down, go ahead, sit, you and Libby can look at 'em together while I write it down."

There were photographs of Emma Green and her friends in a pickup truck at a beach. A sheet was spread on the sand, held down at the corners by six-packs of beer. Others were of Emma in the stands of a highschool stadium, in backyards and porches, one of a teenage Emma standing with a laughing group in an arcade of pinball machines. Libby hung over the back of the chair, pointing over Selby's shoulder, identifying her mother, naming friends she remembered hearing about.

Emma's hair was black then. She was small and slim and pretty, with a direct, confident smile. Her daughter pointed to those pictures with particular pride, the ones where her mother was smiling and showing her perfect white teeth.

While Selby looked through the album, Emma Green put her drink aside and covered page after page in her daughter's notebook with childishly round handwriting. She then told Libby to leave off studying the old pictures and go down to the church and get the minister and his wife.

Emma Green smiled tensely at Selby, not bothering to cover her damaged mouth. "I told you you shouldn't fool us, mister. We too dumb for good fun. Look what I'm doing. I'm writing it all down about that fucker Earl. See what I mean about *dumb?*"

Selby turned off the highway at an exchange near Camden and called home from a pay phone at a gas station.

It was late afternoon and overcast; it had taken the Reverend Elmer Davis, an efficient but simmeringly angry black man, almost two hours to type up Emma Green's deposition and to have the documents duplicated, witnessed by his wife and Selby and notarized by a local bank officer.

At the end of the block was a small meadow covered with shallow water, natural terrain enclosed by industrial grime. Birds swam and fed among the stubby weed patches. Currents moved in sluggish waves over the sheaths of dirty ice. Fine for ducks, Casper would complain, if there weren't so many cars and gas pumps and people around. But nothing would look very cheerful now, Selby knew, with the memories of her broken smile and the daughter's shy goodbyes.

Mrs. Cranston answered his ring and told him she was glad he'd called. Not that anything was wrong. Davey was home from school and Miss Brett was driving Shana back from East Chester.

But a Sergeant Wilger phoned and wanted Mr. Selby to call him as soon as he could. She gave him a number Selby didn't recognize. It wasn't the Detective Division or Wilger's apartment.

He dialed and waited. From the booth he could see gas pumps, a littered street, rows of auto body and repair shops.

A phone was lifted. Wilger said, "Selby?"

"That's right."

"Where are you calling from?"

"I'm in a pay booth."

"Okay, so am I. I didn't want to use the office or my place. How'd it go?"

"She's gun-shy, like you said. But I've got it in writing, witnessed and notarized. What good it will do is something else."

"I called her place trying to get you but you'd left. Then I left a message at your home. I picked up something at the Hall you should know. Another of them funny links. Word is, the defense is bringing in a witness from Germany who'll blow

Brett's case out of court. Also I heard the psychiatrist is testifying for Davic tomorrow and Brett told me it could be rough. So I had a double Scotch and thought screw Slocum. I'm going to the airport to see who else is interested in the GI from Frankfurt."

"So you know who it is? Do you know his name?"

"Sure. He's Derek Taggart, Ace Taggart from Rockland, General Adam Taggart's son."

The shore birds had settled in for the night; the cold, gray meadow was quiet.

"Thank you, Sergeant," Selby said. "I mean that."

It was almost dark when he left the phone booth. A glare of traffic rose from the Camden Pike. A last fading light lay across the stretch of marshland, which spread like a cracked and smudged mirror under the gently drifting birds and frost-white weeds.

CHAPTER TWENTY-EIGHT

Early the next morning Selby drove Shana into East Chester. Brett had asked them to come to her office before court convened; she needed the time to prepare Shana for Dr. Clemens's probable inferences and conclusions.

But when they arrived Brett's secretary told Selby there was a call for him from Senator Dixon Lester's office in Washington. He took it in Brett's reception room.

"Mr. Selby? Mr. Harry Selby? I'm Victoria Kim, Senator Lester's staff coordinator. Do you have a moment to talk, Mr. Selby?" Her voice was full of energy, and flat with an unmistakable midwestern accent. Without waiting for his answer she said, "We've been monitoring the Earl Thomson trial as a matter of course, Mr. Selby. The senator's committee has an ongoing investigation that includes George Thomson."

"Yes, I've read about that."

"Our interest in the trial was routine until yesterday when the defense introduced the transcript of the Jonas Selby court-martial. That shifted the emphasis from a local defense of Earl Thomson to a personal attack against you and your late father. I sent off a record of that testimony by jet courier to Senator Lester last night. The senator's in Belgium presently. He called later to ask if you'd meet with him and discuss this development."

"What 'development'? I'm not sure I understand—"

"Has the defense offered you any inducement to drop the charges?"

"You mean some kind of bribe, a payoff?"

"Mr. Selby"—her voice sharpened with impatience—"I can make the eleven A.M. shuttle flight to Philadelphia. We have a suite at the Hamilton on the Fairmount Parkway. Do you know the Hamilton?"

"Yes."

"Would it be possible for you to meet me there, about twelve-thirty this afternoon?"

"Miss Kim, I'm on my way to court for the morning's hearings. I didn't know anything about the committee's interest in this trial *or* in my father's court-martial. I was never able to get a copy of that transcript myself, as you may know. But the defense had no trouble getting it, and it seems you didn't either."

"I'm sorry if I've caught you at a bad time, Mr. Selby. I can't discuss this on the phone, but I do urge you to cooperate. If the Hamilton isn't convenient, I'll meet anywhere you suggest."

"No, the Hamilton's fine." Selby looked at his watch, then said, "Miss Kim, I need help. I'm willing to trade for it. If you understand and agree to that, I'll see you around twelve-thirty."

"Can you give me an idea what you'd have to trade, Mr. Selby?"

"I'll bring it with me."

After hanging up, he returned to Brett's office and explained that he was driving over to Philadelphia but would try to be back as soon as possible after his meeting with the senator's assistant. He gave Shana a kiss, nodded to Brett and headed for the elevators.

When court convened at ten o'clock, Counselor Davic addressed this question to the defense expert witness, Dr. Leslie Clemens.

"In your monograph, Doctor, which appeared last February in the *Psychiatric Review,* you used the terms 'victim-signal' and 'victim-language.' You also stated that in assault and rape cases, some victims are, in fact, crying out *not for help* but for abuse and humiliation. Would you explain these concepts more fully to the court, Dr. Clemens?"

328

"I'll try. Studies of sexual pathology contain case histories characterized by these so-called victim-signals. In my article I was referring to body language and facial expressions, combined with certain clothing and terrain by which women advertise their availability as willing partners in unconventional erotic activities."

To the intent jury and spectators, Dr. Leslie Clemens was drawing—under Davic's questioning—a portrait of a specific class of female with whom the plaintiff, Shana Selby, might logically be identified.

"At first glance," the doctor continued, "the signals may seem artless or even unconscious, but the literature of abnormal sexual tendencies, not to mention plain commonsense, tell us these advertisements, these sexual alerts are more often than not deliberately and cleverly planned."

Dr. Clemens adjusted his cuffs and shifted his position on the witness stand to more effectively keep in view the jurors. "I have examined Miss Selby on three separate occasions. Each interview lasted an hour or more. I'd like to state that my judgments fall only within the parameters of probability, but my conclusions are supported by numerous accounts of sexual dysfunction that I am familiar with as a physician and which, in certain instances, I myself have authored . . ."

Tall and slender with short brown hair, graying in patches above rather knobby ears, Dr. Clemens, except for a head somewhat larger below those ears than above—cheekbones and jaw more prominent than temples and forehead—was handsome, with pleasant, if somewhat formal manners.

He went on to explain that the death of Shana's mother, coinciding with Shana's own onset of adolescence, and burgeoning womanhood, had surely been a traumatizing blow to the young girl . . . A causal relationship was very common in such situations. When a mother's death occurred at the time of a daughter's passage into sexual maturity, that new sense of life that otherwise might be so welcome became a guilty burden. A kind of rebuke to the dead mother, causing and reinforcing feelings of responsibility for her death. Such daughters tended to feel they had stolen this precious gift, the power to conceive and nurture life, from the departed mother. Now Shana Selby had experienced her first menstrual period just one month after her mother's death. Studies of sexual disorders ranged extensively over this specific subject—the theft-association between the approach of menses and the death of a maternal parent. In such situations it would be unlikely that a daughter could enter into sexual relationships in a normal manner, since a pleasurable experience might be an unbearably guilty reminder, to her, of what she had presumably stolen . . . Such bruised psyches tended to take refuge from their sexual desires—which they often found punitively keen and insatiable—by retreating into emotional connections with *idealized, unavailable* figures—or into other fantasy worlds where their sexual drives might be internalized. But at other times such damaged young females might deliberately place themselves in jeopardy situations and send out *victim*-signals to alert males to their presence, availability, *thereby* provoking attention, aggression, and even sexual attacks. This way they could at once satisfy and be punished for their sexual drives, which at the onset of menses would be straining powerfully. They might well encourage a chance male to molest them, to abuse and assault them, even to commit rape on them but—*crucial* to their simultaneous need for a virginal self-image—they would *insist* that they had been *forced* into those acts against their wills.

At this point Davic asked Clemens to be more specific about the victim-signals.

The vocabulary of this system of communications, Dr. Clemens said, was clear and extensive, although it couldn't always be interpreted accurately, especially by understandably protective relatives and parents.

The doctor commenced to tick them off on his fingers . . . jeans, tight, constricting jeans were obvious. Belts made of leather and ropes and chains were another, pulled painfully tight across creased and sucked-in stomachs. Wedged soles that made running (flight) impossible, foot gear with thongs and straps binding ankles and calves in painful cincture, all were potential "advisers" to the stalking male, signaled a willingness to participate in a kind of bondage. Any female who permitted herself to be tied up and gagged—no easy matter without at least a certain unconscious cooperation or submission from the so-called victim—was very possibly signaling her readiness to accept not only sadistic sex but other humiliating punishment that

330

her, in effect, invited guest might want to inflict . . .

Under Davic's prompting, Dr. Clemens gave as further examples women who exercised "in brief attire" in front of undraped windows, used washing machines in basement laundry rooms or public laundromats late at night because they had supposedly forgotten or postponed that chore during the day, loitered in poorly lit stacks in public libraries, allowed their cars to run out of gas on deserted highways or turnpikes, or hitchhiked along such highways . . . or rode a bicycle at dusk on lonely country roads, even short distances from their homes . . .

A pause as Davic looked at Shana, and then at the jury.

These were not *accidents,* Dr. Clemens said . . . no, they were contrived situations in which the elements of seduction were gathered together with premeditation—subconscious or not—in a place favorable to sexual combustion, just as if paper and dry twigs and kindling had been piled high and splashed with flammable liquids, needing only the single chance spark to set them off. . . .

At that point Counselor Davic thanked his witness and announced to the bench that he had no further questions. With a pleasant smile he addressed Dorcas Brett with an old-fashioned legal phrase, "The People may inquire if they so wish." Then he sat down at the defense table.

Brett's face was white with anger. She stood up and said, "The People certainly intend to inquire, Mr. Davic. We will examine the *expert* witness and his novel speculations. We—"

Judge Flood interrupted with a glance at the wall clock. "If it's agreeable, Miss Brett, and to you, Mr. Davic, I think tempers might cool over a recess for lunch."

Victoria Kim was a striking Eurasian in her early thirties, Selby judged, with a narrow, elegant face and graceful hands. Her clothing and eyes heightened her exotic appearance; a slim pink cashmere suit, heavy coral bracelets. Her eyes were dramatically emphasized with blue eyeliner and a velvet sheen of mascara on her thick lashes.

They met in a suite with a view of the river and its sculling boathouses. A suede coat and pieces of matching luggage were in the adjoining bedroom. After they introduced themselves, Miss Kim lifted a receiver and dialed room service. "Would you like coffee and sandwiches, Mr. Selby, or something to drink and a decent lunch?"

"Just the coffee, thanks," Selby said. He hadn't been eating regularly, and while he was hungry he couldn't rid himself of a vague suspicion that he might be accepting hospitality in the camp of the enemy. There had been so many evasions and lies to this point that he accepted a sense of paranoia as his only practical defense against them. If you didn't suspect that the pulling guards had homicidal designs on you there would be no need for face guards and helmets.

Selby unwrapped the package that contained his father's diaries and placed the weathered notebooks on a coffee table.

After explaining how they had come into his possession, he said, "As far as I know, Miss Kim, no one has seen these but my father and the lawyer in Truckee, California. I took them to Summitt City but never had a chance to show them to Jarrell. This is my part of the trade. Now here's what I'd like in return . . ."

Her smooth oval face and dramatic eyes remained impassive as she listened. Then, in her incongruous idiom and accent, she said, "Hell, that's no problem, no sweat at all, Selby. There's nothing like a call from a senator's office to lubricate the bureaucracy."

Dialing Senator Lester's office in Washington, she tapped a narrow suede pump impatiently. As she waited she told Selby the senator would be joining them later; he was flying in from Brussels and a car would pick him up at the Philadelphia airport . . . To someone named George in the senator's office, she said, "Call Albany right now and get hold of Bill Touhy. He's chief of the section that bonds and licenses private eyes, armed couriers and so forth. I want everything he's got on two investigators. Here's their names. Aron and Ben Cadle." She spelled the last name carefully. "Got it? They're believed to be in the Philadelphia area and may be undercover using aliases. Find out where they're staying, who they're working for, what they're driving, leased or personal, everything. And George . . . tell Bill Touhy that Senator Lester is personally interested. It's urgent."

A knock sounded and Miss Kim opened the door to a white-jacketed waiter who pushed in a service cart. She signed the check, and when the waiter left she lifted the silver cover from the small sandwich tray, saying, "It's Kim, or Vickie, if you like, Mr. Selby. Victoria was my grandmother's name. She was born in Hong Kong and married a Brit who ran a souvenir shop and sold tons of Empress Victoria dolls to cockney sailors. I grew up in Evanston, Illinois, and was a cheerleader at Northwestern, pom-poms and all."

She poured their coffee, excused herself with a smile and began to look through Jonas Selby's diaries. Her dramatic eyes reminded him of clicking camera shutters; they embraced a page at a time, apparently fixing in her mind the words with one sweeping glance.

"We're already in the picture on a good bit of this, Mr. Selby." She closed the books and sipped her coffee. "The major, who is George Thomson, of course, the court-martial and the chief, who was—and is—General Adam Taggart. The railroad names and songs seem like grace notes, a kind of lonely poetry but don't mean much to us . . . So, why do you think the defense introduced your father's court-martial into your daughter's trial? That's what our deal is about, right?"

"To influence the jury—that's logical, isn't it? To convince them I'm out to nail Thomson for something done to my father by his father . . . something that has nothing to do with the attack on my daughter."

"But just to save Earl Thomson's sweet buns?" Kim sipped her coffee. "Somehow I doubt it. There's an old Chinese saying, Mr. Selby, which goes . . . 'If a piece of paper gets dragged into a courtroom, two teams of oxen can't drag it out.'"

Frowning, she put down her cup. "So why Davic would use K.S. 36663864 still beats me. But let's get to *our* deal."

Settling back on the couch, she tucked her legs under her. "Before the senator gets here I can tell you this much from what we've pieced together from the records, some letters and from telephone conversations Senator Lester had with your father. Jonas Selby served his five-year sentence in Seoul, then was transferred to a rehab center in Colorado. That wasn't done by the book. He'd received a dishonorable discharge and wasn't entitled to further army treatment. But somebody needed to keep him under surveillance."

"In other words, he was a prisoner those additional years."

"Technically, yes . . . Please hear me out. When he left Boulder, your father moved about and finally settled in Truckee. He was married by then, Jarrell was a young child. His wife, Rita, died about thirteen years ago. Jonas Selby, ill or not, or whatever he was, saw your brother through highschool and into college."

She studied him with her remarkably vivid eyes. "Which brings me to an important question. When were you last in touch with Jarrell?"

Selby told her about the call from the motel in Quinton, New Jersey. Kim made a note on a pad.

"But you didn't actually talk to him?"

"No."

"Then anyone could have called and given that message to your housekeeper?"

"That's true."

"She wouldn't have recognized his voice?"

"No. But I want to know why you're interested in my family now. You weren't there when my father needed you. You saw that in his diaries. He wanted help the night he was killed. Where was Lester then, and the other *elements* that are supposed to *lubricate* the bureaucracy?"

"Mr. Selby, we aren't adversaries." She chose her words carefully. "Please believe me. But I can only tell you what I'm allowed to by security restrictions. The senator has considerably more leeway. Your father trusted Senator Lester. Jonas Selby realized, eventually, that he'd been the victim of a rigged court-martial, and the reason was that he was a cog in something too complex for him to understand. He got in touch with Senator Lester by pure coincidence, if you believe in such things. Living alone in Truckee, he happened to watch a network television show that exposed certain U.S. Army experiments with LSD on unwilling, unknowing military subjects. A black sergeant, it was demonstrated, had had his head turned into a psychedelic merry-go-round by chemicals added to his food. Your father realized then that his brain had been scrambled in some similar way in Korea, and in Colorado, accounting for his lapses of memory, his failure to defend himself, even to understand the charges. He wrote to the network. His letter was forwarded to the late Senator Mark Rowan's committee, where it was tucked away in an inoperative file. Senator Lester didn't see that letter, and the two that followed, until after Rowan's death when Lester succeeded him. A secretary found the file when they were changing offices. Lester immediately phoned your father, who told him he could cite names, dates and specific instances of illegal use of drugs on captured South Korean soldiers.

"They arranged a meeting to put those charges on tape. One week before that meeting, your father was shot to death in his cabin by so-called prowlers."

At which point in her chilling narrative Senator Lester arrived, accompanied by a bellhop toting his luggage. Tired and travel-worn, the senator looked smaller than he did on television; the camera emphasized his high coloring, his square jaws and the military brace of his shoulders. Now he seemed slight if trim alongside Selby. Strands of gray-black hair fell across his forehead. His deeply set eyes were shadowed with fatigue.

He asked Miss Kim for a Scotch and tossed his topcoat over a chair. Excusing himself, and carrying his drink, he went into the bedroom with his aide and closed the door.

When the senator returned moments later he had freshened himself, brushed his hair and changed into slippers and a loose cardigan sweater. "Fourteen hours from Brussels to London to Philadelphia. I'm beat, Mr. Selby. Jet lag is winding up with the common cold on the list of things we can't do much about. Thanks for coming over here to talk to us. I know you've got demands on your own time."

His eyes turned to the stack of diaries on the coffee table. "Your father never mentioned these to me. We'll have a close look at them, you can be sure. In a case like this any lead can pay off. It's pretty difficult to say in advance what a so-called reliable source will turn out to be."

An urgency in Lester's manner communicated itself to Selby; it sounded in his husky voice and animated his distracted gestures. He held up his glass. "A tad more water, Vickie. I didn't eat since Brussels, a straight whiskey would put me away . . . An investigation like mine, Selby, attracts tipsters, informers, vindictive gossip, people with grudges, ex-wives, power-brokers in Intelligence . . . Who was Deep Throat, for instance?

What's a highly placed official? Who are those people the press and TV quote like Holy Writ? Cleaning women selling shredded papers to Jack Anderson? A maintenance man eavesdropping in an elevator? But your father was an *authentic* source, Selby. He was a *living example* of what they'd done."

The senator settled back and put his slippered feet on a stool. He rubbed his forehead. "Vickie, would you order me something light. A steak sandwich and a salad would be nice . . . Mr. Selby, we've run a quick check on you. Miss Kim tells me you never had any direct contact with your father. Unless there's something in his diaries Vickie missed, this could be another dead end, one more lead that didn't pay off. Still, I'm grateful for your cooperation . . . Now tell me this. When you were in Summitt City last October you met a friend of your brother's, a girl named Jennifer, a model or photographer, something like that. Have you had any further contact with her? Vickie tells me there was one ambiguous phone call from Jarrell. Could have been anyone, for that matter. But I'm wondering if you've heard anything from that girl?"

"You also must be wondering," Selby said, "about what I'm wondering about."

"How we knew about this Jennifer in the first place? That what you're thinking? As I told you, Selby, a case like this has an effect on information like a magnet on metal filings. Things can come flying in from everywhere. But you're entitled to more than that kind of bullshit, pardon my pidgin French, Vickie. We've got an agent undercover in Summitt City, have had since we started looking into Harlequin. A routine procedure. Never mind whether it's a he or a she—it's our source for your brother's friend. But we don't have much. So I'm curious about her, thought you might know something."

"Sorry I can't be helpful—"

"You don't know anything more about her?"

"No."

"Did she mention how she met your brother?"

"Said something about a disco party, they met, started talking."

"Your brother tell you anything else about her? How she happened to be there that particular weekend, for instance?"

Selby said no. He'd been trained, it occurred to him, to

336

stand for the national anthem, to regard pretty cheerleaders waving pom-poms on sunny fall afternoons as the quintessence of healthy and innocent American values, and, it followed, to trust members of the United States Senate. But it struck him that Senator Lester was not being altogether truthful with him. Why all this curiosity about Jennifer? Why so little, really, about Jarrell, or Harlequin, which they were supposed to be investigating? He had been told—by the senator *and* Miss Kim—a judiciously edited story . . . They also hadn't revealed what Jerry Goldbirn had found out in an unofficial inquiry, that Jennifer's last name was Easton, that she lived at an expensive address in New York on Sutton Place South and had an unlisted phone protected by a high priority seal. Such basic information had to be available to anyone with Senator Lester's contacts. If they were keeping their own counsel on those matters, Selby would keep his.

"If your check on me was as thorough as I imagine it was," Selby said, "you'll understand I've got to be back in East Chester this afternoon." He stood and picked up his coat. "So you'll both have to excuse me now. Thanks for the coffee, Miss Kim."

CHAPTER TWENTY-NINE

An expectant silence settled as Brett walked to the stand to begin her cross-examination of Dr. Leslie Clemens. The sharpened interest was understandable because it was obvious the People's attorney was angry; a combative energy was evident in her posture, and her eyes narrowed as she studied the witness.

"Dr. Clemens, how much are you being paid for testifying in this case?"

"I can't tell you exactly, the case isn't over yet."

"Then you are paid on an hourly basis?"

"Yes."

"Plus expenses?"

"Yes."

"How much are you paid by the hour, Dr. Clemens?"

"My fee is one hundred dollars per hour."

"Is that for an eight-hour day?"

"That depends on circumstances. They vary from case to case. On occasion, my working day begins at breakfast, reading transcripts and so forth. Sometimes it doesn't end until I retire—"

"What is your schedule in this particular case?"

"I'm not exactly sure. Close to full time."

"Which means a twelve- or fourteen-hour day?"

"You'd have to check my office for those specifics."

"You are staying at the DuPont Hotel in Wilmington, Delaware?"

"Yes, I am."

"In a suite?"

"Yes—I need a sitting room for reading and writing, dictating notes and so forth."

"A chauffeured limousine brings you from your hotel suite to the courtroom each morning?"

"Yes, it does, but—"

"And returns you in the evening?"

"*Yes.*"

"And these expenses, the hotel suite, all meals and gratuities, the chauffeured limousine—these are paid for by the attorneys who represent the accused?"

Davic stood. "I object, Your Honor. These questions are obviously designed to exaggerate the plain fact that expert witnesses are in heavy demand and are paid accordingly. There's nothing unusual or culpable in such arrangements."

"Your Honor," Brett said, "I think it's only fair that the jury be given a clear picture of these financial arrangements. Nothing in my questions has suggested that they are unusual or culpable. Those are Mr. Davic's words."

"Your Honor," Davic protested, "I just *denied* that such payments were unusual or culpable."

Judge Flood then said, "Since you first used those terms, Mr. Davic, the court cannot hold People's counsel responsible for repeating them."

"Thank you, Your Honor . . . Dr. Clemens, isn't it true that while your fee is one hundred dollars an hour, you will not accept commitments at that rate unless they are computed on a weekly basis?"

"That's generally true, I believe." The doctor crossed his legs. "But circumstances vary, as I've pointed out. In any case, these matters are handled by my office . . ."

"I can understand the demands on your time, Doctor, but isn't it a fact that you are being paid for a *full two months* for your testimony in this trial?"

"That may be true, yes . . . but I'm at a loss to understand your persistence. You must be aware that flexible fees and schedules are of necessity standard—"

"And you have earned on your flexible schedule—if my artithmetic is correct—only three hundred dollars in professional fees for talking directly to the plaintiff, Shana Selby, for three hours. Is that right, Doctor?"

"Your arithmetic is fine, Miss Brett. Three times one hundred is three hundred."

"But in another phase of this flexible schedule, Dr. Clemens, you will receive close to seventy-five *thousand* dollars. Is that correct?"

"Yes, for many days of preparation, for additional extensive reading in recent studies in adolescent sexual psychology, for the time I need to analyze and confirm my impressions of the plaintiff, to modify those concepts, and to refine my definitions and evaluate any possible ambiguities. Yes, I'm paid extra for those contributions."

"The suite at the DuPont Hotel at two hundred and sixty dollars per night, is that also one of the extras? *All* of your expenses for two months, in fact?"

Davic objected angrily. "Your Honor, this line of inquiry is trivial and irrelevant. People's counsel knows the cost of services of expert witnesses has escalated in the last few years in just about direct proportion to the number of unmerited rape cases that have recently burdened our judiciary system, thanks in part to so much publicity from well-meaning women's groups who—"

"Your Honor!" Brett stared at Davic. Someone in the rear of the crowded gallery began clapping. A stir of laughter, and Judge Flood sounded his gavel. "Now, Miss Brett, I think you have made your point in regard to the remuneration of the witness. Please move on."

Brett inclined her head to the bench and turned back to the witness. "Dr. Clemens, you testified that the plaintiff, Shana Selby, was especially troubled by the death of her mother—damaged, you said—because the loss occurred just before the onset of Shana's own sexual maturity. Are you saying that Shana was compelled to seek out a sexual experience—even if it meant being tortured and raped to get it—*because her mother died?*"

"I believe my testimony is quite clear and explicit on that point."

"I disagree. I find your testimony both obscure and diffuse."

"With all respect," the doctor replied, "you may not have the qualifications in psychiatry or medicine to support your differing views."

"Perhaps . . . Dr. Clemens, did Shana Selby tell you she wanted and needed intimate relationships after her mother's death?"

"No . . . not explicitly—"

"Did she suggest that she was eager for such relationships no matter how violent or dangerous they might be?"

"Not in so many words—"

"Did Shana imply that she was compelled to find partners for violent and dangerous sexual activity?"

Dr. Clemens cleared his throat. "Not in such vivid terms."

"Then would you please tell the court how you knew with such accuracy what this fourteen-year-old child was thinking and feeling? How, in short, you reached the conclusions you testified to?"

"My conclusions, please remember, embody a class of sexually pathological females, not necessarily one specific individual—"

"But you weren't hired for seventy-five thousand dollars to examine a *class* of sexual psychopaths, were you? You were hired to examine one teenaged girl, Shana Selby, which you did, for the fee of three hundred dollars. Now I'd like to know, and I'm sure the jury wants to know, exactly what scholarly qualifications you employed to refine and localize your general observations so that they applied *precisely* and *exactly* to the plaintiff, Shana Selby. Just how did you go about that, Doctor?"

"I'm a psychiatrist. My adult life has been spent in the field. You have to understand that what *isn't* said by a patient is frequently more revealing to the professional observer than those things that are said."

"Are you telling us, Dr. Clemens, that your conclusions are based on what Shana Selby *didn't* tell you?"

"The significance of inferential information is an accepted fact, and is widely used as an aid in many areas of psychiatric interpretation."

"Then it's true, isn't it, that *some* of your conclusions are

341

based on your own inferences—not on things that Shana Selby said to you?"

"Yes . . . that's true—"

"You analyzed her *silences.* Is that it?"

"That is only *partially* it."

"Did you also analyze Shana's body language, Doctor? Her so-called victim-signals? Her clothing and shoes for evidence of potential collusion?"

Davic came around the table, glaring at Brett. "I object, Your Honor. This litany of questions is rhetorical and derisive. It is insulting."

Judge Flood rapped his gavel. "Mr. Davic, there's some validity to your objection, but I have allowed Dr. Clemens a deliberate leeway in his testimony. This is a consideration a court does well to extend to expert witnesses. We shouldn't inhibit scholars with procedure. The doctor has, as an expert witness, made certain charges by inference against the plaintiff's emotional balance. In fairness, I will allow Miss Brett to protect the People's interest with a correspondingly extensive and flexible inquiry." He tapped his gavel a second time. "The People will proceed."

After collecting her thoughts, Brett said, "Dr. Clemens, I'd like you to explain what you meant when you stated that damaged females often sublimated their sexual drives into safe areas. And then tell us how you concluded Shana had retreated into such an unrealistic sanctuary?"

"Yes, of course. The girl admitted as much to me." The doctor's small smile invited the jurors to share his self-assurance. "She told me she had a collection of pictures in her bedroom, virile young men, athletes, in fact, who were—it so happened— fit objects for safe fantasies because all the young heroes enshrined on her wall"—the doctor's smile was now rueful—"all of those powerful young men were dead. Israeli athletes murdered at the Olympic Games in Germany some ten years ago."

"You found *this* suspicious?"

"That's a pejorative word. I would prefer revealing. It follows that a dead person is a safe object of idealized love—harmless and nonthreatening."

"Did Shana tell you how old she was when she cut out those pictures?"

"She was four or five, as I understand. But the significant fact is that she has *kept* them all these years, don't you see?"

"No, I don't, Doctor. Shana's mother was not deceased *then*, and Shana was not sexually mature—which are the conditions you told us typified damaged females seeking release from their guilty sexual drives by exposing themselves to sadists and rapists. How could your explanation hold water for a child of four or five?"

Dr. Clemens cleared his throat again. "You are simplifying my conclusions."

"I'm glad to be of help, Doctor."

"I object, Your Honor, to the sarcasm."

"Sustained."

"Doctor, why do you consider it significant that Shana kept the picture of those Israeli athletes all these years?"

"To me, it reveals her need for relationships that are unobtainable and therefore safe and reassuring. Those dead athletes are real to her in one very important sense. They cannot hurt her, they cannot disappoint her, they can never be the living agents to satisfy her rebellious though unconscious sexual needs—"

"Excuse me, Your Honor." Brett returned to her People's table and poured herself a glass of water. Her hand trembled slightly as she drank it. When she put the glass down she squeezed Shana's arm. In a low and conversational tone, she murmured, "Shana, wipe your eyes. Don't let them make you cry. They're abominable, disgusting . . ."

"Miss Brett," Flood said, "if you wish a conference with your client I will recess for that purpose."

"Thank you for your consideration, Judge Flood, but I would like to complete my cross of the doctor." Squeezing Shana's arm a second time, Brett straightened and walked back to the witness stand.

"Dr. Clemens, you have given us a comprehensive and perhaps necessarily subjective profile of the plaintiff." Her expression was composed, but as she paced in front of the witness, there was an edge of hostility in the precision of Brett's movements. "I sense an absence or omission in your testimony, Doctor." Her words were as measured as the sound of her footsteps. "In all this speculation about the victim, in this pawing over and

343

prying into her innermost private and sensitive feelings, *there has not been one word* about the person who committed the crimes against her. A young girl has been tortured and raped. Tell us, Doctor, what class of perverted *male* indulges and delights in such atrocities? What pictures would you find on *his* wall? What parental influences drive him to these violent, sadistic assaults on young—?"

Davic objected, his face flushing. "Dr. Clemens is here to testify to the mental condition and emotional credibility of the *plaintiff*. He is here for that reason only. People's counsel knows that—"

"Your Honor," Brett cut in, "the defense counsel begrudges me the opportunity to examine his expert witness on the motivation of *rapists as a class*. I understand Mr. Davic's concern. He has paid seventy-five thousand dollars for Dr. Clemen's selected opinions. Naturally, he does not want to share his witness's expertise with me."

"Objection, Your Honor."

"Sustained. Miss Brett, I've ruled that you avoid this matter of expenses."

"But the fact is, Your Honor, those damaged young females were not alone when they were attacked and raped and savaged. They didn't strap themselves to beds and beat themselves black and blue and bloody with their own fists. Someone *else* broke their teeth, burned their flesh with cigarettes and raped and sodomized them, but *that* class of perverted, sadistic criminal has remained anonymous in these hearings—no profiles of that class of felon has been drawn or even hinted it—"

Judge Flood sounded his gavel."

"—except for a reference by Dr. Clemens to collusion, by which I gather he means that forcible rape is somehow a deal between equally suspect participants—"

"Miss Brett!" Judge Flood brought his gavel down firmly. "That will be enough."

Brett drew a deep breath; her face was pale; in contrast her gray eyes were almost black, shining with angry intensity. "Your Honor," she said, "I have not meant to offend the dignity of this court or test the generous limits of your patience. But I am forced to speak out because the *victim* in this case has been treated as if she were a criminal, not by the court, but by the license given defense counsel by our laws. Shana's background, her sexual capacities, even the intimate furnishings of her bedroom, all this is not only available and presumably relevant to the defense, but is also subject to clinical probings by their expert witness, Dr. Clemens, who has not spent three *minutes*, let alone three *hours*, examining the *defendant* sitting in this courtroom and charged with torturing and raping Shana Selby."

Davic stood. "I *insist* that Your Honor put a stop to these outbursts. The function of Dr. Clemens in this trial is proscribed by statute. The doctor *cannot* answer any questions in regard to the defendant. If such questions are put to him, I will instruct him *not to answer them.*"

"But, Your Honor," Brett said, "the doctor has referred to the literature of sexual pathology and rape, and studies of sexual disorders. Those are descriptions which embrace males *and* females. I have no specific questions to ask in relation to the defendant. But if a psychological portrait of *rape victims* as a class is admissible, then fairness suggests that a similar portrait of *rapists* as a class be presented to the jury."

"I object, Your Honor."

"Mr. Davic, I have pointed out that the People must be given a reasonable leeway in cross-examining expert witnesses."

"I submit you are giving her more than *leeway*, Your Honor. I object to the court's indulgence in this matter."

"Overruled."

"Exception."

Judge Flood nodded at Davic and glanced across his steepled fingers at Brett. "Counselor, you may inquire of Dr. Clemens as to rapists as a class. But your questions must not relate, Miss Brett, even tangentially, to the defendant. Is that understood?"

"Yes, Your Honor." Brett addressed the witness. "Dr. Clemens, does the commission or rape, in your judgment, represent primarily a need for sex or a need for violence?"

"The latter, in almost every instance. The rapist's basic need is to physically dominate and humiliate a woman. The rapist does not want sex from a woman. It is probably the last thing he wants, because his fears and hatred of women make it impossible for him to sustain a relationship with a female that is based on pleasure or tenderness or mutual respect or confidence."

Davic looked like he would have liked to kill his witness, whose apparently compulsive grandstanding, and was now helping the opposition.

"In your opinion, what is the underlying cause for this sort of fear and hatred?" Brett said in a respectful tone.

"Well, as with most pathological behavior, there is seldom one clearly definable explanation. That applies to other disorders, of course, such as alcoholism, obesity, depressions, recurring nightmares, psychosomatic illness, tendencies toward violence and suicide, even murder. As a rule, they erupt from not one but a mixture of chaotic impulses."

Earl Thomson leaned across the defense table and whispered fiercely to Davic. The attorney nodded but placed a light restraining hand on Earl's shoulder.

"Well, is there any *observable priority* in those various morbid functions?" Brett asked. "A litmus paper test to determine and define sexual psychopaths?"

"No, I'm afraid not, Miss Brett."

"You spoke about the father in relation to the rape *victim*. What about the molding influence of the mother in the formative years of the potential rapist?"

"The mother," Dr. Clemens began, "is of course a major influence toward emotional stability or the lack of it. If she is unable and unwilling to—"

Davic broke in. "This is too much, Your Honor. People's counsel has ignored your injunction. Her overzealous and hectoring persistence surely demands a rebuke from the bench."

Judge Flood said, "The court has been more than generous, Miss Brett. Mr. Davic's point is valid. You have exceeded the limits of inquiry I outlined." Flood made a note on his pad. "Do you have any further questions for the People?"

"If it please the court, I have one last question."

"It will probably not please us . . . but go on."

"Thank you, sir. Dr. Clemens, you mentioned the pictures of the Israeli athletes on the wall of plaintiff's bedroom. You gave us your explanation for their presence there. But there are other pictures in that bedroom. There is a portrait of Franklin Delano Roosevelt, a picture of the late comedian Jimmy Durante, and there is a framed collection of snapshots of Shana's nine-year-old brother, David. I ask you, Mr. Clemens, will you tell the court what *these* pictures reveal to you of Shana Selby's innermost private feelings and sexual yearnings?"

"Objection, Your Honor."

"Dr. Clemens," Brett said, "we would *value* your expert judgment. And I will write my *personal* check for three hundred dollars for that enlightenment . . ."

Laughter began in the gallery. Judge Flood brought it under control by striking his gavel. When order was restored, he said, "You have managed to exceed the limits of my patience, Miss Brett. I will permit no further questions of this defense witness. Dr. Clemens, you are excused. Thank you for your cooperation."

When Brett returned to the defense table she was lifted by Shana's discreet smile, and even more by the solid presence of Harry Selby seated in the gallery directly behind his daughter.

CHAPTER THIRTY

When Selby's bedside phone rang, he lifted the receiver quickly, hoping the sound hadn't waked the house. He heard Blazer growling on the stairs, and saw a faint light on his windows.

It was Jerry Goldbirn in Las Vegas.

"I tried to get you yesterday, Harry. Your housekeeper said you were over in Philadelphia." Selby heard Goldbirn draw a deep breath and release it slowly. "We were tough cookies in our time, my friend, played hurt, missed curfews, messed around but still kicked ass when the whistle blew for game time. But that was quite a while back, Harry."

"Is that your deep thought for today?" Selby said. "Where the hell did it all go?"

"Speaking of time, loyalty's got a statute of limitation on it too, pal, ever think of that?"

"Would you like a violin accompaniment, Jerry? Everything is fleeting, snow melts, Christmas and Hanukkah are coming closer together every year? Fishing isn't as good as it used to be and never was?"

"Go on, make me laugh," Goldbirn said. "You could work a lounge act here with your great sense of humor."

"Okay, what the hell is it?"

"A long time back you took me out of a practice play so I

348

rode the bench and stayed alive. So for auld lang syne, Harry, I leaned on that flake from New York Bell Telephone. I got a number for Jennifer Easton. A switchboard at a convent in upstate New York, a place on the Hudson near Hyde Park. I owed you one, Harry. Well, we're even now. I came across a name so hot I goddamn near dropped the phone. Simon Correll. Jennifer Easton is his personal foldout, his mistress. Correll could push a button and flush my casino and my bank accounts right down the drain. All of Vegas if he wanted to. I'm out of the game, Harry. Back on the bench. You can do me a favor, if you want, tear up my phone number. Sorry."

The phone clicked in Selby's ear . . . So that was what Miss Kim with her big eyes and cheerleader's legs had kept back. And what Senator Lester had decided not to tell him—that Jennifer Easton, who loved boats and not belonging to people, wasn't a model or photographer or casual friend of Jarrell's at all, but the mistress of the man who ran Thomson and Harlequin, the Correll Group and, of course, Summitt City itself.

Before court adjourned that morning, Selby joined Sergeant Burt Wilger in a bar on a side street off the parking mall. It was a cops' hangout, with a pool table covered with plyboard for the lunch buffet and specials chalked on a blackboard beside the cue rack. A private phone was connected directly to District Attorney Lamb's office and the Detective Division.

But at this hour the place was empty except for a waitress and a crippled black sweeper. Nevertheless, Wilger put a record on the jukebox and sat in a rear booth. He ordered coffee for two and a bowl of pretzels. He told Selby that he'd had no word on the Cadle brothers, that his informants had come up dry. "Which could mean the Cadles are split by now, or are registered somewhere under other names," Wilger said.

The night before Wilger had tailed Davic and Earl Thomson to the Philadelphia airport, where they'd picked up Derek Taggart off a Lufthansa flight from Frankfurt.

"That was about nine P.M.," Wilger said, biting into a pretzel. "The little faggot was in uniform wearing a theater ribbon they give you if you get off the boat without drowning and a

349

Good Conduct Medal, which he probably got cornholing some local *herren*. Okay, okay," Wilger went on, interpreting Selby's impatience, "I'll skip the social comment. But all the same, Selby, it made me mad to see a guy like young Taggart wearing captain's bars when my nephew sweats out 'Nam in a vets' hospital in a wheelchair."

Selby drank his coffee and waited.

"They dropped Davic off at his hotel, Thomson and the cocksucker with the medals. They went for dinner to Bookbinders, the old one, then hit a joint near Arch Street, Hell for Leather, that peddles porno magazines, posters, condoms in all colors and flavors, some with jokes on 'em, blow the man down for navy types. Dirt-chute express. Cute stuff. Also they got pinchers, clamps and restraints for cocks and balls and tits, plus cassettes and booths to watch flicks in and listen to porno songs. Place is owned by a man named Petey Komoto. The songs and flicks are raw, not like the ones I remember as a kid—*The Tiger's Revenge* by Claud Bawls, or *The Open Kimono* by Seymour Hare. This joint is for rough trade, bull dykes, heavy leather studs, SM types. Couple of years back Komoto got his ass chewed up in the disposal by taping what went on in a screening room. He had two-way mirrors put in too. Tried the scam on a pair of vice squad officers and they broke it off in him. It was pretty loose surveillance," Wilger admitted. "I couldn't work too close, Thomson's probably seen me 'round the Hall. I staked out the place from my car across the street. They rented some film, disappeared into a booth. When they came out, they bought some magazines and drove back to the Thomson place in Wahasset. Earl's in court now ready to testify.

"Santos and young Taggart left the Thomson house early this morning, drove over to the Pilgrims Trust Bank in Wilmington. I don't know where else they went. I had to get back to work."

Wilger finished his coffee. "Davic's about to put Thomson on the stand. Brett's got to break him on her cross. It's her last chance, maybe your kid's. She's got to smash their goddamn lies. The time element and the disappearing Porsche are what she's got to work on. I been checking quarries, junkyards, closed-up warehouses, looking for the car. I got zilch. She's got to break them open, Selby . . . but what could get broken in the process is her neck."

Earl Thomson had been thoroughly coached, Selby saw, groomed with meticulous care—sincere, polite, quick with "sirs," attentive to Davic's questions. His clothing matched his relaxed but deferential manner; flannel slacks, a gray tweed jacket, loafers buffed to a high gloss.

Thomson told his story in a direct, effective manner. Leaving The Green Lantern about five-thirty, he discovered that his car was gone. He wasn't particularly concerned; a rally of sports and antique cars was scheduled at Longwood Gardens, many of his friends were in town for it. They might have spotted his Porsche 924—they would recognize it, of course—and taken it as a prank. Or . . . with a rueful smile . . . as an object lesson because he'd been stupid enough to leave the keys in it.

Having promised his mother he'd join her for dinner, he'd called Santos and asked him to drive over to Muhlenburg and pick him up.

No, he hadn't notified the police. The theft was reported the next morning.

Earl filled out this simple story with supportive details. The gun he had hoped to buy from Charlie Lee was a double-barrel 20-gauge Parker. The family chauffeur was over in New Jersey, which was why he'd asked for Santos.

Davic knitted the threads together into a neat and credible package, concluding with the defendant's account of the events at Longwood Gardens.

The lawyer paused then, pacing between the jury and the witness stand.

"Earl, you told Captain Slocum you'd never heard of a farm called Vinegar Hill. Is that right?"

"Yes, sir."

"Lieutenant Eberle asked you if you were familiar with landmarks near that place. You told him you were not. Is that also correct?"

"Yes, sir That's what I told the lieutenant."

"What time did that interrogation take place?"

"About two o'clock in the morning, sir."

"Had you been asleep prior to their arrival?"

"Yes, sir. For several hours."

"I see." Davic paused again. "Now tell me, Earl—*not* at two o'clock in the morning, *not* when you've been pulled out of bed by police officers without a warrant—tell me *now*, in this orderly courtroom . . . *do* you know of a farm called Vinegar Hill?"

"Not by that name, sir."

"Ah." Davic nodded slowly. "Then you knew that farm by another name. Is that what you're telling me, Earl?"

"Yes, sir."

"What name do you know it by?"

"The Taggart Place, sir."

"Under what circumstances did you know the Taggart Place?"

"It belonged to a friend of our family, General Adam Taggart. The general's son was a classmate of mine at Rockland. We called it the Taggart Place. Or the General's Place. When I was at college, some of us used to go there to hunt pheasants."

"I want to emphasize one particular point now, Earl. You did not *lie* to Captain Slocum that night, did you?"

"No, sir, I did not."

"You did *not* know of a place called Vinegar Hill, did you Earl?"

"I certainly didn't, sir."

"Your Honor"—Davic addressed the bench—"there are other specifics of the People's evidence I can't refute at this time although I intend to later. But in fairness to my client, I would like to defer this examination. A witness for the defense has been delayed enroute to these hearings. His testimony is crucial to the proof of Earl Thomson's innocence."

"All right, Mr. Davic. But understand that People's counsel may cross-examine the defendant on the portion of his testimony now part of this trial record."

"Yes, Your Honor. I understand. Thank you." . . .

They needed time to rehearse Ace Taggart, Selby thought, that had to be why Davic was stalling. Obviously they'd convinced young Taggart it was safe for him to take the stand and lie. In whatever Davic and Earl Thomson had told him, in the time at the Hell for Leather, the trip with Santos to the Pilgrims Bank in Wilmington, somewhere in that welter of people and

352

places was the proof that had convinced AC-DC Taggart there was no risk in perjuring himself. But they also might be building a house of cards with a marked deck, Selby felt. It was like a trapeze act where the performers worked happily and skillfully without a net or safety straps until they found out that one of them had a trick knee or a hangover or was just a little short on nerve or guts. Then everything and everybody could collapse. One break was what his side needed. When they spotted the marked card, or the fingertips missed connections, the whole thing could go down . . .

At the recess Burt Wilger joined Selby in the corridor outside Superior Nine. "There's a call for you in the pressroom," he told him. "They switched it down from Brett's office."

A desk lined with phones had been moved against a wall in the temporary pressroom. Noise and smoke clogged the air. A girl in jeans extended a phone to Selby, mouthed his name inquiringly.

Victoria Kim did not identify herself. She told Selby what he needed to know about the Cadle brothers and broke the connection.

Selby picked up his coat and left the courthouse. From a pay phone he called Wilger and asked him to tell Brett he was on his way to Philadelphia. He forestalled the detective's questions by saying a hasty goodbye and hanging up.

Maybe he'd already spotted one of the marked cards, Selby thought as he drove out of East Chester and followed the traffic into Philadelphia. The smiling athlete in the trapeze act with the trick knee he wouldn't admit to, the blurred vision or fears that hit him in the morning when it was dark and he couldn't get back to sleep . . . Who was it? Santos? Ace Taggart, or the little Sicilian, or Thomson's mother, or Eberle, the drunk cop? Or Thomson himself? Or one of the Cadles. Who would crack first? Or was he whistling in the dark? Would *anybody* crack? He had to believe it. He couldn't give up . . .

The clerk intoned, "All rise."

After seating himself Flood said, "People's counsel will bear in mind that cross-examination of the defendant will not extend beyond the testimony on record."

"Yes, Your Honor."

"Please proceed then."

Brett began casually. "Were you upset, Mr. Thomson, when you left The Green Lantern and discovered your car was missing?"

"I wasn't upset, ma'am, but I was puzzled, I'll admit."

"I've checked several local dealers who handle Porsches, Mr. Thomson. Considering that your car was equipped with" —Brett picked up a note pad from the plaintiff's table and read —"internally vented disc brakes, an electronic digital ignition system and so forth, the dealers' consensus was that your Porsche Turbo 924 would be worth around thirty-five thousand dollars at current prices. Does that sound like a fair estimate?"

"I believe so, ma'am."

"Some of the terminology is beyond me. Perhaps it's not relevant, but would you mind explaining what turbocharging means?"

Thomson's smile was confident; he was very comfortable in this role. "There's a density in the charge supplied to any internal combustion engine. To put it simply, a turbocharger increases that density to about twice the normal atmospheric pressure. In contrast to a naturally aspirated engine of similar size —well, to put it simply, turbo engines increase horsepower by thirty or forty percent, which gives better performance all round."

"*Thank* you, Mr. Thomson." She paused. "But you weren't upset, merely puzzled that someone had made off with your very expensive turbocharged car?"

"Let me explain that. What I meant was that I wasn't *worried,* ma'am. That Porsche is a very distinctive car, and I figured it would turn up."

"What did you do when you discovered it was stolen?"

"As I said, I didn't realize it was stolen until later."

"You assumed some friend had driven it off as a joke."

"Yes, ma'am."

"Being the victim of that joke, what did you do?"

"I walked to the Bellflower diner and called home. I told Miguel Santos what had happened. Our regular chauffeur wasn't there . . ." Earl smiled. "I have the feeling we've been through this, ma'am."

354

"Do you find it tiresome, Mr. Thomson?"

"Not at all. I'll dot every *i* and cross every *t* if you want me to. I told Miguel where I'd be waiting and told him to come over to Muhlenburg and get me."

Brett adjusted her black-and-white-checked scarf with a seemingly distracted gesture, as if she herself weren't quite sure of her next question. Then she said, "Why did you choose The Green Lantern for your meeting with Charles Lee?"

"I figured that would be convenient for both of us."

"But The Green Lantern is seventeen miles from your home in Wahasset, Mr. Thomson. It's more than nine miles from Hosckessin in Delaware, where Mr. Lee works. What made you decide The Green Lantern was convenient for either of you?"

"Let's put it this way. I knew where it was. That's probably why I suggested it. At least I was sure I could find it."

"You know that area well then?"

"I've driven by there, yes."

"You know that The Green Lantern is only a half mile from Fairlee Road then?"

"Objection, Your Honor. The question is irrelevant."

"Sustained."

Brett said, "According to your testimony, Mr. Thomson, you parked your expensive car in front of The Green Lantern. It was in clear view of at least a dozen homes and shops on Route One. Correct?"

"I wouldn't swear to the exact number, but if you say a dozen I'll take your word for it."

"Did you go to any of those shops or houses to ask if anyone had seen who drove your car away?"

"No, I didn't. I've told you, I was running late."

"That jokester acted with a lot of confidence, wouldn't you say? Acted just as if he owned the car. Knew how to start it, shift gears and so forth. Isn't that how it must have appeared to the people in those shops and homes?"

"Maybe, ma'am. I wouldn't know."

"Do you have a jokester friend who physically resembles you, Mr. Thomson?"

"Well, I've got lots of friends, ma'am. Maybe some of them do look a bit like me."

355

"Then any witnesses to the taking of your car might have thought it was you yourself climbing so confidently behind the wheel, and driving off so expertly? Isn't that a possibility?"

"Objection, Your Honor. That insinuation is unsupported by any evidence."

"Sustained."

"Mr. Thomson, when you discovered your car was gone, did you suspect which friend of yours had borrowed it?"

"I told you, ma'am, I didn't know who'd taken it and I didn't waste time worrying about it. I half expected to find it waiting for me at home."

"What was the *other* half of your expectation?"

"That was only a manner of speaking."

"Did you half expect your car to turn up where it *did* turn up that night? At Vinegar Hill, or the Taggart Place?"

"*Objection,* Your Honor. I ask the court to admonish People's counsel for that inference."

"The question will be stricken. The jury will ignore it."

Brett inclined her head, a gesture of submission in marked contrast with the apparent confidence in her expression. "Mr. Thomson, I find your lack of interest in the whereabouts of your expensive automobile difficult to understand. Weren't you worried that your jokester friend might have, say, been involved in an accident?"

"I wasn't worried, no. That suggests a careless attitude, you may assume. But people worry because they don't know how to think. That's what they drilled into us at Rockland. My car was gone. That was a *fact* I couldn't change. So I didn't waste time worrying about it."

"Let's go back over what you've told me. You left The Green Lantern, found your Porsche gone. Being late for your dinner engagement, you walked to the Bellflower diner, called Miguel Santos and told him to drive over to Muhlenburg and pick you up. Is that it?"

"Yes, ma'am."

"But, Mr. Thomson, the Bellflower is more than a mile from The Green Lantern. Why didn't you go back into the Lantern and call Mr. Santos from that phone?"

"I don't think you'll understand my answer to that but I'll try . . . I'd had my fill of that place. I'd gone out of my way to keep an appointment there, Charlie'd stood me up for one of his sort's typical reasons. He could have sent that shotgun over with a friend, or hired some Puerto Rican to stand in at the mushroom shack. But Charlie took the short-range view, make a buck today, let tomorrow take care of itself. It never occurred to him that I'd adjusted my schedule to suit him." Thomson's mouth tightened with exasperation. "It may not seem logical, ma'am, but I didn't feel like asking favors from The Green Lantern crowd."

"Even though *not* using their phone would make you that much later for dinner with your mother?"

"She would understand, I was sure."

Changing direction, Brett said, "Isn't it true, Mr. Thomson, that you told no one in Muhlenburg—no one at The Green Lantern or the Bellflower, no one in the homes and shops in the area—that your thirty-five-thousand-dollar car had been stolen?"

"You say stolen, ma'am, even though I've testified I didn't think it was. But, no, I didn't tell anybody my car had been borrowed."

"What time did you call Miguel Santos?"

"About six o'clock, I think."

"What time did he arrive in Muhlenburg?"

"About six-thirty."

"Where did you wait for Mr. Santos?"

"On the sidewalk in front of the Bellflower."

"It was beginning to rain, then, wasn't it?"

"Yes, ma'am."

"You waited in the rain for half an hour?"

"I didn't want Miguel to miss me."

"To your knowledge, Mr. Thomson, did anyone see you standing there in the rain?"

"Maybe somebody did. I wouldn't know."

"Did you speak to anyone?"

"I don't remember. Maybe I nodded to someone, I don't know."

"You weren't tempted to get out of the rain and wait inside the diner?"

"Objection, Your Honor."

"Sustained."

"Mr. Thomson, did you speak to anyone in the diner when you made your telephone call? Did you ask the cashier for change?"

"I had no reason to."

"No reason to speak to *anyone?*"

"I was in a hurry, ma'am. I was in no mood for small talk."

Brett pushed her wooden bracelets higher on her wrists and glanced thoughtfully at the big wall clock behind Flood's bench. "Mr. Thomson, your mother testified that you returned home from Muhlenburg shortly after seven o'clock. You showered and changed then. When you returned to her suite, she testified, you were not wearing your wristwatch. Is that also your recollection?"

"Yes, that's right."

"Miss Cluny from The Green Lantern testified that you were wearing rings and a chain necklace in addition to your wristwatch. You removed them too before showering?"

"Yes, ma'am."

"When you joined your mother, how did you know what time it was?"

"There are two clocks in her room. One is electric, the other is solar-powered—"

"You assumed both clocks were correct?"

"Why would I doubt it?"

"In your own words, you were running late. Then you walked that unnecessary mile to the Bellflower to make your phone call. Isn't it possible it was *later* than seven-fifteen?"

"*No.* I'm sure of the time."

"But how did you know your mother's clocks were accurate?"

"Objections, Your Honor."

"On what grounds, Mr. Davic?"

"People's counsel is implying that someone might have tampered with those clocks."

"People's counsel has implied nothing of the sort," Brett said. "You're not listening to my questions, Mr. Davic, or you're twisting them around for reasons of your own. The defendant was not wearing his wristwatch. It was logical to verify his knowledge of the time."

358

Unexpectedly Earl said, "Your Honor, may I clear this up?"

"By all means, young man."

"I checked my wristwatch after I showered. It was about seven-fifteen then. So it couldn't have been more than a minute or so later when I joined my mother. Her clocks had to be right. That should put an end to the idea that my mother jumped out of bed and ran around her room turning back those clocks."

"Your Honor," Brett said, "I understand the defendant's concern for his mother's testimony. That does him credit. But for the record I have never questioned her testimony. Nor have I referred to *anyone* resetting clocks, manipulating the time. Those suggestions come directly from the defendant *and* his attorney. The thought is theirs, not mine."

Royce hastily scribbled a note and gave it to Davic. Glancing at it, Davic nodded. His expression was impassive but he couldn't mask the anger in his eyes as he withdrew his objection.

Brett then asked Earl Thomson if he had called any of his friends that night to find out who had . . . as he said . . . borrowed his car. Earl answered that he had waited until the following morning.

"Did you call your friends then?"

"No, because it seemed clear by then it wasn't a joke."

"So you reported the theft to the East Chester police department the next morning?"

"It was reported then, yes, ma'am."

"That wasn't what I asked you. Did *you* report the theft of your car to the police?"

"No, an associate of my father's reported it."

"May we have that person's name?"

"Sure. He's an old friend of our family, Mr. Dom Lorso."

"Is he the only person you told that your Porsche had been stolen?"

"I also told my father."

"But when you called Miguel Santos from Muhlenburg you testified, and I'll quote . . . 'I explained to Santos what had happened.' What did you mean by that?"

"Well . . . I explained I needed to be picked up, that's all."

"But you told this family friend, Dom Lorso, that your car was stolen?"

"Yes."

"Why did Dom Lorso report the matter to the police? Why didn't *you* report it, Mr. Thomson?"

"What difference does it make?" Earl's voice was hardening. "An executive can tell his secretary to report something missing to the police. The point is, the theft was reported, ma'am, and you know it was."

"Is Mr. Lorso your secretary?"

"You know damn well he's not."

The gavel sounded. "Mr. Thomson, your attorney assured me that your conduct will be consistent with the standards of this court."

Davic stood up. "Your Honor, I make no excuse for my client's language. People's counsel's questions seem designed to provoke such a rejoinder. Dominic Lorso is a respected businessman, a member of numerous charitable organizations in the community. He has served on—"

Flood said, "Miss Brett, Mr. Lorso is obviously not the young man's secretary. You know that, I presume."

"Your Honor, I am attempting to establish the relationship between the defendant and the only person he apparently trusted enough to report the theft of his car to the police. That car, which now seems to have disappeared from the face of the earth, was an instrument in a crime the defendant has been charged with. The People need to examine the relationship between Earl Thomson and Dom Lorso."

"Then go on, Miss Brett, but defense counsel has made a reasonable point about provocative inquiry."

"Thank you, Your Honor. Mr. Thomson, how long have you known Dom Lorso?"

"I told you, he's like a member of the family. I called him Uncle Dom when I was a kid."

"Would you say he was like your godfather, Mr. Thomson?"

"Objection, Your Honor!"

"On what grounds, Mr. Davic?"

"People's counsel surely understands the pejorative implications of her last reference."

"You mean godfather, Mr. Davic?" Judge Flood rubbed his

chin. "I don't know. Perhaps we're becoming too sensitive. I believe the word godfather is a useful term for a respectable relationship. Overruled."

"Yes, he was like a godfather to me," Thomson then stated. "He's the most decent man I've ever known besides my own father."

Brett said, "I want the jury to understand your confidence in Mr. Lorso—why, in short, Mr. Thomson, you went to him about your stolen car instead of the police."

"I can only repeat what I said earlier. Dom Lorso is an old friend. I respect his advice. In this instance he chewed me out. Told me I should have called the police right away. But since I hadn't, Mr. Lorso said he'd get the information directly to Captain Slocum. That would save time, he said."

"Did Mr. Dom Lorso ever give you similar good advice in the past?"

"Yes. Quite a few times."

"When you failed to report a matter to the police which should have been reported?"

"Objection, Your Honor!"

"Sustained."

Brett walked to the People's table and glanced at her notes. "At Longwood Gardens, Mr. Thomson, did you take the plaintiff's accusations against you seriously?"

"Not at first, ma'am."

"But when the physical confrontation occurred, you took the matter seriously then?"

"Yes, ma'am. I did."

"In fact, you attempted to run away—or drive away—on a motorcycle, didn't you?"

A line of pressure appeared around Thomson's lips. "I've never run from anybody in my life."

"But Officer Summerall testified by deposition that you did just that."

"I left the area, I didn't run away."

"Perhaps I phrased the question carelessly. Would you please tell us in your own words just what you *did* do?"

"I'd be happy to, ma'am. But to put the matter in perspective, I should tell you I've had considerable military training."

At the defense table, Royce quickly wrote another note to Davic. Davic barely glanced at the paper, but his eyes became alert and watchful.

Earl continued, "I attended Rockland Military College for four years and was graduated First Cadet in my class, with the rank of cadet colonel. I qualified as expert with rifles and machine guns. I've run obstacle courses with live ammo firing over my head and I've been in simulated combat conditions."

Earl's manner had become expansive. "It's strange," he went on, "that no one has asked about the shotgun I tried to buy. I'm a gun collector. Certain elements think those are code words for Fascism or racism or something like that. But a gun is a tool, no better or worse than the man using it. Charlie Lee's Parker, I'd heard, had its original stock replaced by one made from wood grown in the Balkans. Charlie got the gun from an old Romanian refugee he'd worked for. A gift, I suppose. The best wood for gun stocks comes from the Balkans. They bury scrap iron around the root systems of young trees. Over the years the rust and bits of metal grow right into the tree's circulatory system and it makes natural iron burls and fissures in the grain of the wood—"

Judge Flood cleared his throat. "Mr. Thomson, our interest in these matters is not unlimited. Please get to the point."

"Yes, sir. The thing is, I sized up the situation at Longwood like a soldier. Her father, Mr. Selby looked dangerous to me, dangerous to everybody. Until I could analyze the situation I didn't want to risk anybody getting hurt. So I retreated, which was the strategic thing to do under the circumstances."

"It was a military move then?" Brett suggested.

"Yes. It was only bad luck I was thrown from the motorbike. But you can't run a military exercise by computers. Chaos is often the rule in combat. My father explained that to me. No matter how trained and motivated troops are, there is always an X in the battlefield equation—how the individual soldier will react to gunfire, to wounds or to the appearance of the enemy at an unexpected place or time . . . Well, I *didn't* panic when I saw her father, because I've been trained to anticipate the disorder that is the essence of violence. Physical combat is the last place a hero can define himself—I'm speaking of the heroic ideal, ma'am. There is nothing vain or personal in this. But that ideal has declined irreversibly since the Greeks worshipped the heroes of the *Iliad* and the *Odyssey.*"

Thomson hesitated, a trace of uncertainty in his expression. Flexing his hands, he said, "I didn't run from her father, ma'am. I'd never run—from anybody."

"You are proud of your own father's military background and record, Mr. Thomson?"

"Yes, ma'am."

"Did he discuss the details of his military career with you?"

"I found his discharge papers and service ribbons and Bronze Star when I was just a kid. They were in a musette bag in a storage room." Earl paused. "My father told me a military unit was the fairest thing ever conceived. You were read the rules when you joined. The Articles of War. If you broke the rules, you were punished."

"Did your father ever mention the name Jonas Selby to you?"

Tension hardened Earl's mouth. Davic half rose, then settled back in his chair. The courtroom had become unnaturally silent.

"To the best of my knowledge," Thomson said slowly, "the first time I heard that name was here in this court."

"Did your father tell you that he had presided over military courts in Korea?"

"I . . . I believe that came up in our talks."

"Your father never mentioned the name Jonas Selby during those conversations?"

"To the best of my knowledge, no."

"Mr. Thomson, as a cadet colonel at Rockland Military College, you occasionally gave lectures on military topics to underclassmen. Correct?"

"Yes, ma'am. All upperclassmen gave such talks."

Brett picked up a manila envelope from the People's table and unwound the waxed string from the metal disc on its flap. On a corner of the envelope was a glossy decal of an armored knight with a black shield. Opening the envelope, Brett removed a volume in gray cloth with crimson edges. The lettering on the cover was plainly visible to Earl Thomson and the attorneys at the defense table. It was a Rockland Military Col-

lege yearbook, the school motto arched in black capitals: THY
COUNTRY IS THINE HONOR.

"Mr. Thomson, do you recognize this volume?"

"Yes, ma'am. It's our college yearbook."

"Would the court stenographer please note," Brett said,
"that the witness has identified the Rockland Military College
yearbook for the year 1974. The book contains two hundred
sixty-two pages of general information about the school and
faculty. Plus fifty-eight photographs of the graduating class of
the year 1974. The lectures you gave, Mr. Thomson"—Brett
nodded at the book she was holding—"are listed here in your
biographical sketch. You conducted seminars on military justice
and punishment, and several others on the rights of defendants
and the responsibility of officers in summary and general courts.
That information is correct?"

"Yes, ma'am."

"In those seminars on the courts-martial system of the U.S.
Army, did *you* ever mention the trial of Jonas Selby?"

"*No, ma'am.* To the best of my knowledge, I did not."

"To the best of your knowledge? Then to the best of your
knowledge did you discuss in those lectures the role your *father*
played in the court-martial of Jonas Selby?"

Davic objected. "This line of inquiry is totally extraneous,
Your Honor. I move that it be stricken from the records."

"On the contrary, Your Honor. The court-martial of Jonas
Selby is crucial and relevant to the issues at court—*according to
Mr. Davic himself.* He argued to have K.S. 36663864 made part of
the record. If Mr. Davic now believes that transcript is extraneous, I ask why he went to such trouble to have it released from
an Operative-Classified category and introduced as a defense
exhibit. He insisted that truth was the heart of his defense. That
motive was the heart of that truth. It was Mr. Davic who advised
the jury that Harry Selby's *father* had been prosecuted and sent
to prison by Major George Thomson. He insisted that Harry
Selby had known and hated the Thomson family long before the
rape of his daughter. That the seeds of the persecution of Earl
Thomson lay deep in the past in Korea—or so Mr. Davic argued.
Very well, Your Honor, let the People have the opportunity to
turn that question around. What did Earl Thomson know of the

Selby family before that savage attack on Shana Selby? May we not ask what he—"

Flood cut her off with his gavel. "I have not yet ruled on Mr. Davic's objection, Miss Brett. I will review my notes on K.S. 36663864. We will recess for fifteen minutes for that purpose."

George Thomson and Dom Lorso waited for Davic outside the courtroom. The corridor was crowded but the police had roped off the entrance to Superior Nine. When Davic appeared there were shouted questions and the flash of camera bulbs.

Lorso drew on a cigarette, his nerves shredded from the hours of enforced abstinence, then said quietly, "She's playing him like a yo-yo, Davic. Didn't you tell him to stick to yes and no, for Christ's sake?" Thomson nodded vigorously.

Davic presented a fixed smile to the cameras. Barely moving his lips, he said, "The defendant doesn't want any disruptions from me, Mr. Thomson. Those were his words. Your son is running things. It wasn't my decision to introduce the court-martial transcript that gave Brett a green light to cross-examine. She's taking full advantage of your generosity. Your son is damaging himself, Mr. Thomson, but I can't stop him."

Thomson blinked uncomfortably as flashlights exploded in his eyes. "Then tell Slocum to stop *her,*" he said very quietly.

The three men stood together facing the reporters and photographers. "Give us a break, gentlemen," Davic said pleasantly. "I don't have a statement to make now. When I do you'll be covered, that's a promise."

"We've waited long enough." Thomson rubbed his mouth to muffle the words. "Earl can't handle it. Tell Slocum to cut her legs off before it's too late."

"Yes, of course," Davic said, and with a genial wave to the press, returned to the courtroom.

CHAPTER THIRTY-ONE

Judge Flood sounded his gavel with deliberate emphasis and instructed the People to make no further inquiries into the accused's knowledge of Jonas Selby.

"The young man was not born at the time of that trial in Korea," Flood said. "It's inconceivable those events have no bearing on him now. Miss Brett, please go on to something else."

"Exception, Your Honor. With respect, the People have a right to examine evidence which was introduced by the defense for the sole purpose of ascribing a felonious motive to the plaintiff's father. If the court-martial of Jonas Selby was ruled pertinent to the *defense,* I hold that it must be pertinent to the *People.*"

"Miss Brett, it is not your place to hold on points of law in relation to my rulings."

Brett's answer was to drop the Rockland yearbook into a wastebasket.

During the recess, she had scrubbed her hands and combed out her hair. A few drops of water still glistened at the temples. She had polished the tips of her bone-colored pumps and dabbed cologne at her wrists. As she studied the witness, her manner was now openly skeptical.

"Tell me, Mr. Thomson, do you have any theories to explain the continued disappearance of your car?"

"Theories? No, ma'am."

"You told us it was a distinctive automobile. You told us you were sure it would turn up. Are you surprised it hasn't?"

"No, ma'am. Whoever ripped it off probably stripped it for parts or got rid of it."

"Did you get in touch with Porsche owners' clubs around the country? Did you advertise for information about your stolen car?"

"I didn't think it would do any good, ma'am. So I didn't bother."

"Have you offered a reward for its return?"

"No . . . no, I haven't."

"Mr. Thomson, this may be only a matter of grammar or usage"—she stopped and watched him—"but do you realize we've been talking about your car in the past tense?"

"What does that matter?"

"It matters because it suggests you believe that car doesn't exist anymore. Is that the fact of the matter—?"

"Objection, Your Honor."

"Sustained."

"Mr. Thomson, you told Captain Slocum that you did not know Shana Selby or anyone in the Selby family. The tapes were played in this courtroom only a few days ago. You remember your statement to Captain Slocum?"

"Sure. I didn't know the girl who got so hysterical at Longwood. So I certainly didn't know her family."

"In regard to your testimony about those events, did you see Shana Selby shoved to the ground?"

"No, I didn't. That weird character with her started the trouble and got decked. I think she knelt down to help him up."

"You didn't see anyone strike her or push her?"

"No, ma'am."

"But you observed a man coming to her assistance?"

"Well, yes, I saw that much."

"You observed that man help Shana Selby to her feet?"

"Yes."

"Then you ran away from him?"

"How many times do I have to tell you? *I didn't run away from her father.*"

Brett walked from the stand and stood with her back to the plaintiff's table. "I remind you that you are under oath, Mr.

367

Thomson. I will now ask you to explain two things. How did you know the name of that stranger at Longwood? How did you know his relationship to the plaintiff?"

Earl made a dismissing gesture with his hand. "Well, everybody knew that—" But he stopped there, a curiously numb expression appearing on his face.

Brett remained motionless. Earl moistened his lips and clenched his hands. Brett said, "Would you like time to think about it, Mr. Thomson?"

"I don't need any favors." He spoke quietly, the words carefully enunciated. "Everyone knew," he began, but stopped again, staring at his tight fists. "Everybody heard how he sent his daughter over there to say I raped her."

"At that time, how did you know that man was Harry Selby?"

"I assumed—" Earl shrugged and looked at Brett, his eyes sharpened by anger. "Maybe I saw a picture of him somewhere. Do you remember every man you ever saw in your life? Every man you may have—"

Flood's gavel cut him off. "Mr. Thomson, you will answer the People's questions in a responsive manner."

Brett said, "Mr. Thomson, on three occasions you referred to Mr. Selby as the girl's father or her father. I'll repeat the question: How did you know—at that time—that he was *Harry Selby* or that he was Shana's *father?*"

"I don't know." Earl's voice was rising. "The girl called his name, maybe, or he yelled something to my friends about being her father."

"The truth is," Brett said coldly, "you knew Harry Selby and recognized him on sight, didn't you? Wouldn't you prefer to ease your conscience now and tell us how you knew him? And everything you know about *Jonas* Selby?"

"Objection, Your Honor! *Objection.*"

"Sustained." Flood rapped his gavel.

But Earl's voice was rising again. "I'll answer your question, ma'am. Don't think I'm afraid, *don't ever think that.* I don't want pity from *anybody.*"

"Your Honor, if you please—"

Earl's powerful voice overrode Davic's. "Pity and charity,

they're the virtues of traitors, of faggots and cowards. You're like that, miss, coddle broken-winged sparrows, let the eagles die. Heroes are comic-strip figures to you. You'd destroy your country for the worst at the expense of the *best*. Your hero's Don Quixote, a bungling fool to laugh at—"

The gavel sounded to no purpose, marshals stared at the bench for instructions.

"Or you'd prefer Dante of the *Inferno*, the impotent observer of death, a voyeur in hell—"

"*Mr. Thomson.*" Judge Flood struck the gavel so hard that it started a ringing tremor in his crystal carafe.

"You hate men with guts enough to *act* because they make you realize your helplessness, because they—"

Davic was at his side now, and when Earl tried to rise the lawyer gripped his arm and forced him back into the witness chair.

"Your Honor," Davic said, "I must ask for the court's understanding. My client is under a severe emotional strain. I believe that justice as well as decency would be served by a recess of these hearings until tomorrow morning. It's a cruel burden, as I'm sure Your Honor knows from his long experience on the bench, for a witness to be forced to defend himself —as Mr. Thomson has—against charges that practically deny him membership in the human race, that strike at the very core of his honor and self-esteem."

Judge Flood motioned to Brett to approach the bench. "You've heard Mr. Davic's request. What do you say, Miss Brett?"

"I agree that a brief recess might be in order, Your Honor. But the defendant is in a responsive mood and willing to testify. This is an opportunity the People have a legitimate right to pursue. My examination was designed to get at the facts in a logical sequence, and within a contained time reference."

"I understand, Miss Brett, but nothing will be lost, I assure you, by adjourning until tomorrow morning."

Judge Flood sounded his gavel and interrupted whatever else Brett had begun to say by standing and stepping down from the bench.

"All rise," the clerk said.

The late afternoon sunlight streamed across the Quaker and Indian murals, almost masking Counselor Davic's now more relaxed expression.

Brett returned to the plaintiff's table and smiled for Shana's benefit. She noticed a sheet of memo paper on her legal pad.

"A court officer left it there," Shana told her.

After reading the brief message, Brett looked away and said quietly, "Something's come up, Shana. I'll have Sergeant Wilger run you home, okay?"

"Sure."

The message requested an immediate meeting with People's counsel on an urgent matter. It was initialed by East Chester's chief of detectives, Walter B. Slocum.

Brett paced her office with her arms crossed tightly in an effort to control the tremor in her hands. On her desk was a sheaf of typewritten yellow pages, undated and unsigned. Next to them were Xeroxed copies of arrest reports, a magistrate's booking sheet, detectives' summaries, letters written on university stationery and a small stack of news clippings.

Captain Slocum came in and settled himself comfortably in her visitor's armchair, smiled and propped a large Gucci loafer against the side of her desk. Unwrapping a cigar, he said, "It's the time of day to relax, Miss Brett. If I was home now I'd probably be watching the news and having a beer or even something a little stronger."

Lighting his cigar, the captain savored a mouthful of heavy smoke, allowing it to drift slowly around his moist and slightly parted lips. "Would you like a drink by the way? A little touch to smooth the edges after a long, hard day?" Rolling the cigar between his lips, he studied her with an appraising smile.

"I've got a bottle for medicinal purposes in my office. Suspects go into shock sometimes. I have to be prepared for that. Or we could drive out to a place I like on the river. Seafood joint, make hot canapes with oysters and ham, very tasty. Bartender also knows how to build a very solid martini, uses dry sherry instead of vermouth. It makes a difference. Adds a sweet tartness. No reason why we shouldn't combine a bit of pleasure with business. Right?"

370

Still smiling, the captain nodded at the documents on Brett's desk. "You took a look at them, I guess."

"Yes, I have."

"They kind of speak for themselves, don't they?"

"As much as any anonymous accusation does, Captain."

"In most cases, your point would carry some weight, but the photostats of the operative reports *are* signed, Miss Brett." Slocum blew a streak of smoke at his leather loafer, watched it swirl about the decorative brass links. "I'm just a cop, Miss Brett. Never mind my rank. I'm the muscle, you're the brains. But while we've got different roles to play, there's a need for teamwork between the muscle and brain in a department like ours." (He actually chuckled, she thought with disgust.) "I used to try to explain that to my little girl when she was learning to ride horseback. If you point a horse for trouble, he'll damn sure take you there. If you'd put us in the picture of the Thomson case to start with we could've worked together. But you went your own way, all brain, no muscle. Now we got ourselves a problem."

Slocum nodded at the material on her desk. "Wouldn't you agree, Miss Brett, that the horse has the bit in his mouth now, and you're just hanging on for dear life?" He smiled. "Just a manner of speaking, you realize."

Brett sat down in her swivel chair. Her back was to the window and she either felt or imagined a draft of icy air. Her shoulders were cold, and so was her spine, the coldness went all through her, from her neck down to her ankles. A sharp pain tightened her stomach muscles. Her mouth was dry, and she was experiencing the self-fullfilling fear that she would stutter when she tried to explain the documents Slocum had delivered to her office.

"Would you tell me how you got them?" she said, and to her relief her voice sounded cool and assured, even casual.

"They came direct to my office, addressed to me personally. Copies were also sent to Mr. Lamb and to Mr. Davic."

"No sender's name, no return address on the envelope, of course."

Slocum shrugged. "Of course. But the envelope was post-marked in Philadelphia last night at seven thirty-five."

Brett picked up the letter that had accompanied the various

371

photostated documents. "This was typed on an old machine," she said, "by someone who misspelled simple words like 'various,' drops the *i*, and 'annual,' only one *n*, but does perfectly fine with 'accusatory' and 'judicious' and 'inflammatory.' A clever fellow pretending to be dumb. Do you know anyone who fits that description, Captain?"

Slocum laughed softly. "About half the politicians I've ever done business with, Miss Brett. But people like that understand teamwork. They know that muscle and brain make a good combination. Like I told my little daughter, the horse will take you places, but sometimes it's not where you'd like to be. Brains can make intelligent decisions, I'll grant you. Or sensible ones. But muscle puts 'em to work. Let's get down to business. You look scared, Miss Brett. But there's no *need* to be . . . According to these reports you accused a man named Toby Clark of trying to rape you. That incident happened when you was just a kid in college. It was in the gym, right?"

"In the women's dressing room."

"You'd been in the pool. Alone. There was no one around but you and this Toby Clark. No other witnesses."

"The gym was locked up while I was swimming," Brett said. "Toby Clark had hidden himself in the locker room." She moistened her lips and resisted the impulse to light a cigarette. "I'm sure you haven't found Toby Clark, Captain. Or did you even look for him?"

Slocum laughed. "Why should I bother looking for him? That's all ancient history so far as I'm concerned. I'm just interested in how this could affect the Thomson case."

"I was waiting for you to get to that."

"I'm a realist, Miss Brett. Don't hold it against me. You had Toby Clark arrested. You accused him of trying to rape you."

"Among other things, Captain."

"Yeah. There was a scuffle, I gather. Rolling around in the locker room had to raise a bruise or two."

"There were bruises, as you put it."

"But the thing is," Slocum said, and he was no longer smiling, "you charged Toby Clark with trying to rape you, and then dropped the charges. But that change of heart came too late to help Toby Clark. He was fired from his job at the school. Never mind the nice letters some professors wrote for him, or that he

372

was cleaning up the locker room like he was paid to, picking up after rich little bitches, when you strolled in and peeled off your bra and G-string—"

"It took considerable investigative work to assemble those records, wouldn't you say, Captain? Police reports, newspaper clippings, copies of the magistrate's hearing?"

"That's not the point, Miss Brett."

"What *is* the point, Captain?"

"As a lawyer, you sure must know the answer to that. Everybody on that jury was questioned by you and Judge Flood and Davic about their personal experiences with rape cases. All the women were asked if they'd ever been victims, the men whether it had happened to their wives or daughters, nieces or cousins. Any prospective juror with experiences like that would sure as hell have been disqualified on the grounds they'd bring their fear or prejudice into the case against Earl Thomson . . . But nobody asked *you*, Miss Brett, about *your* personal experience with rape or attempted rape, and you didn't volunteer that information, did you?"

"That's not required of counsel."

"I'll take your word on that. But I know what Davic plans to do with this information. Tomorrow morning he'll move to disqualify you. Mr. Lamb is aware of all this. He wants to talk to you now. He's in his office."

"Davic's motion has no legal validity," Brett said. "He knows that, and so does Mr. Lamb."

Slocum turned his hands up in an innocent gesture. "Like I said, you're the brains, I'm just the muscle. But all the brains in the world can't stop Davic from filing. If Flood dismisses the motion, fine. But the jury is going to know that the woman prosecuting Earl Thomson for rape also accused one Toby Clark of trying to rape her, and then thought better about it."

"The charge was *true*. It was a question of proving—" Her tongue felt like a wad of cotton in her mouth. Her spine seemed frozen solid. She wanted to throw something into Slocum's blandly smiling face, but, ridiculously, she thought, most desperately of all she wanted *not* to light a cigarette. A trial of will or courage, an inquisitor's test of innocence.

She put the pack in her desk drawer and locked it.

"You see," Slocum said, "if you stay on the case the jury

will be wondering if Earl Thomson's life might be wrecked just like Toby Clark's was, because the rape charges turned out to be nothing but some horny kid's imagination working overtime."

He knocked a length of ash into Brett's clean ashtray, but his aim was off . . . the ashes missed the tray and scattered a film of gray flakes over the photostatic reports on her desk.

"Sorry about that." Slocum stood and smiled at Brett. "My wife's always getting on me about spilling ashes when I'm watching TV. We've got a rug, it's Oriental, and she's particular as hell about it." He stopped in the doorway. "If you happen to come down with a cold tonight, a fever, say, I'm sure the police surgeon could get your assignments canceled, arrange a few weeks of recuperative leave."

"I don't feel a fever coming on," Brett said.

"These things hit pretty sudden. My kid used to argue with me about that. She'd come in soaked from riding, but didn't want to rest up, miss school. The important thing, Miss Brett, is that nothing hurts the Thomson case. Right? If you step aside, it could be all to the good. Otherwise Davic files first thing when court convenes. I'll see you in Mr. Lamb's office. We need your decision tonight, so he can assign a back-up deputy. It's been a long day, everybody wants to get home. Don't keep us waiting."

When the door closed, Brett put the back of her hand against her forehead. Her skin was cool and dry as ash. She looked at the photostats on her desk and tried to fight back her memories, and her tears.

After a moment she drew a deep breath and dialed the Selbys' home. No matter what she decided, she owed an explanation to Shana. If a new counsel for the People against Earl Thomson had to be appointed, Shana must be prepared for it.

CHAPTER THIRTY-TWO

Selby phoned Shana from the lobby of the Franklin Hotel in Philadelphia.

His daughter's voice was subdued . . . Brett had called to tell her that she seemed to be coming down with a heavy cold and might not be in court tomorrow. "She sounded sort of strange," Shana said, "but she told me it would be okay if one of the other deputies took over—"

"Was she home when she told you that?"

"No, she was at her office. But she seemed okay today. Super, in fact. When are you coming home?"

"I expected to be back before this." Selby looked at his watch; it was after eight. The Cadles had been out that afternoon but had checked into their room a few minutes ago. "I'll be home in a couple of hours."

"Well, everything's fine here. Mrs. Cranston and Davey are watching TV, and I've been looking up Switzerland in the map book. I found a town called Beaurive near Lausanne, it has hotels right near the ski lifts. I'm going to write for brochures and holiday rates. I'll write a letter in French and have Miss Calder check it out so I don't say something about putting ski wax on the plume of my aunt. I'll ask Miss Culpepper to make me a checklist of books from the library."

If the fantasy of white slopes, Christmas lights and chocolate in a Swiss village could help distract Shana, Selby thought, so much the better . . . she still had Davic's cross-examination to face. But as if sensing her father's thoughts, Shana's voice became shaded. "I want to talk to Kelly tomorrow," she said, "there's something I've got to tell her."

"A couple of aspirin and a night's sleep can work wonders, honey."

"Well, I'd better talk to you anyway. Will you wake me when you get home?"

"Sure thing."

"No matter how late?"

"No matter. It's a late date . . ."

After the hanging up, Selby dialed Sergeant Wilger at the Division in East Chester.

"Can you talk?"

"Go ahead."

"What's up with Brett?"

"I wish to hell I knew. She's in a meeting with the DA and Slocum. A secretary they sent out for coffee leaked that they're moving to get her off the Thomson case. Slocum for sure, and Lamb is leaning that way. The private muscle from New York, Davic's investigators, have come up with something that apparently gives the defense the opportunity to file a motion to disqualify."

"Any idea *what?*"

"No . . . where are you?"

"Philadelphia. I spent part of the afternoon talking to Petey Komoto at Hell for Leather. You sure we can talk?"

"Who knows? They could have a wire up my ass. But go ahead. You told Komoto you were a cop, is that it, Harry? Used a police badge from a crackerjack box?"

"I didn't need to. Petey spotted you the other night. He described you as a thin nervous guy with glasses parked across from his spot. Made you for a cop and figured you were interested in Thomson and Taggart because you split when they did. So Petey Komoto decided his operation was under surveillance and I was part of it. I let him assume whatever the hell he wanted. It seems Thomson and Taggart rented a film called *Knots and Lashes,* a four-reeler about a modern cruise ship. Lady pirates in boots and bikinis board her. Nautical fun and games, seamen walking the plank, cat-o'-nine-tails. But Thomson didn't screen *Knots and Lashes*. He had another can of film. Komoto heard Thomson tell Taggart he'd put it together from a master print."

"You got this for contributing to Petey's favorite charity?"

"Yes, it's called the Komoto Foundation. Two hundred in cash. But Komoto didn't see any of Thomson's film—"

"Hold it, I got a party on another line. Where can I call you?"

"You better not. I'm at the Franklin but I'm about to pay a social call on the Cadle brothers. They're registered here as Ed and John Nelson."

"Don't be stupid." Wilger's voice became angry. "You don't know what you're into. This isn't amateur night. That prick Taggart testifies tomorrow, and Goldie Boy. Davic will put Shana through the wringer. What good will you do if you're in a body cast? Sit tight, Harry. I'm off duty in two hours. I can be in Philly—"

"I'll be all right." Selby hung up and walked down a flight of steps to the men's room. He checked his duffel coat with the attendant and splashed water on his face and smoothed down his hair, which looked copper-tinted in the fluorescent lighting. He dried his face and hands and adjusted his tie and absently touched the white scar on his cheekbone.

After brushing his jacket, the attendant knelt and took several dextrous swipes with a towel at Selby's L.L. Bean dark brown country shoes. A black man with pleasant eyes, the attendant thanked Selby for his tip and assured him he'd keep an eye on the duffel coat. Selby told him he'd be back in about an hour.

He took a self-service elevator to the fifth floor and knocked on the "Nelsons'" door. The man who opened it wore dark slacks and a gray sports shirt. His black hair was cut so short his scalp showed through it. His wrists were almost as thick as his forearms, and his shoulders filled out the shirt without a wrinkle. Life or poor digestion or something had made a pessimist of him, Selby decided. Cadle's flat, hard eyes looked hostile out of sheer habit.

Selby's name generated neither interest nor recognition.

"Okay, so you're Harry Selby. What d'you want?"

His body partially blocked the door, but behind him Selby

saw a TV set and a table with bottles, glasses and a cardboard icebucket. A man's legs sprawled out in view on the bed.

"I'm looking for one of the Cadle brothers," Selby said. "Aron or Ben."

"Wrong room, sport." The man started to close the door.

Selby checked it with his hand. "You're registered as Nelson, but you're one of the Cadle boys. Aron or Ben, one or the other."

The eyes changed, became watchful. "Where'd you get the name Nelson?"

"That's not important. Are you Ben or Aron?"

"Tell me about Nelson. Nothing else, sport."

"Aron, who the hell *is* that?"

The voice came from the man on the bed. His thick bare legs were furred with reddish hair. He wore white socks.

"Well, if you're Aron, I guess that must be Ben," Selby said.

The hairy legs swung off the bed, the wide feet in dirty white socks came down on the floor. "Who's the clown, Aron?"

Ben Cadle was the younger of the brothers, shorter than Aron but thicker through the arms and shoulders. His body was solid with heavy bone and muscle. He wore jockey shorts and a white T-shirt. His hair was a flaming red, red as paprika. It lay flat over his broad head like a skullcap.

"Look, Selby," Aron Cadle said, "I think you're confused about something. You look like good people, so come in and tell us about the Nelsons, okay?"

Selby said fine. An air-conditioner hummed in a window. The room's meaty smell was sharpened by the tang of whiskey. Selby turned his back to the TV set. "I want to know who's paying you. I've got a message for whoever it is, and I want you to deliver it."

Aron Cadle put a hand on his brother's arm, closed the door. "We can't tell you that, pal," he said. "There are rules about it." Moving away from the door, Aron stood so that he and his brother faced Selby. "We can't tell you about our clients. They pay us for privacy, for discretion. We wouldn't be any good to them if we didn't live up to those rules. But you're not bound by 'em, sport, so you can tell us how you found out we'd registered here."

"Look, we can settle this thing without the hard-nosed

stuff," Selby said. "I'm trying to find out about the pressure on a trial my daughter's involved in. She's fourteen and she was raped. You maybe have heard about it. You've made some calls to the deputy DA handling the case. Let's start with that."

They shifted their positions until they stood on either side of him. Aron Cadle said mildly, "No, Selby, we got to start back at square one. I'm gonna be frank now. I don't have any idea in the whole world what you're talking about. Ben and me are licensed private investigators with out-of-state permits for guns, surveillance equipment, police-band radios. What we do is by the book and strictly legal. We haven't bothered your DA pal with phone calls."

"And you didn't try to run her down—her name is Dorcas Brett—in the black Lincoln you drive?"

"What's that name again?"

"Brett, Dorcas Brett."

"Funny kind of name, Dorcas. Never heard that one before. Ben, you know anybody by that name?"

"Dorcas? No way."

"Selby, you *are* confused," Aron said. "We drive a Volvo, not a Lincoln. You got no reason to be bugging me and my brother. Which leaves the Nelson business."

"That's the important thing, right?"

"Yes, it's a matter of security. We went to a lot of trouble to check in here without anybody knowing. But somebody found out and told you. So who was it, sport?"

"Maybe we could swap stories."

"Let's try it that way." Aron smiled. "We don't want to beat it out of you. If you get your kicks getting roughed up, I'd advise you to go bust up a bar or try to punch out some cops. We're businessmen, we don't go in for that. But we've got to know how you found us. The rest is shit, Selby. The phone calls, your fourteen-year-old who got raped, the Dorcas lady, that's all shit. You understand what I'm telling you?"

"I did some checking," Selby said. "I found out you have an agency on Forty-fifth in Manhattan, between Fifth and Sixth. It's called Atlas Investigation." Selby watched their faces tighten as he told them the information he'd gotten from Victoria Kim. "You were bonded by a bank in the Bronx. The trust officer who signed the paper is your third cousin. That, by the way, is known to Mr. Touhy in the Bonding Section in Albany. Neither of you is married and you both belong to a queer health club in Queens, play racquetball on weekends. Aron's got a girl, though, a legal secretary who works for a firm on Wall Street. It's your turn now. What have you gents been up to? Never mind the fag health club, or the legal secretary . . . just the important details . . ."

They were not as professional as Selby had anticipated. Their reactions were blurred, splintered by a kind of frenzy.

Ben threw a looping punch at Selby's head. It was a feint, of course, the trigger to turn Selby toward Aron. But Ben's execution was clumsy, his grunt too theatrical. Selby stepped back and the blow missed him, as it was intended to. You were usually suckered like this in your first year up in the pros, worrying about speedy blocking backs who hit you and were gone, a distraction to make you forget what was right behind them, the pulling guards with ten-flat speed and shoulders like the fronts of trucks.

He was expecting Aron's punch and took it on his shoulder instead of the face. But the man's fist was only partially deflected and bounced off Selby's forehead with painful force. With the heel of one hand, Selby rammed Aron's jaw up and back. With his other, he hit him in the stomach.

He hit Aron as hard as he could, hoping to knock the wind out of him, but he did better than that; the punch landed in the soft triangle of the big man's rib cage, and after one long gasp Aron coughed hoarsely and slid to the floor, hugging himself carefully with his arms.

Selby was hit from behind then by Ben, a blow that numbed his shoulder. He ducked and swung his arm in a back-handed slap that caught the redhead in the neck and tipped him back over the bed.

With surprising agility Ben lunged for the lamp table, clawing at the drawer pulls. Selby caught him and dragged him onto the floor, but the drawer came away in the redhead's hands, spilling out a deck of playing cards, bottles of pills . . . and a revolver in a spring-clip holster wrapped in a webbing of black harness.

Selby knelt on Ben Cadle's back and turned up the television. A burst of laughter exploded from the set as teenagers carried a yappy dog into an immaculate kitchen. Aron watched Selby. His face was swollen, flushed a dull crimson. He held his body cautiously, as if he were cradling a fragile package.

Selby pounded Ben's shoulder and neck and the top of his fiery red head. It was not textbook combat; there was no room for that. Ben heaved under Selby's weight, squirming first in one direction and then the other like a giant crab trying to dislodge a heavy net from its back.

Selby hit him wherever he could, jarring him with short punches, kneeing him in the kidneys and ribs. Holding Ben's coarse hair, he slammed his head against the floor.

Aron watched the proceedings with a glazed indifference. The flush of color had receded from his face; he was very pale now.

Selby put a knee into Ben's back, shoved his face into the carpet and held him until Ben's mouth opened wide and he stopped moving.

"I want you to be quiet," Selby told him.

Ben couldn't close his mouth. His eyes met Selby's and he nodded with his eyes.

Selby released him and pushed him against the wall beside his brother. Picking up the revolver, he went into the bathroom and tossed it into the toilet.

A knock sounded on the door. Selby came out of the bathroom and looked at the Cadles. Ben's mouth was still open. His head was twisted at an awkward angle. Blood glinted on Aron's lips.

The knocking sounded again. Selby turned down the television and opened the door, his body filling the doorway.

A bellboy stood in the corridor. He looked up at Selby and tried to peer around him, a slender youngster with a pointed face and knowing eyes.

Selby said, "I guess you heard it too."

"Heard what, sir?"

"I'm not sure," Selby said. "It was like somebody fell. The ceiling shook. I was going to call the desk."

"I guess it was on the next floor then," the bellhop said.

"Could've been a drunk. What's your name?"

"Karl, sir."

Selby took out his wallet and gave him two twenty-dollar

bills. "We'll need room service in about an hour, Karl, a bottle of bourbon. Will you take care of us?"

"You bet. Any particular brand?"

"I'll leave that up to you, Karl. About an hour, okay? No hurry."

"Yes, sir."

Selby closed the door, locked it and slipped the night chain into place.

He sat on the footstool in front of the television set and watched a plump lady who chuckled indulgently at the cartoon figure of an armored knight holding a floor waxer like an upraised lance.

Loosening his tie, he took out a handkerchief and patted his forehead where Aron had hit him; the broken skin stung when sweat touched it.

"You gents have me at a disadvantage," he said. "This is your kind of action, not mine."

"Something else," Ben Cadle said. "We're expecting calls. Lorso will check in, so will Davic. If you plan to hold us here, you got real problems—"

"Let me finish. You're the professionals, with police-band radios, guns, surveillance equipment. But there's something else that's more important." He watched the blood come from Aron's lips, crimson blisters that filled up and popped with the rhythm of his slow, heavy breathing. "What's important is for you to realize that this fight's over and you guys lost. All that can happen now is for you to get hurt even more—"

"Tell Dom Lorso that, you creep," Ben Cadle said. "And Slocum and—" "You'll find out about hurt . . . I promise you . . ."

"I think I'm wasting my time," Selby said. "But I'll keep trying . . . breathe slow, Aron. It won't hurt so bad—"

"It's my ribs," Aron said, "they're killing me . . ."

"I know . . . sit quiet, you'll be okay for a while. One of them splintered when I hit you, maybe a couple of them. Your lungs are filling up with blood now."

Selby took a sheaf of papers from his pocket and smoothed out the creases. "You're drowning, Aron." He handed Emma Green's deposition to Ben. "Read that," he told him. "Read it to yourself. I've been through it one time too many. *Hold it,* " he said as Ben Cadle started to crumple the deposition. "Please don't do that. You've only got a few loose teeth, Ben, but if you press me . . ." He shrugged. "So start reading. Your brother is hurt. I know about things like that. Players do the real damage to themselves *after* they're hit. Macho bullshit about getting taped up and back in the game. First time they take a lick, they're gone for the season. Maybe for life."

"You crazy fucker, call a hospital," Ben said. "You gonna sit and watch Aron bleed to death?"

"Emotional reaction to injuries tend to aggravate them," Selby said. "A team doctor told me that. Ethnic and national characteristics also play a part. Italians, for instance, you can't keep them on the bench hurt unless you nail them there. Blacks will play hurt if it's a close game, but not for show. That's what the good doc told me—"

"I'm German," Aron Cadle gasped. "So is Ben."

Selby nodded. "Good. The Germans I played with were very sensible. Followed instructions very well. All right . . . Ben, talk to me. I want everything Davic knows. Don't leave anything out."

"Suppose I tell you to go fuck yourself—?"

"Then we'll sit here and watch your brother drown in his own blood."

"Jesus, tell him," Aron said softly, his breath whistling over his blood-flaked lips.

It didn't take Ben long. When he was through, Selby said, "Now call Mr. Davic and read Miss Green's deposition to him. When you're through I'll talk to him. If he asks about me, if he wants to know, for instance, if I'm in a violent or reckless mood, I suggest you give him an honest estimate. He's entitled to that. So are you."

Selby picked up a pillow, put it against Aron Cadle's chest and carefully folded the man's thick arms around it. "Hold it close to you and breathe very slowly," he told him. "We'll call an ambulance after I have a word with Counselor Davic."

CHAPTER THIRTY-THREE

It was after midnight when Selby got to Dorcas Brett's. Winds off the Brandywine mill-race rocked the trees and caused shadows to leap away from the iron streetlamps.

From behind the heavy door her voice was low and tense. "Yes?"

"It's all right, it's me, Harry."

Tumblers fell, a chain came unlatched. She opened the door. A log burned in the living room fireplace. She wore a tan robe with yellow piping over dark velour pajamas. The sofa was made up with blankets and a pillow. A book was on the floor.

Her phone was off the hook, he saw, the receiver lying beside the cradle. He had tried to call her twice before leaving Philadelphia. Now, even above the crackle of the logs, he could hear the faint beat of the busy signal.

She watched him anxiously as he took off his coat. "What's the matter, Harry? What happened to you? Your forehead's bleeding."

"I bumped my head in a phone booth."

"Is anything wrong?"

"Everything is fine, everything is great. Relax."

"Sure. You just happened to be driving by and noticed my lights . . ."

He lifted the receiver from the desk and placed it in the

cradle. "I can't promise you'll never get a wrong number, or your sister won't call to tell you a poodle had pups, but I promise you won't hear from the Cadle brothers again."

She stared at the phone, as if testing its strange silence. "You're sure? You talked to them then?"

"In a phrase from a century when they did things better, I called on them."

"You know Davic intends to move for a disqualification?"

"I knew that, yes."

"And you know why?"

"Yes."

Her dark hair and the firelight made her face seem unnaturally pale, made her high cheekbones stand out.

"Then I guess you know my whole story, Harry . . ."

"No, because I don't know what you plan to do."

"Well, haven't you at least guessed? That would have been a vote of confidence, of sorts."

"All I knew is what you told Shana. It was a flip of the coin then."

"Well, I've decided not to run a convenient fever."

"I'd have taken the odds on it."

She smiled. "Thanks. I told Lamb—after a speech about team spirit and loyalty and some less subtle crap from Slocum, that I wouldn't quit. If I don't take Allan Davic's flak tomorrow, if I crawl away from it, it would make a lie out of everything I've let Shana be put through. So don't worry . . . or maybe you should be . . . but I'll be in court with her in the morning."

"I wasn't worried. Not about you."

She looked at him, not altogether convinced. "Look, Harry, *I'm* worried, and scared, and tomorrow Davic's going to turn the lions loose on us . . . You've been in a fight, it's obvious. Please don't give me any more stuff about bumping into yourself in a phone booth. Tell me all of it. Please. You talked to Davic, didn't you?"

"Yes. First he told me if I tried to pressure him with Emma Green's deposition I'd be personally subject to serious legal reprisal. His very words. Second, he said that the deposition was inadmissible in this case. I told him I knew that. I told him you'd explained it to me. I also told him the matter wasn't negotiable.

I quoted what he'd told me himself about Poland in another context."

"Harry, would you like coffee? You sound high."

"I am high. I told Davic if he filed against you tomorrow he'd find fifty copies of the Emma Green deposition stacked in the pressroom and that I'd hand-deliver the original copy to Earl Thomson's mother in her private suite. I left it up to him. In the end he agreed there was nothing to negotiate."

She said quietly, "But you didn't answer my first question, Harry. You do know my whole story—"

"I don't know anything, Brett. It was *your* experience, your truth. If you want to share it with me, well, then it becomes ours, I guess."

She studied him, and either her eyes had become darker or her skin whiter, he couldn't be sure which.

"That's a nice way to put it, Harry. Let me get you a drink. A Scotch, isn't it?"

A row of brass animals stood on the coffee table, tiny antlers and hooves glinting in the firelight. A pack of cigarettes was beside them, but Selby saw no ashtray or matches.

She came from the kitchen with his whiskey and water on a lacquered tray. Seating herself cross-legged on the sofa, she pushed her hair away from her shoulders.

"It's not just sex, is it, Harry?" She picked up the pack of cigarettes. "That's a tiresome question, I know, but it isn't ir-relevant. I'm not smoking," she added defensively. "That's the phrase the book advises. Not to say you've quit, but just that you *aren't*. It's got something to do with the hang-ups you create if you can't stick to it and start sneaking a few puffs. She put the cigarettes back among the brass animals. "You've got more in mind than one-night stands in motels, right?"

He was accustomed to her verbal zig-zags, these seemingly erratic detours. "That's true, but I wouldn't rule out the motels altogether."

"You're serious, you're serious about *this* at any rate, so let me try to explain why the motels might be okay but more might be difficult." Drawing a deep breath, she said, "You've got a lot locked up in your past, Harry. Come and sit here with me, please."

He sat beside her and she touched the scar on his cheek-

386

bone. "I told you that things heal over, that the pain goes away, but I don't think you really believe that. The wind on the water in Spain, the colors . . . that's the perfect place, sealed off in your memories. It belongs to you and nobody else is allowed to go there, not even to visit. It wouldn't matter if we just shared a motel room and a drink. I could think about something else if you wanted to tell me how beautiful it was back there with her. But if we were serious, I'd feel second class. I'd hate that. I'd start looking for what was wrong, the bad weather, the rainy days . . ."

"Brett, if you're accusing me of being loyal to my past, I can't argue about it. But if *you* don't want a permanent relationship, don't blame it on the phantom lady in Spain."

Her hand strayed to the cigarettes. "Friendly psychiatry, Harry? Behind the battered facade of the All-Pro whatever—"

"For Christ's sake, let's be honest about this. Tell me what you're thinking and feeling."

"I *can't*, goddammit." She uncrossed her legs in a single fluid movement and began pacing. Picking up the cigarettes, she broke open the pack with a clumsy gesture. Flakes of tobacco sifted over the brass animals. "I *want* to tell you what I'm feeling. I'm not afraid of much when I'm with you, I'll say that. But if I could put things unemotionally in a clear precise way . . ." She dropped the pack of cigarettes and sat down again. "I can *lecture* about my feelings, but that's just a suit of armor. I can quote laws and statistics about rape like a sociology professor, use antiseptic sentences, draw diagrams on the blackboard with chalk . . ." (Selby realized she was close to tears.) "But when I talk and think about it personally I start to stutter or cry or get mad . . . I have, it seems, a need to please people and a need for privacy, which turns them away . . . I'm trying, Harry, bear with me . . . Look, I found nothing unusual in my father's occasional dissatisfaction with me and my sisters for not joining the Green Berets or something to avenge the fallen warrior I was named after, Paul Dorcas, a college classmate of his who died of pneumonia at Fort Ord, Kansas, during basic training." She looked down at her hands. "Do you know what the hell I'm talking about, Harry?"

"I think maybe you're inching up on telling me what happened with Toby Clark. Well, I'm telling you that still belongs

387

to you and nobody else. It's your pain. You can do what you want with it."

"You really are a nice man, Harry . . . and wouldn't it be nice if more people felt that way. But some kinds of pain are as public as a sidewalk." She brushed impatiently at her eyes. "All right, I won't—stutter or get mad. No stats or lectures. I was hurt like Shana was, but not as brutally or sickeningly. And I was nineteen, I have five years on her and so could put things in a little more perspective. A little . . . I'm *still* not sure how I feel. I admire Shana tremendously for giving her testimony. That's what takes guts. Telling your story at high noon in the village square, knowing the skeptical grins you'll get. I have trouble talking to you in my own living room. You noticed I said I was *hurt?* That's what I say after *nine years,* like it was a tennis elbow or a twisted ankle."

For a moment she stared into the fire, then . . . "All the other girls got out of the pool on time that night. I'd been studying hard, or something, I wanted to swim a few more laps and relax. But then I was alone in the pool and it was dark except for the door of the dressing room. A light was on in there. It filled the hall and made a tunnel to the pool. But I didn't want to go into the dressing room and take off my suit. Why not? That interested the police. Why didn't I want to go into the clean, well-lighted dressing room? My father was curious about that, too. The reason was I knew someone was in there. Someone who shouldn't be. So then the question was, *how* had I known? And if I'd known, why had I gone in there? Had I been looking for him? My father thought those questions were reasonable. Where there's smoke, there's fire. That's what people would say, he told me. He felt a trial would only make things worse."

Brett pulled a pillow over her legs. "Those brass animals were a gift." She nodded at the figures on the coffee table. "I've had them since I was Shana's age. For years I had dreams about that pool, the smell of chlorine and the bright lights in the dressing room. When I saw Shana that first time at Vinegar Hill, it seemed I was reliving both our experiences." Brett's body was rigid, except for her hands moving restlessly on the pillow.

"A teacher gave me those little animals for memorizing something or other. Coleridge, I think . . . 'The Ancient Mariner.' I couldn't find my towel that night. I'd dropped it beside the pool when I went in. I walked around trying to find it, but trying not to look down the lighted hallway to the dressing room. It was cold and my suit was sticking to me. Finally, I got my nerve up. I *made* myself walk into that bright corridor. I decided it was my imagination after all. The dressing room was empty. I had my suit off and the clothes basket out of my locker before I heard the door click shut behind me. It was Toby Clark. He worked at the school with the maintenance people, washing windows, cutting lawns. He told me he knew I'd waited for him. Then he said he wouldn't hurt me. I tried to get away. How *hard* I tried was another thing the detectives were interested in. I hit him and he knocked me down. What was lucky about being nineteen and having read some books," she said dryly, "was that I knew he was looking for an excuse to get angry. He needed that, and by resisting, I gave it to him. He tried to rape me. He hurt my arms and my hips and my pelvis and cut my mouth. Something stopped him or distracted him. Strangely enough, or not so strangely, come to think of it, it was a church bell ringing, the college chapel sounding the hour."

Selby took her hands. "Let me get you a glass of milk or a drink or something. You better get to sleep."

"I drove myself to the police station that night . . ."

Her voice was steady and quiet; she apparently hadn't heard him.

"I told a detective what happened. I signed a charge sheet. They picked up Toby Clark at his rooming house and called the Bryn Mawr Hospital and my father. Toby Clark told the police he'd been in the dressing room picking up towels because he thought everyone was gone. Then I'd come in and laughed at him and pulled off my bathing suit. The detectives asked more questions. Fortunately my arm was in a cast and my lips were badly swollen. That was a plus," she added bitterly. "But a captain suggested to my father that we should probably drop the attempted rape charge. Which we did. My father was glad to, I realized. Toby Clark was given a suspended one-year sentence for simple assault. He was also fired, which some of the university staff thought was a rotten thing for a poor young man just starting off in life. Some of them wrote letters for Toby, character references, pointing out that he was a good worker. That's what the Cadles got hold of. The Bryn Mawr police reports."

389

She sighed. "What I'd said, what he'd said, the charges filed against him and dropped by a privileged, hysterical—Toby Clark is dead, by the way. He was shot in a woman's apartment in Fresno, California, four years ago. He was forty-two. We'd all thought he was about our age."

Selby rubbed her shoulders. Her muscles, tight as coiled springs, loosened some under the pressure of his hands.

"You're something else, Brett. You actually dredged up that nightmare to help Shana."

"Yes . . . in a way . . . I told her about the pool and the darkness as a sort of metaphor to let her know I understood. I didn't tell her about Toby Clark. I wouldn't add that to what she'd been through."

"But you still went into court each day knowing those bastards at the defense table, including Earl Thomson, knew about Toby Clark."

"That wasn't courage, Harry . . . It might have been just the opposite. A way of escape, doing something for Shana I hadn't been brave enough to do for myself."

"You can play Freud on yourself, I'm telling you that I think it took tremendous guts."

"Whatever . . . Harry, the thing is, I want Shana to be able to come to terms with her anger." She tightened her grip on his hands. "Anger doesn't give you confidence. It doesn't make you a better or nicer person. When I was fourteen I knew I was attractive. I didn't care whether I *was* or *not,* I *knew* I was. It was just a comfortable fact. I didn't mind being wrong or taking chances. I could be reckless and make a fool of myself if I wanted to. But the kind of anger I'm talking about changes all that. You become an expert in limitations. You're afraid you won't be believed or liked or accepted, so you retreat into anything that's secure, even if it's restricting or deadening. You find yourself specializing in dull economies . . . not risking honestly felt passion. *They* say you've been profaned, you feel like a victim of some new and awful original sin."

"Maybe there's something that's still too important for Shana to give up, something she won't talk about. I can understand her fear . . . your talk about Spain makes me afraid I won't know all the old campfire songs."

She brushed at her eyes. "I could buy a used Camelot, but

I'd want to knock some walls down and—"

"Don't talk anymore," he told her. "That's enough now." He took the pillow from her, plumped it up and turned down the blankets, then went into the kitchen and turned on the lights.

The rear garden was dark, with reflections shimmering on the shrubs. He opened the refrigerator and took out a carton of milk. In a cupboard he found saucepans. He filled one with milk and put it on the stove. Maybe she did know more about pain than he did. But he knew how love between people ended. It ended in pain. People got tired of each other or betrayed each other or died. Someone was left with the pain.

He put the glass of milk on the table beside the brass animals. Brett was lying slack as a spent child, one narrow foot trailing off the sofa. Her hair was curled and damp at the temples. She was breathing deeply, each breath stirring strands of hair across her cheek and throat. When she listened and talked her features were irregular, swiftly expressive. But in repose, they were exquisitely proportioned. He realized he had never heard her laugh.

He straightened out her arms and legs, put the covers over her and tucked them around her. He was surprised how light her body was. He sat on the edge of the sofa and looked at the shine of her tumbled hair on the pillow. Watching the rise and fall of her chest, he remembered how touching it had been to look at his children sleeping . . .

He leaned over to kiss her forehead, and she raised her chin without opening her eyes and kissed him on the mouth. Her arms went around his shoulders and drew him down to her, her lips opening.

He held her very tight, and when she pulled back, saying only his name, he felt the place inside him that had been cold and empty so long beginning to fill with a rush of expectation, and a longing for the profound warmth that was almost always too much to hope for, but never too much to accept and believe in . . .

A silver light glistened on the dewy shrubs in the rear garden. Selby looked out and saw the trees beyond the house moving against a still dark sky. A river wind created a shrill but musical sound on the windows.

He made fresh coffee. Pulling on his duffel coat, he poured a second cup. Sipping it, he looked at a bulletin board beside an herb rack. A quotation was typed on the back of a business card partially hidden among messages and recipes. It read: "He was an old man who fished alone in a skiff in the Gulf Stream and he had gone eighty-four days without taking a fish."

He poured orange juice into a glass and filled another cup with coffee. As he looked for a tray, her light footsteps sounded on the stairs. She wore a short white robe.

"I was going to bring up a tray," he said. "I thought you'd sleep until the alarm went off."

She put her head against his shoulder. "Look at the garden," she said. "The light, I mean. I've never seen it so clear. On the other hand, I've never seen the river mist so . . . misty." She laughed, and Selby was almost startled by the sound, so strangely unfamiliar and exciting coming from her.

"You're a nice person to be with," she said quietly. "I'd like to walk with you somewhere for a long time and talk until there wasn't anything left to talk about. Then just go on walking."

"You'd get very tired," he said.

"We'd stop then. Sit on the beach and watch the waves."

"What about winter? How are you and skiing?"

"I'll have you know I spent most of my growing-up life in Maine, Harry. I liked cross-country better than downhill. Maybe I had more stamina than nerve. I learned to ski on a hill behind our house. That's one advantage of having older sisters. They taught me, and I was pretty good. Why?"

The phone rang then, sending its shrill insistent demand through the early stillness. Brett's hands shook suddenly. Coffee splashed into her saucer.

Selby took the cup from her. "It's okay, it's a wrong number or the poodle's having pups. I'll get it."

It was a woman's voice, a familiar one. He remembered mascara and spiky eyelashes as he listened to Victoria Kim say, "I'm calling for Senator Lester, Mr. Selby. Hold on a moment."

Selby covered the phone and waved to Brett, who was watching from the doorway. "Pick up the extension . . ."

"Here's Senator Lester," Victoria Kim said.

392

Brett had already lifted the receiver in the kitchen.

"Selby? I've been here since we got the word, St. Anne's in Philadelphia. A deputy chief called us. The Easton girl was in the operating room then. They've transferred her to intensive care now—"

"What happened?"

"They think she tried to kill herself, Selby. Looks that way now. She wrote your name out for an intern and spoke it clear enough to a nurse. She jumped—well, they're not sure, jumped or fell from the terrace of her apartment. Hit a railing or ledge couple of floors down. Selby, if she wants to see you, it could be important to us. How soon can you get here?"

No mention of Jarrell, no mention of Summitt City or of Simon Correll, still the evasions and omissions.

"Will she be okay—?"

"Sorry, no . . . the doctors say too much is damaged. I'll arrange a police escort to pick you up."

"Never mind, I can get there faster on my own."

He hung up. Brett stood in the kitchen doorway, small and bare-legged, still holding the extension.

"Tell Shana where I am and good luck," Selby said. "Call me at St. Anne's at your recess." He opened the front door and turned up his collar against the raw river winds. "You were right, you know. It was the first thing I noticed. The light this morning, it was clear as I can remember it. Now lock this door after me."

CHAPTER THIRTY-FOUR

The doctor's name was Kohl. He was short and stocky with a clipped moustache and calm, brown eyes. Dr. Kohl waited for Selby at the nurses' station in the intensive care wing of St. Anne's Hospital. A young policeman stood outside Jennifer Easton's room.

"She's not conscious now," Dr. Kohl told Selby, "but you can go in. So far we haven't located any family. I gather she was alone when it happened. Senator Lester is in my office. I'll tell him you're with her."

Jennifer lay in a narrow bed beside a shuttered window. The room was gray with early light. "If your relationship with the patient is close"—Dr. Kohl paused to study her charts—"I'm sorry to tell you her condition is very critical."

Her eyes were closed. Strands of blond hair showed from the bandages around her head. Jennifer's lower body was held in a cast of mesh fabric. A neck brace forced her chin up and back with rigid pressure. Tubes stretched from her slack arms to bottles of liquid suspended from an IV frame.

Selby watched her features for any flicker of recognition. She looked like an old child now, her skin smooth and taut but her face tiny between the neck brace and head bandages. Only her full, somehow defiant lower lip suggested a remnant of stubbornness and will.

A tall nurse came in and out of the room several times to

check the intravenous tubes and mark the charts. In the corridor metallic voices paged doctors and floor nurses over an intercom. The sun was glazing and warming the tall windows.

Court would be in session now, Selby knew, and Ace Taggart would be on the stand to swear to whatever lies were wanted from him . . .

Her lids fluttered, but Jennifer didn't open her eyes. "Harry Selby?" She barely moved her dry lips.

"Yes, I'm right here."

Her eyes opened, tried to find him; the neck brace held her head as fixed as an ornament on a pedestal.

"Harry Selby?"

"Yes."

"Don't play tricks . . . please. Are you Jarrell Selby's brother . . . I can't see you too well."

"I'm Jarrell's brother, Jennifer. I'm Harry Selby. You and I spent some time together at the edge of a lake. There was a baseball game." Her eyes seemed to clear some and focus on him. "Yes, you're his brother. I lied to you, Harry, lied . . . it bothers me . . . he was so frightened . . ."

"What did you lie about, Jennifer?"

"There were no horses to ride . . . no sailboats on the Sound . . . no flags. It was all different. I lied about all that . . ."

"You said he was frightened. You mean Jarrell?"

"Yes. I knew him . . . one night, two. He was afraid . . . I didn't want them to hurt him, you know that . . ."

Jennifer's curved fingers opened, her hand turned toward him. Tears were in her eyes.

"What, Jennifer? *What is it?*"

"He's dead . . . your brother, Jarrell's dead."

"What? When . . . ?" Selby's voice sounded in unison with the stroke of his heart. "Jesus . . . how?"

"It was—" she stopped.

"It was what? *Who*, for God's sake?"

"All of them . . . they all killed him—"

"*Who?*"

"And I couldn't stop it. I saw it but it was too late—"

"You *saw* them kill my brother?"

"Yes."

"When, Jennifer? Where?"

395

"You wanted to help him, talk with him."

"Who killed him?"

Her eyes were glazing over. "You listened to me, you were kind . . . you wanted to find me. You called the convent at Mount Olivet . . ."

Apparently she was confused . . . she had to be thinking of Goldbirn's call to Mount Olivet . . . "Jennifer, do you know why Earl Thomson hurt my daughter? Do you know what they're afraid of now?"

For several moments she didn't answer. Then she said, "I couldn't reach Jarrell, I had to sit and watch . . ." She closed her eyes. Selby held her hand gently and felt the desperation in the grip of her fingers.

Later Dr. Kohl came in and said, "We can't do much more for her, Mr. Selby. She may regain consciousness again, but it's hard to say. Harder to say for how long." The doctor made a note on her chart. "The senator would like you to join him, Mr. Selby."

But as they left Jennifer's room a nurse stopped Selby. "There's a call for you, sir. It's a Dorcas Brett from East Chester. You can take it at the nurses' counter if you like."

"Thank you."

Brett's tone was flat.

"The officer they flew in from Germany, Captain Taggart, has given his testimony and I've finished my cross." (Selby checked his watch, surprised how long he had been with the dying girl.) "Taggart," Brett said, "swore under oath that he and Earl were together at Vinegar Hill in September, just before Taggart was shipped overseas . . ."

In the elevator going down to Dr. Kohl's office, Selby realized from what Brett had told him that Derek Taggart had blown away one of the last remaining props of the case against Thomson. No past resentments had deterred the general's son from doing his lying duty. Not the humiliating time he'd spent upstairs in Emma Green's room shuddering with fear and impotence, of being stripped naked with a whore's blood on his face. They had all been overlooked or forgotten in the service of the greater cause of saving fellow-soldier-in-arms Earl Thomson's ass. And in the promise that if he didn't it would be *his* ass . . .

Brett had described the scene. In a dress uniform with the theater ribbons and a Good Conduct Medal, Captain Taggart testified that he and Earl Thomson had been at his father's farm in mid-September, which, of course, explained the presence of Thomson's fingerprints in the garage.

Taggart's story was a simple one. He had been on leave from his last post in Boston, had decided to look up his old friend and classmate. Furlough papers and motel bills and rental car receipts were introduced by Davic to support this.

The captain made a plausible witness, Brett told Selby. Polite, he had impressed the court with his sincerity.

The "old boys" from Rockland had talked the night away at Vinegar Hill, drinking wine and broiling steaks. Earl had dug around in the garage for the barbecue grill and charcoal. What emerged without embarrassment, with a certain indulgent good humor, in fact, was that Earl had got drunk on that occasion, overstimulated by the warmth of friendship and wine.

The night had receded completely from his thoughts, and resurfaced only under the pressure of false accusations and the ordeal of the trial.

Brett's last words were: "I couldn't budge his story, Harry. Furlough papers, expense vouchers for gas and motels, they all checked out, dates, amounts, everything."

"Where's Taggart now?"

"I'm not sure. He left immediately after he testified."

"Can you get Burt Wilger to call me here, Brett? Can you do that?"

"Yes, I'll find him."

"He can reach me in Dr. Kohl's office or Jennifer Easton's room. She's unconscious now, Brett, but she knows something, she tried to tell me. I want to give her that chance. Tell Shana, will you? How is she?"

"Sick of their lies, of listening to them. We all are, goddammit. But she's okay, Harry. At least I think she is."

"All right . . . well, tell Wilger to call me as soon as he can."

Victoria Kim stood at a receptionist's desk looking through her briefcase. She smiled impersonally at Selby. "Did the Cadle dossier help?"

"The health club in particular. Thanks."

She nodded toward the inner office, where Senator Lester was pacing. "Selby," Lester said, "what did the Easton girl tell you? What did she want to talk to you about?"

"She told me, Senator, that my brother is dead."

"How? When did it happen?"

"She couldn't say."

"Understandable, her confusion, I mean. She's sedated, must be in pain. But what else did she say?"

"Not much more than that, Senator."

"According to the police," Lester said, "she jumped from her terrace, or stumbled and fell. Kohl tells me her blood shows an alcohol content of .14. Did she say whether she was alone up there?"

"No."

"Somebody could have been with her. The police checked the whole place, the lobby guards and so forth, but there's a self-service elevator in the rear of the building that goes from the penthouse down to the garage." Lester stopped pacing and stared at Selby. "You're the only person she's talked to, only person she *would* talk to. What's your guess? Was it a suicide attempt, a drunken accident, or does someone want her dead?"

Selby said evenly, "She's not a model, she's not a photographer and she wasn't a close friend of my brother's. But she *is* Simon Correll's mistress. You didn't mention that when we were chatting on about jet lag and Deep Throat and my father's diaries."

Lester shrugged. "I could tell you I don't know who the hell she is, but you wouldn't believe that, of course."

"Why should I?"

"Now, goddammit, Selby, hear me out." Wrinkled grooves scored the sides of Lester's mouth, adding to the appearance of tension. He was pacing again. "Order us up some coffee, okay, Vickie? I haven't lied to you, Selby. I also haven't told you everything. There's a difference . . . all right, here's how I got into the picture. The Harlequin investigation was dumped in my lap when Mark Rowan died. I was the senior member of the committee. I'd wanted to get my hands on those files for a long time. I've been on national television telling not very interested audiences that it's in the national interest. Well, in a way, I suppose that's an exaggeration. Unless you believe that oil and steel and billion-dollar lines of credit grow under cabbage leaves, you know that conglomerates are a fact of life. The Correll Group is no exception. Anyway, when they acquired Harlequin that became part of our files. The Correll buy-out of Harlequin was preceded by a fraudulent inflation of company's stock, a run-up accomplished by forged receipts from the Correll people for synthetics, epoxies, drilling components, other products delivered—but only on paper. Harlequin's cash position escalated at a cyclical rate. George Thomson resigned and sold off his stock before the windfall. Six months later he bought back his company, with stock options, at an enormous profit. A six-month hiatus satisfied the Securities and Exchange Commission but it didn't satisfy my committee. It was a transparent insider deal. We wanted to know why. I'm being as frank as I can, Selby," the senator went on. "We've got a lot of links, but no chains. We do know now somebody didn't want me to talk to your father. The Harlequin jet flew to Oakland, California, the day he was killed. Our people found that flight plan in company records. George Thomson and a Sergeant Ledge were the passengers on that flight. Our guess is they drove to Truckee for a meeting with Jonas Selby. Maybe Jarrell was on hand. We don't know that. Your father says he was expecting someone, it could have been George Thomson and Ledge. Maybe they shot and killed him. If they did, we haven't been able to prove it.

"But our investigators saw the tip of one iceberg after another. More links, stretching from Van Pelt in Brussels to a Mies Kraager in South Africa. And some people in Britain and the Argentine."

Vickie Kim brought in a tray of coffee and placed it on Kohl's desk. "Black, Selby. Right?"

"Yes, thanks."

"That's all I'm authorized to tell you, Selby." Lester accepted a cup from Vickie. "My people, my investigators, turned out to be on a collision course with an ongoing inquiry by the State Department. In certain instances, State takes precedence. That means I back off. The amount of money Simon Correll represents is like a whirlpool that can suck under legislative committees, even whole countries for that matter. State's team is headed by an old hand named Ferdinand Bittermank, who's got his own leads to Correll. And he's a friend of Bishop Waring. But that aside . . . he's asked me for just one thing out of this meeting, something only you can help with, Selby. Bittermank wants to know whether what happened to Easton was accidental or deliberate. Did she say anything? Suicide would be the preferable alternative to murder here . . ."

A phone rang in the reception room. Vickie came to the door. "It's for you, Selby," she said. "He wouldn't give his name."

Selby took the call on Kohl's phone.

"Harry?" It was Burt Wilger. "What's up?"

"Do you know where Derek Taggart is?"

"No, not right now."

"Can you find him?"

"I heard at the Division he's scheduled to fly out of Philadelphia on Lufthansa around two-thirty."

Selby looked at his watch. Almost noon. "Can't we stop him, Burt? If Taggart leaves today, it's doubtful he'll ever be brought back. He's the linchpin of Thomson's defense, right?"

"In a way, yes," Wilger said. "Santos perjured himself on the time and the pick-up. Thomson's mother supported those lies. But Ace Taggart explained away the fingerprints at the scene. And I don't have to remind you they've got Goldie Boy in the wings, Harry. They'll still want to discount Shana's positive identification of Thomson."

"Burt, given the risk Taggart's taking, his whole career, doesn't it make sense that he had to be shown exactly how Thomson can and will protect him?"

"I suppose . . ."

"But you can't stop Taggart from leaving for Germany this afternoon?"

"You said that, I didn't. I'll be at the airport when he gets there, Harry. It's a question of holding a suspect for interfering with an officer and resisting arrest. It's also a question of me losing a pension. But don't worry, Ace Taggart won't be flying off to any Teutonic blow job, pal. I'll be in touch."

As Selby hung up, Dr. Kohl appeared in the doorway.

"Miss Easton is conscious, and she's asking for Mr. Selby. We don't have much time, I'm afraid."

In Superior Court Nine, Oliver Jessup sat in the witness chair, his strange, milky eyes focused on an invisible spot above Shana's head. The preacher, also known as Goldie Boy, answered Davic's questions in measured tones, but his controlled voice threatened to soar at any moment toward more accustomed evangelical notes. His impassive face, the blank eyes, the controlled voice, were like the steel buckle and canvas straps of a self-imposed straitjacket.

He was pure trouble, Brett knew.

"I was in my church, on the occasion you ask me to give witness to," Goldie Boy was now saying in response to Davic's invitation to relate events in his own words. "I was collecting hymn books. The Tabernacle was dark. Suddenly a light played on the ceiling. I knew it was the light of man, not the light of the Lord. In the street, in front of my Tabernacle of the Golden Flame, a car had stopped. Its lights touched the church."

"And what action did you take then, Reverend Jessup?"

"I went to the front window and looked out. I thought perhaps some lone soul wished to pray with me. That isn't uncommon. A church closed to those in need is as unfeeling as a mother's arms closed to a hungry or lonely child . . . I saw it was a red automobile, flashing and glittering in the street light. A girl, no, a woman, stepped from that car. She was laughing, her head flung back, hair loose, light shining on her lips."

"Is that girl, that person, in this room, Reverend Jessup?"

Ollie Jessup nodded and pointed to the prosecution table. "She is sitting there, next to the lawyer lady."

"I'd like the stenographer's record to show that the witness has identified Shana Selby," Davic said . . . "All right, Reverend Jessup, did you observe the man who was driving the red automobile?"

"Yes, sir."

"Is *that* person in this courtroom?"

"I don't see him, sir."

"In that case, would you describe the driver of the red car?"

"Yes, sir. He rolled down his window, the street light was

401

full in his face. The man was middle-aged, around forty, I'd say. His hair was gray, face fleshy, high colored. He wore glasses and he blew a kiss and threw it with his fingers to the girl. She laughed, a harlot's laugh—"

"Objection."

"Sustained."

"You say the girl was laughing, Reverend Jessup?"

"Yes, sir. She laughed and blew a kiss back to the man. She started to walk away, and the car drove off. I knew they were sinners and—"

"You are sure of the time, Reverend Jessup?"

"Yes, sir. It was a few minutes before ten o'clock in the evening."

"Your Honor, I have no further questions."

Judge Flood made a note on his pad and looked to the People's table. "Your witness, Miss Brett. Will you inquire?"

"Yes, Your Honor. I surely will."

A chill afternoon light streaked the windows of Jennifer's hospital room. The day was overcast and the winds rose with gusting sounds against the building. A delicate, keening tremor shook the windowpanes.

"Harry . . . ?"

She had spoken his name several times since he had sat down beside her bed, but when he leaned closer to tell her he was there her eyes became confused, vacant, and her words dissolved into murmuring fragments.

And then she said his name again. "Harry . . . listen to me, can you hear me?"

"Yes."

"I lied . . ."

"Yes, Jennifer, I understand."

"You must know—" Her voice was abruptly clear, even resonant, and Selby thought with a chill of Casper Gideen and his talk about death crops . . . gnarled, ancient trees sucking their last harvest of blooms and flowers from the earth before fading, withering and dying. An act of defiance. Or life itself, and its instinctive drive to go on . . . Jennifer's voice was like that now, strong and full inside her broken, dying body.

402

"I lied to so many people," she said. "I shouldn't have lied to Simon. I loved him. Can you understand? Lies on one side, lies on the other . . . That's why I understood your brother . . ."

She closed her eyes for a moment, breathing with difficulty. Her forehead looked fragile as an eggshell.

"Jennifer . . . you saw someone kill my brother?"

"Yes."

"How was he killed? Where?"

"They shot him . . . they shot all the little mice. I saw it . . ."

"You watched it?"

"You don't *understand* . . . it was over then, it was over when I saw it . . ."

"When did you lie to Simon Correll?"

She laughed softly, a strange sound under the circumstances . . . "I didn't lie to him, but I let *her* listen to him. His Excellency told me to do it . . ."

"Jennifer, you said it was over when you saw it . . . did you see my brother's death in a picture. Is *that* what you're telling me? Some kind of . . . film?"

Her fingers went slack in Selby's hand, she began to breathe with an effort. A monitor at the nurses' station in the hallway recorded her responses. Within moments an intern and nurse came in.

"I don't think she'll regain consciousness," the intern said after checking her pulse and eyes. "Nurse, page Dr. Kohl."

When the intern went out Selby looked at his watch; it was three-fifteen. He tightened his grip on her hand, there was no response in her chill, thin fingers.

"Jennifer? Can you hear me?"

Her face was like a small mask, so white that her lips seemed unnaturally vivid. Even her blond eyebrows looked dark against her pale skin.

A figure shadowed the doorway, and Selby looked up to see Wilger standing there, hat in his hands. The cold afternoon light from the windows seemed to splinter against his glasses.

He looked at Jennifer. "Can she hear us?"

"I doubt it . . ."

"I got done like a Christmas goose, Harry. Taggart wasn't

403

on Lufthansa like Slocum let me find out. Taggart left on a MATS flight from Dover a couple of hours ago. It's airborne, and the little faggot's gone, on his way nonstop to Frankfurt . . . Well, I talked to Brett from the airport. I checked again on my car phone coming here." He gave Selby the substance of Ollie Jessup's testimony. "In her cross," Wilger said, "Brett pounded at why he waited so long to come forward to tell his story. Jessup rolled those weird eyes of his and swore he'd never *heard* of the trial, never *saw* anything on TV, never *looked* at the newspapers. The good Lord told him about it a couple of nights ago, the Lord fixed it so he'd hear some talk on the radio. So preacher did his Christian duty and went to the police, direct to Slocum. He swore he'd witnessed it right in front of his church. Saw Shana get out of a red Porsche, the guy was middle-aged, they were laughing, blowing kisses. Brett couldn't shake him. Ollie got wild-eyed and crazy, said he was exposing evil, doing the Lord's holy work . . ."

Wilger looked down at Jennifer's small, white face. "Anything from this little lady?"

"I think she's been trying to tell me she saw Jarrell's death on a film . . . she said she watched it and at first I didn't understand . . ."

"Doesn't do Jarrell much good. Or Shana." Wilger put on his hat. "It's guesswork, and we need more . . . And now Davic re-calls Shana. He can hit her with any damn thing he wants. The only way Brett can keep her off the stand is to drop the charges . . . But I hear Shana won't have any of that, even if Brett wanted to give up, which she doesn't. She's taking the stand. Gutsy girl . . . You going back with me?"

"I'll be there. And thanks."

"For nothing, I'm sorry to say." Wilger fumbled through his pockets and brought out a sealed envelope. "Almost forgot. Shana asked me to give you this. See you back in East Chester." Selby took the envelope, Wilger left the room.

Well, there it was . . . a dead brother . . . a murdered brother? . . . and a daughter who would have to be subjected to disgusting abuse on the stand . . . Selby looked down at the slim body on the hospital bed . . . motionless . . . then at the cold, glazed windows dividing them from rows of cheerless gray buildings. His thoughts became like a Kaddish to the dying girl, the brother he'd never known, and the lonely figure common to them both . . . the father he'd glimpsed beyond the shadows of the hills and the streams all crossed—

He felt a pressure against his hand, put Shana's note in his inner pocket. Jennifer, surprisingly, had tightened her grip, like the appeal of a child being left alone, scared of the dark.

"Harry . . . ?"

"Yes, I'm here, Jennifer . . ."

"I heard, I'm sorry." Her voice became momentarily stronger. Her eyes opened, clearing for what would be the last time. "A master print . . . it's still at Summitt. Correll, Thomson, they knew Earl got a copy. It's what he's got over them . . . I'm not lying now, I promise you . . . I only really lied about the sailboats . . ."

She had turned her head toward the windows, and she had stopped breathing when Dr. Kohl and the senator came in.

As the doctor made his final check and a nurse began to detach the IV tubes from Jennifer's arms, Selby and the senator waited outside in the corridor. A uniformed police sergeant had joined the patrolman at the door to Jennifer's room.

"Patient's in pretty bad shape, I hear." The sergeant nodded respectfully to Senator Lester and raised his hand in an awkward salute. "Kiley, Senator. Central district."

The young patrolman said, "Beautiful young girl, you'd think everything to live for . . ."

The senator took Selby's arm and led him into a small office adjoining the nurse's station. Closing the door, he listened to Selby for a moment, trying to take in what Jennifer had said in her last moments.

"Well, dammit, Selby, I can't send in the Marines on the basis of that. She *could* have been hallucinating. There's no justification for search warrants or any other legal action because a dying girl mutters something about a murder. If I acted on what she told you the State Department could and would nail my ass to the floor . . . but then, you don't much give a good goddamn about such matters—"

"No," Selby said, "and I'm not interested in epoxies and phony stock deals and the icebergs your committee's running into. If Earl Thomson goes free, my daughter is marked for life as an hysterical, perverted liar."

"Give me credit for understanding that," Senator Lester said. "I sympathize with you, Selby, but the problem's got to be handled realistically—"

"I'm going to act on what the Easton girl told me. There's a master print at Summitt. She said that and I believe it. She knew she was dying, she told me the truth," Selby said. "And, if it matters, I don't think she was murdered . . . she seemed to be sick of her life, of the lies—"

"Then you're going to Summitt City, is that what you're telling me?"

"I'm telling you I don't have any options. If the judge instructs that jury to return a directed verdict of not guilty the rest of it's academic. Earl Thomson is home free for life. I'm not going to let them do that to my daughter. And this is my last chance to stop it."

Lester rubbed his chin. "All right, dammit, you're not even a constituent and I'm going out on a limb for you . . . we can't justify it officially, but I guess we can at least be silent partners. Our man down there is Lee Crowley . . ."

Selby remembered Crowley, a square-faced Irisher, first at the baseball diamond with the black youngsters and Stoltzer, then discussing local fishing conditions that same day at the commissary.

They were still talking when a light tap sounded on the door and Victoria Kim looked in. "Senator, I've got two wire services on hold. They know Miss Easton was admitted here. They want to know if her *accident* has anything to do with your presence here, and your investigation."

"Just tell them . . ." The senator opened the door and walked into the corridor, where the patrolman and sergeant were still on hand. Dr. Kohl and two orderlies were in the late Jennifer Easton's room. "Tell them, Vicki, that we don't have any statement to make. The condition of the patient will have to come from hospital authorities. And after that book Mr. Selby on the next available flight to Memphis, and send a coded message to our Summitt contact to expect him. Like I told you, Selby, I can't send in the Marines, but I'll back you up as best as I can."

Victoria Kim glanced at Selby. "I'll make your reservations

immediately. The senator's car will be waiting for you downstairs at the lobby entrance in five minutes."

"Thanks," Selby siad. "I've got just one call to make first."

From a pay phone in the corridor Selby dialed his home and through the smudged glass door of the booth saw the patrolman step aside, watched the orderlies wheeling a stretcher from the room Jennifer had occupied. A question surfaced, and nagged at him. What had made Jennifer, even in her confused state, think *he* had tried to call her at Mount Olivet? Jerry Goldbirn had made that call. Jerry had told Selby that when he called him at the farm from Vegas. Who else could have known about it? Only someone who had overheard the conversation . . .

A click sounded and Mrs. Cranston answered. Selby told her he had a message for Shana.

"All right, I'll get a pencil, I don't trust my memory anymore—"

"Never mind, tell her I'll call her later, okay?"

"Sure, Mr. Selby."

Selby waited a moment, then dialed his home again. He heard it clearly this time as the phone began to ring—a tiny metallic click, barely audible but rhythmic and steady.

"Yes?"

"Sorry to bother you again, Mrs. Cranston, but I'd like to leave a message after all. Just tell Shana I'm all right and that I love her."

Selby put the receiver back on the hook. There was a tap on his line, he was sure of it now, someone was monitoring the calls. And he suspected it wouldn't be smart to trust Brett's phone either. Now he couldn't tell Shana or Brett where he was going or what he intended to do.

He took an elevator down to the lobby of the hospital. Senator Lester's limousine, as promised, was parked waiting for him in the circular driveway. . . .

CHAPTER THIRTY-FIVE

The sunlight in Judge Flood's courtroom was thin and pale. Its reflections bronzed the pine floors and bleached color from the mural of the Indians and Quakers on the shores of the Brandywine.

Counselor Davic stood in front of the witness, pinching the bridge of his nose as he collected and ordered his thoughts. Shana sat facing him. Her eyes were shadowed with fatigue but her shoulders were straight and square, and she made a conscious effort to breathe slowly.

Davic broke the expectant silence. "Miss Selby, in trying to get at the truth in the issues in this trial, you and I are forced into an adversary relationship. There's nothing personal in this, it's a system that provides the best possible guarantee of a fair trial. It protects the rights of everyone. It is the best way we know to arrive at the truth."

He looked at Shana thoughtfully. "Now, you have heard the testimony of Captain Taggart and Reverend Oliver Jessup, correct?"

"Yes, I was sitting right there at that table. But I didn't know he was a reverend until you called him that."

Davic ignored that. "Captain Taggart, an officer in the United States Army, explained that he and Earl Thomson had been at Vinegar Hill several weeks before your unfortunate experience. You understood the implications of that testimony, didn't you?"

"Yes, I guess so."

"Well, put simply, it means that Mr. Thomson's fingerprints were in the garage for very normal reasons. Is that clear?"

"I understand what you're saying, Mr. Davic."

"And you heard the Reverend Jessup describe the *middle-aged, gray-haired* man he saw wave a friendly goodbye to you in front of his church?"

"Yes, I heard that but—"

"Just answer my question. You heard that testimony?"

". . . Yes."

"Then, Miss Selby, are you now prepared to tell the truth?"

"Objection, Your Honor."

"Sustained."

"Miss Selby, we think that you made a *mistake* in identifying Earl Thomson as the man who abducted and raped you. Will you now finally agree that you *did* make a mistake? That you were wrong in accusing Earl Thomson of such crimes? That the truth is that Earl Thomson has never harmed or molested you in any way whatsoever—?"

"Objection, Your Honor. Counsel has asked the witness a string of incriminating questions but hasn't given her a chance to respond to even one of them."

"Sustained."

Davic pointed directly to Earl Thomson. "Miss Selby, is it *still* your testimony that this is the man who ran you down in his automobile on the sixteenth of last October?"

"Yes."

"That he forced you into his car and drove you to a secluded house called variously during this trial Vinegar Hill and the Taggart Place?"

"Yes."

"And that at that place, Earl Thomson committed the crimes on your person specified in the indictment?"

"Yes. Yes, he did."

"Miss Selby." Davic's expression hardened now, like a disapproving, wounded parent. "You left Pyle's Corners at about ten o'clock according to witnesses. But it was almost three

409

hours later—*three hours,* Miss Selby—before you arrived at your friend's home in Little Tennessee, which is scarcely a ten-minute walk from Pyle's Corners. Where—and how—did you spend those three hours, Miss Selby?"

Shana hesitated. "I've tried to remember . . . I walked up Fairlee Road, it was raining. I didn't want to get wet. I turned off the road and sat in an old car. In a kind of junkyard. The windows were broken. But it was dry. I could hear the rain on the roof."

"You sat all alone for *three hours?* Listening to the rain?"

"I . . . was thinking."

"What were you thinking *about,* Miss Selby?"

"I'm not sure. My hand hurt, it was bleeding."

"Did any cars drive by? Were there any pedestrians or hitchhikers who might have noticed you?"

"No."

"Then we have only *your* word that you were all alone in that abandoned car?"

"Maybe somebody saw me. I don't know."

"You didn't go *anywhere* else during that time?"

"No."

"But since you're so vague about so many things, Miss Selby, how can you be *sure?* More important, how can *we* be sure that you didn't go somewhere and spend time with someone else during those three hours you have no way of accounting for?"

Brett jumped to her feet, her face white.

"I object, Your Honor. I object to this entire line of inquiry. After the ordeal the plaintiff was forced to endure, it is ridiculous to ask why she didn't behave logically and reasonably. If Shana Selby had *not* retreated into shock, if her senses and nerves were not numbed and unreliable, *that* might warrant speculation. But Mr. Davic's present attack is both cruel and unethical—"

Judge Flood rapped his gavel, but Brett ignored it. "I will stand here, Your Honor, and object and object and *object* until the marshals remove me physically at each and every attempt by Mr. Davic to demand an accountability and justification from the *victim* which should, in fact, and in justice, be required *only* of the defendant."

"Miss Brett, you will be in order, and refrain from these

410

speeches and challenges. But you do have a point." He then reminded Davic that in his opening statement he had stipulated the grievous nature of Shana's injuries. "You will, therefore," he instructed him, "bear in mind the physical condition of the witness that night."

"Yes, Your Honor." He was satisfied that his insinuations had gotten through to the jury. "Miss Selby, if I have upset you, I'm sorry. But truth is at the heart of Earl Thomson's defense. And, as everybody knows" . . . he looked at Brett . . . "finding the truth can be a painful process." He paused then, as if searching for words. "Miss Selby, if we are to believe everything you've told us, it's logical to assume you were terrified of the man who attacked you that night. Correct?"

"I was. Yes."

Davic paused a beat, studied Shana. "Would you tell the court, Miss Selby, if you had any contact with Earl Thomson *after* he allegedly attacked you?"

"I didn't see him again."

"Answer my question. Did you have *any* contact with him? Did you, for example, try to *talk* to him?"

"Yes."

"Speak up, Miss Selby."

"I called him, I called him on the phone."

"Why?"

"I wanted to . . . meet with him."

"Would you please tell the court what prompted you to call Earl Thomson?"

"I saw his picture in the paper. I recognized him."

"Then you believed you had met him on some previous occasion. Is that what you're telling us?"

"Yes, he was the one in the car. The man who . . . knocked me off my bicycle—"

"The very same man who abducted and assaulted you so brutally?"

"Yes."

Davic placed his hands on the arms of the witness chair and stared into Shana's eyes.

"If you believed Earl Thomson was the man who had done those terrible things to you, Miss Selby, *why* did you phone him and try to arrange a meeting with him?"

Judge Flood rapped for order as a murmur swept through the court.

Davic turned away from Shana. He studied the faces of the jurors. "Miss Selby, would you like me to repeat my question?"

"No . . ."

"I'm waiting for your answer then. *Why* did you call Earl Thomson to arrange a meeting?"

"I . . . I wanted help." Shana's breathing was more rapid, spots of color appeared on her face.

"I'm relieved that we're finally getting at the truth, Miss Selby. How many times did you call the defendant?"

"Two times."

"Did you call him twice on the same day? Or on successive days, or what *was* your schedule?"

"I called him first about a . . . about a week afterward."

"A week after *what*, Miss Selby?"

"A week after he hurt me."

"When did you make the *second* call?"

"Five or six days later."

"Both these calls were made *prior* to your accusations against the defendant at Longwood Gardens?"

"Yes."

"Would you speak up, please, Miss Selby."

"Yes." Shana cleared her throat. "Yes."

"*After* you saw his picture in the paper, *after* you called and asked him to meet you, *after that* you went to Longwood Gardens and shouted in front of several witnesses that he had assaulted and raped you. Is that the sequence, Miss Selby?"

"Yes—"

"Did you identify yourself to Earl Thomson when you called him on the phone?"

"He knew who I was."

"How did you know that? How *could* you know that?"

"I knew."

"May I ask you once again why you called Mr. Thomson?"

"I told you . . . I wanted him to meet me."

"Did you have anywhere in particular in mind?"

No answer.

"What was Mr. Thomson's response to your invitation, Miss Selby?"

"He didn't say anything, he just hung up."

"And *then* you went to Longwood Gardens and publicly accused him of kidnapping and raping you. Isn't that exactly what you did?"

"No, *no.*" Shana said, and then shouted, "No, I wanted to understand what had happened. I wanted him to help me understand it."

"I'm sure the jury," Davic remarked dryly, "will form their own opinion of what you wanted, Miss Selby."

"*Objection.* I've tried to control myself, Your Honor, but—"

"Sustained."

"Miss Selby, didn't you accuse Earl Thomson of raping you *after* you'd phoned him for the express purpose of inviting him to meet with you somewhere?"

In the deepening silence, Davic looked at Shana's bowed head. "Miss Selby? Isn't that the truth?"

"Yes."

Davic dropped his hands and returned to the defense table. "I have no further questions, Your Honor. If it please the court, the defense rests."

Earl Thomson stretched his legs and settled back in his chair as Davic sat down beside him.

When Brett stood up, Earl watched her with a speculative smile. Judge Flood said, "On the basis of what presumably is surprise testimony, People's counsel has the right to cross-examine her own witness if she choses to."

"The testimony of Shana Selby," Brett said, "came as no surprise to the People's counsel, Your Honor. The witness discussed her testimony with me in detail. I have no need to cross-examine her. But if it please the court, I would like Shana to explain in her own words—as she explained to me—what she hoped to accomplish by communicating with Mr. Thomson."

"I object, Your Honor." Davic was on his feet. "I see no reason for elaboration—"

"But Mr. Davic," Flood reminded him, "you asked the same question of the witness. *Why* did Miss Selby call the defendant?"

"The defense was satisfied with her response."

"The bench was not. You may expand your testimony, young lady, and I'll ask for order and silence." Flood glanced up at the gallery. "As has been said here, the public's presence at criminal trials is a privilege, not a right . . . Miss Selby?"

Shana looked over the silent rows of spectators, then said quietly, "I wanted to tell him, my mother was dead, that she'd been killed in an automobile accident. I wasn't sure why at first. But I finally realized it might make him know that I was just as human as he was, that I wasn't any different from him. I didn't believe he understood that. Because I don't believe a person who deliberately hurts another person realizes the damage he can do. I thought the person who'd hurt me should know how much pain he'd caused. Maybe he didn't understand he'd hurt . . . both of us. I thought if I could make him realize he'd hurt himself maybe even more than he'd hurt me . . ." She stopped and moistened her lips. "Well, then he might understand that what he did went beyond just us. My mother helped me understand that. She said people did things sometimes for reasons we didn't understand or know about, and to remember that whenever we felt real angry or disappointed and wanted to get back at them."

Shana's voice became stronger and clearer. "Dr. Clemens thought I wasn't religious. Well, maybe he knows more than I do. But I think my father is a religious person in his own way, and *I* know that *Purim* means more than *hamantashin* or Haman's little three-cornered hats. And *tagluch* isn't all there is to Rosh Hashanah. I know there's a time in every religion for confession and forgiveness. We were taught about redemption and repentance at home, my mother and grandmother taught us. We learned there's a Book of Life and a Book of Death for all of us, but they aren't kept up in churches or temples by some old man with a white beard. They're in the way we treat each other. There's nothing to the sound of the *shofar,* or to the story of Abraham, who would sacrifice his son for the love of God, or to Christ on the cross if we don't believe it's *wrong* to hurt and kill each other. So if he could tell me why he hurt me, well, I thought I could maybe understand why it had happened. And so could he.

"I thought if I could help him that it would help *me* to understand and get rid of my angers. I didn't want to go on hating him all my life. I knew he hated me, I could feel it. If he found out, like my mother said, what he *really* hated, maybe it would help him. And me. I don't have the right to judge and forgive anybody, maybe, but I can still try to *understand* them. I told Dr. Clemens a prayer of my grandmother's. We called her Tishie. She read it to me from a prayer book and I memorized it . . . 'How can we give thanks when we remember / Treblinka? / The storm ends. / In the sky a rainbow signals hope and new life. / Again and yet again there is a song to sing.' "

Shana pushed back a strand of her hair. "Dr. Clemens told me that wasn't a prayer, that it was wishful thinking. Maybe trying to talk to Earl Thomson was wishful thinking, but I just felt I had to try. I don't have any other answer for what I did, Your Honor."

Shana seemed oblivious to everyone then, eyes fixed steadily above the spectators.

Raising his head, the judge glanced inquiringly at the defense table. Davic responded with a quick, negative headshake.

Flood tapped his gavel. Softly. "The court will hear closing statements tomorrow morning at ten o'clock. Court is adjourned until that time."

In her office Brett turned on the burner under a Silex of water and set out coffee cups and bowls of sugar and cream. Traffic noises in the mall were muted. The lights of the city gleamed beyond the windows.

Shana sat in the chair at Brett's desk, her legs curled under her. They knew from Burt Wilger's report that her father had planned to return from St. Anne's Hospital to East Chester that afternoon. They had no other news until Shana called home and learned that he had talked twice to Mrs. Cranston, leaving messages of support for his daughter but no further information.

Brett said, "I know you're worried about him, and so am I. But let's concentrate on *our* job. I want to point out something about Davic's cross-examination that you may have missed. A lawyer seldom asks a witness a question unless he himself knows the answer to it. Or is prepared for whatever answer he gets. Which brings me to this . . . how did Davic know you'd phoned Earl Thomson? He was certain you had, no doubt about that. So please, Shana, try to remember if you mentioned it to anyone except me or your father."

"Honestly, I didn't. Not even to Normie."

"One call was from the phone in your bedroom, the other from a pay phone, right?"

"You know all that."

"Please be patient with me. I can't emphasize how important this is. Think hard. Did you say anything to Davey about it? It would be natural enough if you did, he's your brother."

"But I didn't tell *anybody.*"

"All right. But is there any chance he overheard you calling Earl Thomson?"

"I'm sure he didn't. My bedroom door was closed, and I was talking very quietly. Why is it so terribly important?"

"Because Davic *knew* you'd called Thomson. He knew in substance what you said to him. Otherwise he'd never have risked that line of questions."

"Mr. Davic overheard the conversation, is that it?"

"Someone did, Shana. There was, probably still is, a tap on the phones at your house. Whoever installed the tap, well, they could have cut into a terminal on a telephone pole a mile away, or sent someone around in a gas or electric company uniform to check the line. Picked a time when the family was away and told Mrs. Cranston it was a routine service inspection in the basement or attic."

Shana's frown cleared, her eyes were suddenly alert with relief and excitement. "Then daddy must have known about it. He must have found out. That's why he wouldn't leave a message with Mrs. Cranston, to tell us where he is."

"That's my guess too," Brett said. "We'll have to wait for him to tell us how he figured it out. But he doesn't trust those phones now any more than I do."

She put two cups of coffee on her desk and settled down in her leather chair. Resting her chin on her hands, she looked at Shana. "Now, would you like to tell me what's troubling you? What you want to talk about?"

Shana sighed, looked down at her hands. "I should have told you right away. I wish I had." In a careful voice she said, "I won't mind so much if you just think I've been dumb and childish and scared. Honestly I won't. But I'd hate it if you, well, disrespected me."

"It's been a long day, honey." Brett smiled at her. "Drink

some coffee, you need a lift. Or maybe it would be better if we freshened up and went out for some dinner somewhere. We could talk about it then."

"No, I'd rather explain everything now."

"Fine, that's what we're here for. But drink your coffee. It could use sugar by the way. It's very bitter."

"I've already written this to my father. I sent a note to him with Sergeant Wilger." Shana sighed. "That was easy. I could pretend it was like a composition outline and make headings and subheadings and try to make it all clear." She drew a deep breath. "I was selfish, I know that now. I could have helped all of us, but I kept thinking too much about myself. Sometimes I can be a pain."

Shana took a small tissue-wrapped object from the pocket of her blazer. Unwrapping it with care, she placed a shining ornament on a broken chain in front of Brett. The light glittered on the silver cross of the swastika she had torn from Earl Thomson's neck the night he had raped her.

"It was the only proof I could trust," she said. "Not just that it happened the way I knew it had. I had to be sure of something else, that I'd fought back, that I'd tried to stop him from doing it to me. That I . . . didn't just let him. Can you understand why I kept it, Brett? Please. Can you?"

"Yes, of course." Brett swallowed with difficulty. "Of course I can, Shana."

"It happened at the place he took me. He untied my hands and pushed me toward the cot. I hit him and kicked him while we struggled around. The silver cross was right in front of me, flashing in my eyes. I grabbed the chain and it broke. The edge of the crosses cut the palm of my hand, but I didn't know it then. I had nightmares about it. On the tapes Davey made I heard my voice screaming, 'Mommy, it's evil. I'll kill it . . .' I don't know if I said it to him then or whether that's part of my nightmare. Earl Thomson didn't know I had it. I made a fist and kept my hand closed around it, even when he tied me to the bed. I wasn't thinking about proving anything then. I wasn't thinking at all. But when daddy took me home that night, I still had it, and I knew that no matter how long I lived I'd be sure how it was and how it happened."

Brett picked up the swastika and examined the dates and

417

initials engraved on the back of the right-angle arms of the rotary crosses.

"In preparing this case"—Brett's voice trembled, she cleared her throat and took a sip of coffee—"I came across a newspaper item about this." She nodded at the swastika. "It was in a Philadelphia paper. There was a small local scandal because Earl Thomson, with his usual delicate sensibilities, went to a Jewish jeweler, a Phil Gelb on Spruce Street, to have it made. A reporter got hold of the story. Mr. Gelb not surprisingly refused the job, but Thomson found someone else."

Standing, Brett paced behind her desk, watching the light on the swastika, the edges still dark with traces of Shana's blood.

"Let me tell you something," she said. "We're going to be in a hell of a fight in court tomorrow. No tricks, no theatrics, I'll have to go straight at him with this evidence."

"It isn't too late?"

"We're alive until the jury returns a verdict. What you told the court this afternoon about why you wanted to talk to Earl Thomson, what you said about your father and mother and your grandmother, and about yourself, by the way, was simple and honest and in a way very beautiful. But, Shana, compassion and sympathy and understanding may excuse Earl Thomson on some higher plane, but there is no way in the world it will convict him. And justice, dammit, demands that he be convicted. We need the whole truth for that. And this swastika is part of the whole truth. Does anyone else know about it?"

"No, only you and my father."

"You realize this will mean Davic can put you back on the stand? Demand to know why you suppressed this evidence? Demand to know why you waited for months to mention it?"

"I know, and I know Earl will lie about it. He'll say he lost it somewhere, won't he? Or that it was stolen from him. But I know he's been looking for it around Fairlee Road."

"So does your father," Brett said, and then added, "yes, indeed, it will be a fight. They're real confident now . . . Davic, Thomson, all of them. Well, we'll make that work for us, the fact that they think they're home free, that the verdict from the jury tomorrow morning is a mere formality."

A footstep sounded in the reception room, and Burt Wilger walked into the office.

"I played a hunch, Brett," he said, and nodded with an awkward smile to Shana. "Called St. Anne's a couple of more times, couldn't get anything but doubletalk so I tried the airport." He began polishing his glasses. "Harry Selby, I mean, your father, Shana . . . he left on a flight for Memphis a couple of hours ago. And then, I'd guess, he'll be off to Summitt City."

CHAPTER THIRTY-SIX

At dawn a yellow cab slowed and stopped on Broad Street near Market in Philadelphia. Enough light shone from cleaning crews in office buildings and the gray skies to outline the statue of Benjamin Franklin on top of the town's massively ornate City Hall.

Selby paid and tipped the driver, an amiable black man who wanted to get into the electric garage-door business. He then walked to Chestnut Street and stopped and looked at his watch. The center of the city was quiet and empty until a garbage truck rumbled by.

A red-haired woman on the wooden bench at a bus stop wore boots and purple knickers and a tight suede jacket with fringed wrists. She smiled at Selby and moistened her lips. "How come you're studying your watch?" Her tone was good-natured, appraising. "Only time means anything is party time. Would you care for some party time, friend?"

"No, no thanks," Selby said.

"Don't mention it. Thought I'd ask, that's all. But *party's* the word, big guy, not *time*. Wouldn't take long. My van's parked over on Spruce Street, just a short walk. There's some records, a bottle of this and that."

"Thanks again," Selby said, "but I'm expecting someone."

"There's no big, bad pimp to worry about. I'm a good judge of people. Never got messed up with anyone I couldn't handle."

She glanced at her watch. "I could drop you back here in a half hour."

"No, it's not our night," Selby said, and tried to smile.

"I'm a fool to ask, I suppose," the red-haired woman said, "but be honest. Are you fuzz, or don't I turn you on?"

"It's not that." Selby looked up and down the empty streets.

"The knickers okay then?"

"They're fine, they're really okay," Selby said.

A car turned off Broad Street and stopped across from them. A slender man with glasses got out and waved to Selby.

The redhead said, "Fuck you, big man." Collecting her shoulder bag, she stood and moved off into the shadows of the shops around City Hall, the click of her heels fading into the silence.

Sergeant Wilger crossed the street and joined Selby. "Anybody I know?" He stared after the woman. "The hooker made me, right?"

"I guess she did."

"I look like an unemployed druggist when I see myself in shop windows," Wilger said. "Everybody else sees cop. It's probably glandular. You sure you weren't tailed back there?"

"I don't think so. After I called you I got on Flight 10 to Memphis. Just before takeoff I told the stewardess I'd forgot something, had to make a phone call. I said I'd try to get back in time but told her not to page me if I didn't show. I stayed in the men's room until Flight 10 was airborne. I killed the rest of the time in an all-night movie out on City Line."

They crossed Chestnut Street and got into Wilger's car. "I called Petey Komoto twice on my car phone driving over," the detective told Selby. "He's not home. Talked to his lady. Her name's Maria-Encarna. She's from Tijuana. I got that from Vice here. Petey's sitting up with a sick friend, she says. Putting splints on busted flushes, I'd say. They live on Pine Street, near Rittenhouse Square. We'll wait for him."

Swinging off Chestnut Street, Wilger turned into Broad. They drove through the early light past the Bellevue Stratford and rows of closed shops and bars.

"It worked like you wanted," Wilger said. "I did what you told me. But there's something could screw it all up, Harry. Better tell me your end of it first."

"I've *got* to be right," Selby said. "Thomson hid the tree in the middle of the forest. Nothing else makes sense."

"Fine," Wilger said. "The film could be at Komoto's. But that's not the only problem."

He turned off Broad onto Pine. A newsdealer was opening his corner stand, the bang of the shutters loud in the early morning stillness. An *Inquirer* truck swung in front of them and a man on the tailgate threw off a wired bundle of newspapers.

After routinely cursing the driver, Wilger said, "What about the bank?"

The preceding afternoon, when Selby left the hospital, Senator Lester's limousine had been waiting for him in the driveway. So had the senator, in the rear of the big car, holding a phone.

"Get in," he'd said, and then to the driver, "Clem, drive around for five or ten minutes before you take Mr. Selby out to the airport."

He'd then explained in detail about his committee's single undercover contact in Summitt City, Lee Crowley.

"We've had Crowley down there less than a year," the senator told Selby. "He wasn't in town the weekend after you and Jennifer met with your brother. He got sent up to Wilmington on what seemed a routine business trip. But Crowley *was* in Summitt a month or so later when Earl Thomson made a quick trip into town. He helped Thomson get a copy of the film he was looking for, arranged lab passes and clearance, ensured him some privacy. Crowley included that incident in his report, but he never actually knew what the film was all about."

The senator's limousine drove slowly through the center of the town and then into Society Hill on narrow streets with refurbished old row houses and budding spring trees.

"I can check out half of it." The senator nodded at the phone in his hand. "I've got a call through to Judge Dowd, district court here. A federal court order is required to open Thomson's safe deposit box under these circumstances, but you'd better be guessing right."

"The master print has got to be at Summitt to start with," Selby had said. "Jennifer Easton wasn't lying. But Thomson showed the copy to Derek Taggart at a porn shop here in Philadelphia, then returned it to the bank. Or let us *think* he did that."

"But if you go down to Summitt like some goddamn

gunfighter," the senator said, "you'll wind up with your jewels in the wringer."

"Right, Senator, but when I played in the pros we still faked people out with Statue of Liberty plays. If they're expecting me in Summitt City, and your man, Crowley, plays along, that could nail them in place for a while."

The senator spoke into the phone. "Yes, it *is* important, goddammit. Tell Judge Dowd it's Dixon Lester, ma'am." He turned and stared at Selby. "But how in hell do you convince Davic and Thomson you're really on your way to Memphis?"

"Just get me to the airport now, Senator," Selby said. "I can handle it from there."

Sergeant Wilger turned out of Rittenhouse Square and parked in a street of renovated four-story homes, their fresh paint and cleanly blasted red brick fronts shining in the early sunlight. Komoto's house was dark. Wilger turned off the motor.

"One thing, when Komoto shows, he belongs to me. It's my job, understand?" Wilger looked at Selby. "So what about the bank?"

"I talked to Lester from a phone booth in City Line," and Selby explained what he had learned then. With a federal court order, the senator had inspected the contents of Earl Thomson's safety deposit box in the Wilmington bank. No film of any sort was there, only Xeroxed copies of Thomson's driver's license, school report cards, personal papers.

"In which case," Wilger then said, "it looks good, Harry. The tree's in the forest, like you guessed."

"What we need is stashed away somewhere at Hell for Leather." Selby studied the detective's frowning face. "So what's bothering you? What went wrong?"

Wilger hesitated, watched a Chrysler LeBaron driving slowly past Komoto's house. "Okay, you called me at the Division from the airport," he said when the car turned toward Rittenhouse Square. "You knew your home phone was wired, you didn't trust Brett's, but you figured nobody'd dare tap the phone at police headquarters, right? Okay. Brett was in Superior Nine then, Shana was testifying. I made a quick check of Brett's office, swept it for taps. The bug was under her back desk

423

drawer, a tidy job, probably Eberle's work, he's good at that. I didn't touch it, I left it in place." Wilger rubbed a hand over the back of his neck, twisting his head to relax the muscles. "After court adjourned I went back up to Brett's office. Shana was with her. I dropped in on them, like you said to. Told Brett and Shana you were on your way to Memphis. We went downstairs and sent Shana home in a squad car. Brett was excited, told me she finally had something damaging, maybe conclusive to hit Thomson with." He checked his watch. "Which will be in just a few hours . . . What happened, Harry, was this. Before I got to Brett's, Shana had explained to her everything about Thomson's swastika, just like she told you she wanted to in that note I gave you at the hospital. They were talking right into the bug, probably direct to Slocum's office."

"Christ," Selby said softly.

"That's about what I thought," Wilger said. "So I sent a detail of uniforms out to your place for the night, and a squad over to Brett's. They're okay—"

"But Brett goes into court with three strikes against her," Selby said.

Wilger opened the glove compartment and took out a half pint of Old Granddad, unscrewed the top and offered the bottle to Selby. "Davic and Slocum," he said, "know every goddamn card she's holding. Brett understands that. I told her about the bug right away. She knows she's got to stall them until this deal pays off."

Selby took a sip of whiskey and returned the bottle to Wilger. "Davic's had all night to come up with a cover story," Selby said. "Thomson will say he lost the swastika somewhere, and he'll have friends and cops to prove it."

"Yeah, Brett knows she'll be firing blanks," Wilger said, and tilted the bottle and took a swallow of the whiskey. "Look, friend, it's rotten, in fact it stinks. But she'll fight, she told me that. She'll do anything she can to buy time." Wilger drank again, his thin, pinched face beginning to redden a bit. "Let me give you some free insight into cops, Selby. We're thieving bastards or knights on chargers holding back the jungle from civilization—take your pick. I could care less. But some cases have mile-high no-trespassing signs around them. Cops with white canes looking the other way. There are pushers in East Chester I can't touch. They shove that shit into schools, onto army bases, a river of garbage all over the country. I pick up kids and army recruits, their heads are filthy with it. I can't do a fucking thing . . ." Wilger's voice was high and angry. "A lot of cops feel that way. It hurts, so they take a drink and forget it. But a case like Shana's, that's different." He pounded the rim of the steering wheel. "It *should* be different. No pressure, no white canes. They shouldn't try to stop us from dragging a sonofabitch like Thomson in by his heels . . . The reason for this speech, Selby, is that maybe you think you ought to thank me. Don't. There's not a guy in the Division, well, check that, there's Eberle, but the rest would rather be sitting right here with me. So unless Petey Komoto strikes a blow for justice and *cooperates,* he'll wish to fuck he's stayed in Nippon drinking tea with his shoes off."

Wilger smiled at Selby then, his face cold and humorless. "Know what else Vice told me? Petey pays off the right people, but his lady, Maria-Encarna, is dripping wet. Know what that means? No papers. She's a wetback. A word to Immigration and they'd give her a pair of water wings and throw her back into the Rio Grande like a river carp."

"Let's hope we get it from Petey. She could be an innocent bystander."

Wilger looked at him curiously. "You'd make a lousy cop. If she's standing around a scumbag like Komoto, she's not innocent."

A yellow Cadillac Seville stopped in the block. A stocky man in a camel's hair topcoat got out and walked past the dark houses and put a key into Komoto's front door. When he went inside, lights flashed behind the windows.

"I'll talk to him," Wilger said, and got out of his car. "You sit tight."

"No way," Selby said. He opened his door and joined Wilger. "Komoto might have some friends keeping his lady company."

Wilger judged the stubbornness in Selby's face, then shrugged and said wearily, "Okay. But listen . . . I'm nothing special to look at, Selby. I'm a skinny redhead with glasses and dandruff. You know that. So, goddammit, when we're inside, *don't look at me.* Watch *them.* If the wetback opens a drawer or cupboard unless I tell her to, break her arm. That's how cops get

425

called brutal pricks, but it's also how they stay alive sometimes. Shit, I'd rather do this by myself, Harry."

"Don't worry. I'll try not to embarrass you. Let's go."

Simon Correll's quarters at Summitt City included communications equipment and a master suite whose windows opened on the lakes and golf courses. The early morning light gave a glossy sheen to the beige carpeting and brushed suede furniture.

Correll had not been to bed; he still wore a gray silk lounge suit, a creamy white shirt and a maroon tie. His cologne was blended of cedarwood and cinnamon. At the window he stared out at the smooth, dull water, thinking of Jennifer: an informant at the hospital had told them of her death.

Swimming pools sparkled along the fairways. In the hazy sun they stretched like orderly blue beacons, resembling the markers that defined landing strips. A runway would be useful here, Correll thought. It was a detail they'd overlooked. He made a note of this on his desk pad. Near his hand was an enlarged photograph of the postcard his mother had treasured as a young girl in Portugal, a turreted chateau on the river, purple on that distant afternoon the picture had been taken, pointed and leaded windows gleamed in the River Loire's reflected lights.

His mother had been dead a week now. He did not grieve for her, but he missed her presence at Mount Olivet. Everything ended; that was her ultimate gift to him, a pervasive resignation to that one simple fact.

His car was parked beyond the terrace, a classic blue Bentley, the only nonelectric car allowed in Summitt City. The side panels were painted midnight blue, but the fenders and trim were of a lighter shade of the same color, a combination Jennifer herself had chosen. He already thought of her in the past tense, how she had danced, the pleasure she had taken in rainy weather, and certain physical stimulants.

Correll's thoughts turned on these poignant and harmless considerations to keep his suspicions at a distance. But he was only partially successful; he knew something had managed to slip through their defenses.

426

He wasn't surprised when Sergeant Ledge came in a few minutes later and said, "Sir, we've got problems. I've been on the phone to Quade. Selby wasn't on Flight 10 from Philly. Quade waited at the Memphis airport for the next flight, a local that stops over at Nashville and Richmond. He didn't show on that one either."

Correll said, "You're sure of the contact in Philadelphia?"

"Yes, sir. Kiley was outside Miss Easton's room at the hospital. He knew she'd asked for Selby. He heard the senator tell his aide, that slope who works for him, to make Selby's reservations to Memphis. A lobby guard at St. Anne's saw Selby leave in the senator's limo. Quade is out now looking for the staff on the flight Selby was booked on. Some of them must be laying over in Memphis."

Watching Correll appraisingly, Ledge added, "That's all we've got, except that the press is interested in why the senator was at the hospital." After a deliberate pause, he added, "there is one other thing. Kiley informed me an autopsy's being performed on Miss Easton now. At the hospital morgue."

Correll let out his breath. "When Quade checks in, patch the call straight through to me. Understand?"

"Yes, sir."

After Ledge left, Correll opened his attache case and glanced through a codex of classified numbers. He noticed automatically the loaded Beretta in a spring release holster, and beside it the Madonna in its globe of glass and glycerine and fairy snowflakes.

It saddened him to study the touch of pink on the Snow Virgin's cheeks, applied so deftly (but with what pain?) by his mother's arthritic old hands. Yet his melancholy was paradoxically lightened by the built-in despair that had been her most important gift to him. Human life *was* transitory, meaningless . . . it was Correll's rebellion against that dreadful emptiness that, he felt, had given him the purpose and strength to protect human frailty in havens like Summitt City. To protect people from themselves. Particularly from themselves . . .

He punched out General Taggart's number and was patched immediately through to the general's priority phone at Camp Saliaris.

"General," he said, "you can tell our people the second

427

installation is ready to go on-line. We're phasing out here."

"Damn, I always thought of Summitt as our flagship. You're sure it's compromised?"

"Certain enough not to take any chances."

"I've been in touch with the Cape. But what about a mix? Kraager's people and Van Pelt's?"

"I'll leave that up to you." Correll then mentioned the detail that had occurred to him earlier, the advisability of landing strips and hangars at projected experimental bastions. "Everything muted and coordinated with the general ambiance, of course."

Taggart agreed it was an excellent idea. "The other installation won't have the convenience of a nearby Saliaris," he said. "I'll secure everything according to your instructions, Mr. Correll, but what have we got to get so windy about? What's coming loose?"

Correll hesitated, dismayed by his sudden reluctance to trust even the general. "I'm not quite sure yet," he said. "I'll be in touch when I have more information . . ."

Petey Komoto was first and foremost a businessman; everything was relative in his view, pain and pleasure, good and evil, these had varying and negotiable values depending on when and where and under what circumstances they were traded for—just as the price of dollars and francs and yen fluctuated on the boards of an arbitrage firm.

As the city came to life that morning, Petey Komoto let Selby and Wilger into his shop on Arch Street.

"Leave the CLOSED sign in the window," Wilger told him, "and phone your clerks and tell them not to bother to come in."

Komoto's eyes were bland, his complexion the color of dandelion wine. He said, "Yes, but that will cost me money—"

"Bullshit," Wilger said. He was staring with distaste at a display of thin whips done in pastel leathers with finely ornate ivory handles. "Snap shit, Petey, or your wife will be back entertaining tourists in Tijuana."

"I will make the calls, of course," Komoto said. He even bowed slightly to Wilger. "But I don't understand your resentment of me and my merchandise. I am a businessman. I didn't create people's urges and the needs that make them enjoy such little aids or watching group sex acts. I am the grandson of fishermen. Bento Komoto. If I sold gin and whiskey, would you blame me because my customers drink too much?"

Selby said, "Make those calls, Mr. Komoto. I'm not interested in your philosophy. You're making me impatient."

"That wasn't bad," Wilger nodded approvingly as Komoto hurried into his office. "Kind of gentlemanly shit, but you're big enough to make it go down."

The Hell for Leather shop sprawled through four ground-floor rooms of an ancient building that was within walking distance of Wanamaker's famed department store and the Old Reading Terminal. The two rooms fronting the street were lined with glass shelving and counters which displayed dildoes of various sizes, along with inflated, multicolored condoms stuffed into vases like flowers. Jars and tubes of creams and jellies were heaped in pyramids on shelves, some containing alleged aphrodisiacs, others mingled with properties guaranteed to cause itching or burning or numbing sensations.

"Jesus Christ," Wilger said, looking at life-sized rubber dolls that stood about like pink, blank-eyed spectators, fully equipped with male and female genitalia.

The rear rooms were walled with shelves of tapes, film and cassette sets. Neatly lettered signs, like something in the public library, Selby thought, were thumbtacked to the shelf edges to identify various categories: Disciplines, Fetishes, Bondage, Group Activities, Aphrodisiacs. In some cases there were sub-headings—Corporal Punishment, Girls' Schools, Gloves, Shoes and Slippers, All-Men, All-Women; Stimulants (Friction, Drugs, Alcohol, etc.).

At the end of the corridor, a half dozen screening rooms were furnished with couches and chairs. All were scruffed and dusty and in need of cleaning. In each screening room was a projector that could be operated from inside the booth, but the activating tokens had to be purchased from Komoto at the main cash register to run the machines for half-hour interludes.

"Otherwise," Komoto had explained, "the kinks would stay all night."

On the drive over, he had already told them as much as he knew about Earl Thomson. But Komoto's information had only outlined the dimensions of the problem; it hadn't solved it.

Thomson had rented a film cassette from the files titled *Knots and Lashes*—"very pretty porn, pirate ladies in G-strings, captured, tied to riggings, flogged"—but Earl and his friend, the army officer, hadn't screened that film because, as Komoto explained, it was new and the seal on it hadn't been broken.

They'd rented a private booth, paid for one activating token and looked at other footage, a film Earl had brought out of the booth with him later, a cassette with the name of a city on it . . . Summitt City, Komoto remembered the words stenciled on the brown plastic cover in block capitals.

Komoto returned from his office. "My clerks will take the morning off, but it will cost me a lot, you know."

"Cheaper than Encarna's swimming lessons," Wilger said. He looked at Selby. "You believe this character? Or should we try some of those tickle whips on his yellow ass?"

Selby said, "I told him to name his price for that film. If he knew where it was, he'd be interested. He's a businessman."

Komoto smiled gratefully at Selby. "Precisely. It's buying and selling, nothing more. Would you care for coffee while you look around? It's a chicory blend. I obtain it cheaply from sailors up from Panama. They keep me supplied."

"Stuff your coffee," Wilger said. "Let's go to work, Harry."

Earl Thomson, according to Komoto, had asked if he could leave his cassette in the files at Hell for Leather. He'd paid for that, naturally, a storage fee. But Komoto had no idea where Thomson had put it.

"The shop was very crowded, you know that." He glanced accusingly at Wilger. "You were parked across the street watching. You saw the people, sailors, a florists' convention was in town, a man tried to take a live chicken into a screening booth. It was that kind of day. Very much business. I don't know what Mr. Thomson did with it."

He gestured at the shelves of cassettes. "I can't help you." He laughed showing strong, white teeth. "You would have to tear the place apart to find it."

Wilger removed his coat and folded it neatly over a rack of kid porn magazines. "You said that, Bento, we didn't."

Selby said, "You start with *A* to *N*. I'll cover the rest of it."

"That gives me *assholes* to *nookie*. Bento, you wanna help?"

"Most certainly, sir. This is only a business matter. But please handle these items with care. Many of them are irreplaceable."

Wilger smiled grimly. "I'm very glad to hear that, you kinky little bastard."

A cool light spread across Summitt City's blue lake, and the green belts glistened under sprinklers. Miniature rainbows formed brilliant arches within the crystal water cones.

When Correll was informed that directions to the screening room had been left at the north gate for Harry Selby, he drove directly to the theater.

The cameras on the buildings were motionless, their slim barrels fixed on the horizons. The shopping mall was empty and silent, but golfers were already on the course, tiny figures dotting the fairways.

The theater was a stone-colored, windowless structure landscaped with firs and spreading shrubs. Correll parked and went inside.

Wall clocks in the auditorium recorded the time in New York and a dozen world capitals. An electronic island contained projection equipment and a control panel with rheostats, speakers and microphones. Clear light streamed from panels in the acoustically treated ceiling.

A cassette of film had been inserted in the projector. Correll snapped a switch, and twin beams illuminated the large screen. Music sounded and scenes of Summitt City appeared in smooth sequences: children playing baseball, passengers getting off electric buses, homes with colorful gardens, window boxes bright with flowers. The film had been shot in clear fall sunlight, a brilliant day in October. Correll had watched it at Camp Saliaris with Jennifer, surrounded by the world delegates chosen to participate in the Ancilia Four program. On that occasion, General Taggart's sardonic voice had counterpointed the images on the screen.

Correll stood alone now, watching residents of Summitt City in their plants and shop and recreational areas. A baseball game was featured, then couples in drifting canoes. Sailboats skimmed along the water, dissolving into shots of the shopping arcade. This was what he had created, Correll thought, a prosperous community, with a controlled, industrious and harmless population. But now everything was at risk.

His suspicions had hardened to conviction. From the start he was resigned to some degree of personal failure, but that genetic despair had been flawed by unrealistic hope, an unreasoning optimism that his own inevitable defeats would result in a victory for his species. Until now he was blinded to the betrayal he had intuitively been certain of. A vacuum had always existed . . . an emptiness, rather, of love, of confidence, of warmth and esteem between himself and the world, himself and Jennifer, and a darkness had rushed in to fill it.

Ledge had been informed by their Philadelphia intelligence that Harry Selby was on his way to Summitt City. A pass from Lee Crowley was waiting for him at the north gate. And in the screening room the crucial record, the film itself, had been inserted in the projector, waiting only for the touch of Selby's fingers on a switch. The stage was set, the curtain had risen . . . but where was Harry Selby?

On the big white screen, the film cutting had become sharper and faster but the effect remained harmonious. Ducks bobbing on water, children splashing in a pool. People entering a church, quiet hospital rooms and bright sun porches. An American flag strained splendidly above the administration building.

In the empty theater, General Adam Taggart's amplified voice sounded from speakers.

"What you will witness," Taggart had explained to the delegates, "is an experiment in controlled human behavior, disciplines based on scientific conclusions. I stress," the general's voice now rumbled through Summitt City's empty screening room, "that these disciplines are an application of observed scientific principles. Nothing you will see was invented or discovered. A thief doesn't discover the silverware in a home. Gravity, motion and light weren't invented or discovered, they've existed forever. Men of curiosity and learning have come to understand and put to use their relationships and functions. Progress is usually a matter of replacing one error with another, if you will, but progress is inevitable. Whatever exists on this earth, no matter how cunningly nature has hidden it, will be

432

found and understood and put to use by man, for good or ill, it doesn't matter one goddamn."

The streaming flag dissolved into a montage of fresh images. Cameras picked up the baseball game, cutting from batter to pitcher to infielder. Adult spectators lined the diamond, cheering and clapping. The scene dissolved to the lake shore, where a swarm of starlings settled with a rush of wings into tawny trees. A medley of pop tunes sounded distantly from the arcade. Children skipped beside their mothers, a black woman, slim in tailored jeans, bought a snow cone for her daughter.

Simon Correll opened his briefcase and picked up the weighted globe that contained the Snow Virgin. Tipping it sideways, he watched the flakes swirling about the Madonna.

On the screen, the cameras had panned back to the action at the baseball game. The pitcher kicked high, let the ball fly. The umpire's hand shot up.

"Strike one."

The batter checked the third base coach, a middle-aged Puerto Rican whose sunglasses had broad, milk-white rims. The coach signaled to his infielders by touching the peak of his cap, kicking the dirt and clapping his hands. The shortstop yelled, "Bunt! Watch for a bunt!"

The first baseman, a black youngster, crept down the line like a cat, eyes fixed on the crouched batter. Spencer Barrow. His brother was named Dookey, Correll remembered. Summitt's laboratory mice. It was such concepts that had appalled Jennifer. Human lab mice were a reality she couldn't absorb or come to terms with. They were from Chicago, the Barrow brothers, products of ghettos, juvenile detention halls, foster homes, their records "lost," their family's whereabouts unknown and virtually untraceable. Brought to Summit to visit with an "aunt" . . .

A phone in the control panel rang. It was Quade, calling from Memphis. "I've talked with the stewardess on Flight 10 from Philadelphia, Mr. Correll." Quade's voice was light, a surprising contrast to his wide, thick body. "She's staying at a motel near the airport. Unfortuntely she maintains that company policy prohibits any discussion of passengers by flight crews. But I'll try to make her understand that an exception is necessary— excuse me a moment, sir . . ."

As Correll held the open phone, General Taggart's voice sounded around him from the speakers. "Dr. Einstein, near his death, told us nuclear power had changed everything but the way people think. But modifying how people think, well, naturally that's permitted only in authorized churches and legislatures."

The camera picked up golfers on a green, children exercising in groups to the beat of drums. General Taggart went on. "It's an untested article of faith that human nature can't be changed. Attempts to modify the only *thinking* element in nature are considered useless. Instead we've tried to change the machine that transports us through space. We break open mountains, turn rivers and lakes to hardpan, but nature can't be changed. We've got to change the basic responses of the humans living on nature's machine. *That is the function of Ancilia Four.* Some of you may have feelings of outrage about this film. If so, then you don't understand what we've achieved. We are demonstrating to you the indifference of a treated, controlled population to the spectacle of *both* youth and minorities being brutalized. To prove that those two traditional weaknesses in the average human psyche have been chemically anesthetized. Because laudable as it has been made to seem, *in fact, aiding the underdog screws up nature's plan for survival of the fittest.* Chivalry is an infection. We've found the antidote for it. The participants in our Ancilia program have no compulsion to become personally and emotionally involved in the inevitable misfortunes and tragedies of life. Live and let live applies only to themselves, the people who *count.*

"Our treatment turns the stuff of horror into the stuff of dreams—"

Correll turned down the sound, the images on the screen flowed in silence. Quade was speaking again. "Harry Selby got off the plane in Philadelphia, sir. He told the stewardess that he had to make a phone call, but specifically asked her not to page him if he didn't return. They took off without him."

"You believe she's telling the truth?"

"Miss Avery is doing her best to cooperate with us, sir. I think she's told me everything she knows."

"Have you checked charter flights, Quade?"

"Yes, sir. I've made inquiries of the unscheduled carriers

operating out of Philadelphia. I've been in touch with private airfields in the Memphis area. It's extremely unlikely that Selby left Philadelphia."

"You'd better take the next flight back to New York, Quade. If you don't hear otherwise from me, have my jet on stand-by at LaGuardia with a direct clearance for Brussels."

Correll broke the connection and froze the frame on the screen. The flag was locked into rippled immobility, golfers were caught in mid-swing, the shining hair of pretty girls blew out stiff and straight with the gusting winds.

The rear doors of the theater opened and Sergeant Ledge joined Correll, his boots noiseless on the thick carpets, the strong light glazing his sharply cut features.

"I'm telling you straight out. I monitored your call on my car phone," he told Correll. His smile was tight and ugly. "I like to know what's going on. That's how I've stayed alive this long." He had dropped the "sirs." "We've been fucked over good." Ledge nodded to the projector. "Lee Crowley loaded that film. He checked it out of the lab. Then he left the pass for Selby. In Philadelphia they made a point to let us find out Selby was on his way. Crowley's gone, his apartment's cleaned out. Every move they made was to pin us down here. Who sold us out, Correll? You figured that one yet?"

Correll had been nodding thoughtfully. "Not all of it, Sergeant. Not quite."

With an unhurried move, Ledge drew the .45 from its holster and held it leveled at Correll's chest. "Step back from that projector."

"You're right, of course," Correll said. "We *were* set up. But I'd advise you to trust me now—"

Ledge gestured with the automatic. Correll shrugged and stepped aside. The sergeant moved to the control panel and pressed a button to activate the film. The images flowed again, the boats on the lake, the playing fields and brightly striped buses.

"I soldiered with George Thomson," he said, as if mechanically repeating a litany. "The best time of my life, soldiering with the major in Korea. I shot and killed Jonas Selby. I always hated that stubborn bastard. Thomson watched me. We trusted each other. We were soldiers. We doped Jarrell Selby and got

435

him on the plane back here like we'd been told, good soldiers taking orders."

Correll studied the sergeant and chose his words carefully. "You deserve every credit. You did exactly what I wanted. Jarrell was a second-generation product. It was essential to keep him close, to study the genetic properties, endowments and liabilities that connected the father and the son . . ."

On the blazing white screen in front of the two men a stocky figure in a gray twill uniform appeared, Indian features hawklike and vigilant. The image of Ledge.

"That's what connects *me* to Jarrell Selby," Ledge said, nodding at his image on the screen. "And that's what could hang me."

Correll said quietly, "You must trust me, Sergeant, the way you trusted the major."

On the screen, the image of the sergeant drew the .45 from its holster. A pair of golfers pulling carts waved and smiled at him.

"It's C and A time, Correll," Ledge said. "Cover Your Ass. Earl Thomson's never going to serve an hour in prison. He goes free as a bird. So does Lee Crowley. He'll be south of the border on a government pension with lifetime PX privileges and travel cards. I heard your orders to Quade. He's split for New York, and your plane is fueling up to wait for you at LaGuardia. It's a free ride out for everybody but the old sergeant."

"You're thinking only of personal survival," Correll said. "I understand that. But the preoccupation can blind people to intelligent action, Sergeant."

On the screen, a camera tracked abruptly from the golf course to a stretch of shoreline across the lake. A shadow moved among the trees. Unexpectedly the figure of Jarrell Selby stepped into view, tense as a wild creature, his eyes desperate, dirt and scratches streaking his sensitive face.

Sergeant Ledge pressed a button that froze the frame on the screen. *"He's* the danger for me," Ledge said. "Him and the nigger kids you called your little mice. Don't bullshit me about survival, Correll. That's my game, and I play to win, just like you do."

With a hand on the control panel, Ledge erased the images

from the screen. The flat white mat cast a shimmering light through the theater.

"I'm disappointed in you, Sergeant," Correll said. "You drew your gun from habit. Shooting me would be another mechanical reflex, triggered by panic or fear, which aren't very reliable impulses."

Ledge looked steadily at Correll, pressed a flat red button marked ERASE, and listened impassively to the whirring sounds of the film reels as they reversed and irrevocably obliterated and wiped clean every frame of the film shot months earlier in Summitt City.

"I won't add to my problems by killing you, Correll," the sergeant said when the erasure was complete. "You and the general have done a fair job of covering ass in Summitt and Saliaris, but I'm not leaving proof around to stretch this stringy neck of mine. I know there's a copy somewhere, but I'm trusting the major to liberate and destroy it."

"I'm seriously disappointed in you," Correll said again. "You're abandoning the disciplines that made you such a formidable soldier. You're acting like a green recruit. In the face of the enemy, you're falling apart. You don't have the guts to trust and believe in me. You've got the mentality of a regular army stiff." Correll's voice rose with anger. "You know we've been betrayed, but you lack the imagination to try to understand the scope and enormity of that betrayal."

Correll lifted the Snow Virgin and smashed it violently against the counter supporting the control panel. The globe shattered, shards of glass skittered about and a pool of glycerine spread in a small, thick circle around the broken plastic base. A metal cylinder no thicker than a matchstick lay beside the cracked figure of the Virgin. Another floated on the surface of the fluid seeping from the broken globe. Batteries . . .

The black plaster base had parted in two sections, as cleanly as if cut by a finely powered saw. The interior of the base contained a tape recorder no larger than a poker chip, with its side angled to fit a beveled receptacle cut in the foundation of the Snow Virgin.

Correll picked up the curved section of the plaster base. The two men studied the hollowed-out section, precisely fitted with reels and fine-spun metal tapes.

437

In his heart, Correll had expected this. His suspicions had winnowed out every other possibility. It was the only explanation he could conceive of, and yet a protective instinct was still helplessly seeking innocent justifications for these batteries and wires and tape. But all his defenses couldn't sidestep the inevitable truth. His heart pounded with dangerous, impotent anger. The plastic base was repellent to his touch, as cold and slick as the treachery itself.

Correll placed the broken section on the counter, then watched indifferently as Ledge removed the tape recorders from them and held them in the palm of his big hand.

The day after Jennifer returned from Summitt City she had placed the Snow Virgin on his desk while he'd talked to the dying Senator Rowan. Jennifer had told him about sleeping with Jarrell Selby, about her ambivalent feelings for Jarrell's brother, and even then the tiny reels had been spinning silently beneath the pious figure of the Virgin. And spinning, spinning, spinning, at his meetings with Thomson, his sessions with General Taggart, his calls to Van Pelt . . .

The Madonna, whose eyes and cheeks had been painted by his own mother, had been listening.

Ledge was backing away from Correll. The older man seemed barely aware of him now.

As a child, Correll had often puzzled over the riddle of whether the universe was one or many, a flock of birds, for instance, was that one thing, one swooping, darkly cohesive unit, or was it simply a thousand willful creatures soaring and nesting together for a common need and purpose? Was a tree one thing, its leaves another? Jennifer, Fabius, His Excellency, the bishop . . . Had there been one betrayal or an infinite number and variety of them?

Yet even with this thought, Correll couldn't bring himself to believe his own mother had been part of the conspiracy, that her dark demons had not been electrocuted in the therapy clinic after all . . .

Sergeant Ledge had retreated to the main doors of the theater. Holstering his automatic, he put the tape recorder in the inner breast pocket of his twill jacket.

"I told you I'm an expert at survival," he said. "I've been the good soldier, I never questioned orders, *sir*. But I know where you and General Taggart plan your next move, and I'd even sell that to save this ass of mine."

"Sergeant, I'm asking you one more time to trust me," Correll said. "You're a part of this world we've tried to make. You can't betray all that for a personal reason—"

Ledge shook his head and pushed open the doors of the theater. At the same instant Correll lifted the Beretta from his attache case and fired two shots which struck Sergeant Ledge in his shoulder and thigh and caused him first to grunt spasmodically and then to turn and fall clumsily through the open doors.

Correll stepped forward and fired a third shot into the sergeant's struggling body. Doing so was a necessity, nothing more. The shot went cleanly into Ledge's upper chest and through the pocket of his twill jacket.

The lights clouded in front of the sergeant's eyes. His .45 was in his hand, a soldier's reflex, and he managed to fire a shot that went crashing into the ceiling and splintered those dimming lights before the scary darkness he had known on so many battlefields closed around him, finally and forever, just as he had always been afraid it would. . . .

The fenders and grille suffered the most severe damage when the Bentley swerved from the road and crashed into the big tree. Near Correll, on a green belt, Frisbees soared through the air, and children ran after them.

He'd acted hastily with the sergeant, he realized that now. He should have tried to explain how essential it was for both of them to understand and embrace the width and breadth of the betrayal, examine its patterns and significances and, most importantly of all, identify the players and ferret out their varying motives and loyalties. But it was too late for regrets; it was done, the man was dead.

The phone on the dashboard was dead too. He'd tried to raise the operator but it was useless; no hum sounded from the instrument, not a crackle of static. A wire must have snapped or pulled loose when the Bentley went off the road and stopped with a crunch against the huge tree.

His hands were moist and slippery on the leather rim of the steering wheel. He needed the sergeant; there was work to do. Alert his people, put Belgium and London in the picture. But Correll couldn't do it, he was hurt, he might be dying for all he knew. It's my own fault, Correll thought. He should have tried to make the sergeant comprehend the enormity of the breach in security, a tape recorder in a ridiculous Madonna, on his desk, in his traveling case, in his goddamn bathroom perhaps, the wires spinning and listening and repeating everything for the monk Fabius at Olivet, and his tedious superior, His Excellency the Bishop Waring. "Is the lap dog an improvement over the Siberian wolf, Mr. Correll . . . ?" Christ! Correll felt an encouraging surge of energy and anger. He should have taken the sergeant into his confidence. Made him understand. Instead he had shot the man, destroyed the tapes in his uniform pocket. But the sergeant's own last despairing reflex had pulled the trigger of the .45 and the bullet had hissed around the projection room like an angry wasp, recoiling from surface to surface until it found a safe, soft home at last in Correll's narrow, pulsing chest . . .

His mother had been disappointed in him when he was a child because she insisted he had no conscience. This had perplexed him. If he had no conscience, why had he been disturbed by the lack of one?

Put London in the picture. Yes! Call the general . . .

General Taggart knew the Lord Conestain and the Murray clan. Was impressed by their link to the British peerage. Their ancestors had fought one another in various skirmishes and wars, the Taggarts and the Murrays, and wore ribbons and rosettes and medals to celebrate the death of pikemen and lads in the colonies. Drink had done in the boys at Wexford . . . the general sang that song, and Correll remembered Taggart singing in his loud, cracked voice about someone who'd slain the Earl of Murray, in the highlands and the lowlands, and laid him on the green . . .

Stepping with great care and difficulty from the damaged car, Correll hailed a foursome of golfers and asked them to phone for a service vehicle. "I'm hurt," he explained with an apologetic smile.

Their cheerful glances chilled him. They didn't understand, they didn't believe. As they walked off, one turned and waved good-naturedly, while the others continued to discuss the advisability of using an iron club to carry the water holes at . . . Their voices faded away.

Correll looked at the neat hole in his vest where Ledge's bullet had found him. A stain no larger than a silver dollar surrounded the point of entry. Opening the vest, he studied the blood on his shirt. He tried to analyze it as he would any problem, any endangered sector.

The north gate, his apartment, the main plant? Too far away . . .

Summoning his reserves of strength, Correll walked at a measured pace toward the shopping mall with its public phone booths and its streams of people. *His* people, his creations . . .

They had broken Correll's security, which could lead them to Van Pelt. But not to England, to Lord Conestain, blood-linked to the Earls of Murray . . .

Correll stopped a young man carrying a tennis racket. "I need to make a phone call," he told him. "I need your help. I was shot by a security officer. It was a mistake. I have a phone credit number, but I'll need coins to . . .

"Listen," he shouted then. "I'm telling you the truth. I'm Simon Correll, I need to get to a phone. You've got to help me."

The young athlete looked briefly at Correll's blood-stained vest and was, Correll realized with dismay, relieved not to take his anguish seriously, *not to believe in it.* Ancilia Four had reversed his reality signals. Tennis was real. Blood, death were not. With a friendly nod of dismissal, the tennis player hurried on to the courts.

. . . He must phone Brussels. The bishop would be off to Belgium, he was sure, but Fabius would remain at Olivet to sing Masses for the repose of Ellyvan Correll's soul.

How had they turned poor Jennifer against him? By giving her something to believe in, to be part of? Or did it matter?

The problem was not the clever nest at the convent, Bittermank's source, nor was it Jennifer's defection or the Kraagers or Van Pelts or the Murrays . . .

The problem was Harry Selby. He realized that with almost violent clarity. Yes, Selby. He must warn George Thomson. Call him now. Tell him that Harry Selby was not in Summitt City. Had never left Philadelphia. The trial would end this morning, the jury set the young man free . . . Nothing must interfere with—

Some splintered thought reminded him of a noisy tumult

441

in England's Picadilly Circus, a wrecking ball smashing a building to dust, a blind young girl and her crazed seeing-eye dog
. . . Kipper. That was the dog's name. Burdened by a responsibility too great for its nervous system, the animal's discipline and
intelligence had been shattered by the roar and violence and
destruction of the world around him. He must have welcomed
the policeman's bullet in his poor, wild brain.

Correll could sympathize with that cringing animal now. A
thousand thoughts clamored for his own attention and decision,
a billion stimuli were beating on his naked, exposed nerves. But
he must act, he mustn't let the wrecker's ball inside him have
its way . . .

Like a distracted mendicant, Correll went up and down the
length of the arcade, controlling his pain and exhaustion with
an effort of iron will, stopping to speak to shoppers as calmly
and persuasively as he could manage. Cajoling, wheedling and
imploring, he importuned them for coins, for assistance, but
they were incapable of believing in him, he realized, they were
unable to care about the blood on his hands, they were programmed not even to *imagine* his pain . . .

He became enraged and anger gave him strength. He
shouted at the crowds, cursed their indifference. But at last his
steps became slower, his elegantly cut trousers were sodden and
heavy with blood. Each dragging footstep told him that.

Correll possessed a respectable flair for irony, although he
had never appreciated that mordant cast of mind in others; it
had seemed to him a wearisome effect, the epitaph of energy.
But he couldn't escape the irony of this predicament.

He sat heavily on a bench, his back against a window display of scuba gear and fishing tackle. Music was playing, an
up-tempoed waltz, and he thought of rain and snow and Jennifer dancing with distant, pink-lipped smiles.

It was coming at last, he realized, not in darkness but in
deceptively pleasant shades of gray, opalescent lights which
seemed to be trying to filter craftily through his conscious
thoughts.

As long as he continued to think and plan, the darkness
stayed in the distance like a gathering gray mist . . . so he
concentrated on Mount Olivet and someone he loved dancing,
but when he stopped thinking for even an instant of Selby and

Thomson and the telephones, the darkness formed swiftly, and he realized then that the painless oblivion he had offered the world was not a condition he would choose for himself, thank you.

No thank you . . .

A child stopped near him. A girl. Correll felt her presence. Overhead a helicopter circled them, its rotors throbbing noisily.

"Are you all *right?*" the child asked.

Correll fought the darkness and his thoughts leaped with hope. "Oh, no, *no* . . ."

"Then you're all *wrong,* aren't you?" It was her little joke and she laughed with pleasure and ran off.

"Not altogether, I hope," Simon Correll said, speaking clearly and firmly for the last time in his life.

CHAPTER THIRTY-SEVEN

Mrs. Adele Thomson insisted on attending the last day of her son's trial. Her husband's attempts to dissuade her were futile. "You'll tire yourself out, for no reason," he'd said. "It's only a formality. Earl will be home by noon at the latest, the whole business will be over. Wait here."

But Adele was inflexible, she demanded to be taken to court. It would justify her own suffering and helplessness to witness Earl's triumph and vindication. His freedom was the only compensation she could imagine that would redeem, or make some sense of, her own bondage.

Their chauffeur, Richard, drove the family to East Chester well before Judge Flood's courtroom was open to the public. A space behind the defense table, between George Thomson and Dom Lorso, had been cleared for Adele's wheelchair. Her maid arranged Mrs. Thomson's silver-blond curls in a corona about her bony forehead and dressed her in a lavender suit with caped shoulders and amply cut sleeves, which puffed out to camouflage her slack arms. Even Adele's one useful hand was concealed under the plaid, fleece-lined robe pulled over her lap and knees.

By the time the marshals opened the doors, the press section was filled and Captain Slocum had taken a seat beside the bailiff's desk. Spectators rapidly crowded the gallery.

The principals were seated at their tables—Earl Thomson and Davic, the People's counsel and Shana—when Judge Flood appeared and the uniformed bailiff commanded the lawfully assembled company to rise and announced that Superior Court Nine was in session, the Honorable Desmond Flood presiding.

His Honor asked the opposing counsels to approach the bench.

"What's that for?" Adele Thomson whispered to her husband. "Are they talking about Earl?"

"It's a technicality," he said.

"I thought this was a public trial. Don't I have a right to know what they're saying about my son?"

"There's no problem. The prosecution is re-calling Earl. We know about it."

"I don't like her talking to the judge in private, like she's privileged."

"Dammit, I told you to stay home."

Her head turned angrily to Dom Lorso. "Fix my robe, can't *you* even help me?"

"Sure, sure, Adele." Lorso's voice was a soothing murmur. Adjusting the robe around her hips, he pulled it up under her flaccid arms. "Don't worry, everything's fixed, it's all set."

But the Sicilian, whose instincts were still influenced to a certain extent by the smell of garlic in suspicious places, and by the look of roses on funeral altars and the clink of the priest's censer from which poured coils of incense, knew that only fools and children believed things would turn out the way they hoped and wanted, because it wasn't always human hands tipping the scales. But as far as Lorso could see with his worldly cunning, the outcome of this trial was as fixed in their favor as anything in life could possibly be.

At the Park Towers last night he'd talked to Judge Flood in the apartment his honor shared with Millie Haynes, whose days as a drum majorette and tumbler were recorded in photographs on Flood's desk and wall. Millie in short, white boots and silver skirts, her head thrown back. Millie swinging high on bars and trapezes.

To clarify and emphasize their understanding, Lorso talked of the judge's condo in San Diego, and his boat in the marina, both unpaid for and piling up interest every day. He listed the amounts of Flood's unsecured notes to the Camden Finance Company. It was a reminder, like the flick of a whip. Maybe not necessary. Flood intended to rule in favor of Davic's motion to dismiss as soon as the Commonwealth finished questioning Earl.

They knew what was in the envelope of the defense table, the swastika. They'd got everything from Eberle's tap. They were ready, Davic and Earl both. And Harry Selby was down in Summitt City on a wild goose chase. The trial would be over when, and if, he got back.

But there were always things you couldn't see or hear or even understand, and they might hurt you for reasons of their own. His grandmother told Lorso that. The old lady thought airplanes were pictures flashed on the sky by jokers, but Lorso believed her about how life was.

They'd done all they could. It better be enough, he thought. Giorgio had nothing left to fight with. Lorso tried to reassure Adele by patting her cold hand, but she flinched away from him. Screw her, he thought. And wished desperately for a cigarette.

Judge Flood had excused the attorneys by then and turned to address the jury. "As you know, the defense and the People rested their cases yesterday. The court was prepared to hear closing statements this morning. But the People have asked to recall the defendant. Certain substantive information—I can't call it evidence at this time—has come into their hands. The defense has the right to cross-examine, or to call other witnesses. I won't hold a stopwatch on either the People or the defense. It is the purpose of any trial to give both sides reasonable flexibility. A judicial hearing is not a contest that ends after nine innings or four quarters. We will go on as long as the court is satisfied that new and significant and relevant testimony is being developed and elicited. But I will not tolerate unnecessary or frivolous interrogation, or delaying tactics. I will also rigorously exclude subject matter which should properly be included in counsels' closing statement. Is that clear?"

"Your Honor," Davic said rising, "the defense has no further witnesses to call. But we are naturally curious to know why Counselor Brett has so belatedly decided to reopen her own case."

Judge Flood nodded and filled his glass of water. Glancing at the Commonwealth table, he studied Shana and Dorcas Brett, then said, "We will sit as long as necessary in the interests of justice, Miss Brett. But not one minute for any other reason.

446

That wouldn't be fair to the defendant or the plaintiff. I want you to present those inconsistencies you say you have discovered, with due promptness. In short, I want you to conclude this business as quickly as possible and get on to your closing statement. The court will direct its close scrutiny to the area of relevance. Clear, Miss Brett?"

"Yes, Your Honor."

The clerk then recalled Earl Thomson to the stand. "Mr. Thomson," Brett began, "you've testified that you asked Miguel Santos to pick you up in Muhlenburg after your car was stolen. You called Mr. Santos because you thought your family chauffeur, Richard Gates, was in New Jersey. Correct?"

"Yes, ma'am. That's right."

"According to hotel records in Osmond, New Jersey, Richard Gates spent part of the night there and joined your father Saturday morning. Richard Gates checked into his room after midnight. At twelve thirty-five, to be exact." Brett looked at her notes. "Were you aware that Richard Gates didn't leave your home in Wahasset until after ten o'clock Friday night?"

Davic rose. "Objection, Your Honor. At this late date I'd hardly call that a substantive issue." But it was obvious the attorney was unprepared for Brett's line of inquiry. It was also apparent Earl Thomson had been caught by surprise. He was openly relieved by his attorney's interruption.

"I'll withhold a ruling for a moment," Judge Flood said. "What is your point, Miss Brett?"

"Your Honor, Miguel Santos, for the first and only time in his many years with the Thomson family, was asked to serve as chauffeur—at about six o'clock on the night Mr. Thomson's car was stolen. My point is this . . . why was Miguel Santos pressed into service when the family chauffeur, Mr. Richard Gates, was on duty and available?"

Judge Flood tapped his pencil impatiently against his water glass but said, "Well, ask the witness your question then, Miss Brett. Let's get on with this."

"Mr. Thomson," Brett said, "were you mistaken when you testified that you called Miguel Santos because you thought Richard was on his way to New Jersey?"

"Obviously I was, ma'am. Our home is rather large. The comings and goings of the staff aren't announced"—he smiled calmly—"like planes arriving and taking off. Richard was on tap that whole weekend, spoken for, to pick up my father and drive him back from Osmond. I assumed he was gone when I called from Muhlenburg. But even if he was home, I wouldn't have asked him to change his schedule to accommodate me." Earl's voice was confident; after the first uncertain glance at Davic, he had regained his composure. "It may be old-fashioned, Miss Brett, but at our house my father's plans rate top priority."

"In fact, you didn't *know* Richard Gates was in his quarters when you called Miguel Santos?"

"Yes, ma'am, that's correct."

"And the only reason you called Miguel Santos was because you thought Richard Gates was enroute to New Jersey?"

"I object, Your Honor," Davic said. "This line of inquiry is pointless. People's counsel is trying to suggest something sinister in the normal, complex operation of any large, busy household."

"Sustained. Miss Brett, you've established an inconsistency, but I see no relevance in it. The witness needn't answer those last questions. Please get on to something else now."

"Yes, of course, Your Honor. If the court considers the *mistaken* testimony of the defendant and a crucial defense witness, Miguel Santos, irrelevant, I won't try Your Honor's patience by contending otherwise."

Brett returned to the table and picked up her notes. Shana looked up and gave her a barely perceptible headshake. They were expecting a call from her father or Sergeant Wilger. It would come to a pay phone in the lobby outside Superior Nine; Brett's secretary was stationed there. She would give the written message to the bailiff, who had the authority to deliver information and documents to the prosecution and defense while court was in session.

Shana's negative headshake added to Brett's tension.

Her job was to stall as long as possible, as long as necessary, in fact, yet not a fraction beyond the point where Flood would have an excuse to dismiss the witness and instruct the jury that the People had failed to prove its case against Earl Thomson.

The defense, she was aware, was relieved by Earl's controlled response to her questions so far. To gain time, Brett made a pretense of leafing through her casebook, as if searching

448

for a particular item of information. Her small, precise hand-writing, in fact, covered dozens of pages; she had spent hours last night checking her notes on the case, examining every depo-sition, and rereading the complete transcript of the testimony to date.

Ever since Wilger had told her of the bug planted in her office, she had been rethinking her arguments, studying the principals' backgrounds, and later going through her encyclope-dia for military and biographical sketches, using a magnifying glass to examine even the agate type in footnotes, seeking to find delaying facts or incidents that might meet Flood's test of rele-vance.

Her lack of sleep was evident; her face was pale and her eyes were shadowed. Her dark suit and bright scarf only accentuated her fragile appearance. She had jogged two miles along the Brandywine at dawn, with one of Wilger's squads trailing her, but even that exercise and a long, hot shower hadn't helped. Her nerves felt frayed; they practically ached with tension.

Judge Flood cleared his throat. "Miss Brett?"

"Yes, Your Honor." Dropping her notebook casually, Brett returned to the witness. "Mr. Thomson, you testified, didn't you, that the name Vinegar Hill meant nothing to you when Captain Slocum asked you about it?"

"Yes, I did."

"You had never heard of such a place?"

"No."

As Davic rose, Brett said, "Mr. Thomson, you attended a military college with an excellent reputation, I believe."

The abrupt change of subject forestalled Davic's objection. Settling back, he listened warily to the exchanges.

"Yes, ma'am," Thomson replied. "Rockland's senior staff is made up of professional soldiers. Most are field grade officers with combat experience."

"Well versed in military strategy and history then?"

"That goes without saying. They're scholars, and they know the problems in the field from personal experience."

"The Taggart family's military history dates back to our Revolutionary War, does it not?"

"Yes. There've been Taggarts in every war America's fought, drummer boys at Valley Forge, foot soldiers at Shiloh, and officers in both World Wars, the Marne, the Ardennes, Heartbreak Hill and Old Baldy in Korea. The Taggarts are part of all that."

Thomson's response, his drum-beat roll call of place names, had been cool, dispassionate, and Davic seemed reassured, Brett noticed; he relaxed and crossed his arms.

"Mr. Thomson," Brett said, "a famous battle was fought between Ireland and England in the year 1798. The Irish pikemen of Wexford were crushed and destroyed. The Viceroy of Ireland at that time was—"

Judge Flood tapped his gavel. "Excuse me for interrupting, Miss Brett, but can you assure us there is some material point lurking under this welter of detail?"

"I can indeed, Your Honor."

"Then please get to it."

"Thank you." Brett paused and adjusted her blue silk scarf. "Mr. Thomson, the Viceroy of Ireland at the time of that decisive battle in Wexford was Lord Earl Charles Cornwallis who —*earlier* in his career—was a major general in command of British forces during the colonial Revolution. His army raided American troops in South Carolina and Virginia and was finally besieged and beaten decisively at Yorktown. With Cornwallis, of course, fell the British cause in America.

"There were *Taggarts*," Brett said, after a pause, "who fought and died in those battles against General Cornwallis in South Carolina and Virginia and Yorktown."

Again Flood tapped his gavel. "Your *point*, Miss Brett. I insist you get to it."

"Your Honor, the bloodied ground where the British overwhelmed and destroyed the Irish pikeman of Wexford"—Brett paused again—"that patch of high ground, Your Honor, was known as *Vinegar Hill*. General Adam Taggart named his estate on the Brandywine after that historic engagement, where Taggart blood was spilled, as it was at Yorktown and Normandy. I find it curious"—she stared skeptically at Earl Thomson— "that the witness never heard of Vinegar Hill, either from those senior officers and military scholars at Rockland or from his close friend, who flew all the way from Germany to testify for him here, Captain Derek 'Ace' Taggart."

Davic stood to object, but Earl said casually, "I believe it's a question of context, Miss Brett. I've probably heard of a dozen battles between the British and the Irish, but I didn't connect any of them to the Taggart Place. Derek never mentioned it, by the way. But my interest at Rockland was modern military history, tanks and aerial warfare. Pikemen weren't my speciality, I'll admit."

Davic was still standing, but relaxed again, gratified by Thomson's frank and reasonable responses. His attitude suddenly gave Brett a clear insight into their weaknesses—the very superiority of Davic's position was one minus factor, an inevitable overconfidence, and the other was the potentially destructive character of Earl Thomson himself.

"Your Honor," Davic was saying now, but with a good-humored inflection, "I believe I should object to this digression by People's counsel. If she is demonstrating she's done her homework, earned her keep, if you will, fine. But I think we've indulged her sufficiently. These military trivia have nothing to do with the issues at trial—"

"Sustained," Flood said. "Miss Brett, let us consider the history lesson over and done with."

"Exception, Your Honor."

"That's noted." A line of exasperation appeared around the judge's mouth. "Get on with your examination."

"Mr. Thomson"—Brett walked past the witness stand and turned to face both Thomson and the jurors—"you heard the Reverend Oliver Jessup, who is also known as Goldie Boy, describe the man who'd stolen your Porsche, did you not?"

"Yes, ma'am. I did. I also heard Oliver Jessup describe how he blew a kiss at the little girl who—"

Judge Flood sounded the gavel. "The witness will limit his answers to the questions."

"Sorry, sir," Thomson's eyes glinted with confident amusement.

"The thief," Brett continued evenly, "was described as a middle-aged man with gray hair, a red face and thick glasses. Mr. Thomson, do you have a friend or acquaintance who answers to such a description?"

"I don't think so, ma'am. To the best of my knowledge, I don't."

"Have you noticed anyone of that description following you about lately?"

"Can't say that I have, ma'am."

"Would you like to think about that answer a moment? That gray-haired, red-faced man with thick glasses obviously knew a good deal about your comings and goings. He also knew how to operate your sophisticated automobile. Do any of the mechanics who service your car fit the description Oliver Jessup gave the court?"

"No . . . the Porsche is checked regularly in Jenkintown. The mechanic's from Stuttgart, his name is Gunther, he's about twenty-five and he had blond hair and blue eyes—"

"But this gray-haired automobile thief," Brett persisted, "must have known you were going to be at The Green Lantern that Friday afternoon. And he also must have felt pretty sure he wouldn't be interrupted in the act of stealing your car. Aren't those logical assumptions, Mr. Thomson?"

"Objection, Your Honor. People's counsel knows her questions are improper. She has no right to ask the witness to make assumptions about anything at all."

"Sustained. Miss Brett, you assured me that you had relevant and substantial information to introduce. So far you haven't demonstrated anything of the sort."

"I can only ask the court's indulgence," Brett said. "The man described by Oliver Jessup is guilty at least of grand theft auto. He may also be a kidnapper and rapist. I believe it's reasonable and substantial to inquire into the accused's knowledge of that phantom thief and pervert, that sodomist and rapist who is apparently invisible to everyone but the God-fearing eyes of Goldie Boy Jessup—"

Davic was on his feet shouting before Brett finished. "Your *Honor,* she cannot be allowed to impugn the sworn testimony of the Reverend Jessup. Her sarcasm is improper. Her use of the word 'phantom' is derisive and insulting."

"Sustained. The stenographer will strike the references to a phantom thief."

"Your Honor," Brett said. "I apologize for that intemperate remark. But Mr. Davic has repeatedly insisted that Shana Selby mistakenly identified Earl Thomson. If Shana's attacker was, *in fact,* this gray-haired, red-faced man we've been told about, I'd think Mr. Davic would be very grateful for that information."

Judge Flood said, "I'll ignore your sarcasm, Miss Brett. But I am becoming impatient. I don't need to remind you that the defense is under no burden to prove anything. The true perpetrator is properly of no consequence or relevance to them. For the last time, Miss Brett. If you have meaningful points to make, you must do so without any further delay."

Assuming a mildly chastened manner, Brett returned to her table. But no dissembling was necessary when she noticed Shana's white face and the message the bailiff had placed on Brett's casebook. The note had Wilger's initials on it. Her spirits sank to ground zero at the one-word message: "Nothing."

Brett knew she had stalled as long as it was safe and prudent to. The information about the Thomson's chauffeur, the background from the *Britannica* on Vinegar Hill, even her inquiry about the phantom thief, had been smokescreens to buy time and delay her main thrust at Thomson.

But she wasn't done yet; so long as she was the lightning rod for the emotional atmosphere in these proceedings, she felt sure Davic would give her all the rope she needed, enough to hang her, in fact. His confidence was based on the information they'd got from Eberle's wiretap. They knew exactly what was in the white envelope on her table, and Earl Thomson was prepared for it; his responses would have been carefully designed and rehearsed to explain just how Shana Selby had come into possession of that blood-streaked swastika.

Davic would allow her to inquire in "safe" and "unemotional" areas, where there was no chance of a spark to set Thomson off. He seemed composed and at ease now, but beneath his unruffled manner, Brett could sense a dangerously strained anger and hostility.

If, she thought, she could casually lead Earl into areas he was confidently prepared for, into those safe and predictable havens where even Davic might not perceive the dangers, then —she decided grimly—she might use the only weapon available to her, a weapon not in her hands but in Earl Thomson's own violent compulsions.

Gently, she thought, as she faced the witness. Let him run smooth and easy until he has the bit in his teeth, until the spurs of fear struck him . . .

"Mr. Thomson," she said, "the afternoon you were in The Green Lantern, you wore a distinctive ornament about your neck, did you not?"

"If you say so, ma'am, I'll take your word for it."

"According to Ellie May Cluny, the waitress at The Green Lantern, you *were* wearing such an ornament. Would you like the court stenographer to read Miss Cluny's testimony?"

"No, I'll take her word on it, too, ma'am." Earl shrugged, smiled. "I frequently wear things like that, medals, emblems or chains around my neck."

Earl was completely at ease, and so was Davic. They were both prepared for this line of inquiry; they seemed almost eager to harmlessly defuse the prosecution's anticipated bombshell.

Brett picked up the envelope, which contained the broken chain and swastika. Davic and Thomson tensed themselves pleasurably for her next question. Captain Slocum relaxed at the bailiff's table, watching Brett with an expectant smile. They waited with assured and nearly sadistic anticipation for her to trip the wire that would spring the trap.

They expected the swastika now. They were ready for it. And when Brett would finally ask, as ask she must, *when* and *where* Earl Thomson had lost that pendant emblem, she knew his rehearsed answers would dismiss this last shred of Commonwealth evidence. As the fingerprints had been explained, as Shana's identification had been discredited, so the lost swastika would somehow be innocently accounted for.

Brett caught them all by surprise by dropping the envelope and returning to the stand. She said, "Mr. Thomson, are you familiar with the area at the intersection of Fairlee Road and Mill Lane?"

"In a general way." Earl Thomson looked quickly to Davic, who was rising. "I've driven by there."

"The Selbys' home is on Mill Lane near Fairlee," Brett said. "Isn't it a fact that you've driven there at night on more than one occasion—"

"Objection, Your Honor."

"—since Shana Selby was kidnapped and raped?"

"Objection! People's counsel is making damaging insinuations. An adverse effect on the jury could be created by *any* answer my client gives. The answer to both questions is: what *difference* does it make? What possible point is there in my client's knowledge of where the plaintiff lives? Or whether he has driven by that intersection since her alleged accident?"

"Sustained. The jury will ignore the People's last inquiry."

But Earl Thomson said unexpectedly, "I'd like to add something if I may, sir."

The last exchange seemed to have tipped the defendant's careful emotional balance; his voice was loud and unrestrained. "Yes, I drove over to Mill Lane one night a month or so ago, I've got no reason to hide it or deny it. I'm sitting here like a fish in a barrel, everybody taking shots whenever—"

"Your Honor!" Davic overrode his client. "I don't want Mr. Thomson to discuss the matter. The issue raised by the People's counsel is extraneous—"

Earl Thomson ignored this. "Don't I have a right to talk, Your Honor? Implications have been made and I'd like to clear them up."

Dom Lorso leaned forward and said in a bitter whisper to Davic, "Goddammit, can't you put a cork in him?"

Davic murmured behind a well-manicured hand, "No, Mr. Lorso, I can't."

"Very well, Mr. Thomson," Judge Flood said. "The court will hear your clarification."

Thomson said, "I did drive to Fairlee Road one night last month. I stopped and got out of my car. The lady here must know that or she wouldn't have asked. I'm not so ignorant of legal techniques. Maybe someone saw me there, got my license, I'm not denying I was there. I never have. I was trying to visualize what happened. It wasn't morbid curiosity."

To Brett's surprise, Earl Thomson's voice had become effectively and firmly assertive. "Someone stole my car and deliberately ran down a girl riding a bicycle. *I've* been accused of that, and of kidnapping and raping her. I went back to see if I could find something the police might have overlooked. I wanted to get the feel of the place, the mood of the woods and the sky and the terrain, the angle of Fairlee Road where it curves past Mill Lane, the incline of the shoulders. In military science, that kind of appraisal is called the 'sense of the battlefield.' That may sound strange to some of you, but the opponents of Napoleon Bonaparte were intimidated by what they called his eye of

455

battle. He *saw* what others didn't. I can also tell you that General George Patton, one of America's finest commanders in World War II, had the same gift. In his memoirs it's reported that he actually *saw* the ghosts of Roman centurions on the battlefields of modern France. In the Ardennes when his Third Army raced to relieve Bastogne, Patton observed in the fog—"

Lorso reached forward and jabbed Davic in the back. "For Christ's sake!" he hissed at him. *"Do something."*

But Adele Thomson's eyes shone with pride. "It's beautiful, it's true," she whispered.

When Thomson at last finished, Brett asked him quietly, "And were you successful in your search, Mr. Thomson? Did you find any evidence, or glimpse some truth the police had overlooked?"

"No, ma'am, I didn't. But I went there to help them, and for no other reason."

Brett nodded thoughtfully and walked to the plaintiff's table and picked up the envelope containing Earl's swastika. Her eyes went to the closed rear door of the courtroom and the immobile marshals. Her time was running out. She had to work on the knife-edge of the present.

She opened the envelope and unwrapped the sheets of tissue paper from the silver swastika and links of chain. A soft stir of whispers drifted through the courtroom. Flood tapped for order.

"Mr. Thomson—" She held up the swastika by a link of chain; the silver crosses glistened in the clear light. "Is that what you were wearing at The Green Lantern?"

"Yes, it is," Earl said. "You can see it's got my initials on it. I'd about given up hope of ever seeing it again." His smile was bland.

Davic rose. "Your Honor, if the object the People's counsel is displaying is meant to be a Commonwealth exhibit, I ask that she identify it. But if the exhibit is part of this case, it should have been available to the defense during discovery proceedings months ago. Since it wasn't, we've got to ask where it's been all this time."

"You've made several points, Counselor," Judge Flood observed, "but no objection. So we'll take your points in order. Miss Brett, do you intend to introduce that object as a Commonwealth exhibit? If so, would you define it for the record?"

"Yes, Your Honor." Brett raised the swastika so the jury could examine it. "This emblem was the symbol of a political party in Germany before World War II. It is a decorative or symbolic ornament in the form of a cross with equal arms, each of which has another arm turned at right angles to it. The object is silver. It has the initials E.T. on the reverse side of the cross of one arm, a date on another, November 9, 1938. The clerk will identify the object as People's Exhibit Three."

Brett put the swastika on the exhibit table, placing it between the photograph of Earl's license plate and the cards identifying his fingerprints from Vinegar Hill.

Then she said, "Mr. Thomson, did you remove that—necklace on the night you showered before dining with your mother?"

"Yes, I did. I took off my watch, as I've already told you, and my rings, and what you refer to as a necklace."

"You couldn't have lost that object while you were driving from The Green Lantern to your home?"

"Of course not. If I had, I'd have mentioned it to Santos."

"But you didn't tell Santos you'd lost your thirty-five-thousand-dollar automobile, did you, Mr. Thomson?"

"That's different. I've explained often enough that I didn't think the car was stolen. But a piece of personal jewelry, I'd have missed it right away."

"Because of its value?" Brett asked.

"For whatever reason, I don't see what difference it makes."

"Does the date on the emblem have a sentimental or emotional significance for you, Mr. Thomson?"

Davic, Brett noticed, was reluctant to object. Earl's voice was mild, but a potential violence seemed close to the surface of his smile . . . "Miss Brett, I'm sure you know the significance of that date, November 9, 1938. It commemorates an event in Germany called Crystal Night. I'm not sure of the details, but it was some sort of national event. I asked a jeweler in Philadelphia to engrave that date with my initials but he refused to do it. He told me that Crystal Night had offensive memories for him. Like a Japanese in this country might remember Pearl Harbor, I guess. So I got someone else to do the job. There's nothing illegal about that."

457

"Then this emblem," Brett said casually, "couldn't have been what you were searching for on Fairlee Road?"

"Objection, Your Honor."

"Sustained."

Earl shrugged. "No. As you yourself said, it *couldn't* have been."

Davic seemed relieved by his client's apparently calm response. He said, "Your Honor, Mr. Thomson has admitted that People's Exhibit Three belongs to him. But since he also admitted that he lost that object, I respectfully ask you to instruct the People to tell us where they found it. Or how it came into their possession."

Brett said, "If I may anticipate His Honor's instructions, that object was worn by the man who kidnapped, tortured and raped Shana Selby. She tore it from his throat the night he attacked her. It is Shana's blood, dried and blackened, that is still visible on those crosses—"

Davic's objections cut across Brett's final words. "I object to the hearsay, Your Honor, and to the incriminating, baseless insinuations . . ."

"Sustained." Flood sounded his gavel for silence. "The hearsay is not admissible. The jury will ignore it."

"But, Your Honor," Brett protested, "you have already told Mr. Davic he may re-call the plaintiff for further examination."

"But I cannot allow you to paraphrase what Miss Selby herself is best qualified to tell us."

"All right, Your Honor, but how can my paraphrase be defined by Mr. Davic as an incriminating insinuation? I've stated that Shana Selby ripped that insignia from the throat of her *attacker*. By the sworn testimony elicited by Mr. Davic from his own witness, the Reverend Oliver Jessup, that attacker was a gray-haired, red-faced man with thick glasses. Is Mr. Davic casting doubts on his own witness? If not, how could the accusation possibly incriminate the *dark-haired, young* man *without* glasses now seated in the witness stand?"

"Your Honor," Earl Thomson said, "if it's not out of order, I'd like to make a point here."

With noticeable tension, Davic said, "Your Honor, it is not in my client's best interest to respond to any of these inquiries. He is eager to cooperate, which is commendable. But I must

458

instruct him to remain silent. Also, the gray-haired man described by the Reverend Jessup would seem not to have been the plaintiff's attacker—he was more correctly her companion."

"I'd still like to straighten this out, Your Honor." Earl's tone remained amiable but persistent. "I'm a pretty fair judge of what's in my best interest, after all. That's something every soldier learns, if he intends to survive combat." He smiled pleasantly. "Miss Brett is reluctant to call her exhibit by its proper name. I think her confusion begins right here."

George Thomson leaned forward and spoke sharply to Davic. "Can't you get a recess, for Christ's sake?"

"I wouldn't risk it. It's safer to let him finish."

"You better be goddamn sure, Davic."

"We can destroy Miss Brett with two questions. I'm sure of *that*. But it's not safe to cut your son off. I'm even more sure of *that*."

Earl Thomson was saying in pedantic tone, "The young lady representing the prosecution doesn't seem to know what to call the object she's identified as an exhibit. Once she referred to it as a pendant, then as an emblem, in another instance, a necklace and finally as an ornament. I wonder if she knows what its real name is, or if she's afraid or embarrassed to use it. Or perhaps she's shrewd enough to simply let the jury's imagination work overtime. That is a swastika, ladies and gentlemen," Earl said, pointing at the gleaming silver crosses. "A *swastika*. Miss Brett is well aware, I think, that people tend to regard anyone wearing that insignia as some kind of racist or anti-Semite. But that isn't true, philosophically or historically. The fact—"

"Mr. Thomson," Judge Flood interrupted him, "you asked the court's permission to make some point or other. But I fail to perceive any pertinence in these comments."

"If you'll indulge me for just another moment," Earl said courteously, "I'd like to explain that the swastika *per se* is not ugly or obscene. It dates back to Greek mythology. It's been used as a religious and heraldic device in India and in Finland. Great Britain, in fact, used a swastika on postage stamps it issued in Hong Kong some years ago. I'm trying, Your Honor, to make the good people on this jury realize that because I owned and wore a swastika—its more proper name is a gammadion, by the way, a cross made of four gammons—because of that I don't have any particular interest in concentration camps or all the Jews who reportedly died in them."

"*Stop him,*" George Thomson said to Davic.

"They've lied about a lot of things in that war, of course." A faint tic pulled at the corner of Earl's mouth. "They've lied about me during this trial too. She lied"—Earl nodded toward Shana—"she lied when she claimed she got my gammadion the night she was hurt."

With a sudden tension, he went on, "You've lied, too, Miss Brett, and we know that. About things that happened to you, or the other way around."

"Your Honor," Davic said, raising his voice now. "I ask you to consider the ordeal my client's been through these past few months."

Flood sounded his gavel. "Mr. Thomson, the court has allowed you ample latitude. I will now ask you a two-part question, which Miss Brett has delayed asking: *Where* and *when* did you lose that pendant which you wore at The Green Lantern, and which you've heard described as People's Exhibit Three?"

"Your Honor, please forgive me." It was Davic who was stalling now, obviously hoping to ease Thomson's spiraling anxiety. "May I ask one concession? That the court's questions be put singly to my client to give him time to consider his answers *seriatim.*"

"Very well, Mr. Thomson, let's start with the first one. *When* did you lose that object?"

Davic's interruption gave Thomson a saving respite; his expression cleared, the glaze of unreason faded from his eyes, his expression became thoughtful.

"It was a Sunday morning," he recalled, "six or eight weeks ago, cold but sunny. I wore a cardigan over a flannel shirt." He nodded at the exhibit table. "I was also wearing that swastika."

Brett could not stop him now, interrupt or object for any reason whatsoever. She looked at the clock and the closed doors of the courtroom. As she did she caught a glance from Captain Slocum, a look of complacence. There was no malice or triumph in the captain's expression; this is how it is, his cold eyes told her, this is the way it's played, you lose, lady.

Thomson was saying, "Two cadets from Rockland were

with me, Richard Knarl and Willie Joe Bast, both good friends of mine. I'm sure they'll remember what I was wearing that morning."

Brett stood helplessly beside Shana and waited for the final blows. "And where was it you lost that swastika?" Judge Flood said.

Earl replied promptly. "At Longwood Gardens, Your Honor, on the day of that exhibition of Grand Concourse automobiles. Dick and Willie Joe and I went there together. There was an interruption when the girl's father arrived, but we've been through that." Earl smiled at Brett. "Somehow or other," he continued, "the chain broke or was pulled loose when my motorcycle swerved into the side of the greenhouse. When the doctors were checking my eye at the hospital, I realized the chain and swastika were gone, they were on the ground somewhere back at Longwood."

"You reported that loss?" Judge Flood asked.

"I guess I was in too much pain at the hospital to mention it to the nurses or the doctors. But I remembered it after my father drove me home. He reported it to Captain Slocum. Mr. Lorso also called Lieutenant Eberle."

The double rear doors of the courtroom opened. The marshals turned and nodded at Sergeant Burt Wilger. Harry Selby was beside him.

"I was still angry and shaken up," Earl Thomson added, "but I knew if we didn't start looking for my gammadion, there was a good chance somebody could find it and walk off with it."

Sergeant Wilger approached the bailiff's desk and gave the officer a narrow, oblong package with a note in Selby's handwriting taped to it. The detective ignored Slocum's hard, inquiring glance. Meanwhile, Harry Selby took his seat behind the plaintiff's table. Brett and Shana didn't notice; they faced the witness stand.

Earl Thomson was staring with bold challenge at Brett. "If your arithmetic is as good as mine, you'll see that I lost that swastika at least six weeks *after* Miss Selby claims she got her hands on it."

The bailiff crossed behind the press section and placed Wilger's package and Selby's note on the plaintiff's table.

"And," Thomson continued, "if your geography is good,

461

Miss Brett, you'll realize I lost that necklace and swastika"—no one at the defense table had as yet noticed Selby—"at a time and place where the people who've brought charges against me could very easily have found it and, in fact, very probably *did* find it. Or someone could have picked it up and sent it to them to get me involved in their snake's nest of lies—"

Flood rapped for order. "You've answered my questions, Mr. Thomson. I've granted you more flexibility than strict procedure usually permits, but I think the jury is entitled to know something of the emotional pressure you've been under. But you will refrain from any further elaboration." He glanced at Brett. "Does People's counsel have any further questions?"

Brett stood motionless, reading the note the bailiff had brought to her table. Her expression was puzzled. "May I ask the court's indulgence, Your Honor? I need a few moments . . ."

"Very well." Judge Flood looked to the defense table. "Mr. Davic?"

"If it please the court, how much longer must this young man's ordeal be drawn out? If any one fact has been made abundantly clear in this hearing, it is that the prosecution has failed to make even a shadow of a case against Earl Thomson."

Davic continued to speak, but the words were sounds without sense to Selby, vibrations without meaning, because his consciousness of reality was still blurred and distorted by the film he had watched in the projection room in Komoto's pornography shop in Philadelphia.

. . . A black boy played and laughed with youngsters on a green lawn, diamond-bright with drops of water. A blond child in pigtails sprayed them with a hose.

The air in Komoto's screening room was close, the glow from the screen glinted on the sweat on Wilger's forehead.

. . . Sergeant Hank Ledge appeared in the foreground of the screen, striding toward the playing children. Raising the .45 caliber automatic, he fired twice, the sounds of the shattering reports disrupting the laughter of the children and the soft, hissing spray of the water. Dookey Barrow's first screams were hoarse and astonished. The pain did not pierce instantly, although the right side of his face flamed with blood. The little girl laughed and splashed him with water. Crying, knowing like a dumb animal that he was mortally hurt, Dookey ran in circles until his

stumbling feet found a graveled pedestrian walk leading into the shopping arcade . . .

"The presence of Earl Thomson's fingerprints at Vinegar Hill," Davic was saying, "were proved to have been placed there on a casual social occasion *weeks* before the alleged attack on the plaintiff."

As Flood frowned, Davic added, "Your Honor, I know you instructed me not to touch on areas which I intend to include in my closing statements. But if it won't try Your Honor's patience, I would like to briefly mention that . . ."

. . . on the screen in Komoto's shop, Selby recognized Spencer Barrow, the youngster who had leaped so high and exuberantly to catch a pass from him on that distant autumn afternoon. He was at first base when Sergeant Ledge appeared in the film, striding from the outfield. The black bulk of the .45 was like an extension of the sergeant's big hand.

The pitcher threw a strike. The crowd cheered. At that instant, Sergeant Ledge fired a single shot, which blew away the top of Spencer Barrow's cranial vault. The other players stared in mild bewilderment at the body sprawled on the baseline. They turned to the umpire for a decision. Spectators seemed eager to hear his ruling. They crowded around him, gesturing and talking. The umpire blew his whistle, raised his hand, shouted, "Play ball!"

A camera picked up Jarrell Selby running from the woods behind the baseball diamond. Another camera had zoomed in as young Selby lifted Dookey Barrow from a graveled walk. The images dissolved to a young girl in leotards drinking from a fountain in the mall. Music was playing, the arcade was brittle with cool sunlight, streaming with shoppers . . .

"The identification of Earl Thomson by Miss Selby," Davic said, his tone theatrical, "has been discredited by the testimony of a disinterested witness."

. . . Jarrell Selby and Dookey Barrow appeared in the mall. Haggard expressions, bloody clothes. Holding the dying boy in his arms, Jarrell carried him through the crowds. He shouted for help at the people around them, but it was as if a thick wall of glass stood between them. No one paid attention to him or the bleeding figure in his arms.

At the end of the arcade, Sergeant Ledge waited for them . . .

"This tissue of lies and innuendos," Davic announced to the jury, "which we have exposed, were designed to avenge the plaintiff's father, Jonas Selby, against George Thomson."

Brett by then had read the note. She unwrapped the cassette the bailiff had delivered and turned slowly until she met Selby's eyes.

"Your Honor," Davic continued, "the defense moves at this time that the court direct the jury to dismiss all charges against Earl Thomson and free him unconditionally."

"Miss Brett," Judge Flood said, "I must ask you again, before I rule on the defense motion, do you have any further questions to ask before I discharge the witness."

. . . A small breeze stirred Jarrell Selby's brown hair. His expression was perplexed, then despairing, his burden suddenly intolerable. Holding the boy close, he lowered himself to his knees among the shoppers in Summitt City's arcade. Sergeant Ledge raised his automatic and killed Jarrell Selby and the dying boy he was holding with two deliberately spaced shots . . .

They had torn apart the inside of Komoto's shop trying to find the cassette. After it seemed hopeless, after Wilger called East Chester to tell Brett they'd found nothing, Selby noticed that Komoto was watching them with a detached smile. Also, he noticed that Komoto's hands were no longer trembling; when he'd poured himself coffee earlier, the spout of the ceramic pot had almost tipped over the cup.

"Petey, you're not as good a businessman as I thought," Selby said. "You should have at least listened to my offer."

"But I've got nothing to sell you."

"No." Selby shook his head, Wilger watched him with sudden interest. "The fact is, Petey, we could never top an offer from Thomson. He could double it, and I'm sure he promised you he would. We've been wasting our time."

"I know nothing that would help you, truly."

"Maybe. But I don't see why your wife should suffer because you're after the top dollar. I should tell you, we're working with Senator Dixon Lester and he's already opened Thomson's safety deposit box."

"I know nothing of that, believe me."

"The senator is willing to put a rocket under immigration." Selby glanced at Wilger. "I think you should call Maria-Encarna and give her a couple of hours head start. We'll wait here with you, Petey"—he looked at his watch—"until she's on a Grey-hound out of town. *Then* we'll call the senator."

"You're a bleeding heart idiot," Wilger said. "Why the hell do her any favors?"

"Why not, Burt? She's not involved. If she splits now, she'll be a jump ahead of Immigration. A bus to Indianapolis, say, then she can drop down to Houston. I've got a friend in Brownsville, Texas, a Mexican, one of the first soccer players they brought up to our league as a place-kicker. He'll look after her, keep her until it's safe to make a run for it."

Wilger picked it up. "If she starts right away, keeps her mouth shut and stays out of sight, she could be over the border in two or three days."

Komoto cleared his throat. He smiled, but not enough to show his strong, white teeth. "Maria won't believe you, she won't leave."

"Angel Ramirez owns a bar and a souvenir shop," Selby told him. "He's a good man, lots of guts. He didn't know any-thing about contact football, but he tried his damndest. Got his lights shot out a few times. He'll look after her."

"Maria-Encarna never hurt anyone in her life."

"That's why she's getting a break. Ramirez knows *coyotes*, he'll get an honest one to take her across the border into Matamoros. Find her a job, too. Can she do anything that doesn't require a partner?"

They stared at Komoto. He blinked his eyes.

"Poor goddamn beaner, she'll understand why you had to pull the chain on her, Petey. Sure she will . . ." Wilger picked up Komoto's phone and began dialing. "It's business, that's all."

Komoto blinked again. "Would you care for coffee now? Please put the phone down. Maria-Encarna would not under-stand, she has no head for business. She leaves that up to me."

"Hang up, Burt."

The Summitt City film, Komoto revealed, was locked away in his office safe.

"Miss Brett?" Judge Flood's voice was insistent. "You have heard the defense motion to dismiss the charges against the defendant. Do you have any question before the court rules?"

As she returned to the witness stand, Brett said, "Yes, Your Honor, I have several questions to ask the witness."

Holding the cassette in front of her, she paused and watched Earl Thomson react to the stenciled words. He stiffened in the chair, his strong hands tightening on its arms. The tic began to pull at his mouth again.

"Mr. Thomson," Brett said, "is it still your sworn testimony that you had no knowledge of *any* member of the Selby family prior to the attack on the plaintiff? You're under oath, remember."

Dom Lorso turned slowly and looked at Harry Selby. The Sicilian's face was impassive. He studied Earl Thomson, his expression bitter. Picking a fleck of tobacco from his lower lip, he glanced at George Thomson.

"There was another way to handle it, Giorgio. I told you that all along."

Thomson nodded, staring at the cassette in Brett's hand. "Maybe I should have listened, Dom," he said.

The two men looked at each other in silence.

"What is it?" Adele demanded. She was frightened by their sudden silence. Her head swung between them, the blond curls trembling like the petals of a flower on a withered stalk.

"We're beaten, Adele," her husband told her.

"What's happening?"

"I just told you." Thomson smiled wearily. His tone was almost indifferent, as if he were discussing the fate of figures in a landscape. "You heard Dom. There was another way, but we didn't take it . . ."

"But you *promised* me, George. You *swore* my son would be safe, that you'd protect him. You lied—"

Flood rapped to still her furious whispers.

"Mr. Thomson," Brett warned the witness then, "it is my duty to inform you that concealing knowledge of a capital crime constitutes a felony of similar gravity." Brett held the cassette in front of Thomson. "Now. Do you have knowledge of this film? And information relating to events that occurred in Summitt City, Tennessee, on October 17 last year?"

"Objection, Your Honor. She hasn't given the witness time to answer her first question."

"I'll repeat it then," Brett said. "Mr. Thomson, is it still your sworn testimony that you had no knowledge of the Selby family prior to the attack on the plaintiff?"

"I don't think you expect a yes or no to that question," Thomson said. "I'm sure that would disappoint you."

"Mr. Thomson," Judge Flood said, "I remind you—"

But Thomson ignored him. "You'd like the chance to dispense some Christian forgiveness and mercy first, wouldn't you? But I'll have to disappoint you there, Miss Brett, and my father and Captain Slocum. Because forgiveness is the Christian decadence that perverts justice." His eyes were bright. He was obviously savoring this moment, a new excitement evident in his expression. "I embody an idea, a principle, that insists that the elitist decision is the only valid legislator in human affairs. Rule by the best. I acted to save the truth. Everyone else lied to save—"

"Your *Honor* . . ." Davic had been shouting through most of Thomson's tirade. "Your Honor, my client is under no obligation to volunteer . . ." A quiver of panic entered his voice. "Mr. Thomson may invoke the Fifth Amendment, Your Honor. He can and will refuse to answer any further questions on the grounds that such answers might tend to incriminate him."

Judge Flood sounded his gavel. "Miss Brett, you know that the defendant cannot be requested to place himself in jeopardy. His attorney has already stressed that." Turning to Thomson, he said, "You have the right to remain silent on the advice of your counsel. While you consider your position, the court has a question for People's counsel. Miss Brett . . ."

"Your Honor?"

"Is the film on that cassette relevant to the charges and specifications in the indictment against the defendant?"

Brett paused. "They establish, Your Honor, the continuing inconsistencies in his testimony—"

"That would seem to be an evasive answer, Miss Brett. I've told you I would not admit inconsistencies unless they were substantive and relevant, or were probative of deliberate perjury. And as far as the cassette is concerned, I'm not going to admit it as evidence in this case, nor will I permit any further questions about its contents . . ."

During these explanations, Selby became aware of the growing tension around him. It was like the weight that settled

467

in the air before the first storm clouds appeared, a charged tension that was usually shattered by rumbles of distant thunder or a sudden lightning flash.

Selby was something of an authority on tension . . . he had experienced those areas of human response a good deal more than the average person. He had been conditioned for years to the provocative cadence of snap counts and referees' whistles and the sudden warning roar from packed stadiums.

It was the breaking point of those moments that professionals could usually predict and defend themselves against. Amateurs tended to be caught off-balance. But there was a dangerous equipoise in such situations that experts recognized—the compression of emotional elements beyond given flashpoints. There they burst and erupted in spasms of violence.

But with all Selby's experience, he missed the breaking point of the trial, because it came from an unlikely source and spiraled with irrevocable pressure in three unpredictable sequences.

Earl Thomson interrupted Flood's discourse to Brett by suddenly shouting at Shana, "You claimed I hated you, you swore that under oath, but that was *wrong*. I hated something close that I couldn't—"

As the marshals moved from their posts, Earl pointed at Shana. "I didn't hate you. I *disciplined* you. I *controlled* you because I had to. You were a diversion, a tactic—"

His voice broke like a child's, but it rose above the hammering of Flood's gavel. "You didn't know what I hated, why I had to hate it." He was shouting frantically. "Nobody asked me *that*, nobody thought of *that* . . ."

Turning around quickly, Shana said to her father, "Help him, please, I don't care, can't you *do* something, *help him?*"

Selby was so stunned by her outbreak of compassion for this miserable young man's pain, that he didn't immediately identify the object shining dully against Adele Thomson's plaid robe. His peripheral vision was usually automatic, inherited from anticipating a thousand blind-side blocks, but he wasn't aware of what was about to happen until he saw the shocked glaze in George Thomsn's eyes.

There was a gun in Adele Thomson's fragile hand. Dom Lorso was close enough to strike the gun aside, deflect the barrel from pointing directly at George Thomson. But he said in a tired voice, "It's better this way, Giorgio, better for all of us. You know that it is . . ."

Selby threw himself over the railing in front of his daughter and Brett, but the Sicilian sat motionless, his eyes lidded in his gray face, and watched Adele Thomson fire three shots which struck George Thomson just below his heart and sent him crashing backward, already dying, into the arms of the shocked marshals. The bailiff reached Mrs. Thomson then and took the gun from her withered fingers.

Selby held his daughter and Brett close to him and listened incredulously to the sound of Earl Thomson's sudden laughter threading in a senseless counterpoint through the roaring confusion in the courtroom.

CHAPTER THIRTY-EIGHT

In mid-June, some eight weeks after Earl Thomson's aborted trial, Selby sat in Senator Lester's private office, which adjoined a conference room furnished with a bar, a burnished walnut table and a dozen leather armchairs.

Summer was well advanced in the capital. The Potomac was swollen and shimmered with heat and the leaves of the trees on the banks were a lush, dark green, moist with an oily humidity.

In an hour or so the avenues would be circled with streams of traffic, but now Selby could see the famous lighted monuments of the city, the great marble heads and figures of the nation's founders gleaming through the darkness.

In the small kitchen beside a reception room, Victoria Kim made tea and heated breakfast rolls. She could hear a murmur from the executive suite, the senator and Selby's muted voices.

Their work was almost done, the debriefings over; Miss Kim had already confirmed Selby's return ticket to Philadelphia. For several days he had been meeting with operative agencies and committees, giving them accounts of his conversations with his brother, Jennifer Easton, George Thomson and various personnel at Summitt City.

Simon Correll's death, given its circumstances, had created a worldwide stir; the news media had covered the story with obsessive intensity. A plant manager, Clem Stoltzer, arriving in the Summitt mall after the slayings, had theorized that the security guard, one Henry Ledge, had attacked Correll without provocation, apparently suffering from a psychotic seizure. Police and ballistic experts testified only that both men had died in an exchange of gunfire from a Beretta Model 951 and a .45 army automatic, both guns found at the scene. There were no witnesses.

A federal investigation of Summitt City's connections to Camp Saliaris and the Chemical Corps was underway with a panel of general officers. A civilian overview was provided by retired congressmen and public officials. These inquiries were coordinated with a probe at East Chester, Pennsylvania, into the criminal conspiracy indictments stemming from Earl Thomson's confession to the charges brought against him by the People of Pennsylvania.

Civic and political leaders from many nations had commented respectfully on the death of Simon Correll. His Excellency, the Suffragan Bishop Waring, spoke to reporters from his new station, the Abbey of St. Georges in Brussels. The bishop said, "It was my privilege to know Mr. Correll and his family for many years. He was a man of the world, a master of complex enterprises, but with a sense of poetry and imagination. In the words of two great Americans, Mr. Correll 'understood profoundly that injustice anywhere threatened justice everywhere' . . . and that 'in the councils of nations as well as the human heart, the concept of God must be a verb, not merely a noun.' "

The participants in the cover-up at East Chester fell like a row of dominoes. Earl Thomson had involved his beloved mother and Miguel Santos. Oliver Jessup incriminated Lieutenant Eberle and Captain Slocum. Slocum, after plea-bargaining futilely with DA Jonathan Lamb, had surrendered the tapes which proved at least one degree of Counselor Allan Davic's complicity. Davic was suspended immediately by the bar associations of Pennsylvania and New York. Slocum was indicted for perjury and misprison of felonies—specifically for lying about the substance of his first interrogation of Earl Thomson and of withholding information relating to Casper Gideen's murder by Lieutenant Gus Eberle, *and* the felonious assaults by Earl Thomson on Shana Selby.

Goldie Boy Jessup contended in shouting, biblical rhetoric

471

that he had been "possessed" by both Captain Slocum and Lieutenant Eberle. He had been forced to accept their "false gods."
He had lied and accepted bribes only to save his life for the
further service of the Lord Jesus.

On the federal level, the investigation of the Chemical
Corps' illegal fiduciary connections with the Correll Group
were complicated by the fact that General Adam Taggart, after
destroying certain military files and all his personal papers, had
seated himself at his desk and taken his life with his service
revolver.

"That was a plus, of course," Senator Lester had confided
to Selby. "Simplified things considerably."

The general's son had not been extradited by Jonathan
Lamb. The U.S. Army had by then placed its own legal hold on
the officer . . . Derek Taggart was arrested in Germany and
ordered to face a court-martial for conduct described in the
Articles of War as detrimental to the "integrity, good reputation
and best interests of the service." It developed that the young
German carpenter with whom Ace Taggart lived off-base had
been picked up by the German police for trafficking in drugs to
the military and using the Frankfurt quarters he shared with
Taggart as the "drop" for these operations.

The federal panel established that General Taggart,
through Camp Saliaris, had for years been misappropriating
massive amounts of U.S. Army chemicals and classified scientific information. Informed speculation held that this was the
true reason the general had taken his life; his soldier's pride
simply could not and would not face the exposure of his long
and personally profitable links to the Correll Group.

Jonathan Lamb, however, did not need an indictment
against Captain Ace Taggart to buttress his charges against
Slocum, Eberle and the other conspirators. He had more than
enough evidence to convict them all.

Miguel Santos, for instance, had changed his testimony
with almost desperate relief. In his second version of what happened the night Shana Selby was raped, he stated that Earl
Thomson had arrived home alone at approximately eleven o'-
clock, his clothing soaked and mud-stained. He had forced Santos to help him dispose of the red Porsche, threatening to have
him both fired and deported to Cuba if he refused. They had

dumped the car later that same night into a deserted, water-filled quarry near Wahasset. Confronted with subpoenaed bank records, Santos reluctantly amplified his statement and admitted that Thomson had given him twenty thousand dollars for this cooperation.

Mrs. Adele Thomson had perjured herself and supported her son's alibi for reasons which could only be speculated on . . . she had retreated into a state of real or affected shock since her fatal shooting of her husband, and had been judged by a competency board as unfit to stand trial at that time.

A court order, secured by Ferdinand Bittermank, had given the federal government possession of the film cassette Harry Selby recovered from Komoto's shop in Philadelphia. This evidence was of only presumptive value now, since the film stock had shredded and dissolved while being reassembled by government technicians.

"It was an amateur's job from start to finish," the senator had told Selby. "Thomson used a second-grade stock, for some reason, didn't understand the technical aspects of splicing and lighting and so forth."

The content of the film as described by Selby and Wilger was not required in any event, since the film itself was not pertinent to the specifics of Jonathan Lamb's indictments.

The People's case against the principal conspirators was without loopholes. Only Judge Desmond Flood and Mr. Dominic Lorso had so far escaped the wide cast of the nets of justice. But everyone else variously faced disbarment, fines, loss of pension, deportation and prison terms . . . Counselor Davic, Captain Slocum and Lieutenant Eberle, the Reverend Oliver Jessup, Miguel Santos. And Earl Thomson.

Thomson's confession was a vindictive document, with a tone of contemptuous satisfaction in its detailed accusations against those who had lied and schemed and suborned for him.

Ferdinand Bittermank attended the federal committee hearings with Selby and Lester. A strongly built man with a cold face, Bittermank had been assigned to complete the government's investigation of the Correll Group network outside the United States. It was through Bittermank's orders that the photographic technicians at the CIA had attempted to "save" and "restore" the Summitt film but the stock had been grainy and disintegrating, and many of the images so blurred and un-focused (as Selby himself had seen), that it would have been difficult to prove anything conclusive from the shredding footage.

Earl Thomson, speaking through his court-appointed attorney, had denied all knowledge of the film, as had Derek Taggart.

Bittermank's position was that Summitt City was now a closed issue, that the Correll Group had been checked and contained at this point in the United States.

Operating with extensive but confidential instructions, Bittermank had instituted an investigation of the Correll Group's commitments with foreign governments—in particular Belgium and the Netherlands, Africa and South America.

"His authority supercedes everyone's in this area," Lester told Selby.

"Summitt City, as Bittermank sees it," Lester continued, "is at present nullified, dysfunctional, isolated, any or all three. In Bittermank's own words; 'We're vaccinated against it.' By which he means his technicians have clamped a surveillance bell over it. They've got the name of the Correll Group's basic chemical formula."

Bittermank's people had picked up oblique references to the various Ancilia strains from taped conversations between General Taggart and Simon Correll, abstracted from one of the last "Snow Virgin recordings." Still, the technicians hadn't identified the compound other than by name and couldn't determine what residue or discernible effects the Ancilia substance left or might leave with its subjects.

Under the umbrella of a government health inspection program, Bittermank's team had examined a significant sample of the population at Summitt. However, they had found no traces of any determinant elements in bodily organs, liver, kidneys, blood stream and so forth. They had hypothesized then that since the Ancilia strain might be a mimetic synthesis of the human brain's own chemical secretions, electro-brain scans couldn't be expected to detect it either.

As indeed they had not.

Lester said, "The effect of this chemical compound on the people at Summitt hasn't shown up in lab tests, and doesn't seem to be a weighable or measurable entity. But I'm goddamn sure, Selby, from what you told me, that the Correll Group *did* achieve an effective control over the minds and emotions of the inhabitants of Summitt City. Still, that mental straitjacketing apparently can't be tracked by sensors, chemical dyes, or presented on graphs. And Bittermank's people, tops in their fields, haven't even been able to pinpoint the *source* of the infusion element, whether it's the water supply or an atmospheric inhalation from the fern and foliage irrigation system which is part of every building, home and office in Summitt, except—significantly, I'd say—those occupied by company managers, security personnel and the Correll living quarters.

"Ferdinand Bittermank," Lester went on, "has carte blanche to investigate the potential international influence of the Correll Group. But even though I've been officially doubleparked on this, Selby, I still took my own personal look at Summitt, based on what you and I learned."

On his orders, the senator explained, a group of sociologists and psychiatrists from various national health agencies had gone to Summitt to examine the inferences which seemed to be warranted from what Wilger and Selby had reportedly seen in the Earl Thomson film.

These classified reports to Senator Lester had so far been as inconclusive as those of Bittermank's medical diagnosticians. The psychiatrists hadn't observed *any social or exterior pathologies whatsoever* among the population at Summitt City. The eccentricities, or divergencies from accepted customs they'd noted were all on a scale in the "upper limits of normal." Nothing aberrant, incapacitating or asocial had been uncovered.

"But the fact is," Selby reminded the senator that morning in his office, "my father was a living example of what Taggart or Correll's people could accomplish with drugs. You told me that yourself."

"But he was a special instance, Selby. They couldn't be complacent about their accomplishment with Jonas Selby because they'd failed with him."

Senator Lester's office was brightening; a sunny sheen covered the big office windows. The white mass of the Lincoln and Washington monuments stood out radiantly against the gradually widening horizons.

Victoria Kim, in a gray sheath dress and white clogs,

brought in tea and breakfast rolls and gave Selby his airlines ticket to Philadelphia. "I've run Clem to bring the car around," she told him. "If you leave in half an hour, you should have plenty of time. There won't be any traffic."

Victoria Kim poured tea into cups patterned with copper-colored flowers. Senator Lester relaxed in his chair, stretched his arms and said, "The fact is, Selby, the attitudes of the men and women at Summitt don't differ significantly from the national average. Our social experts, of course, hedged their conclusions with the usual on–the–other–hand disclaimers and cop-outs. But their consensus is there's no reliable way to establish what's normal in these areas. Or even to say that selfish concern for one's own immediate welfare is wrong.

"People don't want to be their brothers' keepers these days. They flat out *don't want to.* That's a fact you can't argue with."

"You feel I wasted my time trying?" Selby asked him.

Lester picked up a file from his desk, scanned it briefly, then dropped it in front of Selby. "It's spelled out clearly enough. Emotional isolation, the psychiatrists insist, is not only a typical attitude but a sane and reasonable one today in most American communities. Any compulsion to get involved is suspect. It could reflect some mental imbalance, a dangerous or antisocial refusal to accept or come to terms with the status quo. Given our personal information and what inductive reasoning we can apply to the problem, it's still a matter of conjecture whether the population of Summitt is programmed, permanently or not. The effects of the mimic chemicals may wear off. Or the people may go on indefinitely exactly as they are. It would be difficult to tell in either case, because our experts tell me they'd probably find the same rate of indifference they found at Summitt if they'd taken their samples in St. Louis or Boston or Atlanta or anywhere else for that matter."

"From personal experience," Victoria Kim said, "loving one's neighbor is fine with dead–bolts on your doors and a big Doberman trotting at your side when you're jogging. It won't keep you warm nights, but it can keep you alive."

The senator's phone rang. It was his chauffeur, Clem, on the limo phone from the congressional parking lot. "We'll be right down," Lester told him.

Standing, he said to Selby, "I'll get your father's diaries

476

before I forget. By the way, Bittermank wanted to Xerox them for his files. I was pretty sure you wouldn't mind so I didn't bother checking."

When he went into the conference room, Victoria Kim said to Selby, "You mentioned that your daughter was in summer school. Is she enjoying herself?"

"I believe so, thanks. She got behind in several classes and is working hard to catch up. We're planning a vacation in Switzerland over the Christmas holidays. Shana's determined to get a grip on the language."

"No, thanks."

"I'd better tidy things up. If you're in Washington and need anything, you'll call us, won't you? You have our numbers and extensions, I believe."

"Yes, thank you."

She collected the tea things and left the office.

Selby had been tempted to ask her to use her sources, as she had with the Cadles, to help him locate the photographer, J. D. Parks, who had closed his office and left East Chester six weeks earlier. Parks had never billed Selby for the enlargements he'd made of Thomson's license plates. The German janitor was no help. One morning the office was cleaned out, that was all he could tell Selby. But the old man seemed relieved that the 'Nam vet was gone. The breadcrumbs he'd left on the windowsill attracted more ants than birds. Respect for living creatures was fine, the old German grumbled, but not when it violated sanitary codes.

But it was already part of a past Selby didn't want to examine . . . Dade Road, Vinegar Hill, the helicopter over Brandywine Lakes . . . and so he'd decided to forget it.

He looked at the morning sunshine on the Lincoln and Washington monuments. Emotional isolation . . .

Dorcas Brett had taken an official leave of absence after the interruption of Thomson's trial. She had wanted to resign, but Lamb had asked her to put off any final decision until he had completed his indictments against Slocum and the others.

The last night Selby had spent with her, she had confessed she felt fragmented, as if pieces of herself were scattered everywhere. "I'm more part of your life and Shana's than I am of my own. I can't define myself with any accuracy, and I'd like time to try. I want to talk to my father. That's strange, because I haven't needed him for years. As much as I loathed Earl Thomson, I felt he belonged in a hospital instead of prison. Even my anger couldn't convince me otherwise."

She pulled herself gently away from him and sat on the edge of the bed. The dim moonlight glinted on her black hair falling in a mass around her neat, white shoulders.

"I've got a need to please. I've said that before, and it's in conflict usually with a basic need for privacy, or of wanting to be alone. I don't know . . ." She had turned and smiled at him. "The thing is, I don't know if I need to be needed, Harry. Or even wanted to be. Maybe I'm afraid of that for some reason . . ."

Senator Lester came out of the conference room now with Jonas Selby's diaries and notebooks wrapped in brown paper and tied neatly with knotted cord. They walked together to the elevators and took a car down to the lobby. Selby carried his father's diaries under his arm, which seemed, in a sense, to complete the circle . . . they were, after all, what had taken him down to Summitt City in the first place, such a long time ago.

Clem stood beside Lester's limousine in the congressional parking area. He said, "Morning, Mr. Selby," and stowed the diaries and Selby's overnight bag in the trunk.

The sun was higher now, streaming brilliantly across the Lincoln and Washington monuments. Senator Lester looked beyond Selby to these symbols of the American experience and said with a smile, "I don't intend to pull a Fourth of July speech from my pocket, but we stopped Simon Correll and their conglomerate in their tracks in this country and I'm proud of it. The Congress of the United States is not totally composed of ninnies and frauds and opportunists. Of course it won't put to shame the memory of the Platos and Justice Marshalls and Holmeses of the world either. Congressmen, most of us, despite our rhetoric, aren't passionately concerned about saving whales and condors and exotic spiders, although we do get spastic and apoplectic about gun control and abortions and prayers in schools. But with all our pious speechmaking and expensive junkets we're the best representative assembly of free men in the world and I'm proud of the job we do and the country we serve."

"With all due respect," Selby said, "if that's not a Fourth

of July speech, it's a fairly reasonable facsimile. Would you please spell out just what you're trying to tell me?"

"Simply that there are things you and I have got to take on faith, Selby. In certain areas—and Summitt City is one of them —no one, I repeat, *no one,* is ever sure of more than about eighty percent of the truth. It's guessing at the remaining twenty percent that creates conspiracy theories, which can be as dangerous and addictive as heroin, I can tell you."

"Faith is fine," Selby said, "it moves mountains, but so can doubt, as I think some Frenchman said."

"Selby, speculation feeds on itself. I'll grant you it takes faith, a lot of it, to buy the fact that the most sophisticated film labs in the world, I mean the CIA's, managed to screw up the film you and Wilger turned over to them. But what's the alternative? Reckless, subjective evaluation, that's all I can see." The senator patted Selby's arm, a sympathetic gesture. "All this guesswork and anxiety simply reflects a compulsion to make some sense and order out of situations that are naturally painful and inconclusive. Selby, I personally know intelligent people who've gone to their graves convinced there was not just a second gunman, but a half dozen at Dallas the day Jack Kennedy was assassinated. They just wouldn't be convinced otherwise. They wanted some comforting illusion of conspiracy rather than the truth."

"Or they wanted that other twenty percent," Selby said. "Maybe that's the reason they went to their graves."

Senator Lester shook his head firmly. "I'm not going to leave you on that morbid note. You did what you set out to do on your level, you broke that lying conspiracy of Thomson's, and you probably saved that lovely child of yours a future of heartache. Dammit, Selby, accept that. I'm proud I was able to help. As a matter of fact," he went on, removing his wallet and taking a card from it, "we could make a good team. Here's a number where you can always reach me. I know Vickie gave you the office number and extensions, but this is a priority line. Connects directly to any meeting I'm in, regardless of circumstances."

He closed the car door and smiled at Selby through the open rear window. "Have a good flight, Selby. When you're in Switzerland with a glass of something warm after a day on the slopes, think of me. Take care of yourself, Harry, and God bless."

They shook hands and the senator stepped back and Clem raised the rear window from his front control panel.

Selby turned and glanced around as the car swung out of the congressional parking lot. The senator stood with the warm sun on his face, his head thrown back and staring, Selby decided, with an expectant and defiant challenge at the monuments along the mall, the great and sternly righteous figures of his nation's founders.

CHAPTER THIRTY-NINE

The Selbys' hotel in Switzerland was near Lake Geneva in the foothills of the Jungfrau. At dusk, banks of clouds gathered around the peaks but in the morning the sunlight broke through like splendid yellow lances.

The village had no name; it was a suburb, a cluster of buildings on the narrow road between the towns of Zweisimmen and St. Stephan.

Their lodge was settled in a valley circled by stands of fir trees and smooth white hills. The main street—there was just the one thoroughfare actually, the others were only lanes or footpaths—that single street was packed deep with snow and lined with a few shops and a pair of open air cafes. The architecture was pleasantly uniform; all the buildings were faced with cream-colored stucco crisscrossed with stained brown timbers. A steepled church stood at the top of the street, where the road forked to St. Stephan. In this season the shop windows were trimmed with holly wreaths and silver bells and brilliant, glittering lights.

Shadows deepened in the cafes as the last sunlight slanted over the tallest ridges of the Jungfrau. The hazy light made a dull shine on the steeply pitched red-tile roofs of the village. A few bundled-up tourists were window shopping, but most of the skiers were down from the slopes by now, either resting up in their rooms or sitting about the fireplaces in the lounges. Dogs with thick heavy coats trotted along the sidewalks, stopping as if on schedule for a snack from the few people sitting outside at the open air cafes.

A large horse-drawn sled came down the street, harness bells jingling, bringing in a last group of skiers. The youngsters perched on the high seats laughed and waved like celebrities to the people in the cafes in front of the hotels. Most of the ski lift traffic was routed back and forth in long diesel station wagons, but the huge sled with its hand-painted panels was brought out during the holidays as a reminder of the country's festive old traditions.

The horses' hooves thudded rhythmically on the packed snow. Their snorting breath puffed like streams of white smoke from their frosted nostrils. The decorative brass "irons" on their harness straps were relics of a lost craft, delicately worked with tiny figures of knights and hounds and castles.

Shana sat on one of the highest seats of the sled, between two tall teenagers who carried her skis and poles slung over their shoulders. Their laughing voices mingled with the sound of the creaking harness, the pounding hooves and the Angelus bells on the gusting winds.

Selby looked up and smiled at his daughter. He sat in a sidewalk cafe with a pot of chocolate and the British newspapers. Shana laughed and pointed to the young men beside her; they smiled broadly at Selby and pantomimed bowing from the waist and shaking hands.

When the sled stopped, the young men handed Shana's skis and poles down to her and shouted cheerful goodbyes as she joined her father.

"They're brothers, Jules and Guy Brizzard," Shana said, waving back at them as the horses pulled the sled off. Stacking her skis in the hotel's outdoor rack, she joined her father and took a long swallow from his pewter mug of chocolate. "I had an adventure with them," she said, turning and smiling after the jingling sled and horses. "I lost a binding on that slope they call Bonne Chance, accurately enough, and took a derriere-over-teakettle spill. I wasn't hurt but my knee felt funny, so I stuck my skis in the snow, made a cross of them, the international May Day distress signal, you know, and within seconds, really, the Brizzard brothers came swooping down to rescue me."

She was a pleasure for Selby to look at in a red parka with her blond hair tumbling around her shoulders, glinting now with sun and snowflakes. Her face was pink and tanned with the mountain sun, except where her snow goggles had made a slim white mask across her eyes and cheeks. It gave her an animated and whimsical look, a winter harlequin.

She ate a sugar bun, licked her fingers and drank the rest of his chocolate. Guy and Jules Brizzard were nineteen, she told Selby. They had tucked her skis under their arms, picked her up between them and carried her down the Olympic trail to the lift area, where the doctor said a hot bath was all she'd need, and maybe a day or two off the slopes to rest her knee.

"They're both studying medicine in Lyon," she told him. "They're fantastic skiers. They'd like to come over some time to meet you and have tea with us." She gave him back his empty cup. "When's Miss Brett's train getting in?"

"In about an hour," Selby said. "I just checked, it's on time." Brett had flown to Bern from Paris that afternoon. She was coming over to St. Stephan on the Bern-Montreux Exchange. Selby planned to drive over shortly to meet her.

"I've talked to the hotel manager," he said. "He's put Brett in the room next to yours, on the floor above Davey and me."

"Wonderful. We'll probably talk all night, then we can have a graceful invalid's breakfast on the terrace. I *am* an invalid, you know. I can't ski for two whole days. But we have lots to talk about. She wrote that her sister's poodle had puppies, six of them, imagine. She's bringing pictures. They named them after wines and grapes. Pinot, Margaux, Chablis, Merlot—I forget the others. She says they're absolutely adorable but rascals, into everything. She wondered by the way"—Shana glanced at him —"how Blazer would manage in his dotage with a puppy."

"Blazer's only six, what does she mean?"

Shana picked up another sugar bun but put it down again with a resolute gesture. "No, it would spoil dinner," she said, "and my shrewd intuition tells me dinner might be a celebration of sorts."

"It will be a pleasure, for sure," Selby said. "But there's nothing definite to raise glasses to."

Davey came out of the hotel then and joined them with the afternoon mail. He had filled out in the last year; he was as tall

483

as Shana now, and had the promise of Selby's size in his wide hands and knobby shoulders. Shana told him excitedly of her fall on the Bonne Chance—it was now a "desperate, dizzy slide" —and the rescue efforts by the Brizzard brothers.

Selby sorted through the letters. There were household bills, a note from Miss Culpepper for Shana, a statement from the league's pension plan and a card from Mrs. Cranston.

Everything was fine at home, young Gideen had shoveled out the drive, and some of Shana's friends had made a Christmas wreath of plastic bones for Blazer's doghouse. "It sounds all wrong, but it's really very pretty. The bones are painted red and green," Mrs. Cranston explained.

Miss Culpepper wrote that she had found some new books on Swiss history that Shana might find of interest but would hold them at the library until the Selbys returned. She concluded with a smattering of local news, which Shana read aloud for Davey's benefit:

"Muhlenburg beat Bull Run for the regional finals. Normie Bride scored eighteen points. Weather is cold and blowy, with lots of snow. The new management at Brandywine Lakes is making all sorts of changes. They're mostly young men—by my measure, *very* young—in their thirties, that is, a team of specialists in community planning from Belgium and South Africa. A good deal of construction is going on . . ."

Shana dropped the letter and said, "Davey, can you imagine living with Normie Bride if we make the state finals? You know how *intense* he gets."

Selby picked up Miss Culpepper's letter and glanced through it. He put it in the pocket of his duffel coat. It was dark by then, and time to drive down to St. Stephan to meet Brett's train.

Shana was saying, "Davey, we're having a party tonight. Miss Brett will be here for dinner. Would you go up to my room, please, and—"

"I know she'll be here." Davey's voice was good-humoredly resigned. "I also know she's won about three or four hundred medals skiing, and I'm still floundering around on the bunny slopes."

"You're doing fine," Selby assured him. "Remember, she hasn't been on skis since she was in college. You'll probably have to help her along until she gets the feel of it again."

"Davey, listen, *please*. Will you get my shoulder bag for me? I've saved some money from my allowance, lots of francs, and we should buy some fresh flowers for the table tonight. You can order the wine, that will amuse everyone."

"Very funny, *mam'selle.*" Davey wasn't indifferent to his sister's opinion and occasional sarcasm, but he had lost most of his young sensitivity to it.

"My bag's on the dressing table," she told him, "or hanging on the hook in the closet. Or in the drawer with my sweaters, maybe."

"I'll get a metal detector and sweep the place," Davey said, standing and walking into the hotel.

Selby paid the check and they stood and watched the snow drifting heavily into the street, the flakes spinning through the colored lights from the shop windows.

"Daddy, may I ask you something?"

"Why, sure."

She hesitated. "Is everything okay with you and Brett?"

"I think so, Shana, I think it will be. But there are some things to talk over. Nothing serious from my point of view." He paused. "Brett finds it hard to put in full perspective any problem or issue. I mean that as a compliment. She doesn't blame other people if things go wrong, she takes the responsibility herself. Most people, as you probably know, lean a little the other way. But Brett tends to feel any failure is probably *her* fault. It's made her, well, cautious."

"Can I tell you something?" Shana smiled and suddenly hugged him tightly and put her forehead against his chest. "I'm not going to be the only girl in your life now. So I won't ever say this quite this way again, not ever exactly this way. I love you, daddy, I love you very much. And I respect you more than anybody. Even during the worst of what we went through and when we were angry and said things because of it, I knew you were never really mad at me or disappointed. I always had that to hold on to, I knew we were trying to get through it together. That made the difference, because I knew you were on my side and nothing could ever change that. I wanted to tell you this, I wanted to say it, and now I have."

Selby held her close for an instant, her slim body firm and

485

warm in his arm, and then he let out his breath and smiled and put his hands on her shoulders. "I'm glad you told me," he said. "It makes me feel very good, Shana, and very proud."

It was an important and precious moment because it was so fleeting and impermanent; they were closer than they might ever be again, and they both realized that, with a poignancy matched by the lights of Christmas and the transient beauty of drifting snowflakes.

When Davey came from the hotel with Shana's shoulder bag, she kissed her father on the cheek, and that moment between them was over, the child was gone, and it was a young woman who slipped from his arms and hurried away with her tall brother.

Selby stood and watched them, hearing their light voices mingling with the sound of church bells. A curtain of snow fell across the street, stirred by winds, and Davey and Shana disappeared behind it. He had an impulse to call after them and wish them well. They were growing up, no question of that, they had started their journey, and he hoped people would be kind to them . . . God bless.

The station at St. Stephan was on a spur between the main line from Montreux to Interlaken. A weathered sign gave the town's name. A chalked notice below it listed the arrival of the next Bern connection: 6:35 P.M. A lath and timber building with a narrow clock tower above it, the station adjoined a platform which had a phone booth and several wooden benches.

The stationmaster was tall and thin, with black moustaches waxed to tapering points. He assured Selby the Bern Exchange was on time. The interior of the station was warmed by an iron stove. A group of people stood around it, but Selby decided to wait outside. A glowing red wreath hung above the ticket window, the light falling across the tracks. A wind from the valley sent snow gusting along the platform. But the rails were clear and Selby knew he would see the light from the train when it came around the foothills into the St. Stephan spur.

He sat and reread Miss Culpepper's letter. ". . . the management at Brandywine Lakes is making all sorts of changes . . . community estate experts from Belgium and South Africa

. . . a good deal of construction is going on along the river. They're putting in a landing strip for their own airfield, buying up most of the land on the other side of the Rakestraw Bridge. I've never been opposed to progress, anyone who lives with books as much as I have knows that change is just another way of defining growth, but all growth isn't necessarily an improvement on present conditions, or a congenial addition to the general community. We are losing so much of our natural beauty here, things that seemed to belong to us without question . . ."

Selby heard the sound of the Bern local, a muted, staccato rumble, and saw the headlights turning around the hill into St. Stephan.

He looked at Miss Culpepper's letter again and then—with the feeling he was ridding himself of a worrisome burden from his past—he crumpled the pages lightly in his big hands and dropped them with a sense of relief and finality into the immaculate blue-and-white trash container beside the phone booth.

The train stopped and a conductor swung down and looked at his watch. Several passengers were met by friends and relatives with flurries of holiday greetings and hugs.

Selby went aboard and walked through both cars, and then spoke to the conductor in his stilted French. He described Brett as well as he was able to, holding up a hand to indicate her height, but the conductor shook his head and snapped the cover shut on his watch. In careful English he replied that no person of such a description had boarded his train in Bern or Montreux. Excusing himself, he climbed aboard and the cars started up with a lurch, gathering speed as they began the climb toward Zweisimmen.

Selby called the hotel. Shana's room didn't answer, she would be in the bathtub, he surmised. Davey answered his phone on the first ring. No, they hadn't heard from her, there'd been no message. They'd been to the shop and bought snowdrops and pink roses. The waiter already had them in a vase on the table. Was something wrong?

"Brett missed the train, I guess," Selby explained. "I'll check with the stationmaster and see when the next one is due. Then I'll call her in Bern. Just wait dinner till you hear from me, okay?"

"Sure, dad."

The stationmaster came onto the platform as Selby left the public phone booth. "Mr. Selby? Mr. Harry Selby?"

"Yes, that's right."

"I have a call for you in my office. You can take it there if you like. Come with me, please. This way, sir. It's a Bern call, the Hotel Regina."

The stationmaster's office was small and warm. His desk held a rack of well-cured meerschaum pipes. On the wall a white sign with a gold cross listed church services in various nearby villages. Selby noted these details automatically as he heard Brett's voice, unnaturally high, saying, "Harry, I was leaving for the station, I was waiting for a cab, when the concierge stopped me. I'm still at the hotel. Burt Wilger was killed last night. I'm sorry to tell you like this—" He heard her swallow tightly, heard the tears in her voice. "Like some stupid weather report. He was killed last night in an automobile accident, Jonathan Lamb called me at the hotel here, and the concierge stopped me. I'd paid my bill, I'd left the lobby to get a cab. I was leaving for the train . . . I said that, didn't I?"

"Brett, are you all right?"

"Yes, Harry. It's hit me so hard. I was standing there waiting for a cab. I had presents for Shana and Davey and pictures of Chablis, that's the puppy Kay gave me. Oh, Harry . . ."

"Brett, listen. Would you like me to call you back in a little while? You could sit somewhere and have coffee or a drink."

"No, please. I want to be with you, Harry. There's another train in an hour. Will you wait for me?"

"Yes, I'll be here at St. Stephan, standing right on the platform. I'm just an hour away. We're only an hour apart. But, Brett, don't keep it all locked up inside you until then."

"I'm sorry, Harry. I wasn't thinking of you. But saying it was so hard. Hearing myself say the words made them true. Here's all Mr. Lamb could tell me . . ."

Selby sat on the platform with his coat collar turned up. The station was empty, except for the stationmaster, who was inside at his desk posting accounts in a ledger and smoking one of his curved golden pipes.

Burt Wilger, Jonathan Lamb had told Brett, got a call at the

488

Division toward the end of his shift. Something he had to check out, Wilger advised the sergeant who relieved him. He didn't say who phoned or where he was going. But he'd given the impression it was a continuing case and that he was meeting someone that night.

There was a reminder on his desk pad to pick up some dry cleaning in the morning, and at the Mobil station in East Chester Wilger had stopped for gas around ten-thirty P.M. That was all they had at that end.

Approximately an hour later a man who wouldn't give his name called the sheriff's substation in Muhlenburg and reported that he'd seen a wrecked car on the riverbank at the foot of the Rakestraw bridge. There was somebody inside, but he wasn't moving, the man told the sheriff's people. But he didn't want to get mixed up in anything, he added, and hung up.

The sheriff dispatched a squad and they found Sergeant Burt Wilger dead at the wheel of his car, crushed against it when he went off Dade Road and smashed into the wooden timbers of the old covered bridge. Skid marks were inconclusive, and so were the dents and scratches on Wilger's car. He could have been sideswiped and forced off the road. Or he could have fallen asleep at the wheel. There was no way to say for sure. But there was no trace of drugs or alcohol in his blood.

Selby stood and paced the platform, watching and listening for Brett's train. He thought of her and he thought of the red-haired detective, crushed to death on Dade Road, a mile or so from Brandywine Lakes and Vinegar Hill, lands the Taggarts had owned for generations . . .

". . . let me give you some free insight into cops," he remembered Wilger telling him. It seemed strange to think of the detective on a snowy night in the hills of the Jungfrau while a stationmaster with waxed moustaches and a meerschaum pipe sat adding up his ticket sales. "We're thieving bastards or knights on chargers keeping the jungle back from civilization. Take your pick. Some cases have mile-high no-trespassing signs around them. It hurts, so some cops take a drink and forget it."

Selby thought he heard the far rumble of the Bern Exchange in the hills.

Then Wilger had said, "A case like Shana's, that's different. They shouldn't stop us. Maybe you think you ought to thank

489

me." He looked at Selby with his mild, near-sighted eyes and said, "Don't."

Selby saw the lights of the Bern train flashing around the white flanks of the hills. He walked to the phone booth and picked Miss Culpepper's letter from the blue-and-white trash can beside it. Typical of this immaculate country, it was the only waste paper in the receptacle.

Smoothing out the note, he held it up to the glowing light of the Christmas wreath, then folded it into a neat square and tucked it next to Senator Lester's card in his wallet, a card with nothing on it but a priority number in Washington, D.C.

He put the wallet in his pocket and buttoned the flap over it. The snow was coming down harder, big, star-shaped flakes that had covered the tracks and the platform completely by the time the last Bern Exchange for that evening pulled into St. Stephan.

The windows of the coaches were warm yellow squares against the driving white darkness. Selby saw passengers rubbing mittened hands against the steamed glass and looking out. A wind rushed from the valley and made a metallic whine along the frozen rails.

He watched anxiously as the conductor studied his watch. He didn't see anyone get off the train; the storm had become a blinding whiten-wall, like the snow in the village that had closed around Shana and Davey, sealing them off from him.

He called Brett's name but heard only the conductor shouting orders and calling out the next stop: Zweisimmen.

As the train began to move, the snow seemed to part suddenly like an immense curtain and Brett came hurrying toward him, one hand raised high and waving, and her red scarf and dark hair tumbled and blowing about her in the bitter winds.

Her face and lips were numbed from the cold. He kept an arm around her shoulders as they collected her luggage, a leather overnighter, cheerily wrapped presents, a heavy coat and lined boots.

He stowed her things in the rented station wagon and got in beside her. She asked him how long they were from home, and they both smiled at that choice of word, because they knew it wasn't a mistake, but the simple truth between them now.

They would talk about that tomorrow. And then the rest of it. But not tonight.

On the narrow road through the white hills to St. Stephan, he watched the rear-view mirror and saw their tire tracks filling swiftly with snow and the road stretching out white and empty behind them.

When he saw the lights of the little town beyond the stee-pled church glowing like beacons through the darkness, he touched her shoulder and said, "We're home, Brett."